For testimonials from law enforcement,
visit Carolyn Arnold's website.

ALSO BY CAROLYN ARNOLD

Detective Madison Knight

Ties That Bind
Justified
Sacrifice
Found Innocent
Just Cause
Deadly Impulse

In the Line of Duty
Power Struggle
Shades of Justic
What We Bury
Girl on the Run
Life Sentence

Brandon Fisher FBI

Eleven
Silent Graves
The Defenseless
Blue Baby
Violated

Remnants
On the Count of Three
Past Deeds
One More Kill

Detective Amanda Steele

The Little Grave
Stolen Daughters
The Silent Witness
Black Orchid Girls

Her Frozen Cry
Last Seen Alive
Her Final Breath

Matthew Connor Adventure

City of Gold
The Secret of the Lost Pharaoh

The Legend of Gasparilla and His Treasure

Standalone

Assassination of a Dignitary
Midlife Psychic

ASSASSINATION OF A DIGNITARY

CAROLYN ARNOLD

Copyright © 2013 by Carolyn Arnold
Excerpt from *Eleven* copyright © 2011 by Carolyn Arnold

All rights reserved. No part of this publication may be reproduced, distributed, or transmitted in any form or by any means, including photocopying, recording, or other electronic or mechanical methods, without the prior written permission of the publisher, except in the case of brief quotations embodied in critical reviews and certain other noncommercial uses permitted by copyright law. For permission requests, contact the publisher.

Hibbert & Stiles Publishing Inc.
www.hspubinc.com

This is a work of fiction. Names, characters, places, and incidents are the products of the author's imagination or are used fictitiously. Any resemblance to actual events, locales, or persons, living or dead, is entirely coincidental.

Names: Arnold, Carolyn, author.
Title: Assassination of a Dignitary / Carolyn Arnold.
Description: [London, Ontario] : Hibbert & Stiles Publishing Inc., [2021]
Identifiers: ISBN 978-1-988353-14-2 (paperback 4.25 x 7) | ISBN: 978-1-989706-83-1 (paperback 5 x 8) | ISBN 978-1-497711-35-8 (ebook)

ASSASSINATION OF A DIGNITARY

CHAPTER ONE

They say the past has a way of catching up with you. Mine was in my living room when I came home.

Christian Russo, son of the Italian Mafia Don, Pietro Russo, sat on my sofa making himself comfortable. The side table had a glass of amber liquid sitting on it. He raised it for a sip.

The clock read three fifty. Brenda would be home with the kids soon. I hadn't seen the man in fifteen years.

"What are you doing here?"

"Now is that any way to greet an old friend?" His Italian accent laced each word.

I couldn't show the man fear. This is what he wanted. He craved a reaction. He always had. "If I saw one before me, I may greet him differently."

"Oh." A fake pout had his lips pinched together only a second. He put the drink down and placed a hand over his heart. He laughed when it touched the silk of his silver jacket. "If only I had feelings, Hunter. Maybe you'd hurt mine." Silence fell between us like a cloak. I stood in front of him. He studied my face. "Sit."

"Get out of my house, Christian."

"Sit!" His voice rose, and he straightened his posture as he barked the command.

I sat. I desired to stretch my leg, one over the other, but didn't want to appear too comfortable either. I kept myself leaning slightly forward, apprehensive this would give the impression I was eager to hear what he would say.

"We have a job for you," he continued.

"I don't do this anymore."

"Tsk. Tsk." He raised a finger to his lips. "You don't interrupt me."

"But, I don't…" I let my words trail off into non-existence based on the reflection in his eyes. I wasn't the type who could take a life for a wad of cash anymore. I had too much to lose, too much to live for.

"Pays one hundred k. Half up front."

"I'm doing fine. I have been—"

He dropped a wad of cash on the table between us. I knew from the banding it was ten thousand.

"How can you be fine? After you turn your back on The Family? Surely you must miss us."

I missed the paycheck, the one that padded my bank account with thousands at regular intervals, but not the control they held over me.

"Seriously, there must still be a fire in you." Christian's mouth lifted, slightly to the left as it always did when he schemed manipulation.

His eyes contained more evil than had been there the better part of two decades ago. In all honesty, I was shocked to see that he was the one the Don sent to me. Christian was more hurt than Pietro when I turned my back on The Family.

My eyes scanned my living room, settling only briefly on the family photographs, on the children's school portraits. My eyes came back to Christian. "Like I said, I don't do that anymore. I wouldn't even know how to—"

"Fire a gun." Christian finished my sentence and cocked his head to the side. "You should know better than to lie to me. Want to try again?"

When I was offered a permanent role in The Family's business, I had declined. I saw my way out and took it. There were times the nightmares of what I had done would slither back into the darkness of night, but I worked to shutter them out. I justified my actions as responding to directions. It was nothing personal. A kill never was. I reminded myself they were marks, not individuals. But over the years I had never lost the love for firing a gun. The fall of the hammer and the slight kickback as the bullet exited the chamber.

"I know you go to the gun range." Christian took another sip of what looked to be my Scotch.

I pointed a finger at him. Many men would not dare to. "Don't follow me."

"You tell me what to do now? Things changed, yes?" Christian laughed. "I believe every Thursday afternoon. I trust that's why you're home now and not at the office."

How closely had he been watching me? In fact in such an economy, I was fortunate not only to have a job but to own a modest accounting practice. I chose the career hoping the rumors were true; accountants lead uneventful lives. I looked at the clock. Within fifteen minutes, my family would be walking through the door. My eyes went back to the cash on the table.

"How does it pay you, Hunter?"

"I'm not that person anymore." My last name improvised as my nickname among the Russos. They viewed it as evidence of a life calling. I was predestined to be their hitman.

"You always will be to me." Christian reached into a jacket pocket and pulled out a cell phone. His eyes were on me. "Disappointing."

"Why me?" I didn't know the details yet but wasn't sure I wanted to.

Christian leaned forward and appeared more comfortable than I was, at this moment, in my own home. "You're close to her. You can make this happen."

"Who?"

Christian smirked. "The Governor of Michigan, of course. Marian Behler." He leaned back into the sofa.

My heart beat as a piston in a chamber. It felt ready to explode.

Governor Behler was a client of mine at the firm. Christian obviously knew this just as he was aware of my whereabouts on Thursday afternoons and my active fascination with guns. "I didn't think you killed dignitaries."

"An exception has been made."

My last kill was over fifteen years ago; it may as well have been a lifetime. But when I had been at my finest, I excelled both at close range and sniper hits. The versatility made me a valuable asset. "Pietro Russo ordered this hit?" I knew I was being arrogant, and even courageously stupid, questioning Christian's authority but the directive was hard to believe.

"You used to call him Pops." Christian didn't react the way I had expected, but that was partially what was frightening about the man. He had always been unpredictable.

"My life is different now." I had to stop staring at the clock, but my eyes kept drifting there.

"Different, good? Different, bad?"

I owed him no explanation for the direction my life took or an assessment of its fulfillment.

"We used to be close, you and I. We can be again."

"Did Pietro Russo order this hit?" I repeated my question.

"Why else would I be here?" He held out his cell phone. "Want to speak to him yourself?"

My stomach tossed. One normally didn't leave the Italians without there being recompense. I seemed to have been an exception to the rule. Now I wondered if the smooth transition had been afforded me because of the service I had offered and could possibly again.

"I can dial the number for you."

"Why her?" Behler was the first female to serve as Governor in the state of Michigan.

Christian laughed. He lifted the glass to his lips but lowered his arm again. He rested it on the sofa arm. "You know we don't answer those questions. Yet she must know where her death is coming from. And, to the media it must appear as an assassination."

"So you want it to take place from a distance, or close range?" I asked for clarity. His words seemed to contradict each other, *know where her death is coming from, yet it must appear as an assassination.*

"A statement must be made."

"In-her-face-personal then? And you want the last words she hears to be—"

"From Pietro Russo."

"From Pietro Russo?" The woman must have wronged the man on a personal level. For all of my past close range kills, they would know where their fate came from, but the Don was never explicitly named. I couldn't risk my family's lives being caught up in this vortex. My wife, my parents, no one knew about my past. While I preferred it stay buried there, it might not be an option.

"So what will it be? One hundred thou richer or—" Christian stopped talking as he exchanged his drink for a nearby family portrait. "You have a nice family."

"Don't even think of hurting them." My jaw tightened, the familiar adrenaline rush surged through my blood stream.

"It's not a threat, Hunter." His calm voice conflicted with his words. "If you don't do this, it will be more than that." Christian rose to his feet. "You have until tomorrow morning, 9:00 AM, to decide. After that, I can't answer for what happens."

"You son of a bitch!" I rose to my feet and came at him fast.

Christian turned. The barrel of a .38 was pointed at my abdomen. "Don't think I won't kill you just because you're a friend. I can get new friends."

I wanted to tell him to find a new one for this mission, but with the wildfire in the man's eyes I needed to back down from the confrontation. I put my hands up in surrender and slowly took a step back.

"Smart, Hunter. It would be a shame to lose you. I want her dead within the week."

"The week?" Just when I didn't think my heart could pump faster, or the adrenaline provide more of a high, it exceeded on both counts. I glanced at the clock. *Brenda and the kids.* "If I do this—"

"You're out for good."

"I heard that fifteen years ago."

Christian laughed and finally retracted his gun and placed it inside his jacket pocket. "You have no reason to trust us. Keep that in mind." He stopped at the door, his hand on the knob, and spoke facing it. "The clock's ticking Hunter. Say hi to the family for me."

With him gone, I felt violated. He had been inside my house, my home that I shared with my family. They could know nothing about this. They would know nothing of it.

The clock read four ten. I had about seventeen hours to let Christian know what I decided but did I really have an option? It was either kill or be killed. I knew too much now. Christian had seen to that. I scooped the wad of cash from the table and fanned it. The smell of money lodged up my nose as nostalgia. I tucked it into a pant pocket causing it to visibly bulge.

I poured myself a few shots of single malt and swigged it back in a couple mouthfuls. As the alcohol started to work, my mind assessed the situation. It recalled my past life in detail, the people, the blood, the locations, the intensity I would feel every time I took a life. In a way, it was the type of rush I hadn't experienced since. I wouldn't dare say I missed it, but as the vague recollections transformed to shape, I knew I was capable of doing it again.

The directions were simple: kill the Governor.

But I wasn't that man anymore, and this was different. Governor Behler was my client. I was her accountant. We had grown close. Brenda and I had even been to her house for dinner before.

As the alcohol soothed me, I remembered that Behler had mentioned something about an upcoming trip to Niagara Falls, New York. I looked at my watch for the date. Next weekend I believe. I needed to get downtown to the office.

The front door opened. Yvonne, my fourteen-year-old daughter, was the first one through it. "You don't understand!"

She closed the door on her mother who came in behind her. "Get back here young lady!" Brenda cast me a passing glance as she went down the hallway after our daughter. "I told you not to skip any more classes."

"You don't understand!"

Another door slammed and Brenda returned to me with anger brimming in her eyes. "That girl needs to be disciplined, Ray. She can't go on talking to me like that…" Her words paused as her eyes went to the glass on the side table. "Speak to her."

Max, our ten-year-old, walked through the room carrying a backpack that looked like it would tip him over backward. He waved at me on the way by.

"Ray, are you listening to me?" Brenda's eyes darted from the bar cart to the glass in my hand and back to the table. "You're drinking? And you had someone over?"

I just nodded. To say I had an old friend drop by would be a lie. And, if she didn't like the afternoon drink, she really wouldn't like what I had to say next. "I'll need to go back to the office later tonight."

CHAPTER TWO

Detroit, Michigan
Thursday, June 3rd, 11 PM

Brenda didn't say much through dinner and despite the fact she was mad at me, how would she feel if the Mafia came after us? I took a deep breath. I needed to let Christian know my answer, and as far as I saw it, the sooner, the better. I also wished to discuss compensation in more detail. One hundred thousand for a dignitary was an undercut.

First I needed to go to the office. Hunter & Associates sat on a corner lot of a downtown property that accrued thousands in taxes a month. The building itself was an older house that had been zoned for commercial use before my time. It had been a dentist office when I bought it. Now it served as an office where people got their taxes done and their bookkeeping handled.

I had founded the company fourteen years ago. I never believed in business partners—too much room for disagreement. But I did have one other certified accountant on staff, along with six transient accounting students. Most of them just put in the time, got the experience, and waited for their break to come along.

I struggled with the front lock as it had dictated from the beginning. The deadbolt needed replacing, but it fell down the list of things to do. It just seemed more important things were piled in front of simple maintenance.

Inside the building, it was silent, not even the hum of a computer station. In less than twelve hours, Serena would open the front door and switch over the phones, transforming the static environment to one of activity.

My office was upstairs along with a cubicle area for Serena and an office for the other certified accountant and his assistant. Really, the business should have been named Hunter & Associate, in the singular, but it made it sound more prestigious in its plural form.

The third step from the top was another item that made it on the ever-growing to-do list. It groaned under the pressure of my weight. I went straight to the safe in the back of the room. Like the one in my house, no one else knew about the existence of this one except for the company I had install it. And there was a reason for this. I didn't trust financial institutions. They were fine if your funds were mediocre, but if a large sum was required quickly, they were tiresome. I studied the contents—roughly four hundred thousand dollars. This combined with the fortune I did keep in the financial system, tied up in various accounts and investments, made my net worth somewhere around ten million. Not a vast fortune in these changing times, yet sufficient to retire on for good, or to disappear should the need arise. My wife had no idea we had this sort of money.

I pulled out a few wads of bills and sat them on the credenza. I added Christian's ten thousand to the stack. At the back of the safe, I found what I was looking for. My old weapon—a pen gun. Maybe it had been careless to keep something like this so close, but for some reason it instilled a sense of security having it nearby.

The pen gun held one .22 shell, but if executed properly that was all I needed to get the job done. I fished it out of the case and held it in my hands. The five ounces felt featherish in the palm of my hands. Its overall length was five point six inches; shave about one point four when it was folded and ready to fire. It was made of stainless steel.

From the safe position, or its full length, I pulled out and bent it to expose the small handle and trigger. Holding it, the past rushed over me. I took a deep breath and looked at where the arrow on the barrel was pointed—S for Safe. When it came time to execute the hit, the barrel would be loaded, and at this point, I would move the arrow to F for Fire.

I put it back in its original position and unscrewed the barrel. I held it to my nose and inhaled deeply. I had taken twenty-one lives with this weapon. I put it back in its case and slid it into my pants pocket. I went into the back part of the safe looking for bullets but first came out with a small envelope.

As I remembered its contents, I smiled. It could come in handy, but I would need Christian's help with it. I slid out the fake identification. A driver's license and passport, both of which would need updating. I placed them back into the envelope and put it in my jacket pocket along with a box of .22 bullets.

As the weight of the bullets pulled down on my jacket, I considered my wife and children. They had no idea the type of person their husband and father was, or who he had been. I had kept all of this from them—for their protection. Yet now, everything demanded one final accounting and I had no choice but to pay the bill, as it were.

I stood in the cover of darkness, tucked into a corner untouched by the glow of a street light or motion sensor spotlight. The house was a two-story brick but only home to one man.

A man stood vigil in the corner of the porch. There would be at least one more out back. If Christian hadn't changed, both men would be carrying AK-47s.

But there would be no need to disturb them.

My heart fluttered with the adrenaline rush that used to fuel my soul on a regular basis as I contemplated the ascent to the second floor. There were two large windows that would serve as a means to propel myself upward. The brick's mortar had become deeply inset over the years and allowed for a good toe hold. I could have done things the easy way: placed a call and accepted the mission. But I needed to prove that I wasn't one to mess with either. He violated my home; I would his.

I hoisted my legs onto the bottom window sill and spent a moment thankful I had kept in good physical shape. I stood there, braced in front of the window, back to the world, vulnerable. I heard something ruffle and realized the two guards were moving around. I froze there while I struggled to study their movements by sound. My heartbeat thumped in my eardrums and made it hard to hear. I had to recall my breathing technique. I had to tell myself that I had nothing to lose, just like before. But so much had changed since then. Brenda's and the kids' faces skipped through my mind, and I closed my eyes willing them to obscurity.

The men were still moving around. I strained to hear. As I focused, my heartbeat relaxed in my ears and receded into a dull hum.

"Carlos…pssst, Carlos."

"What are you doing man?"

The second voice sounded paranoid and at unease. Either he hadn't been a soldier or grunt, for long or he had been witness to Christian's evil side.

"He's sleeping man. Relax."

"Go back to your watch," the one named Carlos said.

The more they spoke and the more they moved around, I feared they'd do a full perimeter search. If they did, I would be dead. One bullet to the back of the head, and I'd be fed to Mitchell, Christian's pit bull. At least that's how the lucky intruders were disposed of in the past. Betrayers of The Family never received the courtesy of the gun shot first.

Mitchell had likely passed, but Christian loved the breed and would have replaced him with a younger, hungrier version.

They're good at tearing flesh from bone, he told me. Anything that can do that is worthy of my respect.

"You ever been to Popeye's? The girls are hot." The chatty soldier was from the front door. This much I could tell.

"Please go back."

"You're such a fuckin' pussy."

"Go."

I heard the man return to the front, his feet crunching on the crushed shell driveway that Christian had demanded be shipped specifically for show. Standard gravel would never suffice for a man like him.

I let the rush of air leave my lungs. I placed my gloved hands on the brick and worked the toes of my shoes into the deep groves. I made my way to the second story like a modern day Spider-Man. As I reached for the sill of the second window, I paused and listened. My toe went into a slot, and I extended upward as far as I could reach. I needed to go up another few bricks in height. My hand reached the sill, but as I went to pull myself up, my grip slipped.

Shit!

I was hanging suspended, fifteen feet off the ground, by one arm. I needed to maneuver my legs to the side, get them into a toe hold. My body lost all willpower to move when I heard rustling in the bushes.

Shit!

My arm was aching like a son of a bitch. The push-ups and bench presses at the gym hadn't prepared my muscles for this workout.

I summoned my thoughts to go somewhere more tranquil. They instantly jumped to Brenda—the smell of her perfume and the warmth of being in her arms. The recollections weren't helping as my resolve weakened. I needed to rediscover the killer inside of me, and it wouldn't come from thinking of my family.

There was silence. Not even a blade of grass blew from a breeze. I looked to my left and noticed the silhouette of a guard easing around the back corner of the house. His hands were holding onto his weapon. I couldn't see the one from the front.

My attention back on the hand that still gripped the windowsill, I swung my body.

"I think someone's here." The voice came from the man at the front.

Not good at all. Maybe he never left the side of the house.

Carlos answered, "Nah, you're hearing things. It's your mind playin—"

"Sssh."

"You're such a loser."

For the next few seconds, my breathing labored. The muscles in my arm bit as a scorching fire. I watched the guard from the front move up the side of the house. If he looked up, I was dead. I had to stay perfectly still.

He seemed satisfied from his search and went back to his post. It was time to move, pain or not. I swung again and found a toe hold. I reached up, obtained a hold on the sill with my other hand and hoisted myself up.

I balanced in the sill and worked to pry the window open with a flat-headed screwdriver. The action brought me right back to my days of being a hitman. I would move stealthily and undetected, and the mark would be dead before they could open their eyes to see their killer. At least, those were the lucky ones.

The window was located in a hallway, at the top of the stairs, just as I had remembered. The hallway was dark, but if Christian kept his old bedroom, he was the third door on the left.

As I made my way down the hall, the oak flooring softly moaned my approach. I stopped moving and heard nothing other than the heavy breathing of a sleeping man. Christian.

I stepped inside the room and closed the door behind me. "Rise and shine!" I flicked on the light and watched him struggle to get out from under the duvet in a sleepy confusion. My eyes adjusted to the light much better than his seemed to as he had been roused from a dead sleep.

"What the fuck—"

"Am I doing here? Getting even. Now you know how it feels to have your home violated." I reached into my pocket and turned on the recorder I had also grabbed from the office. I just wanted some insurance in case I needed it.

I heard the moan before I saw her. A woman, who didn't look much older than my Yvonne, sat up. Her eyes were large, and she attempted to crawl behind Christian. He snapped his fingers. "Out!"

The girl didn't move.

"Get your fuckin' ass out!" Christian pointed to the door and slapped her bare ass without restraint as she rose from the bed. She took a shirt from a chair and made her way out of the room, completely naked.

Christian's eyes fired at me. "You better have a damn good—"

"You want me to kill Governor Behler."

Christian rolled his eyes.

"Speak it."

"Yes, my Father demands it."

"And you want me to do this up close, and speak the words, *from Pietro Russo*?"

"Yes." He let the tail end of the word drag out.

I stopped the recorder. "I'll take the job."

He remained unimpressed. "You broke into my house to tell me—"

"I'll do it for five hundred thousand." I had given the amount and the breakdown significant thought. If I were going to do this, I would make it worth my while. My family's wellbeing was already at risk. Taking the job was the only viable option. When it was over, we may need to go far away.

Christian laughed. He was awake now. "Five hundred?"

"She's a person of office. This one's different."

"No different."

To me, Governor Behler represented *different* in several ways. Regardless of her station, I knew her. I was relatively close to her. And she was a woman. I had never killed a woman before. I had to assure myself they died just the same as a man. Obviously they were capable of making enemies the same way.

I took out my pen gun and untwisted the barrel. Christian never moved. He would never acknowledge experiencing fear. But I was also careful about the way I moved. I didn't need him to feel threatened, but I needed him to know I was serious. "Five hundred."

"Fine." Christian's jaw tightened. He rose from the bed and positioned himself inches from my face. "Five hundred." He spat on the floor to the side of me. "Two fifty, less the ten I gave you earlier."

I remained steady. "Five hundred now. Five hundred upon proof of death."

"You must have fallen. Hit your head." Christian stepped back from me and reached into a dresser drawer. He came out with a handgun if you wanted to term it that. A Desert Eagle, ten-inch barrel, likely .357 caliber. He examined it almost as meticulously as I had affectionately handled my pen gun earlier. In a gun battle, mine wouldn't be a match against his.

"You need to start using a real gun," Christian said.

With his words, conflicting energy surged in the room. Reality must have struck him. Killing Governor Behler meant a lot to The Family and he had been entrusted to ensure that it happened. How would he explain to Pops that he killed the hitman?

He placed the gun back in the drawer and closed it slowly. "Five hundred? Fine. Agreed." He looked at me and went to another drawer. This one was full of cash. He tossed wrapped wads of bills on his bed. "How'd you get in past Rocco and Carlos?" Christian kept fishing out the cash. Each wrapped amount valued ten thousand, making for forty-nine of them. "There, that's it." His finger pointed at me, his eyes reflecting with the likes of a human Lucifer. "You better make good."

For an instant, I feared being on the receiving end of Christian's wrath. He was only one year younger than me but held the maturity of a raging hormonal twenty-year-old eager to prove himself to any trespassing mammal. "I always have." I looked at the cash on the bed and at Christian. "I'll also need you to pack this up to go."

"And you never answered my question, what'd you do? Climb up the wall like Spidyman?" Christian's laugh ended abruptly when my eyes responded to the question. "You still have skills."

"That's why you pay me the big bucks." As the words slipped out, it felt reminiscent of my earlier years and the tight friendship that had once existed between us. I handed him the envelope with the fake IDs.

He took it with a smile. "You held onto these. All this time. See, you are meant for this."

"I need them updated right away."

"For certain." The smile remained pasted to his lips.

"And I'll need you on the way out."

Christian led me through the house to the front door; his man there jumped back ten feet when it opened. His gun came up to the ready.

"What the fuck? You shoot your boss now? In the house!" Christian's arms flailed with each word.

"Sorry, Boss. Sorry." When his eyes reached mine, he shook.

Christian snapped his fingers. The man hustled through the front door. With him out of earshot, Christian said, "The rest will be brought to your office once it's done."

As I walked away, I heard the back door swing open. I knew Rocco and Carlos may become pit bull food, but that wasn't my problem. Right now, I had to focus on myself and keeping my family safe—and I would come out one million dollars richer. The bills that I held in the bag were blood money, but they spent just like the rest of it did. I felt the old, familiar tug on the corner of my mouth.

CHAPTER THREE

Brenda gave me the silent treatment through breakfast and left for work without saying goodbye. We normally kissed and hugged before going our separate ways. But I couldn't focus on that; I had to dwell on the entire picture. I'd go into work today, but I wouldn't get much done, at least when it came to clients' financials.

"Good mornin', Ray. The sleepy bug must have bit ya." Serena had come up to Michigan from a southern State and held onto her twang. She followed me down the hall to my office. It was nine thirty, but Serena had the work ethic of a pig farmer—in the trenches early and up to her armpits with shit to shovel.

"I got your coffee ready for ya a while ago now. Let me refresh it." She reached for my cup.

I placed a hand on hers and smiled. "I'm fine."

She withdrew her hand, and her cheeks flushed a modest hue of red. "'K then, I'll be down the hall if ya'll need me."

"Actually, Serena." She stopped and turned in the doorway, appearing ready to please. It was hard to find good help these days, but I struck it rich with her. "Can you close the door on your way out?"

"Course." She smiled, seemingly deflated that's all I requested of her. She was working toward her accounting certificate and was hungry to get any real-life experience she could. I did my best to pass things on to her as she grew in her knowledge.

I loosened my tie as I sat behind my computer. The timeline compressed on me from all sides. One week. I needed to become intimate with Governor Behler's itinerary. I snuffed the conscience that attempted to creep in. It made no difference who she was. All of my marks had been people. All of them had family and friends who loved them. Behler would be no different.

I logged on to my email to verify the date of her trip. My mind remembered the mention of a trip to Niagara Falls, New York, but I couldn't risk a sloppy recollection with fact. I needed to verify everything, and it pivoted on her location.

Scrolling through emails, I found everything but the one I was looking for. I opened up seven from the Governor all in relation to her business account with us.

She owned a florist business by the name of Rose Buds. When she first approached me, we laughed about the name of the company, but she said it always made her smile, and she hoped it would bring joy to others. It must have held appeal because Rose Buds grew from a single location to a nationwide franchise.

I had to shake aside my personal recollections of the woman and dwell on the hard facts. Governor Behler's first name was Marian. She was fifty-six and hailed from a family of six children. Her parents were into scrap metal and had struck a small fortune before Marian graduated from diapers. As with most Governors, she was wealthier than God and didn't draw a salary from the state. She viewed it as her duty to be used in any capacity the State required of her. When I had asked about her decision to get into politics, she told me it's up to each of us to use our talents to the best of our abilities.

I took a deep breath. I doubt she referred to a natural talent for taking people out.

Where the hell was the email where she mentioned going away? I knew she had put it in writing. My eyes went to the phone on my desk. I had no other choice. "Vanessa? This is Raymond Hunter—"

"One minute—"

"No, please don't put me on hold," I said.

"I'll get the Governor for you."

"No, there's no need to bother her."

"Okay." Vanessa dragged out the word.

Vanessa was her assistant for nearly two years. I had met her in person and could envision her biting on the tip of a nail while on the phone with me.

"I just need to verify when she's going away again. I have some papers for her sign. She mentioned Niagara Falls."

"Yeah, she's going this weekend."

This weekend? My heart cinched in my chest. That was tomorrow.

"No, wait a minute." Vanessa paused and laughed. She must have removed the finger from her mouth. "I'm a week ahead of myself. She goes on the twelfth. Well, she leaves on the eleventh, but she'll be gone that weekend. It's been a long week."

It's been a long week? It's been a long twenty-four hours. "Thanks."

"So you want to make an appointment? I can squeeze you in before she leaves."

Maybe I wasn't ready for this mission. "The paperwork's not quite ready. I just wanted to know the timetable I'm looking at. I'll call when she gets back. So she's expected back on the—"

"Fourteenth, yes, Mr. Hunter."

"Thanks." It was merely a token word and served as a closure to the conversation. I had the information I needed. The location and date had been confirmed. Christian would have to accept it was just over his mandated week.

I would be killing Governor Behler.

As the sentence repeated in my head, the main verb punched out more each time. "I'm going to *kill* Marian."

First I had things to do. Whatever the Governor's purpose it was likely I'd need to look the part to fit into her world. Passing Serena's cubicle, I said, "I'm stepping out."

She looked up from her computer monitor. Her eyes said, *but you just got here.* Verbally she just thanked me for notifying her.

I drove to Salvatore's Clothier, a designer fashion boutique with the wealthy man as its target, on the outskirts of the city. They only carried high-end items, with the lowest priced item likely being a belt at five hundred dollars. The effects of the downed economy weren't seen here, and it would be easy to fall prey to the thinking that it held no impact. It was effortless to dismiss troubles when one wasn't personally affected.

"May I help you?" The sales associate must have been a size zero. Her black hair was slicked back into a tight ponytail, and she wore an Armani dress suit complete with stilettos. Her feet must have killed her by the end of the day. My wife bitched enough about heels after a four-hour wedding and reception.

"I need a tuxedo. Armani. Double-breasted jacket. Wing-tipped collar shirt and black cummerbund to match the suit. A bowtie, as well."

The clerk's mouth lifted. Her eyes read of calculating how much commission she'd receive. "Certainly. A size thirty-eight waist, am I right?"

I nodded. She did her best to impress me, but it would take more than that. These people were trained to visually assess a person's measurements.

She came back minutes later, and I walked up to the till. "I want the finished suit to be ready for pick up at your Niagara Falls, New York location."

The clerk's eyes fell. "Sir, we don't have a location there."

"This was a waste of time." I placed my Visa back into its slot in my wallet.

"No, no, sir. We do have an affiliate store. I can arrange this for you."

Now she was starting to impress me. "Good then. I need it ready no later than June the eleventh, noon."

"Of course. We can call you once it's ready."

"No calls. I will just show up, and I expect it to be ready. But you should make note of a new number for the files."

"Go ahead." She smiled. Our connection existing solely on the dollar signs she saw in me.

I gave her my cell number. At least if something went wrong, I would receive the call, not Brenda.

CHAPTER FOUR

Detroit, Michigan
Sunday, June 6th, AM

According to Google maps, Niagara Falls, New York was two hundred and forty miles from Detroit. That equated to just over four hours one way and would have me driving through Canada. My innate fear was that Governor Behler would change her mind about the trip, and I would be left holding the gun, literally. Not to mention have the Russos after me for failure. The thousands I was out for the tuxedo was a small loss by comparison.

I waited until Sunday morning to tell my wife about the "business" trip I had to take the coming weekend. The kids had left the table and filtered back to their rooms for their independent means of entertainment.

I told her it was a seminar on changes in tax laws—a conceivable cover. She didn't understand why I hadn't provided more notice. She went on about how maybe it would have been nice to take the family and make a mini vacation out of it.

"Why not fly at least?" Brenda stood a couple of feet in front of me with arms crossed and one leg slightly forward—the stance she assumed when she was least impressed. The coffee she had been drinking prior to my announcement chilled on the table.

Flying commercial wasn't an option when you were armed. "I can't catch a flight this last minute."

Her jaw tightened and her eyes fired. "Isn't that why they're called last minute flights? They're normally even discounted."

It was a jab at my frugal ways. Since my early days in the Mafia, despite the surplus of funds, I learned to appreciate the value of money. It held power, yet came at a cost.

"And you're leaving me alone with that daughter of yours. She has no respect."

I stepped closer to my wife and wrapped my arms around her. She dropped her head to my chest, and I kissed the top of her head. Her hair smelled of perfumed flowers—some fancy designer shampoo that cost fifty bucks a bottle. She whined about the money for days after each purchase of it but said it was the only shampoo that made her hair shiny.

She only surrendered for a few seconds before her head shot back, and she scanned my eyes. "You're having an affair."

The sound escaped my throat.

"You're laughing at me?" She pulled out of my arms; both of hers rose in a defensive stance. "You are!" The words spat out. "That's why you went to the office late the other night. That's why you were gone most of the night. I know you came in around three AM"

I knew the smile remained. Why was everything about that? Any time a man showed an interest in something other than his wife, he must be cheating. Maybe that's why I never told her about gun range Thursdays. I preferred to avoid the confrontation and ensuing lecture.

I placed my hands on her arms and managed to neutralize her mood. As I made the connection, I felt everything rush in on me—my past, the people I had killed, and how they all had families as well. They never got to come home to their loved ones. I needed to shake the bouts of conscience before it weakened my resolve.

CHAPTER FIVE

Detroit, Michigan
Friday, June 11th, 6 AM

The week went slowly and painfully as I obsessed every hour, rehashing details I knew while collecting more. Brenda only spoke to me when she needed to about the kids, but she had no way of knowing that what I was doing, and going to do, was for us. Maybe once this was behind me, I would feel the need to cleanse my soul, but I didn't put faith in that projection.

I had received my updated fake IDs from Christian and used the days to make calls to the hotels that could cater to the expensive tastes of the Governor. I finally struck gold when The Grandeur confirmed the reservation.

I analyzed my knowledge of Behler. She was a single woman and had never been married. She believed in the sanctity of marriage and spoke publicly about preserving oneself for a committed relationship. Her concern wasn't the broken hearts, but the taxed economic climate that took a hit when people couldn't afford children, or they needed to place them into the system.

Behler had various lovers, none of them serious. I just hoped she wasn't meeting one of them. But from the way she mentioned the getaway, when we were in a meeting, there was more to her getaway than a personal tryst, there was a political agenda. There was no public record of a conference or debate, but it seemed apparent to me that the Governor was headed to New York in some official capacity.

The sun hadn't risen, yet my mind was fully awake. I had watched the ceiling in the dark for the last hour as if trying to derive answers from it. But the level of intensity didn't matter. I still didn't know what I was getting myself involved with being given so little time for research. In the past, I usually stalked the person for a while to ensure there weren't additional causalities or collateral damage. I had been paid to kill one person at a time, and that would be the only person who died. This trip would be no different.

Behler would die alone. I would get in and out without being deemed a threat. I would return to my family and my association with the Russos put behind me. Again. This time for good.

My heart rhythm bumped off course every time I graphically envisioned pulling the trigger inches from her head. I wasn't sure if it came from a buried high that wished to re-emerge or from fear that once it did return, it might be back for good.

Brenda was starting to move around more, and she yawned.

The alarm clock read six. She didn't need to be up for at least an hour. I rolled on my side to face her and found her eyes open. My vision had adjusted to the darkness in the room, and hers must have too since she turned her face away when our eyes met.

"Don't be like that." I moved over to hold her.

"I just don't know why you have to go." Brenda was a thirty-eight-year-old woman, but she could still conjure a decent whine.

I slipped an arm around her waist, slid my hand under her pajama top, and massaged a breast.

"Please don't."

"I love you." I pinched a nipple between my fingers. "I wouldn't go if I didn't have to."

"Would you stop?" There was a teasing quality to her voice. Did her no mean no? I kept my hand in place.

"It's only for today and tomorrow. I'll be back on Sunday. I'll make sure I leave early enough to return for brunch." I wondered for a moment how many hit men had a woman they answered to for their actions.

Her head turned and she looked at me over a shoulder. "You better Mr. Hunter." Her face was rigid, but a smile broke through.

I took this as a sign my hand was fine where it was. She rolled over to face me and wrapped her arm around me.

As our lips met, starting with small kisses and growing in intensity, I knew the passion I had for my wife of fifteen years would be the envy of most people. As we touched and moved together, despite the passage of time, it remained exciting; there was nothing boring or predictable about it. Her breathing deepened and caught; mine in turn. I took her, and we made love like newlyweds, but with the benefit of years of experience and familiarity.

Afterward, still over her, I brushed a strand of hair from her face. She looked up at me, vulnerability written on her features. It was time to reassure her. "You're the only one I love. You know that." I tapped her lips with mine and pulled back to study her eyes. She was crying. "What is it?"

"It's just…" Her words broke through sobs.

Maybe she was tired? Brenda normally wasn't emotional like this.

"I just have a bad feeling."

"A bad feeling like what? I'm cheating on you?" I thought I'd beat her to the accusation.

She slapped my chest and laughed. "No. We've been through that." She paused, and the silence held an uncertain quality.

What wasn't she saying?

"You know I don't like you on the road. I trust your driving, but other people…well, they're idiots. They change lanes without looking, they swerve—"

I placed a hand on her temple and caressed it with the back of my hand. "I will be all right." I sure as hell hoped I could come through on those words. But it wasn't a car accident I feared, it was the possible repercussions if things didn't go according to plan.

"You can't promise that."

Brenda worked with a woman whose life tragically ended when the bulk of a transport made one with her SUV. Since then, Brenda had an unhealthy fear of getting into a car accident. It had been a sunny August day and according to Brenda, people weren't supposed to die on beautiful days. How I wished there was an exemption.

I moved back to my side of the bed; my eyes staring again at the ceiling.

"Well, you can't promise that, can you?" Accusation and anger filled her tone.

"Guess not."

I heard her continue to sob, and my heart ripped at the fact I had to leave her. But I didn't have a choice. I thought of the money in the safe, Christian's smug arrogance as he sat in my living room. Maybe I should have arranged to take care of the Governor in town. Maybe I should have picked another time. The questions rolled through my mind like a spinning Rolodex.

"Well, go do what you have to do." The tears were drying up.

"I'll come back to you." I rolled over and kissed her forehead. "Now, I've got to go." As I rose, a pillow hit me in the back. Turning to Brenda she was laughing, flirting with me as a teenager. I smiled at her and swooped down next to her.

She slapped my chest. "Go now. You must be going." Brenda was laughing, and we kissed some more before she kicked me out of bed. "And you better be back for brunch on Sunday!"

She called out to me, minutes later, as I left the bedroom dressed and with my bag in hand. I had packed everything last night.

I went down the hallway to rouse the sleeping bears. They needed to be up for school anyway. The fact that it was earlier than normal was something they would have to deal with. I went in to see Max first. I found him curled up on the bed on his side, his arms wrapped around his legs.

"Hey, Champ." As I sat on the bed beside him, I wondered how many fathers called their sons Champ. I liked to think of myself and my family as different, special, but didn't everyone think that way? "Max."

He let out a moan, followed by a yawn. The NASCAR logos on his sheets were skewed and bunched up. My son tossed a lot at night.

"I've got to go Buddy."

"Bye." He rolled on his back and placed his arms under his head.

I smiled. I would be back in two days. To him, I could understand he wouldn't see it as a big deal. I repeated the thought myself, *everything would be fine*. I bent over to kiss his forehead.

"Oh gross!" Max shot upward to a seated position. "Don't kiss me, dad!" He was wiping erratically at his forehead. "What's wrong with you?"

I started laughing.

"It's not funny." He flopped back on the bed. "It's early." He wiped at his eyes.

They grew up too fast. "I'll be back Sunday."

"Yeah, yeah. Nite dad. See you then." Max let out a large yawn, fluffed his pillow, and rolled back to his side.

He would need to get up for school soon enough. I stepped out of the room backward, studying it as if I would never see it again. Brenda had a bad feeling and it sought to ratchet my paranoia.

Max's fascination with NASCAR made itself evident in every piece of furniture and accessory in his room. He had the car-shaped bed, the desk lamp, the wall switch cover, and a binder for school—all of which had the logo imprinted on them.

His school backpack lay on the floor by his desk as if it was just dropped there on his way by. It even had an NASCAR logo on it. For the commitment he showed to the sport he should have received royalties for the sponsorship.

He told me his favorite driver was that not just because of winning many championships, but because of his good sportsmanship. I never saw racing cars as a sport. When I had time to pass, I'd rekindle the underlying debate, and the kid would go on for hours. As I left the room, I smiled. He was a good kid.

I flicked the light switch on as I backed out of the room.

"Dad!"

I knew I was the bad guy, but the kid had school and the instilling of responsibility started with regular attendance. At least that's what I told myself; really it was a selfish reason. I wanted some time with the kids.

Down the hall, I knocked on my daughter's door. I had made the mistake of walking in once and got the lecture about how inappropriate that was, and how I needed to respect her privacy. The argument that I paid for her privacy didn't carry any weight.

"I'm coming!" I could tell by her tone, she assumed her mother came around for the wake-up call. She watched her attitude with me.

"It's me, honey."

"Oh, Dad." Yvonne opened the door and walked back to her bed. She dropped heavily and sat there with her legs crossed in front of her as one would around a campfire. She started pecking at the small keys on her phone. Apparently, texting with friends started early. "I can't believe you're leaving me—"

"Yvonne, get out here!" Brenda called from the hall.

Yvonne let out a huff of air. "With mom."

"I'll be back Sunday—"

"You better be. I can't handle her any longer." Her eyes went from mine to the screen of her cell and link to the outside world. She closed it only after hitting the send key and bounced up off the bed. She wrapped her arms around me. She was at a vulnerable age. The decisions she made now would affect her for the rest of her life. I held her, recalling all the years when she needed me to make her decisions. Now she made a lot of them on her own.

Yvonne pulled back. "Be safe." She kept the phone in her hands and shuffled her slippered feet along the hardwood.

Brenda stood in the kitchen doorway, a fresh mug of coffee in her hand. It smelled great. "You have your cell phone?"

The question was the same one she asked every day. "It's on." I came to her for one final hug and kiss.

"Here, I made you a to-go." She extended a travel mug to me.

"I couldn't have a better wife." I kissed her on the lips and pried myself away from her.

"Remember that!"

I had convinced myself over the past week, it would be better to place distance between the kill and my family. But I hadn't even left the driveway, and I couldn't wait to get home to them. They needed me, but even more so, I had become dependent on them. My family—they were my life. Now I needed to get to Niagara Falls and get this mission over with.

CHAPTER SIX

There were a lot of things I needed to take care of once I got to Niagara Falls. I needed to familiarize myself with Behler's itinerary, the hotel, its security, and the building's alternative exits.

At this point all I knew for certain was where the Governor was staying. I still had to obtain a floor and room number, but that would be easy enough once I got there.

As I thought through the scenarios, I knew some factors were irrelevant. The Grandeur had a platinum suite—their version of a presidential suite—and knowing the Governor's taste, she likely had that booked.

My feet slammed on the brakes when a minivan cut me off. Most people would swear and speak of blowing the offender off the road with a rocket. It didn't elicit that reaction from me. Maybe it was because I knew I could shoot the driver from a range of a thousand yards and hit the target accurately, that it didn't hold much appeal to me? Whatever it was, the road rage impulse had abated years ago.

The close call refreshed the fact I needed to focus more on the road now, the mission once I got there. The coffee Brenda had made me was long gone. I was about half way through the trip with two hours to go.

A white sign notified of an upcoming exit that offered service stations and a restaurant. It was coming up in two miles; the city was London, Ontario. I'd allow myself a washroom break and a coffee to go.

"Extra large. Black." I stood at the counter watching the teenage girl impatiently. Every step in the process seemed to take minutes.

"You don't need something to eat at every stop."

I turned in the direction of a woman's voice. She spoke to her teenage daughter who wore black lipstick and had blue highlights in her hair. A man stood with them holding a boy about three in his arms.

I smiled turning back to face the counter, thankful Yvonne hadn't gone the way of the Goth on us.

I took a deep breath and stretched out my neck. If anything went wrong, and the experienced always had to calculate the odds, how could I ever forgive myself? I hated being so far away from my family, but again I had no choice. I needed to shake this negative energy and move forward.

"That will be one ninety."

I tossed the change on the counter and took my coffee. I needed to get to Niagara Falls and get this over with before my emotions took hold and superseded rational thinking. It took years to let go of the past. The feelings of worthlessness, of being undeserving of love, and now, in a span of seven days, my past lifestyle rose to the surface bringing with it that feeling of inadequacy.

I passed the family one more glance as I walked by. What was I doing here?

Hours down the road, focus on completing the task remained difficult. Images of my family kept striking at inconvenient moments. But, again, what choice did I have? I willed myself to remember the faces of my kills—the way their eyes enlarged when they realized their time had come, and how their spirit faded in their eyes.

Maybe the pen gun wouldn't be everyone's choice. But the way I saw it, overkill was wasteful and unnecessary—an amateur's MO. Accuracy and efficiency combined with being able to conceal it topped my list of importance when it came to my choice of weapon. The pen gun fulfilled all those requirements.

It enabled me to carry it without detection. And in cases, such as with the Governor, her bodyguard could even frisk me and not be the wiser. If his hands did feel it, he'd think it was a pen and wouldn't expect it to harness the killing power of any equal .22 handgun. Another advantage was the bullets were untraceable, meaning no striations. The demand to fire it barrel to skin would fragment the bullet inside the victim's head.

I had been a lover of firepower since my early teen years and made my first homemade zip gun by the age of seventeen. The accuracy was pathetic, and honestly, I was lucky I didn't injure myself or anyone else in the process. As the bullet fired out of the barrel, the heat of it singed my fingers, but I got wise and started to wear gloves as I tinkered with it. From there as my love of guns evolved, I came to value the straighter, more precise trajectory of the Remington 700. It made for an accurate shot up to just over six hundred yards away. That meant little possibility of being made—a highly valuable commodity when you were paid to kill and preferred to get away with it. But Christian favored to utilize my talent of killing up close. Maybe he was simply prejudiced from our first meeting.

My cheeks swelled with the passing thought of him. My fingers gripped the steering wheel hard enough to turn the knuckles white. I shook him, and the way everything got started, from my mind. One couldn't change the past. I had to focus on the future.

But first I had a few stops to make, starting with exchanging my car for a rental. I'd pick one up at the airport and leave my vehicle among the hundreds of others that were parked there on a regular basis.

CHAPTER SEVEN

Detroit, Michigan
Friday, June 11th, 12 Noon

If **Brenda** spent one more minute in the office, she'd be telling her boss where to put the spreadsheets. But today it wasn't just him on her case. Everything her coworkers did drove her to the brink of turning physically hostile.

Tina, a woman who shared the front office with her, was unusually chatty today. Discussing everything from what she ate for dinner the night before to what shifts her husband would work for the foreseeable future. As if Brenda cared. Not to mention the slew of personal stories she kept regurgitating.

Normally, on days like this, she would call Ray at his office, or show up for a last minute lunch date. Today, he had left her alone—some last minute tax seminar in Niagara Falls. She still wasn't buying it. But he had been so loving with her this morning. And they had a great marriage, didn't they? At least she thought they did. No matter the number of his reassurances, she worried that he withheld something from her, and if it was another woman the sooner she knew, the better.

He exceeded some husbands' communication skills, who preferred not to talk at all, but there were areas for improvement. She could tell by the way that he'd pull back when she'd confront him about his emotions. His face would distort and he'd shake his head. Most times he'd leave the room. In those moments, she knew her assumptions were fact. And the same thing happened with this seminar. He didn't leave the room; he wrapped his arms around her to shield his eyes from hers. And for an instance, she had fallen for it. But when she accused him of cheating on her, he laughed in her face. A smile danced on her lips now. That meant he was telling the truth and even found her accusation humorous.

As she set her keys on the kitchen counter, she noticed the blinking light on the answering machine. Maybe she'd check it tonight. She had enough messages to deal with at the office.

She went to the fridge, pulled out a package of deli sliced turkey and a jar of non-fat mayo. But the light on the machine kept signaling her. She hated her obsessive compulsiveness sometimes. She sighed as she pushed the button. As she listened to the message, the butter knife fell to the floor.

Niagara Falls, New York
1:00 PM

The streets were crowded with tourists eager to catch a glimpse of the largest waterfall in North America. To me, Niagara Falls was simply a bunch of water cascading over a hill. The draw to witness it, to breathe in any of its supposed beauty, was wasted on me.

The check-in for The Grandeur was four, which should allow plenty of time to look around before the Governor showed up. At least I hoped for that. The disadvantage of choosing a spot outside of my home territory was that the recon mission needed to happen in a close time proximity to the execution of the hit. When the targets were in the city of Detroit, or even when I was single for that matter, there was more time to do the digging around beforehand. Familiarity of the environment could mean the difference between life and death, of getting away or being caught.

Tomorrow night, Saturday, was when I planned on taking out the Governor.

Taking out the Governor? Was I really doing this? I shook my conscience that attempted to tell me that I wasn't a killer anymore. I had to realize nothing changed except a wife and a couple kids. The same heart beat within me, the same brain fired its synapses, and the same lungs brought in the oxygen. Why couldn't I shake the bad feelings? I silently cursed Brenda for even mentioning hers.

I pulled into the parking lot of The Oasis about one in the afternoon. It would be nothing compared to the luxury of The Grandeur, but it would have a bed and a bathroom—the necessary amenities. And most importantly, it was only a short drive to The Grandeur.

The Oasis was a real dive and must have only survived due to the generosity of families seeking some sort of accommodation on their excursion to the Falls. Despite its distance away, it might have held appeal for the price tag of sixty-five bucks a night. It was a single-story, personally owned and operated motel dating back to the sixties. I could envision an oversized heart-shaped sign posted over the front door that would read, HONEYMOON SUITE WITH HEART-SHAPED BED. It didn't have one though.

My tux hung in its wrapping off the backseat hook, and I couldn't wait for an opportunity to wear it. Dressing up for occasions had always been something I found pleasure in doing. However, I would have preferred the moment to be shared with my wife. In this instance, it would be what the Governor saw me in before her eyes closed for the last time.

The thought of her falling backward, dead, had played out numerous times in my mind and was beginning to morph into reality, making it conceivable.

The front desk clerk of The Oasis was an older man in his sixties. His eyes were fixed on the cash I pulled out of my pocket to prepay the room.

"Cash then, eh? No credit?" He spoke as a stereotypical Canadian, adding the word *eh* to the end of his sentences. My guess was he hadn't been in the United States for many years. He counted out the bills I gave him as if they had changed values when I extended them to him.

"That good then?" I asked.

The older man placed each bill individually into the register. "We're good." I noticed his eyes dance to the insignia on my shirt. It was a Polo and had cost about sixty dollars. He was probably wondering why a guy who would spend that much on a shirt would stay at The Oasis.

When he looked back at me his eyes read, *are you in some sort of trouble*, but he never verbalized his inquiry. Maybe it was my mood that placed the insinuation there.

I dropped my bag on the bed in the motel room; it didn't make an impression. I placed a hand on the surface. It was hard as hell. The springs would likely ease their marks into my back when I laid down tonight. I would worry about my comfort later, even postponing that until Sunday, when I could crawl into my own bed. But right now I had a job to do and that took priority.

A long dresser occupied the one end the room with a tube television sitting on top of it. To the middle was a mirror about four feet square. The artwork on the walls was cheap and looked like it had been bought at a flea market. The bathroom was crammed into a space only large enough for a full grown man to back into and reverse out of.

I took the wrapping off the tux and admired the design, the fit, and the fabric. The ordered alterations were perfect. I slapped on fresh cologne and worked at getting myself into the *monkey suit*. To get any access to the Governor one had to project the impression that they belonged in her world. I studied my reflection in the mirror. My brown eyes looked tired from the drive. My hair was dark and shaved short. It had receded more than I would have liked, but my wife said it made me look distinguished. My circle beard complimented my round-shaped face, and if I had to admit it, I was looking quite dapper.

I reached into a pocket of my jeans and pulled out my cell phone. I had told Brenda it was on, and that was not a lie, but I had the volume muted. I looked at the display, zero missed calls. *Good.* I didn't need anything to distract me from what I needed to do.

CHAPTER EIGHT

Niagara Falls, New York
Friday, June 11th, Just After 2 PM

Traffic moved slowly. Not only due to the tourists, but the population of the city had day jobs they needed to carry out. Courier vehicles crowded the roads. A FedEx truck led the way for seven blocks, and at the last minute decided he had reached his next stop. He slammed on the brakes and swerved to the right, bringing his truck to the curb. Road rage surfaced despite my prior illusion of having control. I had to let the tension out of my neck and shoulders.

The Grandeur could be seen from several blocks away. It stood out as a beautiful monument next to buildings of more subdued architectural details. Still I wondered why the Governor chose Niagara Falls as a getaway destination. Knowing her love of the finer things, why not New York City itself? She could experience fine cuisine and award-winning restaurants. Niagara Falls may have been a tourist destination, but I suspected that the Governor hadn't come for the view.

I pulled into the underground garage and looked at myself one last time in the rear view mirror. My eyes had started to change. They were full of sheer determination and reflected my past. I would be killing the Governor and walking away from it a million dollars richer.

She's just another hit. Maybe if I repeated it enough.

I pulled down on my tux as I got out of the car and depressed my thumb on the key fob. The lights flashed and the security system beeped.

An elderly couple had gotten out of their vehicle across the row and smiled at me. I could tell by their faces they respected a younger man who was dressed up. People didn't do that anymore. At least not since grunge became a new standard. I performed a partial nod as a greeting and kept moving.

The Grandeur housed apartments in the base, and the hotel occupied the highest eight floors. I assumed the Governor would be in the platinum suite, but I needed to verify this.

I took the elevator up to the hotel lobby, which was on the first of the eight floors. The front desk was made of marble and had two higher tiers. The clerk sat in the middle of the tiers. In front, there were two wingback chairs for the guests who were checking in. I never took a seat.

The woman behind the counter smiled. "Welcome to The Grandeur. What can I do for you today?" Her name badge read Lauren.

I returned her smile and put on the charm. Her cheeks flushed a pinkish hue. In the words of ZZ Top: *every girl's crazy 'bout a sharp dressed man.*

I left my sunglasses on. I couldn't see the security cameras, but I was certain of their existence. Even if this clerk were questioned about me later, I'd be long gone. "Lauren, I have a friend who is going to be checking in today. I would like to see if she's arrived as of yet."

"Certainly." Her eyes narrowed; a goofy smile lingered on her lips. "Her name?"

"Marian Behler."

"She hasn't checked in yet, but she has until after six before she'd be considered late."

"Are you able to give me her assigned room number?" I leaned against one of the higher tiers of the counter. From this position, I could easily see the phone.

"I'm sorry, but I can't. It also looks like she has a couple of rooms booked."

A couple of rooms? Knowing Behler, she probably did so for privacy. "Well, that's a shame. I had wanted to surprise her. Is her room made up yet?"

She typed a concoction of letters onto the keyboard. "That floor is the first cleaned."

"*That* floor?"

"The twentieth. They always start at the top, work their way down. All floors should be done soon…" Her words stalled when she realized she gave the assigned floor for Behler away. "You're a tricky one." The clerk laughed. As she did, she straightened her posture, and her cleavage became more evident.

"There's no way I could go up? Wait for her? Surprise her? I haven't seen her in a long time."

Lauren looked conflicted between appeasing me and keeping her job. "I really can't." She pressed her lips downward. "I'm sorry."

"Can you at least connect me to her room?" I placed a hand on the arm of my sunglasses, reminding myself not to remove them. The Grandeur, like most hotels, had sufficient light yet its intensity was subdued and with the glasses in place even more so.

"She won't be there."

"Yes, I realize that. But I'm sure you have answering machines in all your suites."

"Of course. All of our rooms."

"Would you call hers for me?" I adjusted my posture so that it gave me a direct line of sight to the keys on the phone.

Lauren smiled. "I can do that. Just pick one of them?"

"If I know her at all, pick the largest suite."

She nodded, and I watched as she referred to the computer monitor and then punched the numbers into the phone.

8. 3. 8.

"Here you go." She extended me the receiver.

I waited for five rings until the phone forwarded to the voicemail system before hanging up.

Lauren looked confused. "You were going to leave a message?"

I straightened my posture and slipped my hands into my pockets. "I've changed my mind. I want to surprise her in person."

Lauren's eyes blinked heavily. "That is so sweet."

"Well, she's not really expecting me." I smiled at Lauren. "Thank you."

"Anytime."

I left Lauren sitting there wondering who this mysterious man in a tuxedo was. But let her wonder. I didn't need my identity known. I lowered my head and walked away from the front desk. I had my room now. And I had something even better.

The hotel occupied the last eight floors of this building. If Behler's suite was on the highest floor, and the maid service cleaned there first and Lauren mentioned they were almost done, I would best be finding them finishing on the first floor—this floor.

I entered the hallway where the rooms were and looked left and right and didn't see a maid cart.

I worked my way around the floor and spotted one at the end of the hallway. The accompanying maid must have been inside a room. When I reached the cart, I heard her. She was singing some Justin Bieber song I recognized as coming from my daughter's room. Her voice overpowered the vacuum she was running. Timing on my part couldn't have been more perfect.

I moved around the cart with two things in my mind—the location of security cameras and the all-access card key. I spotted the closest camera and turned my back on it, and as I did, I noticed the card key dangling from a chain. Again, I was fortunate that the maid didn't have it around her neck. I took out the card reader from my pocket and slid it through twice. The lights went green notifying me that it had read it successfully.

I picked up some bars of soap and a hand towel. To anyone watching from security, it would simply look like a guest who needed more toiletries and helped themselves. I laughed thinking about the conversation that would evolve around it. Man in tuxedo raids maid's cart.

Around the corner, the maid's singing, if you wanted to call it that, could still be heard. She had built up to the chorus line and should she have ever auditioned for American Idol when Simon Cowell was judging, he'd say, *are you serious.*

I slipped into the public washroom, dumped the toiletries into the garbage receptacle, and slipped into the large stall on the end. I pulled out the card reader/writer and my smartphone. I took a blank card from another pocket and brought up the needed application and changed the direction to "write card." The lights turned yellow, and I had just been granted access to every room of The Grandeur for the cost of an app and a card writer.

CHAPTER NINE

The timing couldn't have been more perfect. With Governor Behler not being able to check-in to her suite yet, and with her room having being cleaned, it afforded me the perfect timeframe to get in and do what I needed to do. I still had at least another hour before Behler could access her room.

The hallway on the twentieth floor was silent. I didn't hear anyone in the rooms as I made my way down to number 838. I noticed the security cameras and made sure I was never facing them directly.

I stopped in front of the room and took a deep breath. Moving forward from this point would make all this real. No longer would it be two-dimensional as played out in my mind.

I pulled out the key card and slid it into the card pass. It hesitated and then displayed red lights. Maybe I had done something wrong?

I tried again. The lights on the lock flashed green this time, and I turned the handle. As I walked into a room that wasn't mine, it felt like a betrayal of someone else's space even though that person hadn't claimed it yet. At the minimum, I knew I wasn't supposed to be here. But I didn't have a choice. I needed to go through with the assassination if I didn't want to risk losing my family for good. I lifted my sunglasses to my head and walked around the suite checking out the different rooms.

The door opened to a living area with a matching creamy-gray leather loveseat and chair and a black oak coffee table. Red drapes hung from bulky rods and were paired with white vertical blinds. A large flat screen TV sat on a credenza that matched the table. There was a phone at the end of it.

To the left of the entry was a wet bar with a bar fridge beneath the counter. A coffee pot and serving tray with mugs and sugar packets sat beside it.

To the right, a double-wide door led into the master bedroom. The door trim was also black oak as were the other wood elements in the suite. At the far end of the room was a stately fireplace with another large screen TV mounted above it. There was an ensuite bathroom with double sinks and large mirrors and brushed silver fixtures.

I slipped on a pair of gloves and went back to the phone in the main sitting area. I pulled out a small recording device with an unlimited range of transfer. It was connected to yet another app on my smartphone and permitted me to hear everything.

I placed one on every phone and by count there were three—one in the main sitting area, one in the bedroom, and one in the bathroom.

My heart raced within me just thinking about what I was preparing to do. With the devices in place, I would know what I was up against and whether the Governor traveled alone. I would discover the best way to take her down.

With the latter thought, my family tapped at my numbing conscience. I couldn't allow them back into my line of thought. As long as I was in Niagara Falls, I had no family. I had nothing to lose. To admit to anything else would only weaken my resolve and make room for error. I had never failed in the past. I had no intention of starting now.

I put my sunglasses back in place and left the room. I found a stairwell at the end of the north hallway. It was located further from the Governor's suite than the elevators, but it could prove to be a viable option I might have to utilize.

But for right now, there was nothing to do but wait.

. . .

I went back to The Oasis and ordered in a fresh pie topped with everything from double meat to fresh veggies. I pulled out a bottle of Scotch from my travel bag and settled in for the night. I'd need my rest to carry out what I needed to do tomorrow. Tonight would simply be about establishing direction and listening to everything that came through from the Governor's room. I needed to find out her plans for tomorrow so that I knew when best to strike.

Nothing was coming through, and by seven, I worried that something had gone wrong with the bugs I had planted. Had they been found by her security? Maybe her traveling bodyguard was more diligent than most hired monkeys.

I doubled checked the app, and it appeared to be online. I had placed it on the nightstand beside me with speakers attached to it. It was ready to record anything that went on in that room. I turned the volume up on the tube television. Between the light buzz provided by the Scotch and lack of surround sound, I found it hard to hear. At the same point, I didn't want to overpower the phone and miss anything that came through from the Governor's room either.

"Yes, I'm here now."

The voice came through beside me, and I quickly muted the television.

The clock read ten thirty.

"...seven tomorrow. Don't be late. I can't stand tardiness." The Governor's voice held a serious tone to it.

She was with someone, or at the very least planned on meeting up with someone. This may require an adjustment to my plans. The conversation she carried on was one sided which meant she must have been on a phone call.

She didn't say anything else for hours. And even though I made myself stay awake, all I could hear was her soft snores. I made sure it was still recording and turned the light out. I needed rest myself. I would review everything in the morning.

CHAPTER TEN

Niagara Falls, New York
Saturday, June 12th, 8:30 AM

The curtains of the room did little for keeping out the morning sunlight. My back felt broken in several spots from where the bed impressed its springs like a horrible form of acupuncture. I rose to my feet and stretched.

Nothing was coming through the speakers, but the app was still recording. I'd have hours to study it and plan my next step.

The clock read eight thirty.

Right now I needed coffee. I went over to the machine in the room to find two mugs, one filter, and a little sign that read, COFFEE A BUCK A PACK. What motel charged for coffee and didn't leave any in the room?

Shit!

I needed one badly. I hardly slept at all between the bed and the reoccurring flashbacks to my last kill.

Names weren't important, but I still knew them—for each one of my marks. My last was Bob Riley. He couldn't make good on his gambling bets at Russo's racetrack. His extension had expired, and I was sent in to finish him off.

When I went into Bob's apartment, one he kept for screwing his mistress, he barely clung to life. Russo had sent in the heavy hitters to break his jaw, his nose, his kneecaps, and both of his wrists. The work had taken place over several hours of torture. I never understood why they didn't just take care of it themselves.

Bob was drifting in and out from the pain, but when he heard my footsteps on the floorboards, his eyes opened wide. I raised the gun and took him out with one bullet between the eyes before he had a chance to scream.

But broken bones weren't Bob's only means of torture. His tongue had been cut out as a message to other deadbeats—spoken promises meant nothing. He also had the words TSK TSK carved into his chest with a knife.

I found out later Christian had killed the rest of his family, including his wife and two children at their house in the city. I knew then that there was nothing Christian wasn't capable of. When he had extended the job to me, he presented it as a night of entertainment.

Bob's eyes mingled with Christian's in my nightmares last night. This kill would be a lot smoother. This was the type of thing I had been trained for. This type of kill was what I possessed a natural ability for. I didn't have a problem getting close to my marks. Most killers preferred to keep a distance. I would rather be up close.

"Rick, ensure my reservation at Casa Grande."

I moved back to the bed. The Governor was up and giving directions. Rick was possibly one of her bodyguards. She had a few of them and I didn't know them all on a per name basis.

I pulled the phonebook from the nightstand. Casa Grande was a restaurant specializing in fine Italian cuisine. Based on her comments last night about meeting someone at seven, and now mention of the restaurant, I knew right where to find the Governor tonight. I smiled. I would have another chance to wear my tux.

Nothing much else came through, and when I heard a door close followed by silence, I figured she had left her suite.

I dialed the front desk of The Oasis and got the man who had signed me in yesterday as easily disclosed by the *eh* at the end of his sentence.

Minutes later, there was a knock on my door. "Coffee's here." It was the older ex-Canadian. I started to wonder if anyone else worked here. The man stood in the doorway exhibiting a body language that read he would have stepped into the room if I gave him an inch.

"One buck." He moved his head to the side trying to look around me.

I exchanged a five dollar bill for the coffee packet. "Keep the change." I went to close the door.

"That's a nice tux you have, Mister?"

The word *Mister* came out arched as if he was fishing for a name. "Thank you." I closed the door. Only then did I pick up on the fact that he had seen me in the tux yesterday. Hopefully, nothing more would be thought of it.

I took my coffee black, which turned out to be a good thing seeing as there were no whitener packs, sugar or sweetener in the room and the man hadn't brought any with him.

My first mouthful of the brew was offensive, but I forced myself to swallow it. It was caffeine. And that was something I desperately needed. I stopped the recording and played back what I had missed while I had been sleeping.

"Don't worry. Everything will be taken care of. I promise you that." It was only the Governor's voice again, and I surmised another telephone call. She continued, "…everything will be taken care of…yes, tonight—"

There was a loud banging on my door. I hit pause on the feedback. What the hell was it now?

I looked through the peephole and opened the door a few inches. "What is it?"

"Four more packets of coffee. You gave me five bucks, eh?" The older man smiled.

I pulled the card that hung inside on the door knob, opened the door further, took the coffee from him, slapped the Do not Disturb sign in place, and shut the door. "Good day."

Now back to the recording. I hit play.

"…Talbot will listen to me. Yes, tomorrow night…don't worry I have everything with me."

Talbot? That was the Governor of New York state.

"I have everything under control. I will update you once it's done."

Nothing more was said until this morning when I heard her direct Rick to confirm a reservation. Before that, I heard a running shower and CNN.

I stared into my coffee, deep in thought. What would the Governor of Michigan have to do with the Governor of New York? And what exactly did she have under control?

CHAPTER ELEVEN

Niagara Falls, New York
Saturday, June 12, 6:45 PM

"Welcome to Casa Grande." The maître d' braced his hands on the walnut podium that held a desk light and his reservation schedule. "Name, sir?"

I pulled out a hundred dollar bill and passed it to him. "I trust that should be sufficient."

He looked down to the bill, and when he noticed its value, his thin lips pressed upward. "Table for one?"

I nodded.

"One moment." He held a bony finger up in the air and left his station for a few seconds. He returned with a smile. "Table for one. Right this way. Please follow me."

Aromas of garlic, sautéed onions, and tomato-based sauces saturated the restaurant. My stomach tossed at the smells. As I followed the maître d', I scanned the restaurant. I noticed the back of a man whose head resembled photographs I had seen of the New York Governor. He was balding on the crown.

I addressed the host, "Is that Governor Talbot?"

He smiled with pride. "Yes, sir. We are honored to have him here tonight." He caught himself. "As we are honored to have you." He gestured to a table set for two. "Will this be acceptable?"

The table was a good twenty feet from where the Governor sat but provided a clear line of sight. I nodded, and the maître d' pulled out a chair for me.

I didn't see any sign of Behler, but I had arrived fifteen minutes early. I had been right in piecing the bits of the Governor's conversations together. She had told Governor Talbot not to be late, and he seemed to have kept to her directions.

The man lifted his glass and turned to glance to his right. He seemed to be looking straight at me, but his eyes passed through me. His expression revealed he wasn't impressed to be here and something told me this meeting wasn't his idea.

His drink was of amber color, and he had drunk a good portion of it. So either he had arrived a lot earlier or drank quickly to suppress nerves. Based on the way his hand clutched the glass, he wasn't ready to release it any time soon.

Not that it would make sense that he'd be nervous about meeting with a colleague. Then Behler's words that had replayed several times in my mind throughout the day reiterated once again, *I will make him listen to me.*

I had noticed her before he did. Governor Behler came in from his left, toting a leather satchel over an arm. She wore a simple, black straight line dress that fell just below the knee. Her slender figure complemented the fabric, which draped on her frame elegantly. I guessed the outfit as designer.

For a woman of fifty-six, she could have pulled off ten years younger than that. Her makeup was always tastefully applied. She kept her auburn hair trimmed short just below the jaw line.

She approached the table and when Governor Talbot noticed her arrival, she flashed him a political smile—one she typically reserved for election time. This meeting wasn't a cordial event. Talbot rose to greet her and shook her hand. She took a seat.

"May I get you something to drink?" The waitress's question pulled me from my observations.

"Just a glass of water."

"Perrier with lime? Or without—"

"Just a glass of water."

The waitress nodded, but her eyes gave away her conflict. She might not be getting a large tip from the man in the Armani tux.

My attention went back to the Governors. No one around them seemed to cast them a second glance. In fact it seemed most people did their best to avoid looking in their direction at all. I knew I should hang back and keep a distance, but curiosity got the best of me. I wanted to know the reason why the two Governors, from different states, would meet privately like this. From my understanding, Governor Talbot was a married man. His children were grown. I most certainly didn't sense any sexual chemistry between the two of them. This wasn't an affair.

Behler had a glass of champagne brought to the table, and she flashed another one of those insincere smiles to the staff. She lifted her satchel from the floor beside her and pulled a phone out of it. Talbot tossed back the rest of his drink and signaled for a refill from a passing waitress.

I watched Behler's face. Whatever she showed him on her phone was of relative seriousness. The face she typically reserved for the voting public had disappeared. When she spoke, each word seemed pressured to come out.

"Have you decided what you would like to eat?" My waitress was back.

"Another few minutes." I dismissed her with a wave of a hand.

I needed to get closer to them to figure out what was going on. I knew that the notion was insanity. I had one objective when it came to the Governor. My debate over getting closer to what was transpiring was absurd. And foolish. And careless.

I scanned the restaurant and noticed the signs for the washroom were behind my table. When I turned back to look at the Governors' table, Talbot's refill had been delivered, and he already had the glass pressed to his lips. The other hand that didn't hold the glass was balled into a fist on the table.

I drank the rest of my water as if it would somehow provide the strength and courage to approach them. I swallowed the logic that dictated I stay away from her and just get the job done later tonight. What they discussed didn't matter. I didn't need the Governor to gain access to her room. I just needed to hang back and wait for them to appear finished with their meal. I would beat her back to her suite and be waiting there. Before she had a chance to sense my threat, she'd be dead, and just prior to that, she'd know the reason why.

. . .

Detroit, Michigan

Brenda refused to let her anger show to the children, but with Ray's cell constantly forwarding to voicemail, it became harder to hide. She slammed the receiver back to the cradle.

"Holy crap, Mom." Yvonne walked through to the kitchen.

"Don't speak to me like that."

"Well, you've been a bitch—"

"Watch your mouth!" She would never tolerate her daughter speaking to her like that. And if Ray had been here, Yvonne would be happy to see the light of day. He believed strongly in grounding them for disciplinary measures. Brenda never agreed as to the effectiveness. The kid had everything she needed from the outside world in that room. There was, however, one effective means to mete out correction to a fourteen-year-old.

"Your cell phone now." Brenda held out an opened palm to her daughter.

Her daughter's eyes flashed rage as she tossed the phone on the counter. "I hate you!"

Well, right now I hate your father. Of course, she couldn't speak those words aloud, but the message she got on the machine yesterday made her question everything. He said he wasn't cheating on her. Yet he took off last minute to Niagara Falls and ordered a tuxedo for pick up. Since when did they have that type of money anyhow? He better hope that he just stayed in New York State, because when he did return, she was going to kill him.

...

Niagara Falls, New York

"Raymond?" Behler looked up at me, glanced at the phone she held extended to the Governor of New York, and quickly pulled it into her chest. "What are you doing here?" She smiled at me. Although not her best work, she attempted the full political showcase.

"Just here on some business." It wasn't a lie.

"By yourself then?" Her eyes went up and down my tuxedo. "You clean up well, Mr. Hunter." The complete smile now broadcasted.

"Yourself as well." I returned the smile and cast a glance at the New York Governor. He was flushed, and a rapid twitch pulsed in his right cheek. He avoided eye contact.

"How rude of me." Behler gestured toward him. "This is Vance Talbot, Governor of New York state."

"I must say I recognized him." I extended my hand to the man. He shook it, but his grip was weak. Whatever they had been discussing didn't please him. I glanced at his drink. Another one had almost disappeared. At this distance, I picked up on the scent of Scotch.

"Raymond Hunter is an acquaintance of mine." Behler distanced herself with the introduction. Talbot seemed more interested in people at other tables. His eyes were hardened and glassy from the alcohol.

Behler placed her satchel back on the floor. A tangible silence filled the space, and I saw this as my point of exit. "Good evening." I took a step back from the table.

"Nonsense. Are you traveling alone?" Governor Behler repeated her earlier question that I hadn't answered.

"I am."

"Why don't you join us?" Behler turned to her companion who shot me one of his own political smiles—obviously forced.

"Well, if you're sure."

"Of course." Staff was summoned over. An oversized table for two became a compact one for three.

"What brings you to the fine state of New York, Mr. Hunter?" Talbot asked out of political etiquette; I sensed not out of sincere interest.

"If I told you, I might have to kill you." I spoke the words knowing they'd be taken as a joke.

Behler took hold of the conversation again. "I've known you for what—thirteen years now?"

I took a sip of the water that had been placed in front of me. "Fourteen, but who's counting."

"Wow, I didn't imagine it had been that long. Time has a way of moving forward, doesn't it?" Behler lifted her glass and both Governors exchanged glances.

Instinct told me her reference to time moving forward had a bearing on their prior conversation somehow.

Waiting staff took our orders with the exception of Talbot who said something about needing to leave for a prior engagement. The waitress who had been serving me at my table shot sideways glances at me from across the room. She likely wondered who I was to warrant company with people of such prestige.

"It's a shame you're not staying for dinner. I hear they have a marvellous fusilli with creamed leak and spinach here." Behler spoke to Talbot in a tone of voice that I had come to recognize as one she reserved for moments of intimidation. There was something she sought from the New York Governor. I may never know what.

Talbot ordered another drink before excusing himself for the evening.

Behler waited for Talbot to get out of earshot and flung back the rest of the champagne in her glass. "That man is a sack of lies. He no more has a prior affair tonight than I have the election locked for the next two terms."

She sat her glass down and raised her eyes to meet mine. She didn't blink. She was a hardened version of her regular self.

"Has he wronged you, Governor?"

"Please don't call me that." She smiled. "It's Marian to you." She took a pause and her expression turned serious again. "He takes a stand on the side of the law but fails to see that it takes all types of people to make a society."

"'All types of people?'"

"Of course. You need to have freedom of expression to find better ways of doing things. For example, hybrid vehicles. If Ferdinand Porsche had listened to the skepticism of his colleagues, he might not have invented the technology. And if it wasn't for the Kyoto Accord that made the world agree to reduce greenhouse gases, it might not have realized fruition. We'd still be living in the Stone Age.

"And think of solar energy. Because of entrepreneurial individuals, there are grants provided by the government to individuals' properties, as well as to businesses, to obtain kickbacks for hydro consumption. Talbot is a blind man."

"You're here to discuss political issues."

Her eyes churned with an underlying agenda. "Talbot and I go a few years back. We came to discuss issues that affect both of us in our relative positions."

"Hybrids and solar energy?"

It warranted a hearty laugh. "Hardly. But those are a couple of moot points. He just doesn't see the future with the same vision that I do."

"Isn't that part of what you were just mentioning? A society involves all types of people?"

"You listen too well, Mr. Hunter." She leaned back into her chair. "What are you doing later this evening? Would you like to have a nightcap with me?" She extended a hand and placed it on my forearm. "I know you are a married man. I would never jeopardize that. Just my room for a couple drinks. We can talk politics until you bore of it."

"Or discuss your tax returns."

"Or we could talk politics?" She smiled as she repeated her earlier suggestion for a topic of discussion.

"Sure. Sounds fine." My pulse intensified. As I looked across at the woman I was about to kill, I was numb. Prior instinct had become interwoven with my fibers.

"I'm staying at The Grandeur," she said.

I smiled. "What a coincidence."

CHAPTER TWELVE

Behler insisted that i go back to the hotel in her Town Car. I declined. I needed to do some thinking. In less than thirty minutes, she would be dead and I would be the cause.

As she continued talking through dinner, I almost couldn't wait to silence her. It's almost like the woman loved the sound of her own voice. I noticed that she hadn't traveled with a bodyguard to the restaurant. It made me thankful I hadn't taken the original route and waited on her in the hotel room. She had directed a man named Rick to confirm her dinner reservation. It could have been the concierge or hotel staff, but I doubted it. The interaction was brief but held familiarity.

I came off the elevator on the twentieth floor ready to carry out the job. I walked with determination. I had been in this position before. I had taken lives. I had survived. In fact, I even came out wealthier on the other end.

My stride slowed for a single deep breath when I saw the man outside of her room—her bodyguard. She had left him back at the hotel while she met with the New York Governor. She didn't fear for her life. This displayed an arrogance that hadn't manifested itself in the woman before. I knew the woman was both a politician and wealthy, an elixir for having a superiority complex, but I never recognized a careless cockiness in Behler before. That strength would be her weakness.

The motivation for ordering the hit circulated in my mind. I knew one of her primary agendas as Governor, in addition to improving the stilted economy of her state due to the crippled automotive industry, had been a verbal lash out against organized crime. But from what I could see, it had been a bunch of talk, nothing more.

As I neared the room, the man who stood there placed both hands in his pockets, an unusual stance for someone who needed to be on the ready. The weak display exposed his character. He cared more about collecting his paycheck than the Governor's safety.

He seemed like a rat of a man with shifty eyes and scrawny appendages. He moved to the side of the door, granting me access as I moved closer. "The door is unlocked." He placed a hand on my wrist. "Ray." I looked down at his hand. A Rolex peeked from under the cuff of his shirt.

"Get your hand off me."

The guy lifted his hand and smiled. The way his lips curled, it gave me the creeps. This man wasn't hired by Behler's choosing. This man was put in place by the Russos to make sure I succeeded. No bodyguard for hire would be able to afford that watch. I pulled my hand back and put it into my pocket with the pen gun. I wanted to get this over with and behind me.

He knocked on the door and opened it for me. He whispered at a volume just loud enough to discern. "I hope she begs for her life."

I cast him a glance that told him she wouldn't have a chance. "Don't find her until mid-morning, Rick." Saying his name served as a pre-emptive strike and killed his grin until it gave birth to a high pitched laugh unnatural for a man. It was almost like the man was possessed.

"Oh, it's about time you got here, Raymond." The Governor had slipped into more comfortable apparel. Her heels were exchanged in favor of bare feet, and her dress for silk pajamas. A silk robe hung on her small frame, an evident few sizes too large. "I hope you don't mind that I changed. My entire life is formal. Come in, please. Take off your shoes and loosen your bowtie, if you wish." She flashed one of her sincere smiles, afforded only to those with whom she kept close company.

As I returned her smile, I latched the door behind me, careful to do so with the sleeve of my jacket covering my hand. I couldn't leave a trace. And her wardrobe change only made an easier cover. Investigators would wonder if a rendezvous with a lover proved deadly.

"Maybe I will." My goal was to set her at ease and get it done. My heart sounded like a drum; the familiar adrenaline rhythm keeping beat. I pulled one end of the bowtie and let the silk dangle around my neck. I left my shoes on.

"Well, don't stand by the door all night. You'll make me nervous."

I studied her as she moved through the suite to the wet bar. A few bottles lined the countertop; they hadn't been there yesterday. She turned them around to make sure all the labels were facing out. "I have pretty much anything that would appeal to a man of your taste."

Of my taste? Her word choice struck me.

"You look like a Scotch man." She laughed. "Although I believe most men are." She poured a glass from the bottle of Blue Label Johnnie Walker.

I took the drink she extended me and took a small draw. "Good stuff."

My eyes scanned the room I had been in over twenty-four hours prior. Tonight it was riddled with the Governor's effects. Her satchel sat on the table in the living area as if just tossed there when she entered. It beckoned my curiosity, but I had to remember the reason I came here. First some small talk. "You and Governor Talbot seemed to be in a deep conversation when I showed up."

Behler poured herself a drink before taking a seat on the sofa chair. She adjusted her robe as she did so. I remained standing.

"He's a complex man. As I mentioned at the restaurant, he doesn't see the future." Her eyes fell to her drink and then lifted up to meet my eyes.

"I'm surprised that you would find entertainment in his company then."

She laughed. "Well, we're hardly friends if that's what you assume. We are both in the business of representing our people, our respective states. Leaders can only benefit from expanding their field of vision. I was here to help Talbot with that."

"His vision didn't include the Mafia?"

Her eyes opened wide. She did her best to recover but failed when she lifted her drink.

I continued, "You mentioned all types of people are required to make a society. I would assume organized crime would be no different."

"I don't wish to discuss this." Her brows pinched downward.

"The topic of conversation was your choice." I paced around the room. Her eyes followed me. "Politics. 'We can discuss politics all night.' Weren't those your exact words?"

"Who are you?" Rage fired in her eyes, yet there was no hint of fear. She straightened her seated position, leaning slightly forward, her one elbow on a knee.

I walked over to the wet bar, my back to her and took out the pen gun. I pulled out on it and bent it to expose the trigger. I had already loaded it. I turned the arrow to point at F for Fire.

"Is there something I can help you with over there?" She asked, irritation lacing each word.

The time had come. I turned around and made the distance to the sofa chair in less than a second. I placed the small barrel against her forehead. "Gift from Russo."

"I was one of—"

I pushed up on the trigger. The Governor's head fell backward from the impact of the bullet. Her head came to rest on the back edge of the chair, suspended at an upward angle as if looking to a higher power.

I watched as the blood pooled from the wound and dripped down her face—the china doll's face now stained a crimson red. I slung back the rest of my Scotch. I had never found pleasure in death. Killing had simply served as a means of validating myself to the Russos. For a fraction of time, guilt threatened to seize hold of me, but the woody burn from the drink was enough to dislodge it from setting in. It was time to go.

CHAPTER THIRTEEN

I went over how the night had played out numerous times, and with hours left on the road, I would rehash it several more. I had picked up an extra large coffee when I dropped the rental off and got my car, but it had cooled in the holder.

The clock on the car dash read one fifteen. I was only an hour and a quarter into my journey. It would be a long drive home. At this point I was thankful for the rest I got yesterday afternoon and the solitude I had now. It gave me time to think.

I had been careful to remove all the bugs I had set in place before leaving the room. I took them along with the glass I drank the Scotch from and dumped it off in a garbage receptacle a block from the hotel. No one would be able to forensically trace me back to that room.

Fear held power. And I was counting on that to keep the Governor of New York's mouth shut if he got the urge to mention my appearance at the restaurant. Even if he did decide to speak up about *some man*, he'd know Behler herself introduced us and that we went back years. Either he wouldn't perceive me as a threat, or if he did, he might not speak a word about me out of apprehension. He'd simply be thankful that he didn't share the same fate his dinner companion had. The possibility was also there that he might not remember me. He seemed aloof and into his Scotch.

The highway was barren, except for the odd person who had ventured out, and one could always count on transport truck drivers. Their lights were an unpleasant thing for my eyes. Despite the fact I had become wired from the kill, my eyes were sore, making the rest of me feel tired and drained of energy.

I pictured my wife and the kids as I drove. They had no idea their husband and father was a type of chameleon, pretending to blend into a normal suburban lifestyle while housing a murderous past and volatile present. I needed to make the transient leap back to being the family man they knew me to be. They were all that had kept me moving forward these past few days. What I had done, I did for them.

I couldn't wait to hold my wife again and smell her perfume. If I thought hard enough, I could feel Brenda's touch and the softness of her skin. I could hear her and Yvonne yelling at each other about something trivial that wouldn't matter past dinner. I replayed prior debates with Max over NASCAR.

I inhaled deeply. In less than three hours, I'd be home. I flicked the radio on. It was some pop rock station out of Toronto.

"Up next Justin Bieber."

The tune started, and I changed the station. The maid had been singing that song when I showed up to copy the all-access key. I needed to shake the flashbacks but allowed myself the trespass because the scene was still fresh. I could smell the gunpowder and feel the heat of the gun on my fingertips.

As I thought of Behler lying there, I envisioned tomorrow's headlines, *"Governor of Michigan Assassinated in New York State."*

The text of the article filled in too quickly for my liking. "Did her stand against organized crime have a part to play?"

Bile rose in my throat. The pungent smell of blood filled my sinuses. But there is no way they could tie her murder to the Russos, or back to me. I went through the entire process again from the cleaning of the room to ensuring no trace was left behind.

There was one thing that didn't want to release its hold. Her last words, *I was one of—*.

One of what? I had to dismiss this and put this weekend behind me. It didn't matter anymore. I had done what I came to Niagara Falls to do. I didn't even care if I got the other five hundred thousand. All I wanted was to crawl into bed next to my wife and wake up with her. The thought of settling into the pillow top eased some of the tension in my shoulders.

I turned up the cool air and the radio, anything to keep me awake. Brenda's words of caution came through, *be careful on the roads, come home safe.*

Another two hours went by, and the tunes on this station kept me awake.

"Breaking news…"

It sounded like the new allergy medication commercial that inundated the airwaves these days in Detroit. I had my hand on the radio to change the station when I realized it wasn't an advertisement.

"There's been an assassination attempt on the State Governor of Michigan…"

Attempt? I turned up the volume. What the hell were they talking about? I had shot her skin-to-barrel, bullet-to-brains.

"…law enforcement isn't saying too much at this time. But she was found in a hotel room in Niagara Falls, New York."

That son of a bitch wasn't supposed to go in until mid-morning.

The earlier nausea returned with a vengeance. My chest heaved for a solid breath. My hands gripped the steering wheel, my eyes welded to the road. My heart palpitated, and I questioned whether I was having a panic attack.

How could I have failed? It didn't make any sense. Unless I was set up to fail? My family.

Oh, shit!

I picked up my cell. If Christian heard the broadcast, he would come after them.

The road sign read Chatham-Kent. I was still an hour out. And I still had to get across the border back to the States.

"Pick up!" I yelled into the hollow ringtone. It went to the machine. "Shit!" I dialed again. More ringing.

Where the hell were they?

The dash read three fifteen. I pressed the gas pedal to the floor.

CHAPTER FOURTEEN

Niagara Falls, New York
Sunday, June 13th, 3:30 AM

Major Crimes Detective Dave Clinton had the case that would advance him to Sergeant. As he looked around the hotel room that had been Governor Behler's, a smirk cut into his lips. He would find the son of a bitch responsible for this and put him behind bars for life. He could see the headlines now.

"Detective Clinton?"

"Yeah." He turned to a CSI tech who was thin enough Clinton knew he could likely bench press him.

"I think the guy we're looking for is a professional."

"It's too early to assume anything. Keep looking." Clinton dismissed his colleague with a wave, returning to evidence collection.

Nothing could be presumed or assumed. Clinton needed facts to cement this case.

Governor Behler had been escorted to County General where she was deemed critical and fighting for life. According to the attending physician she had a probability of making it through. When they refused to attribute percentages, Clinton knew it wasn't a good thing. Right now it was a game of wait and see. But he would treat the case as a homicide unless the good news fairy intervened. Solving attempted murders didn't warrant as much clout as solving successful ones.

And he didn't have time to waste. This had been a blatant assault on the life of a State Governor. The FBI, the Michigan State Police, and the New York State Police were already called. There were more offices of law enforcement involved than Clinton cared for. With different branches came territorial conflict. Clinton likely had precious little time to get answers before any of them would rush in and take over. He'd wager the FBI would be the first to assert control.

A staff member of The Grandeur found Behler when he came to deliver food to the room. His name was Paul Hensal. Clinton had some uniformed officers hold him in the hallway. He wanted to see inside the room first. And now he had, it was time to start doing the real work that involved investigative skills and not the aid of technology to match DNA coding and fingerprints. If Clinton was going to get any immediate answers, it was with Hensal.

Clinton stepped into the hall and found two officers stationed outside the door. He didn't see Hensal. "Where—"

"Room next door, Detective. That way." The one young officer gestured to the right of Behler's room, and then let his hand come down to rest on his holster.

"Get your hand off that thing unless you have course to draw it, or lose your badge for being reckless."

The officer lifted both his hands. Red saturated his cheeks.

"Why's the kid next door?" Clinton asked.

"The Grandeur didn't want us all in the hall. They comped the room."

"I don't give a shit what The Grandeur wants." Clinton held up a pointed finger and swiped it to take in the area around them. "You get this entire floor sealed off. I don't want anyone coming or going. Do you hear me?"

He nodded, almost too quickly. Clinton didn't respect those who didn't think for themselves. He viewed this officer—he paused to read his badge—number 8329 as one who could be easily manipulated.

Clinton headed to the other room but stopped when his partner came toward him. Her stride carried a message, as did her facial expression. They were partners for six years, which in cop life equated a small eternity. Her name was Sonya Wingham, and her skin next to his was a creamy white. The guys in the division termed them their salt and pepper team; Clinton was disappointed by their lack of originality.

"Whatcha got?" He asked her.

She stopped a few feet in front of him. Both hands braced on her hips. "They've got security cameras and are pulling the footage now."

. . .

Detroit, Michigan

It took hours for Brenda to fall asleep. She kept thinking about how she was going to approach this with Ray in the morning. He had to be cheating on her. There was no doubt in her mind now. Why else would he go away last minute and order a tux? How was he going to explain that to her? Her stomach rolled as she assumed he'd leave the tux at the other woman's place.

A single tear fell down her cheek as she lay there trying to sleep. Anger suppressed more from falling. She needed rest to have the energy to confront him. The last time she saw on the alarm clock was one, and it felt like she had just fallen asleep.

At first the ringing phone morphed into a dream mentality, but it just kept ringing.

She rolled over, groggy and still half asleep. What she saw at the end of her bed made her stop—paralyzed with fear.

The man wasn't Ray. She could tell by his frame. Her hairs rose on her entire body. Her breath stalled. The man's eyes were watching her.

She had to reach the phone. But she couldn't will her body to move. The phone rang again. The blue LCD screen cast eerie shadows in the room.

The man wasn't moving. He was just staring. She took her eyes off him only for an instant and reached out for the phone. It was only three feet away. She could get it, pick it up, and tell the caller she needed help.

The man came toward her.

Her scream hurled from her toes.

The man grabbed her by the back of the head. He pressed a cloth against her face, and she smelled a sweet aroma. She could still hear the ringing phone as her arms and legs went limp. Her perception of sound began to dull, but not before more screams made it through— the kids'. Then she heard Ray's voice as if out of nowhere.

The answering machine?

Brenda willed herself to scream, but it was as if her mouth and tongue were frozen. She tried to move. She was a prisoner in her own body. Her eyes fell heavy. Everything went black.

. . .

Chatham, Ontario En Route to Detroit, Michigan

Still no answer. I drove like an NASCAR driver thankful I didn't have many other cars to weave through.

One hour away.

It may as well have been twenty. I tried again. Come on. Answer.

Still nothing. If they killed my family, I would make it possible for one man to take them all down. I depressed the number on my phone—Christian's direct line.

. . .

Detroit, Michigan

Christian hated kids. The little one put up quite a struggle for his size and age. Ingo had to slap him around a bit to get him to stop squirming. Once the cloth was in place, he fell asleep.

Christian imagined the kid not waking up. Kids were trouble. But when it came to bargaining power, they held the key.

That's probably why he chose to take care of the wife. It hadn't been hard, and the repeatedly ringing phone had worked to his advantage. It distracted her and gave her hope that she could escape the strange man at the end of her bed.

Hope could be like that—blinding and deceiving. And empowering to those who made hope out of reach. Christian smiled.

Maybe that's why he had decided to make his own future—no one else could make it for him. And if one was too weak to make their destiny, then they deserved others to write it for them.

"This is the last one, boss." Berto carried the dead weight of the teenage girl over a shoulder like an oversized sack of potatoes. For the man, brawn didn't equate with mental prowess. But he was willing to please, and for that Christian kept him around.

Ingo closed the door of the Escalade after Berto inserted his cargo.

"Her hair smells like lilac." Ingo inhaled the air that filtered behind her as a lion stalks its prey.

"Keep your hands off her!" Christian turned on his man. That young lady could be a strong bargaining chip. She was the only daughter. And girls were special to their fathers, weren't they? And if that were not enough, she was the firstborn.

"Boss," Ingo said.

Christian knew he stood there seemingly staring into space, but he was thinking. He would get to know her quite well.

"We should get moving—"

Christian pulled out a Desert Eagle and held it at the man's gut. His words calm. "Don't you ever fuckin' rush me. You understand?"

Ingo nodded. His eyes went large with panic and fell downcast to the paved driveway.

Christian held the gun there for another thirty seconds to emphasize the point—no one told him what to do.

He went back to contemplating in silence, his gun still held in one hand, but it was now down at his side. His men filtered into the Escalade.

Christian affectionately traced a hand down the black exterior of his ride. The street lights refracted off it. His thoughts were on Ray and how he had done quite well for himself getting set up in a decent neighborhood. He put The Family money to good use. It would work out to Christian's advantage tonight, too, because his vehicle wouldn't stand out among the hundred other SUVs; not that anyone in the neighborhood seemed to be awake. And if they had been, they wouldn't know what to make of it anyhow. If a prying neighbor did get involved and called the cops, Christian and his men would be long gone with the entire Hunter family before law enforcement arrived.

Christian's cell rang. A smile spread on his lips when he read the caller ID. No one said the man was stupid. He pressed the ignore call button and slipped it back into his pocket. He rapped his knuckles on a back window of the Escalade. "Just one more thing to take care of."

. . .

En Route to Detroit, Michigan

"Shit!" I pounded the steering wheel. Christian sent my call to voicemail. I could tell by the clipped ringtone.

Fifteen minutes away.

I almost didn't want to go home. I couldn't handle finding them murdered in their sleep. My head felt faint. Every mile brought me closer, but it wasn't happening fast enough.

Even with limited traffic on the roads, the cars that were, moved slowly.

I tried the home phone again. I needed to believe they were still alive. I had seen the work of Christian before, firsthand. I was paid for discretion and skill. Christian possessed no conscience of right and wrong.

All the morbid scenes of my past played through my mind as a fast motion slideshow— faces strewn, blood spatters, broken bones, separated appendages, torture conducive with war crimes. But as all these paraded through, at this moment, I couldn't allow myself a fraction of time to consider them having been inflicted upon my loved ones. I knew Christian was capable, but I hoped that he would give me some consideration based on what I had done for him eighteen years ago. I thought of the five hundred thousand. Maybe if I gave it back the present failure could be redeemed.

Then I thought of Yvonne. She was only fourteen. Christian and his men would love young girls. My stomach churned, and I vomited into my empty coffee cup.

CHAPTER FIFTEEN

Everything looked the same from the outside. But the early morning air felt tattooed by the lingering presence of evil. I took a deep inhale trying to derive strength to move through the threshold. My legs felt weak and grounded. Procrastinating wouldn't change what had happened. To prepare myself, I had to picture my nightmare. Images of them being raped, stabbed for sadistic pleasure, bullets to their faces…I had even known the Russos to decapitate those who betrayed them. I vomited into the garden bed outside the front door.

Somehow, I willed my legs to move. Then my pace quickened. "Brenda!" I went through the house, a man afraid he had lost everything. I saw the blinking light on the machine.

One message. It would have been mine.

The house was silent. *Oh God!*

"Brenda! Yvonne! Max!" I yelled all their names hoping that I had simply overreacted to everything. Maybe this was a nightmare and not a reality. Maybe my tired eyes had closed on the road; I got into a car accident and was in a coma.

Oh God, please let that be the case.

I went to Max's room first and found it empty. My breathing slowed, and my heart rate intensified.

"Yvonne!" I yelled her name as I ran down the hallway. Her door was open. That was not a good sign. She always kept it closed for privacy. She wasn't there.

It felt as if four walls were compressing in on me. My chest was tight. My breathing—soft, broken inhales and exhales. I breached our bedroom door and my breath stalled.

Blood was everywhere. I gasped for air.

With each deep inhale, a vise-like grip restricted my airflow, reducing my lung capacity for the next. It must have been sheer adrenaline alone that made it possible for me to make it the six feet to the bed.

There was someone under the covers. I attempted to steady myself.

For the amount of blood that saturated the white duvet, I could find all of them under there. My brain communicated with my hand to lift the cover back, but I couldn't bring myself to act.

I stood there for seconds, maybe minutes, trying to come to grips with what I had done. If they were dead, it was because of me. I stared down at the bed and distinguished one impression. Only one person was in our bed.

The blood was still wet, not tacky. The kill was fresh. I had just missed Russo's men. I don't believe in coincidences. I believe in cause and effect. To the Russos, the cause, my failed assassination attempt, would result in the effect, my being punished for my failure.

I pulled the duvet up. What I saw took the strength from my legs. I fell to my knees and raised my arms heavenward yelling like a primitive animal.

CHAPTER SIXTEEN

Niagara Falls, New York
Sunday, June 13, 4:30 AM

Detective Dave Clinton didn't like liars. And Hensal had to be. "You're telling me you just found her like that?"

He chewed on the end of a finger. There wouldn't be any nail left if he kept at it.

"You just happened upon her room?" Clinton stood above the hotel staff member while he sat on a sofa chair.

"We received a call. She wanted eggs Benedict."

"And it's your normal service? To offer that at midnight?" He frowned. "Most hotels wouldn't serve anything at that hour."

"We aim to please our guests." His eyes cast to the floor too fast to be believable.

"You aim to please? So you shot her because she asked you to—"

"I didn't. Believe me."

Clinton didn't need to believe one syllable coming from the kid's lips. He knew the video feed was being evaluated as he spoke. Wingham had returned to the security room of the hotel. Her specialty was diplomacy. He didn't operate within the same boundaries. That's probably yet another reason why they made a good team.

She had already called Behler's office to find out whether she always traveled with a bodyguard. Just because it was recommended didn't mean dignitaries never ditched them, but first he had to be cleared. Surprisingly, the message hadn't been returned yet. Clinton had a feeling Detroit's PD was doing their own investigation.

Hensal rubbed at his throat. "Can I have a glass of water?"

Clinton stood there with one hand on the badge he wore on his hip. He made eye contact with the one unie at the door and looked to the sink. He followed the silent directions.

"Who made the call downstairs for food?" Clinton asked.

"A man."

"At midnight?"

"Yes."

"Do you have a recording of this request?"

"Like I said, talk to Karen from the kitchen. She took the order. See..." He fished into his uniform shirt pocket and extended a copy to Clinton. He pointed at the writing. "That's hers. Question her." The uniformed officer handed him the glass of water. Hensal took it and drank as if he'd been wandering the desert for hours.

Clinton dropped the order slip on the table and took a seat across from Hensal. "She's not the one who found Behler. It proves nothing to me other than an order was taken. You could have come in here, made the phone call, rushed downstairs to get it, came back up here to deliver it and *make the find*." Clinton attributed finger quotations to the last two words.

"I'm not that smart."

At least he was aware of his limitations. But stupidity wasn't an alibi. Most criminals had a few dead brain cells. "Who can testify as to your whereabouts for the hour before midnight?"

Hensal drained back the rest of the water and held it in his hand like a life preserver. "I was working."

The snarky delivery didn't warrant him any merit points. Clinton remained silent.

Hensal's eyes fired over. He bent forward and placed the empty glass on the table next to a newspaper.

"You realize we're getting camera feed right now that will prove when you were in her room. That room is being looked over with fine scrutiny by NFPD's best. If we're all lucky, Homeland Security will be here too." Clinton added the latter part to instill fear. He would love to have the entire thing wrapped up before the FBI's plane touched down though.

"Home…Homeland Sec…I'm going to be sick."

The door opened and a man from Crime Scene walked in. He was here to swab Hensal's hands for gunshot residue.

He looked between the investigator and Clinton. "I will say two things. First of all, someone made me do it—"

"Shoot the Governor." Clinton directed the CSI to Hensal.

The CSI put his collection kit down beside him. "Please hold out your hands."

Hensal looked from him to Clinton. "The second thing I have to say is I want a lawyer."

. . .

Detroit, Michigan

Christian smiled as he reflected on the passengers through the rear view mirror—out like a light. His two men kept an eye on them to ensure they stayed that way. Christian had everything under control. This would be his game.

While he derived pleasure from physically torturing his victims—and he had especially enjoyed tonight until the fun had to end in a spray of red—mind games could prove to be an interesting transition. Of course, he only had so much patience before he would bore of it and needed to kill something. He couldn't wait to become better acquainted with the members of Hunter's family. Just thinking of Hunter making the discovery in the master bed made him laugh.

"Boss," Berto said.

"Go back to babysitting. I have a call to make." This call would be the start of even more enjoyment. Christian wondered if he could handle all the excitement. He pressed the speed dial certain he could.

. . .

Detroit, Michigan

My sole scream stopped when all the air had left my lungs. The expulsion drained my energy. All that propelled my thinking in any forward motion was raw adrenaline. When I pulled back the duvet, I had expected to find Brenda lying there. But the man I found sent a loud enough signal. I had signed my family's death certificates.

I rose to full height, careful not to lean on the bed for assistance. The man barely had any recognizable facial features. His nose and ears had been cut off along with a few fingers. But one didn't have to look far for them. All his mutilated body pieces lay on my pillow.

He had been tortured here prior to the slash to his neck. Stab wounds had been strategically inflicted in the joints where they would cause optimal pain yet keep the man alive. Based on blood loss, his body parts were removed while he was breathing.

His limbs were long and scraggly, and a gold Rolex adorned his left wrist. I had seen that watch before in Niagara Falls. I knew this man. This man was Behler's bodyguard—Rick.

Carved in the middle of his chest were the words, TSK TSK. This was Christian's work; those were his words.

What the hell was going on?

Behler had tried to tell me something before I pulled the trigger. She had said, *I was one of.*

Shit! What had I gotten myself involved with? What had I dragged my family into?

Had I been set up to fail? Had this been an elaborate concoction of the Russos to exact revenge for my leaving The Family? But why wait so many years? Why make it so complicated?

For the average person to come across this scene, it would have driven them to repeated bouts of vomiting. They would be in therapy for the rest of their lives. Most people would pick up the phone and dial for the police. I wasn't other people. Instead, adrenaline fueled strength in the power of reason and determination. Law enforcement wouldn't be getting involved. I would mete out my own justice for this invasion.

I would get my wife and children back if I had to take down the entire Russo Mafia Family singlehandedly.

At least that was what the high propelled me to believe—that I was untouchable. Logic reined in the free flow of irrational thinking based on what was in front of me; if I showed my face to Pietro Russo, I would be a dead man. Even though all I wanted to do was storm into the back doors of the bar down at the racetrack, it would be suicide. And even worse, my entire family would pay the price for my stupidity. This situation called for precise thought and exact execution.

I still didn't understand where everything went wrong. I had executed the murder flawlessly. It didn't make any sense at all that she would have survived one bullet straight to the meat of her forehead.

My ringing cell phone grounded my reality. The caller display read CR. A quiver ran through my body not from fear, but from anger. I let it ring three times before picking it up. Waiting on it would hopefully communicate to Christian I wasn't someone to be easily toyed with and manipulated. But each ring burrowed into my mind, further impressing the situation I was in, the situation of my family. I depressed the button yet remained silent.

"Niagara Falls didn't go so well."

To hear his voice, and know that he kept my family company, made me nauseous and light-headed. I remained silent knowing this would upset Christian more than anything I could say. The man was built to cause a reaction.

"She's alive Hunter." He dragged out each word. "I trust that you found my gift already."

"You fuckin' hurt one—"

"Oh temper, Hunter." His voice had a way of transforming to another dimension.

Shivers ran down my back. The words had lashed out providing Christian the upper hand of this interaction.

"You failed me. You betrayed me," he said.

"I shot her point blank." Emotion had eased into the forefront, caution dispersed because of it.

"Well, obviously something went wrong."

"Where's my family?" It took all power to harness the raw hatred that surged in my system.

"Seems to me you owe me something first."

"I'll pay you back—all of it!"

Christian laughed. "Money's of no significance to me." He let the line go silent, and I considered breaking it. He spoke first. "You saved my life years ago, and for that I won't take yours—yet. Your family, however, I have no such arrangement with them."

"You son of a bitch!"

"You try to play hero, I'll put a bullet in their heads. Every. Single. One. Of. Them. Including the boy. Oh, and your daughter, Hunter—" Christian drew in a deep breath.

"You keep your fuckin' hands off her!"

"She smells like fresh lilac."

"I swear I'll kill you myself."

Another arrogant laugh. "You're a dreamer. You still need to finish the job. Non-negotiable."

My mind calculated the odds. Behler's security would have intensified. The bodyguards to replace Rolex would be government appointed servicemen who wouldn't hesitate to take a bullet for their employer and shoot me down to protect her.

"See, it's no longer about the money, Hunter. It's about loyalty. Not that I can expect a man like you to comprehend loyalty. Does your wife even know about your past?" I detected his amusement over the phone. "Does she know your present? How you're a hired hand for the Russos? You have twenty-four hours to get it done. You sold your soul to the Devil, Hunter, and I'm here to collect." The call was disconnected.

I looked at my watch. I had until Monday at 5:00 AM

How I wished I could go back in time and prevent all of this, starting with the first time I met Christian. I should have let that man kill him.

The club's name was Blurr, and they had hired me as a bouncer at the age of twenty-one. Christian was twenty at the time. I knew who he was but respected the fact that he was a mafia Don's son. One night around midnight, Christian ran in with this guy tailing behind him. The man did his best to push past me, and for a while I was able to hold him off. But just before he broke free, I felt the piece tucked into the waist of his pants. He tore after Christian like a bull released from the gate.

Both men weaved through the drunken crowds, and I followed. Christian went into the back room. I entered behind them into the area that I had been told was off limits. The stranger's back was to me, but he had a gun pointed at Christian. I didn't think twice. I pulled out the .22 handgun I carried and drilled two bullets into the back of the man's head. He dropped to the floor.

I had killed my first person. It felt surreal like a video game. But I'll never forget the reaction from Christian. Initially shock gaped open his mouth, but cocky laughter came out soon afterward. Smoke was still steaming from the fired gun.

Christian came over and placed his hands on my shoulders. "You've got to meet my Pops."

Recalling where it all began only increased my nausea. I wasn't in my twenties and single anymore. I had retired from the business when offered a full-time position with The Family three years after meeting Christian. Now I was thirty-nine with a family. I didn't want to kill people for money. I wanted to make up for past sins by living as a decent, law-abiding citizen for the rest of my years. Was it even possible to expect that from a person like me?

My eyes stayed on my bed and the bloody remains of a man who had worked for Christian. He was expendable. With no excelling skill set to warrant special attention, he had been thrown into the field with promises of grandeur. He probably spent his entire first advance on that Rolex.

The people surrounding Christian really meant nothing more to him than slaves to do his bidding. And whether I cared to admit it, I was one of them. I needed to get back to Niagara Falls and finish this. I needed to save my family. And Christian, he would pay for this. I had saved his life once. It didn't mean when presented with a similar opportunity, I would make the same mistake again. No, this time I would take his life instead.

CHAPTER SEVENTEEN

I stood there for minutes wondering what I was going to do. My eyes were burning and my body was succumbing to sheer exhaustion. There was no way I could turn around and drive another four and a half hours. I couldn't take a commercial flight for security check reasons. My thoughts were mingled and clouded from tiredness.

How the hell was I supposed to pull this off?

I didn't even know for certain whether Behler was being kept at a hospital in Niagara Falls, New York. But I surmised that due to head trauma, it would be a risk to fly her home.

There were variables that needed to be reconciled. I dropped myself on the sofa chair in our living room and dropped my face into my hands. My family—my wife, my daughter, and my son—could die because of me.

"Shit!"

Then the thought struck. It never occurred to me to request proof of life. I blamed the oversight on fatigue. But how could I have been so stupid? Christian had mentioned putting a bullet in their heads. What if he already had and was playing me? Without fear of losing my family, I owed Christian nothing. He would know that. I dialed his line.

"Aw, you missed me, Hunter. You want to catch up? Twenty-three hours and forty-five minutes—"

"How do I know they're still alive?" I asked the question while fearing the answer.

Christian laughed. "You don't trust me? Tsk. Tsk." He disconnected the call.

"Fuck!" I wanted to smash my phone into the fireplace on the other side of the living room, but as my arm extended the chimes rang. I had a message. Turning the phone over, the screen announced one video message. I clicked the link.

The quality was grainy and the room dark. There was a cot with nothing more than a thin mattress in the corner of the room. The curled up figure on it was unmistakable.

Max's arms were suspended and cuffed to a fixture on the wall. His head bowed forward, chin against chest. He lifted his head up when someone whistled. It sounded like a canary. They had Max's mouth gagged. His eyes were shadowed. I studied the feed closer, paused it. Both eyes were blackened.

Had they hit my boy? I would kill the son of a bitch who did this with my bare hands!

On camera, Max's eyes opened wide and I heard his moaned cries as heavy footsteps went in his direction. The person was off camera. The video cut out and came back on. Different room.

The feed was choppy and slow. This room was smaller, and there was very little light. Max's room must have had a window or a source of light off camera. This time the figure was in the middle of the room on a chair.

Brenda.

The cameraman's hands were unsteady. The zoom moved in closer. I heard more footsteps. The same ones as were in Max's room. The camera flashed to the floor briefly. The man who shot the video wore beige standard-issue safety boots. The ground beneath them was concrete.

He moved closer to Brenda. She was tied to a chair, wearing nothing but her bra and underwear. My stomach knotted and twisted. This was my fault.

The cameraman stopped beside her. The lens focused on her chest, the rise and fall of it. Her breathing quickened the longer the man stood beside her. Her eyes were covered.

"Pretty lady," the man said, hissing the words into her ear. He pulled back quickly and whistled the tune of a bird—a canary.

Heat made its way up the back of my neck. I felt the hairs rise and my earlobes catch fire. The same boots and the same whistle from Max's room.

The cameraman brushed Brenda's cheek with the back of his hand. "Early Christmas gift."

The video feed was cut.

I wanted to hurl the phone, discard the video as if by doing so, it would make it all go away. But my eyes were fixed on the screen. My grip on the armrest of my chair tightened, the fabric became embedded under my fingernails.

"Help!" The cry came before the video feed; it was muffled yet easy to discern.

I rose to my feet. "Yvonne!"

"Daddy!" Her subdued plea for help transformed into sobs.

A door opened. I realized the camera had been on the entire time but had been shrouded in darkness. Light from inside the room revealed my nightmare was a reality.

Yvonne's room was much like Max's. Another cot was in the far corner of the room. There were shackles on the wall above it. Her wrists were handcuffed to it. She, like Brenda, was in her bra and underwear. She wasn't alone on the bed. A man was beside her; he was dressed in black. He stroked her cheek.

"No need to be afraid." The man's voice was different. This was Christian.

My heart stalled, taking with it my next breath. Revenge would be the only restitution.

He moved a hand down her torso, touching her in a soft manner as would a lover.

I would kill him myself!

He went in closer to her, putting his face into her long hair. "Smells like…lilac."

Yvonne's head moved away to avoid contact. Christian moved in closer. He reached around behind her head and pulled off the gag from her mouth. As he did, he spoke to her. "Not one word."

The cloth fell. The cameraman moved in on her face. Her chin trembled, and tears fell. "Pleeeassse…."

"Just do as I tell you." Christian spoke in whispers.

Yvonne let out a heartrending scream that tore fiber from muscle, muscle from bone, bone from flesh.

Christian's response was instant. The gag was put back in place. He leaned his face into her hair again. "Tsk. Tsk."

End of feed.

I sat there watching the blank screen.

Anger pulsated through my veins, wincing like the snarling jowl of a mad dog. I would get my family back alive. I would kill the Governor and come back to take Christian and every one of them down.

I rose on instinct and made my way to the basement gun locker. My wife had no idea of its existence. She didn't even like the concept of a gun being in the house. She said they were dangerous and asked for bad things to happen. Maybe she had been right because trouble had come our way—almost enough to equate the amount of gun power I had on the premises.

The house we lived in had been custom built, everything according to our specs. I had the contractors make a hidden room off the furnace room. Its front was an electrical panel because I knew Brenda would never go near it. She had commented on there being two before, but she seemed satisfied with my response that it was a big house.

I opened the panel. Breakers lined the inside as if it were real. I removed three from the bottom right-hand corner to reveal a number pad. I entered my eight digit code and heard a small click as the tumblers released.

The room was fireproof and housed fifteen guns and their accessories. Ammunition of various calibers was sorted and organized in a chest. There were silencers, scopes, bore brushes, holsters, and a large assortment of magazines. Gun were catalogued based on size and type. My collection included H&K, Beretta, Smith & Wesson, and Kimber among others. I even had a CZ 75 P-01 which is all over Europe but not as well known in the United States.

I picked up my .44 Auto Mag and two magazines. That would give me fifteen rounds counting the one in the chamber. This would be for my defense when I went to retrieve my family. Even with the job completed, Christian wouldn't surrender them. I knew him better than that. They were witness to too much. I would die for my initial betrayal. The rest of this was simply a game to him. He would be sorry he called this to his doorstep. Yet I would still finish the job with Behler.

I went to the shelf to where I kept my rifles and chose one I had customized from overseas. It was a very special single shot which was built according to my specs. I had purchased it years ago and it cost a small fortune, but it was about to prove its worth.

The twenty-eight-inch barrel would provide the bullet with sufficient velocity to keep its trajectory flat enough to be practical six to seven hundred yards out. It had been powder-coated black to reduce glare and had been threaded to accommodate a suppressor. But one of the greatest advantages was it broke down easily into three components—the stock, the barrel and scope, and sound suppressor. This feature made it possible to carry in a relatively small case.

It was chambered in the commercial .243 Winchester, but I wasn't too worried about the fired bullet falling into the hands of law enforcement. They would be able to classify the bullet, but the rifling would be unique making it impossible for them to know what kind of gun they were looking for. Since I hadn't used the gun in any previous hits, their databases wouldn't flag any matches to past cases.

I placed my hands on the rifle case and opened it to ensure everything was enclosed even though I knew it would be. My guns were more than simply toys that satisfied a grown man's interest. They were respected.

I ran my hand over the scope. The plan was to take Behler out in her hospital bed. Most hospital rooms had windows for the purpose of letting the sunshine in to cheer their patients and for safety reasons. This would be an architectural necessity I would exploit. The thought had crossed my mind that the curtains may be closed, but they may not have expected a long distance threat, as the last attempt was done at close range.

I knew I could assemble the weapon in seconds because I practiced weekly. I went to a long distance shooting range and fired it monthly. It would feel like a natural extension of my arms.

As I packed up my artillery, I did a lot of thinking, and it kept rolling back around to the same fact. None of this made sense. How could a bullet to the head allow one to walk away? And why did Governor Behler *need* to die? The

Mafia normally didn't target dignitaries. In fact, most of the time, if a member acted alone to take one down, they would be murdered by The Family. Yet, here, I faced orders for Behler's murder from the Don himself.

I secured the door to the safe room behind me and exhaustion from the hours on the road threatened to sap my strength to the point of collapsing. There was no way I could go without sleep for twenty-four hours. I needed to get this over with. My eyes were burning and my limbs were weak. I couldn't drive back to Niagara Falls. It would kill me.

I needed to call in a favor from the man I would kill. I dialed the number.

"I trust you saw your proof of life." Christian's smug voice made me conjure images of slicing off his head.

"I need a plane."

"Your daughter. She is beautiful. Your wife too."

"You want me to do this for you—"

"You talk like it's an option, Hunter. No option. You kill the Governor. You and your family live."

"I can't drive back." I knew I wouldn't sleep on the plane, but even if I could rest my eyes. The tired made mistakes. The emotionally compromised did too, but I couldn't dwell on that.

"Not my prob—"

"It is actually. You want her dead."

"You speak bravely for a man who could lose everything."

I didn't speak another word.

"Fine. Wheels will be ready to go up at 0800. I'll send you the coordinates." He paused but then continued, "Consider yourself paid in full too, Hunter. Providing airfare and the rising fuel costs. Oh, and one more thing, the clock's still ticking."

As if I needed the reminder.

The line went dead. At least I had my way back to Niagara Falls. Now to find out what went wrong and why. I barely made it to the front door when my phone chimed to notify me of the message—GPS coordinates to a place on the outskirts of the city.

It would take every minute to make it there in time for eight. I grabbed the original travel bag I had brought along the last time. The action reminded me of the murdered man in our bedroom. But I didn't have time to do anything about him. As Christian had said, *"The clock's still ticking."*

CHAPTER EIGHTEEN

Niagara Falls, New York
Sunday, June 13th, 5:15 AM

Detective Clinton hated when suspects called for a lawyer. The entire case took a pause while waiting for the legal right to continue. With this case there wasn't time to spare. The target had been a Governor of State. No one would be going home until this matter was resolved. And Clinton had every intention of getting this case solved quickly—preferably before the full involvement of other branches of law enforcement.

He popped a few Tic Tacs in his mouth and stood while keeping his eyes on Hensal. Hensal wouldn't return his gaze and watched the floor as if it was a marathon special and he was spellbound. His arms were crossed.

Clinton curled an index finger in a gesture for the uniform to approach. This was the same one who had gotten water for Hensal earlier. "Get this guy a phone book."

"Sure."

"Don't let him out of your sight. I'll be back."

"Of course."

This uniform warranted Clinton's respect. He held an energy that denoted respect for superior officers, but the fire in his eyes told Clinton he would stand up for himself if need be. Clinton placed a hand on the officer's shoulder on the way out of the room.

He wondered what was taking his partner so long in securing the video footage. Sonya had left nearly two hours ago now. The guests in neighboring rooms had been questioned and no one had heard anything that stood out to them. The Governor's room didn't look tossed and combed over. The only thing out of place was a missing hotel glass. They had confirmed with maid service that the woman assigned to the suite had checked two glasses off the inventory. This left Clinton with the feeling the killer took it with him. Crime Scene would be checking all garbage receptacles in the hotel to see if the killer had a lapse in judgment and tossed the glass on his exit. The video may show something as well.

Based on gut instinct, this didn't seem like a robbery gone wrong. Despite the Governor's silk wear, it didn't speak of a lover's rendezvous that went awry either.

Clinton walked through Behler's suite trying to envision what exactly happened. He turned back to the door. There was no evidence of forced entry. That meant whoever had shot the Governor had either been let in or had an all-access key.

Two factors that made Paul Hensal appear guilty. He would have one and he had made the discovery. Did this other person he talked about even exist?

Clinton's cell rang and he answered.

"You've got to come down here now." His partner's voice held conviction like she had already solved the case.

"We've got our guy on camera?"

"Actually, we have three."

CHAPTER NINETEEN

My mind replayed everything like a slideshow presentation. Pictures of my family faded out to ones of the Governor and morphed with Christian's face and smug smile. I would wipe it off his face permanently if he hurt my family.

Included in the flashbacks were clips of speech, the scream from Yvonne overshadowing everything and impressing the severity of the situation. But I also heard the Governor's last words to me, *I was one of.*

She was one of what? That answer still hadn't been satisfied and might never be. But if I had to go back to kill her, I wanted to know what made her a target.

I knew the woman spoke out against organized crime. Had that been enough to warrant a target on her back? Maybe she inadvertently came down on one of Russo's men? But any recent bills she passed had more to do with financial restructuring. She hadn't declared herself as against organized crime by providing laws for the state to lean upon. She hadn't passed any pertaining to gun control, gambling, or drugs. All three of those were huge sources of business income for the Russos.

They had their restaurants and clubs, construction companies, laundry facilities, trucking, and garbage hauling firms, but a large source of the Russo Family income came from their racetrack. Distinguished thoroughbreds graced the half mile track, enhancing excitement among the patrons and encouraging them to put down money at high odds.

As I followed the directions provided on the GPS, I turned the radio on hoping to catch an update on the Governor. Now minutes into the drive, a broadcaster came on.

"Governor Behler remains in critical condition in New York State. As she recovers, our thoughts and prayers go out to her friends and family, and the great state of Michigan." A second of dead air was followed by another song on the playlist. I turned the radio down.

Critical condition.

It still didn't make sense that she had survived a shot to the head at the range of barrel-to-forehead. Part of me feared failing again. Would a long range rifle with the power of a hundred grain bonded bullet be enough to do the trick? I knew the insanity of the rhetorical question, yet it formed anyhow. None of this really made any sense. I needed to find out more about the woman I thought I knew so well over the last fourteen years.

I turned left as indicated by the GPS. The country road was nestled between trees and farmer's fields; the air was ripe with the smell of cow manure. Twenty more minutes down the road, I saw my destination.

A large farmhouse was to the front of the property with a hangar out back large enough to house a few planes with minimal effort. I couldn't see a runway from this vantage point, but I knew it would be there.

Adrenaline intensified as I got closer.

Christian's words came to mind. Basically, money was of no significance to him. The job just needed to be finished. Translation: the target Behler had on her back was written in indelible marker.

A woman was sitting on the front porch of the farmhouse holding a mug in her hand. Her hair was black and the length of her jaw.

As the gravel crunched beneath the car tires, she turned to study her visitor. Her aura was inquisitive. I sensed nothing much escaped her watch and that she was fully aware that her tarmac and planes catered to The Detroit Partnership, or in the very least the Russo Family.

I kept driving until I reached the hangar. The message from Christian said to see Landen. A plane sat on a runway that didn't look long enough for takeoff, but it must have been sufficient.

I let myself inside. Two more planes were in there.

A man stepped out of one barely fitting through the doorway. He had to duck to get through. He wore a business suit and came out with a briefcase in his right hand. Strange thing to see for Sunday morning at seven-thirty, but it didn't matter. I was only here for one purpose. "Are you Landen?"

"What's it to you?" The man kept walking to a nearby table where he placed the briefcase. He stood in front of it as if protecting it from a threat.

"Here for a flight to Niagara Falls, New York." My .44 tempted me to make a move. I hated silence, and I didn't appreciate the way this man was looking at me.

The man smiled. He said nothing. He noticed my gun but didn't fear it. The door that I had come through opened, and the man's eyes went over my shoulder toward it.

"Who are you?" The woman from the front porch came hustling through the hangar, the heels of her shoes clicking with each step.

Concrete.

My mind melded the connection with the video of my family. Yet concrete was found in many places. I glanced around and noticed a few doors that came off the hangar, likely offices or maintenance rooms.

"You must answer me." She came to a stop in front of me, both hands on her hips. Her eyes were piercing emeralds. She had seen death and possibly even been the one to inflict it.

"Safe flight." The large man walked off, laughing.

Did his voice sound familiar?

My attention only left her for an instant. I noticed that the large man left the briefcase.

Her hand went to my face and stayed there as she spoke. "This is my hangar, my planes. Who are you?" She shook my face before removing her hand.

"I'm looking for Landen."

"Who are you?"

"Hunter."

"Ah, see now we have no problem. This way." She wore a pair of leather pants that must have been painted on and a fitted leather shirt. As she led the way to the plane outside, I couldn't help but think she reminded me of the barrel of my rifle—slender, efficient, and deadly.

She snapped her fingers, the noise carrying in the hangar. A man peeked out of the aircraft. She spoke to him, "He's here. Get ready to leave."

She turned to me. "The plane on the tarmac is yours until your business is finished. We ask no questions. We want no answers. Understand?"

I nodded. I wouldn't be disclosing anything anyhow.

"Very good then." Her eyes went from the .44 in my waist holster to my duffel bag and rifle case. She walked away a few steps and then stopped. She didn't turn around. "You call Christian when the job's done. He'll arrange for your return." She didn't wait for a verbal acknowledgment and resumed heading for the exit.

Hearing Christian's name only registered the level of hatred I felt for the man. I missed my family with a dull ache that was only exceeded by the heat of vengeance.

I shall repay.

I boarded the plane and dropped my luggage on the facing seat. My eyes went to it. I thought of my primary cell phone, the one Brenda knew the number to, and how I had it turned off all this time. I just wished I could hear my wife's voice again.

The engines started up. We were getting ready to leave. I went into the bag, took out the phone, and turned it on. Sitting here, my heart ached, but there wasn't anything more I could do—at least not right now. The time would come when the Russos would wish they had left me alone for good.

I settled into the oversized chair and found my body thankful for the reprieve. I hadn't slept much at all within the last twenty-four hours. Waiting for the phone to power up felt like an eternity. I hoped Brenda had tried reaching me and had left a message. I would at least be able to hear her voice. Ten missed calls. Only one number. Home.

Could I have prevented all of this from happening if I had picked up? Could I have warned them? Of course I knew I wouldn't have been able to. Christian was already in our house when the news hit the radio. He would have known beforehand from Rick; he would have flown him back to Detroit for his death.

My breath went shallow as I pressed the button to listen to my voicemail. Two messages. The first was a click, but in the second one, Brenda spoke: *"Ray where are you? I've tried reaching you a hundred times. Please pick up. We need to talk. What are you doing in New York? I know it's not a tax seminar. I called your office and…"* Her voice cracked albeit it slightly. *"A men's apparel store called. Why do you…why do you need a tux?"* She hung up the phone, leaving a definite click at the end of the message.

Salvatore's Clothier didn't update my file as I had requested. I saved Brenda's message and held the phone as if it were her hand I held. I needed to explain a lot of things to her. To hear that pain in her voice sliced through me. She thought I was cheating on her. She felt betrayed.

The plane started down the runway, and as it did my head fell back and I shut my eyes. I only had so little down time. I would have to take advantage of it while I could. But even with my eyes closed there was a slim possibility of actually falling asleep. My mind kept churning with what the next few hours would hold.

CHAPTER TWENTY

An Hour And A Half Earlier...
Niagara Falls, New York
Sunday, June 13th, 6:30 AM

The security pen of The Grandeur wasn't much larger than a prison cell. Monitors were stacked around the room. Computers hummed, and the smell of rotten cheese lingered in the air. Given the fact it was early in the morning, it had likely saturated the room due to the night shift personnel.

The security technician was Wayne Devries. His hair was pulled into a ponytail at the base of his neck. His voice held a small lisp and he pronounced his s's with a slight hissing noise.

"We have an unobstructed view of the elevator and hallway." Devries pointed at the monitors. "This is the twentieth floor, outside of the Governor's room."

Dave Clinton stood there with his back arched and his arms crossed. "What time is this?"

"This right here is ten forty-five."

A man stood outside the Governor's suite with his hands in his pockets. He only took them out when he saw her approaching. His stature was lanky and approximately six feet as he wasn't much taller than Behler when she brushed by him into the suite. Behler was five eight. There was no interaction between them, not a glance or one word.

Wingham, who was seated beside the security guy, turned around to talk to Clinton over her shoulder. "Bodyguard?"

Clinton pressed his lips downward. "Seems like it, but that raises a few questions. The primary being, where is he now?" Clinton turned to the hotel security guy. "Do you have camera access in all parts of the hotel? Can we trace his steps from here through to when he leaves? What about facial recognition software?"

The security tech's eyes crinkled as he smiled. "We're not in Vegas." His smile faded when he noticed Clinton wasn't amused. "I can trace his steps, but it will take time."

"That's fine. We'll need that footage." Clinton gave the direction. Wingham turned back around to face the monitors. He knew she didn't like it when he came in and took over, but he couldn't help it at times. It was nothing personal. "Okay, so this guy stays outside her room..." He gestured to get the conversation moving again.

"Until this guy shows up." Devries fast forwarded the video.

"Time now?" Clinton asked.

"Eleven."

"He's a little dressed up."

"Date?"

Wingham pointed to the monitors. "Except he seems to be avoiding the camera. He turns his head just before he comes into range every time."

"What about the elevator? Does it tell us any more?"

"Same thing. He's really careful about hiding his face."

"Follow him through until the time he leaves as well. We need to find out for certain who these men are."

The tech resumed play.

Wingham narrated, "Now Tux—we'll call him Tux—leaves not even half an hour later." She always had to attribute a nickname to people.

"So he went in, got his rocks off, came back out," Clinton said.

Wingham turned to study her partner's eyes. "I think there's more to it." She turned to the tech. "Can you go back and zoom in on him?"

"Yeah, but you're not going to get anything." He maneuvered things around, and they were almost close enough to see ear hair if the feed wasn't so fuzzy. "That's it. That's all you're getting."

David wondered what nickname Wingham would have for this security guy—Tech Geek, Boy Wonder? He was certain it would come out.

"Whoever this is he doesn't want to be seen." Wingham slapped a hand on the table in front of her. "That's what makes me want to see him even more."

"You said there were three men," David did his best to steer her back.

"Well, the employee at the hotel, Paul, he goes in—" Wingham changed direction and directed the security tech. "Go to him—"

The tech hit a button and the video went backward. The time stamp read ten thirty.

"Stop!" David put both hands on the back of Wingham's chair.

The tech jumped, startled by the outburst. "What is it?"

"That's Paul. What room is he at?"

"That would be 836." The tech's face scrunched up. "Yeah, that would be it."

"Who rented that room?" Wingham asked.

Devries called down to the front desk. His face was pale when he delivered the answer. "Marian Behler. They said she had rented out a couple of rooms. She preferred her privacy."

"A lot of good it did her," Clinton said.

Wingham bit down on a lip. "Was Paul Hensal in the Governor's room before he found the Governor?"

On screen, Paul entered into the neighboring room with the serving cart.

Devries shook his head. "He goes in that first room at ten thirty, leaves for a couple hours and comes back with an order for the Governor at twelve forty. As you know, that's when he found her."

"So he goes away for a couple hours and shows up later to find the body," Clinton reiterated.

"We're still missing motive with the hotel employee. And the Governor is still alive." Wingham narrowed her eyes.

Technically, she still was... "Is there a door that connects the neighboring room to Behler's suite? He could have gone through there."

Devries shook his head. "None of our rooms have connecting doors."

"Paul says someone made him do it—"

"Shoot her?" Wingham asked.

The tech watched them banter back and forth.

"No, come back with food two hours later for the Governor's suite," Clinton said.

Wingham stood and joined Clinton at the back of the room. "Someone made him," She paused a second. "He had to for fear of his life. He was set up to find her."

"Forward the video. Does anyone other than Paul Hensal come out of that room?" Clinton asked.

Devries sped up the feed a bit.

Five minutes later, Hensal left the room.

Clinton smiled when he saw the man who left about another five minutes behind him. It was the man who had been posted outside the Governor's door at quarter to eleven. "Bingo!" Clinton slapped his hands together. "The Bodyguard, we'll call him that, approached the kid in the privacy of the hotel room. I'll be damned. The kid wasn't lying. And that guy right there—" Clinton pointed a finger at the screen. "If he was Behler's bodyguard, where is he now?" The footage replayed and they watched Behler enter her room and Tux not long later. The two men had a brief interaction outside of the Governor's suite and it included the bodyguard touching Tux's arm. "Something huge is going on here. We are looking for a professional."

"And a collaboration. Looks like we can let Paul go. I don't think the kid was in on this. You check his background?" Wingham asked. "And what would his motivation be?"

"The check came back clean, but it doesn't necessarily mean anything. He could have just gotten away with things before now."

"Serious—"

"More importantly, we need to find this man—" Clinton nodded toward the monitor where Tux stood with his face averted "—and man two." He gestured toward the stringy man who filled the main screen. "But right now, number three's the only one we've got."

CHAPTER TWENTY-ONE

Hours Later...
Niagara Falls, New York
Sunday, June 13th, 9:30 AM
Less Than 20 Hours Until the Deadline

"Wake up sleepy head." The words were accompanied with a shove on my shoulder.

My body must have shut down from pure exhaustion. My eyes didn't want to open, and when they did focusing was another issue. I wished it had all been a nightmare, but I knew it wasn't when I saw the bag across from me. I looked down to my hands which gripped the cell phone as if it would bring my family to me.

"Time to go." The voice that had called to me while I was sleeping grew impatient.

I turned my head toward the man and noticed the .38 tucked into the waist of his pants. My hand instinctively went to my holster. The gun was still there.

What time was it anyway?

I pressed a button on the phone. Nine-thirty in the morning.

Nineteen and a half hours left.

The flight had taken about ninety minutes. I fended off a yawn and started to move.

I scooped up my luggage from the facing seat and exited the plane. Stepping out, I noticed crop fields were all around. "Where are we?" My groggy state let the question escape. It was obviously another private hangar on the outskirts of the city.

The man laughed. "Sleeping beauty must have taken a tranq."

Another man came up behind him. He didn't say anything but watched me with unwavering attention.

"I realize we're somewhere in Niagara Falls," I said.

The silent man held his hands together and performed a sarcastic golf clap.

"When I'm finished here, where do I…" I had to shake the blurry feeling in my head. "Where do—"

"Don't worry about it." The man who woke me up patted me on the back and pointed to a car on the tarmac. "Gift from Christian."

Gift? My thoughts cleared to stark alertness. The rage came up my throat like bile needing to be excreted. I swallowed hard. The man in the video with my wife had referred to her as an early Christmas gift. My hand tightened around the handle of my gun. The action gained attention from the one man who responded by placing a hand on his piece.

"A what from Christian?" I wanted to hear him say the word one more time.

"Gift." He said it giving each letter enunciation.

While anger clouded my vision, my breathing hesitated and became shallow. If I killed this man or made a move, my family would be dead. I had one option right now. Play by Christian's rules.

I brushed past him. An Asian man from the Town Car came toward me, all of five-foot-five, wearing a uniform complete with hat. He extended his arms for my luggage. I kept walking. I shoved all my baggage into the back seat and slammed the door behind me.

The fact Christian had arranged for a car never surprised me. He would want to limit his connections between him and the crime— the murder I was about to commit. I assumed the ride would only take me so close before dropping me off at some random location. But for the man to say, *a gift from Christian*—he spoke those words from a script provided by Christian. They were part of his mind game.

I watched as the car made turns and replayed them backward with every change in direction. The last turn made my destination very clear.

Anger swirled with nerves. So much for Christian keeping at a distance. The car pulled into the parking lot of the crappy motel I had stayed in Friday night.

How had Christian known where I was staying?

Then I thought of the mutilated man on my bed at home. The rat was two-timing between keeping me in line and babysitting the mark.

"What are we doing here?" I asked. "Turn around, take me somewhere else."

"Sorry, sir, but this is where I've been told to take you. I must follow the rules." He pulled to a stop.

I had my door open before the hired driver came around to it. I held up a hand to him.

The Asian man placed both of his hands on his chest. "My 'pologies." His accent dropped the *a*. "I told to give you this." He extended a key and nodded toward the hotel. "Room 11." He smiled. "They say that's your lucky number."

I could tell by the cheesy innocence lit all over him, the driver of the Town Car knew nothing about me. As far as he knew I was a businessman coming in for a meeting or a rendezvous. He had also been well trained to respect the privacy of his occupants. Most drivers, even though trained to, would have made some comment or betrayed themselves with eye contact over the shape of the motel. What sort of businessman has access to a private plane, a Town Car, and gets dropped off at The Oasis?

I tried to dismiss the driver's latter comment but couldn't. Room 11. I turned the key chain over. The number was etched into the red plastic in white; most of it had worn from use. This was the same room I had stayed in over the last two days. Christian knew everything.

"Good day, sir." The driver dismissed himself with a lift of his hat and started back around to the driver's door.

The older man from the hotel came walking over. "You're back."

The driver's steps stalled, and I noticed the slight glance over his shoulder toward the motel, and the man coming toward me before he got into the car and drove away.

The manager had a huge smile on his face. "You loved your stay with us, eh?" The Canadian speech hadn't been lost in the last twenty-four hours.

I walked toward my room furious at the stupidity of Christian—same motel, same room.

Was he trying to get me caught?

"You hear about the Governor?" The manager asked.

My legs stopped. I didn't turn around. My job was to kill the Governor, not collect collateral damage, but if it meant the difference between saving my family or not, I wouldn't hesitate. I shut my eyes, searching for strength and patience.

"She was shot here, in the city, last night. Kind of scary. No one's safe these days."

The comment he had made was simply that, not an accusation. His tone gave him away. I resumed walking.

"Things are getting worse every day. Violence is on the rise. Things can't continue to carry on like this, eh—" He put a hand out in front of me just before I reached the doorknob. "Wait. If you're going to be a regular, what should I call you—" His words stopped; his eyes on the gun in my holster.

I was happy that I had paid the man cash before. He was asking too many questions, and I was starting to wonder if his bringing up the Governor was a coincidence or evidence of suspicion.

"Peter Williams." I stepped into the room and shut the door behind me. All his ranting about the world's escalating violence and coming to an end... if only he had any idea the type of man he housed within four walls of his motel.

The first thing I needed to do was find out the Governor's hospital room number. That would be a tricky enough manipulation given the fact she'd have intensified security and be surrounded. There would be no unauthorized access in or out of her room. But there were always ways around the system, and I already had it figured out.

I called for a cab to shuttle me down to County General. I knew from a quick look online that one of the things they specialized in was head trauma. She would likely be there.

There was little doubt in my mind that her condition would have stabilized. I didn't see how it could. Of course, I still found it hard to accept that she remained among the living—a mystery I would have to rectify and honestly solve for my self-esteem.

I hated the fact I was two hundred and forty miles from my family. I hated even more that I had to leave them in the hands of Christian and his men to manipulate and torture. Anger surged through me and mixed with a painful longing for their touch and laughter. I redialed my voicemail and listened to my wife's message. For now, it was all that I had to hold onto. I hated the fact the last time she tried to reach me she couldn't and she was upset. They would all be so afraid right now. I sensed their fear and related to their feelings. My family was so close to me, it almost felt as if I were experiencing it myself.

. . .

Unknown Location
Around 10:00 AM

The shadows were all that provided Yvonne comfort. She woke up in a darkened room only graced with a flicker of light when the solid door opened. She had been subjected to touches and advances from men her father's age. It made her sick, but she swallowed the bile, allowing it burn down her throat to avoid the risk of making them angry. She feared that more than anything—especially when it came to the man who whistled as a bird. He drove fear into her.

Maybe it was something in his eyes when he looked on her—the way they traveled down her body and seemed to envelope her into his own state of rapture.

If it hadn't been for the other man earlier, he would have raped her. This was something a woman, even of fourteen, knew. Her heart fluttered with anxiety remembering his hands on her. The tears came from the memory as she relived the moment again. He had come close. Her only rescue was an Italian man with clipped speech and an accent, and even he had briefly touched her when they were videotaping. What if he wasn't around the next time?

She hadn't even been with a boy, but she had come close to wanting to with Craig. She only made out with him, heavy kissing and some touching. She should have just hooked up with him. Her mom pretty much accused her of it anyway.

Shivers ran through her. She felt so cold and damp.

She couldn't hear anything despite straining to hear something, anything. When the door would open, she did her best to focus on something that would tell her where she was, but between the man's footsteps and his whistles—nothing.

And why had she been allowed to see their faces? She knew that wasn't a good sign. She sat huddled in the corner of the room wondering if the rest of her family was alive. She could even handle a hug from her mom right now.

She knew hours must have passed; it felt like she had been here for a lifetime. All she remembered prior to this room was sleeping in her bed and a blur of shadows as someone came toward her.

When she came to, she remembering screaming loud enough to rouse the dead; her yells muffled by a gag quickly tied in place, her hands cuffed and secured to a fixture above her head.

But each time the whistling man crept into her room, she used flirtatious charm to free her way from the confinements. She had promised to keep quiet.

She sat huddled on the bed, which was in the corner of the room, her legs tucked in and her arms wrapped around them. The position brought her some peace. She felt safe. She knew he'd be in again, but she hadn't been able to set an exact time interval to his visits. She just knew that when she heard the heel of boots scuffing along the floor, she needed to start focusing on something else other than the here and now. She leaned harder into the wall when she saw the door handle turn and heard the whistling begin.

CHAPTER TWENTY-TWO

It didn't sit well with me that for the third day in a row—considering I checked out last night—I was back at The Oasis in the same room. And now that the manager had firsthand knowledge of the piece I carried in my holster, it had likely raised some suspicions.

I worked on obtaining clear vision. I would need it to pull the trigger at a potential six hundred yards away.

A knock on the door jarred my thoughts, actually making me jump, if only slightly. I pulled my gun. The banging had been heavy, deliberate. It would be too soon for the taxi to have shown up.

What if Christian chose to cut his losses and wipe out the entire Hunter family? He obviously knew where to find me.

My breathing quickened as I wondered if an assassin had been sent after me—although we didn't normally knock and why not just kill me back in Detroit.

I pressed against the door and glanced through the peephole. I sighed and opened the door holding my gun behind my back.

"Coffee for you on the house." The older man smiled at me. "For repeat business." He extended a couple of packs of coffee toward me which I took with my free hand. His eyes went to my waist. He searched for the gun he saw earlier.

The obvious visual investigation made me weary.

When he seemed satisfied it wasn't there, he backed up from the doorway. "Have a good day, eh? Supposed to be sunny and warm—"

A honk interrupted him. A yellow cab jolted to an abrupt stop only a few feet from where he stood. The manager slapped the hood. "Watch where the hell you're driving!"

I smiled. Here was the man who minutes ago was a preacher's advocate about how bad times were getting yet he had a bit of a temper.

The cabbie hauled the upper half of his torso out the window. "Don't touch my cab!"

The manager put another flat-palmed hand down on the hood. "What are you going to do about it, eh?"

"That's enough!" The cabbie got out of the vehicle and came after the manager with intent to do some harm. I knew eyes, and I knew how to read body language. The manager was too proud to back down.

I took a couple steps outside the hotel door. That's all it took.

The cabbie looked at me, halted in his approach. He spoke to the manager. "I didn't hit you." The driver's eyes narrowed with a threat as if saying, *you might not be so lucky next time.*

"We've got it from here. Thanks for the coffee." I nodded toward the manager and thanked him for something I would never use. If everything went according to plan, I would be two hundred and forty miles away from here before the next sunrise.

The cabbie watched me unload my luggage just as he had when I crammed it into his ride. There was no way I would be carting everything around with me, and there was no way I would be leaving it behind at the motel for the manager to rummage through. In fact, I wouldn't be returning.

I must have been tired to bring all of this with me anyway. All I really needed was my rifle case and bullets. Nothing more, nothing less.

"You must be a hunter."

I was in mid-sling of placing the duffel bag over my shoulder. I held the case in my other hand. I turned to face him and his head nodded toward my waist and the .44.

"Something like that." I had him take me to the Greyhound bus station where there would be a lot of people and public lockers for rent. It also served to sever the connection between me, the motel, the taxi, and the hospital. But just the way he kept watching me, I feared another suspicious person.

"That will be forty dollars," he said.

"Forty? That sounds like a lot—"

"Gas keeps going up."

As I counted out the bills, I thought of Brenda and how she would jab at my frugalness. She might have a different viewpoint now that Salvatore's Clothier notified her about the tuxedo.

How I missed her and the kids!

I extended the bills to the driver and our business transaction had been concluded.

He stood there for a minute, and I held concern he might attempt conversation, but after counting the cash he left. There were no more glances to the piece on my waist. This cabbie lived in his own world and preferred to stay there. He could almost be a hired driver for a Town Car the way he seemed to respect privacy, except for that one inquiry.

He drove off and I glanced down at the case I held in my hand. It had been customized to look like a man's briefcase with no shiny aluminum or other telltale sign that it held a sniper rifle. Its interior shell was forged titanium to make it a lighter weight, but the exterior had been overlaid with genuine leather. To the untrained eye or the uninterested observer, it would be viewed as nothing more than a business case and me nothing more than a traveling businessman… with a huge weapon holstered to my hip.

I needed to lose the .44. It had given me confidence when this mission had started, but it drew too much attention—and attention wasn't a good thing when you needed to be invisible.

. . .

3 Hours Earlier...
Niagara Falls, New York
7:00 AM

The security tech offered his chair to Clinton, who took it without a nod of appreciation. His thoughts were on getting the son of a bitch who shot the Governor and thought he'd get away with it.

"All right, so start this up again. Go back to around eleven when the Governor came back to the room."

Devries reached past Clinton and pressed the appropriate buttons.

They watched the video play out in fast forward from ten thirty. Hensal, the hotel staff member, delivered food to room 836. Clinton passed a glance at his partner whose eyes were fixed on the replay. She lightly bit her bottom lip, the way she did when she was in deep thought.

The video caught up to where the Governor showed up around ten to eleven.

"Okay, so the Governor comes back to her room. Lanky's standing vigil at the door," Clinton said.

Wingham faced him now, a smile only lit in her eyes. She must have felt proud for rubbing off on him with the attribution of nicknames. "Standing vigil? What sort of bodyguard do you know who stands with his hands in his pockets?"

Clinton's eyes went back to the screen. "Stop the video." The tech wasn't moving quickly enough. Clinton rose to his feet. "Go back to where she's outside the door." Clinton paced while the feed was reversed. "Now, play it frame by frame." He stopped moving.

"What is it?" Wingham's tone flickered with the hint of a whine.

"Pause it." The tech hurried to accommodate Clinton's request. "Look at her left hand." It was the one opposite from the camera angle they were watching from. "Is there another angle?"

"Ah…" The tech pressed some keys on the keyboard and clicked the mouse a few times. The mirrored image came up on a screen beside the paused feed.

"Enlarge that—"

"Please." Wingham added the pleasantry to her partner's directive. It warranted a look from Clinton.

"Just as I thought." Clinton walked out of the room into the hallway. Wingham followed. He heard Devries's inquiries about whether they'd be back. Wingham responded and told him to stay put. Clinton was already on his cell phone.

It didn't stop her from talking to him. "What are you doing?"

Clinton held up a hand and listened to the person on the other end. After a few seconds, he had the answer he needed, not necessarily the one he wanted.

"What is it?"

Clinton could picture his partner stomping her one foot. Her patience level had a lower threshold than his at times. And just for that, he'd take his time. "The Governor was on a cell phone."

"Yes." She dragged out her *s* almost like the security tech. "So what? Don't most people have them these days? And she held a position, does hold, a position of power. It was likely tied to her ear most of the time."

"Crime Scene never found one." He stated his revealed jewel matter-of-factly.

"What? That doesn't make any sense." She paused. "So our guy kills the Governor and takes her cell phone?"

"Well, not just any cell phone. A smartphone."

"Are you a spokesman for the industry now?" There was the faint detection of amusement in her voice.

"They're utilized for a lot more than simply conversations. They have hundreds, thousands, of apps for them. They can store files."

"The killer wanted what was on her phone," she said.

"Bingo."

They stood there silent for a few seconds. Clinton's attention was on the wall across from them and Wingham's was on the carpet.

She took a deep breath. "This raises a lot more questions."

"And opens up a lot more possibilities." Their eyes connected now. "First of all, the question I raised earlier, why was the Governor out without her bodyguard? I mean she obviously recognized the guy. She never gave him a second glance when she saw him standing outside her doorway."

"We need to find out why the Governor was here. I'm getting the feeling it wasn't official business," Wingham said.

"I tend to agree with that assessment. And I'd also wager that the reason for her being here might be tied to Tux and to something on her phone."

"I'll see your bet and raise it with the fact she must have been killed for it."

Clinton's lips pressed downward. "I'm starting to think so."

CHAPTER TWENTY-THREE

The public washroom made the perfect retreat for removing my piece and placing it into the duffel bag. I studied my eyes in the mirror as I headed for the oversized cubicle intended for those with health restrictions. My eyes had changed and glazed over with a man reborn into a former life. I would kill the Governor without hesitation and get my family back alive. There would be no mistakes, no misses this time. She would die.

My realization came with a slight pause when I placed the holster and .44 into the bag. I almost forgot I even had this; I held the Governor's smartphone in my hands for a few seconds before stuffing it back in the bag. What was on there really didn't matter right now. Getting my family back alive was all that did.

. . .

Navigating through the bus station was a struggle. People never stuck to the mentality of defined lines that should separate one direction from the other. Someone's elbow went into my side, and my instant fighting reaction had them pinned with a raised fist in front of their face. Of course, I never acted on the thought and they kept walking as if they never even noticed they cut me off.

The interaction quickly gave way to the situation my family was in—because of me. I would never forgive myself for this, even for as far as things had already progressed, my family kidnaped. If something actually happened to one of them, if Christian killed any of them or physically harmed them, I would never recover.

Despite the forward momentum and how far I had truly come in a short amount of time, nothing was coming together fast enough. Twinges of pain pulsed through my body—the heartbreak that came from the uncertainty. I would get revenge for this. I just hoped that my family would come out on the other side with me.

I took another cab to County General. When I reached my destination, I performed a scan of the area and looked into the distance, taking in the surrounding buildings and analyzing potential perches. First, of course, I needed to determine exactly which room the Governor was in. That would be the easy part.

Walking through the revolving door, I noticed the vacant spot at the front desk that at one point would have been manned by a human being. Now a message board sat on top of it beside a phone, which listed numbers to call should you need assistance navigating through the corridors of the hospital. A layout of the hospital had been enlarged and framed and was displayed on the wall behind the desk.

Given the fact the Governor's injuries were to her head, I scanned for the appropriate wing. It didn't take long to realize I needed to be on the other side of the building.

As I took elevators and wound through the maze of hallways, I was aware of each step I took on the glossy, tiled floor. They hadn't been scuffed up yet, resulting in a mild squeak from my shoes.

The elevator chimed and the doors opened to the third floor. The embossed sign read, MENTAL HEALTH AND HEAD INJURIES.

I remembered from the board, the wing took up a couple floors of the hospital. I had been conflicted about whether I would find her in this wing or down in the emergency area. According to the last update, she was in critical condition, but that was hours ago.

I took a deep breath and stepped off the elevator.

I had too much to lose, and it could compromise the mission. When emotions factored into the equation, it normally meant failure. I wasn't afraid of getting caught and going to prison, although I'd prefer not to experience that, but it couldn't happen or my family would be killed.

Each step a heartbeat, each lift of the legs a stymied exhale.

The way I saw it, I wasn't looking for the Governor, I was looking for her security detail. They would be easier to spot than one lone dignitary. When I found them, I had her.

I was just thinking about moving to the next floor when the last turn in the corridor revealed what I had been looking for. Two government agents, apparent by their suits, stood guard outside of a room. One faced me and the other watched the hallway in the opposite direction.

My heart raced. I needed to get closer if I was going to get the room number. I needed to get this taken care of now. Time wasn't on my side. It worked against me. I took a deep breath. I was used to getting close. That was my specialty. I could do this.

The agent facing me raised both hands. "Sir, I'm going to have to ask you to step back."

I did my best to conjure a confused look. *"Je suis de l'extérieur de la ville et ici pour voir un parent."* I knew little French, but I was thankful for what I did remember. I told him I was from out of town and came to see a relative.

The agent appeared unfazed. "You will not find them here." He braced himself, stood straight, and put both hands on his hips—providing himself close access to his holster.

Getting shot wasn't what I had planned for this morning. *"On m'a dit—"* I was told.

"Sir, I'm not going to repeat myself." The agent's patience had worn thin. I relaxed my posture. The agent was prepared to fire with deadly force if necessary—it was in his gaze.

"Sorry." I let my eyes drift to the floor for a second, and when they came up, they met with the agent's. He was analyzing me. *"Bonne journée,"* I said. Good day.

I turned around to retreat down the hallway and felt his stare on the back of my head. But I had to hold this together. My entire family depended on me. And I had to act quickly for a couple reasons now. I think he might have been on to me, which would mean they'd be arranging for a room change.

I studied the numbers as I made my way back to the elevators. The Governor would be in room 315.

My heart resumed a regular rhythm, but my breathing remained unsteady. I hated the necessity of getting so close to the authorities, but by the time everything went down, they would have no idea where to find the French-speaking man looking for a relative. At least I sure as hell hoped not.

CHAPTER TWENTY-FOUR

Detective Clinton walked back into the room where Hensal sat with his head cocked to the side, resting in one hand. The other held a phone to his ear. He lifted his head when Clinton and Wingham walked in. His eyes were bloodshot. He slammed the receiver back on the cradle.

The man had transformed over the last three and a half hours. He was no longer the weak, fragile person who had discovered a woman clinging to life. Clinton found the transformation to be enlightening. But as he had learned over the years, you could never accept anyone at face value. People only projected what they wanted others to see.

"Finding it tough to get a lawyer on a Sunday." Clinton more or less stated it, rather than raising it as a rhetorical question. Hensal said nothing.

Wingham and he had spent more time looking at the video footage and had been called in by the Chief to head downtown. The FBI was here now. They were supposed to cooperate with them and the Michigan State Police. But so far, Clinton and Wingham had the lead.

MSP had tracked down Behler's bodyguard. He was a man by the name of Kevin Biggs and he had worked with her for ten years. His record was clean. They found him at home, and he provided a solid alibi for the time the Governor was shot. He said that Behler had told him to take the weekend off and had added that she had other bodyguards accompany her periodically. Apparently, Behler found them on her own, without the formal interview process, and was very private about their identities.

Clinton pressed the flat of his hands on the front of his trousers as he took a seat.

Paul crossed his arms, licked his top lip, and turned to the right. "Where have you been? I've been held up here for hours."

Clinton disregarded his statement. "We know that someone talked you into going into the room."

Hensal's eyes made contact with Clinton's but quickly diverted to a sofa pillow.

"You were delivering food to room 836," Clinton continued.

Hensal's jaw went askew for a moment. He didn't speak a word.

Clinton settled into the couch, crossed a leg. Most men didn't make it a habit of sitting that way, but he was comfortable. And in his case, the rumor about the package being smaller in a man who did held no truth. "We know someone approached you. Maybe even set you up."

His eyes dashed to Clinton's. Wingham stood at the side of the room with one hand braced on a hip.

"I want a lawyer," Hensal said.

"And that's your choice kid."

His brows furled as if to say, *I'm no kid.*

"But, what we need is your help—"

"Why should I help you? You're going to twist what I say. I watch those…those…" His hand moved emphatically. "Those shows. I know what you cops are capable of. I won't go to jail."

A smile formed on Clinton's lips. He fought to stifle the laugh that lingered behind it. Hensal must have picked up on it. Seriousness grazed his expression.

"You can't make me talk." His arms tightened in front of his chest.

"No." Clinton paused for dramatic effect, uncrossed his legs, and leaned forward. He loved it when he had a suspect or witness within his grasp. "But you don't want to be responsible for letting the Governor's killer go free, do you?" Clinton heard the deep exhale of his partner, but didn't acknowledge it by looking at her. To him, it was only a minor technicality that the Governor was in critical care. "I mean that wouldn't be a good spot to be in. You could have helped but chose not to." He paused for effect. "Because you were afraid."

Hensal's jaw tightened. The message his eyes tried to convey was, *I'm afraid of no one*, but Clinton saw through the veneer.

"This is your shot, kid. Your chance to be—"

"I'm not a kid. Stop calling me a kid." Hensal uncrossed his arms. Both of his hands went to the edge of the sofa cushion and picked at the cording.

Clinton waved a hand of apology. Anything to sway this kid to speak.

Hensal's eyes flitted to the sofa, back up to meet Clinton's. "A guy approached me."

Wingham took a seat beside Clinton who moved over to allow her room. Couches weren't built like they used to be, or people weren't; somehow they seemed shorter in length.

Hensal's attention dodged to Wingham.

Clinton forced eye contact back on him. "Someone approached you?"

"I don't want to go to jail."

Clinton let out a loud exhale and rose from the couch. It was time for his partner to take over—the one with the more delicate touch.

Hensal watched Clinton get up and pace around the room. There were seconds of silence as he seemed to debate whether to proceed.

Wingham leaned forward, her elbows on her knees and clasped her hands. "Paul, we really could use your help. You would be bringing justice to the man who shot the Governor. You would be in newspapers and headlines around the world—"

"This kid doesn't want to be famous," Clinton interceded.

Hensal's eyes iced over as he cast a glare at Clinton.

"All he wants is to get back to his simple life. No responsibilities."

"Listen, so what, you don't want to be famous. I'm not so sure I would want to be either. But I'd want to do the right thing." Wingham gestured toward Hensal. "And I know you're that type of person too."

His face relaxed and he nodded.

Clinton respected his partner's means of delivery. She held the soft touch while he didn't possess that trait. Maybe for a brief stint as a child before the world impressed upon him its cruelties and how no amount of whining or heartbreak would make an ounce of difference.

"Can you tell us exactly what happened?" Wingham sat perched mid-cushion and stretched out her back for a few seconds.

"I was told to deliver food to room—" He seemed nervous that somehow he'd get the facts wrong and looked to Clinton. "Room 836. The guy in the room—"

"This guy? Can you describe him, Paul?" Wingham asked.

His eyes danced around her face. Clinton surmised he knew what the kid was thinking. She wasn't hard to look at.

Hensal rubbed at his arms as if he caught a chill.

"He threatened you?" Wingham asked.

This was taking too much time. Clinton came around to the front of the couch and took a seat again. He leaned back into the sofa, crossed a leg and his arms. Wingham and he shared a look. She would continue with the questioning.

"What did he say to you? Did he have a gun?"

The rubbing of his arms intensified as if Hensal was trying to create a spark to start a fire with two sticks. He nodded.

"He threatened to shoot you if you didn't cooperate?"

"Yes."

"Had you seen this man before last night?"

"Never."

"How long were you in room 836?" Wingham asked the question aware of the answer.

"Five minutes or so."

"What did he want from you?"

"Just said to come back and deliver a food order to room 838 in about an hour. He said he would be calling it from room 836."

"Did he tell you why he was doing this?"

Hensal cocked his head to the side. "I just figured it was some rich guy goofing around. He said there would be a big tip in it for me if I just did as he said."

"Rich man?"

He pinched the tip of his nose, released it. "He wore a gold watch. I think it might have been a Rolex. I never did get my tip either."

"So you never saw this man again?"

"When I came to deliver the food he was nowhere around so I let myself in."

Wingham and Clinton shared another look.

"Do you remember anything else specific about him? A tattoo, a scar, the way he talked?" Wingham asked.

Hensal sat quietly for a few seconds. Clinton could almost hear his brain grinding away and picture smoke coming from his ears.

"He had an Italian accent." He seemed proud with his second offering.

Enough of wasting time. "Lots of people have accents. What stood out about him?" Clinton asked.

Wingham sat back with a deep exhale and a flash of evil intent in her hazel eyes. Clinton didn't care.

"You need to think of something that will help us."

"Go do your job then! Stop looking at me to do it for you!" Hensal closed up; his arms crossed tightly.

Wingham flashed a look to her a partner as if to say, *are you happy now?* She stood up and took a seat beside Hensal. "Sometimes, he gets a little moody."

"A little?" He gave her a sideways glance.

"He's just a driven guy. He wants the answers; he wants the guilty to pay for their crimes." Wingham softened her approach even further.

"Governor Behler could die, Paul. Now we know that's not your fault." They matched eyes. "But you're the only one, besides her, that might have had direct contact with her killer."

His cheeks flushed as if he was suddenly aware of how close he sat to the female detective. With Wingham leaning forward, their knees were less than a foot apart. Clinton fought a smile. The kid was attracted to his partner.

"The fact you told us he had an Italian accent and a Rolex, those are great leads but do you have something else to give us?"

"Sorry, no."

Wingham placed a hand on Hensal's shoulder and rose. She thanked him for his help and insisted that he stay in the city in case they had any further questions. Clinton and she went into an adjoining room. She spoke first. "How does a bodyguard afford a Rolex?"

"I think I chose the wrong profession."

"I ditto that. I wonder if Behler's regular has one." Wingham paused, tucked a strand of her red hair behind an ear. "Do you find it strange the guy had an Italian accent?"

"Why would I?"

"Mafia?"

Clinton laughed hard but stopped when he noticed her expression. She took her statement seriously. "Why would they concern themselves with a Governor? And because the guy has an Italian accent, it must be the mob?"

Wingham attempted to cover up the seriousness of her comment with a weak smile and a slap on his arm. "I wasn't being serious. Dave, you didn't think I meant that?"

Clinton knew her. Wingham only verbalized her theories when she felt they had merit.

CHAPTER TWENTY-FIVE

Niagara Falls, New York
Sunday, June 13th, 11:45 AM
Just Over 17 Hours Until the Deadline

I had the perfect place picked out. It was a modest apartment building a few blocks away. It had an unobstructed line of sight which would afford me distance from the dead Governor and secure my getaway. I had moved quickly through the streets to make it to this point, metaphorically one eye ahead and one behind.

The energy that came from the government agent at the hospital didn't give me any sort of warm reassurance. He suspected the hint of a threat with my approach yet not enough to warrant subjecting me to hours of interrogation.

Thank God for that.

However, I still didn't trust that he wouldn't relocate the Governor based on a gut instinct. I needed to act quickly. My heart wrenched as if my voodoo replica had been stabbed by a sword.

Yvonne.

I stood outside the apartment building looking up. Based on distance, trajectory, and the velocity of the bullet, I needed to be on at least the fifth floor. I had estimated the distance from here to the hospital based on the length of my stride, which I knew was approximately three feet. And accounting for the fact there was little to no breeze today it would make the shot an easy one.

The front door opened and a woman wearing a gray-pleated skirt and a black blouse came out. She held a Bible clutched in her hands as if relying on it to provide meaning and direction to her life. I remembered holding onto my cell phone in the same manner—as if it would somehow subdue the reality of my living nightmare.

She scanned me from my shoes to my head, back to the briefcase. Her foot stayed braced in the door as she held it open. "Jehovah's Witness?"

Her comment made me speechless. My mission was hardly one of preaching and teaching, it was one of reconciliation on man's terms.

"You guys always find your way into locked buildings." She nudged her foot causing the door to open wider. She nodded me inside the building and smiled. "God's way is the only way. Good day to you."

"Good day." The words came out in an automatic reply. I was still in shock. There were always ways into a secured building, but this had been a stroke of luck.

By the time I recovered from the ease of access to the building, the woman had made her way down the street a good fifty feet. A smile formed on my lips. Now it was time to do what I had come for. And I doubted God would be happy about it.

Clinton called out his partner. "You were serious when you said the Mafia."

Her lips contorted. "Kind of." She revised her answer to insert more conviction. "Yeah, I was. I mean, why not? They're still around."

Clinton refused to let his amusement show.

"I know it sounds crazy." A hand went to her hip. "It sounds crazy to me."

"And it's quite the leap."

"And it's quite the leap." She reiterated his words. "But, it is a possibility. Most bodyguards don't make enough money to afford Rolexes. And they most certainly don't run away when their detail has been shot."

"Unless they're the one who did it."

"Exactly. And it seems he wanted Paul to discover the Governor."

"Only thing is, though, the Mafia doesn't make mistakes. And normally the body's never found," Clinton said.

Her head cocked to the side. "They're still people. There are still too many questions and not enough answers."

With her statement, Clinton was renewed with zealous determination to get the score settled—one answer to every question.

"And we still don't know anything about Tux."

Clinton heard her words, but his mind was elsewhere. They needed to find out why the Governor was here in the first place. If they could get the answer to that, they'd be on their way to solving this thing.

CHAPTER TWENTY-SIX

Unknown Location
Sunday, June 13th, 11:45 AM

The tears had dried up hours ago. Brenda's eyes were now itchy and sore, the back of them tender as if they were bruised. Light was seeping through the cloth they had covering her eyes. The sun must have been up and illuminating this darkened hell hole she had been stashed in.

She hadn't heard Yvonne for a while and feared for her daughter's safety. Her heart burned with maternal anxiety wondering if both of her children were alive. Instinct told her they were. They had to be.

She could hear men walking. She knew from the heavy stride and the impact on the concrete as they moved, the one man possibly wore a pair of safety boots. The other man's footfalls made relatively little noise so he either wore loafers or running shoes.

She had counted a total of three men. The one who also whistled wore the boots. Based on the projection of his voice as he'd approached her, he was of average height and build. One man had a larger build and exuded a presence that could be felt from a distance. And the third man hadn't come to see her since she had been here but she heard his voice in the hallway. He held a thick Italian accent and, by the way, his energy read she took it that he was in charge. She also pegged him as the man who had been in her bedroom.

His steps made a soft tap-tap noise. It was hard to pinpoint the type of footwear, but it sounded like a thin leather sole.

Over the last few hours, she replayed all that she could remember and fought for some sort of normality in all of it. She had long ago let go of the premise it was her imagination and a bad dream. A shiver ran through her. In dreams, you never felt cold. No, this was one hell of a reality.

She wanted to wrap her arms around herself, but both wrists were bound to the arms of the wooden chair she sat in. Her legs ached from being stationary and had long ago recovered from the pins and needles sensation. Her rear end was numb.

She didn't remember much before waking up here. Her head hurt from the crying, and from the intense stress and pressure she put upon herself to piece it all together. And all she could remember was the ringing of a distant phone and the presence of a man who smelled of expensive cologne—the same man from her room with the tap-tap shoes.

She'd listen when the men talked and walked. In her mental picture, she was in a room with some sort of opening to the outside. Based on the increase of light, it wasn't a four walled room without an aperture.

The men's voices dulled, yet she didn't feel they were far away, maybe even just outside the area where they kept her. She knew there was a door to the room as it would creak lightly when it was opened.

But it didn't seem like a normal hallway. It seemed cavernous as their voices were mostly absorbed. For this reason, she had concluded the building they were in was large. She also surmised they were somewhere in the country as the smell of manure would periodically creep into her sinus cavities.

She found it fascinating how with her vision taken away, her other senses were piqued and more attuned. She would have preferred not to ever experience their full capability. All she wanted more than anything was to be home again with her family, for all of them to be safe and secure. Where was Ray? Had they killed him?

She didn't care if he cheated on her anymore. They would work their way through this. There were worse things in life, and she was afraid they might face the reality of that before they had a chance at reconciliation.

The straps on her wrists bit into her flesh as she attempted yet again to waggle free of her constraints. She thought of her little boy and could picture him huddled and afraid, scared and alone. But her worst fears came out of concern for her daughter. Yvonne portrayed herself as tough and indestructible, yet Brenda knew her daughter wasn't. It was simply a front she would erect. Her daughter was fragile and vulnerable.

More chills went through Brenda's body. She needed to get her family out of here. She see-sawed her arms back and forth and howled like a wounded animal when she felt them slice through her flesh. She stopped moving and sat there crying without tears.

CHAPTER TWENTY-SEVEN

Apartment 516 would make the perfect location for setting up, but when I approached the door, I heard a screaming baby. I would have to settle for a less than ideal place—the neighboring apartment, 514. It was silent, but it could simply mean the occupants were sleeping.

The knocks were heavy, but after three of them, there was no answer. I proceeded with caution, standing tight to the door as I pulled out my pick, which worked flawlessly for unlocking dead bolts. When I heard a door close down the hallway, I stopped moving and stepped back, pretending I had knocked and waited for an answer. I couldn't see anyone; it sounded like they headed the opposite way. I moved back in close to the door. I felt the tumblers give way with a definitive click and slowly turned the handle.

One benefit to the modern age and of sticking to one's own personal matters, with little or no regard for your neighbor, was actually an advantage in some instances. People were less likely to pry their nose into what didn't directly relate to or concern them. If someone had noticed me picking the lock, through a peephole from the other side of the hallway, it was unlikely they'd even call the police. Of course, I hated the uncertainty of not knowing.

I opened the door with purpose as if I was an invited guest who had a copy of the key. Once inside I moved slowly; my ears strained for any indication the tenant was sleeping. I heard nothing. The place was empty.

Whoever did live here, though, placed no importance on keeping the place up. The kitchen was to the immediate right and dirty dishes lined the counters along with takeout containers and pizza boxes. A couple of empty beer boxes sat on the linoleum floor while the drained bottles were scattered randomly around the apartment.

The place definitely belonged to a guy. No woman would ever live like this no matter how creative a mind she had. At a point long before now necessity would have forced her hand to tidy and clean. I inhaled with disgust as the mingled smells, similar to a gym locker and days-old pizza, hit my nose.

All these assessments were computed in fractions of time. My goal was to get this assassination over with. The window I would set up in was in the living area straight across from the apartment's main door. I relocked the door and slid the chain across and made my way to the window.

Clothes were strewn on the couch and coffee table. I propped open the window, first flicking beer bottle caps out of the sill and moving a coffee mug which had some sort of science project brewing in the bottom of it. This place was a hazardous material den.

I kicked a pile of magazines that were stacked on the floor and pushed the television stand to the right to make more room. I stood in the window and took a deep breath. I could see the hospital with a clear, unrestricted view without the scope.

I moved quickly to assemble the rifle. For the final touch, I attached the suppressor to the barrel and readied myself. Looking through the scope, I could see her clearly. The Governor's head was wrapped in white bandages. A government agent stood beside her, but I still had a clear shot. It seemed crazy to me that for a woman of her station, who had just faced the bullet of an assassination attempt, had open curtains.

Stupid, stupid, stupid.

I steadied my breath and pulled back on the trigger.

. . .

David Clinton wasn't going to let the lack of answers get in his way of solving this case. He would gather every last one of them and formulate a clear picture of what really happened in the Governor's room. It went beyond what the job required of him. He had a personal drive compelling him.

Wingham's cell phone rang, and by the expression on her face the news she was receiving from the caller was enlightening. Her eyes sparkled as if she were examining a fine diamond in rays of light. "You sure…all right… keep the file ready for us to see." She hung up. "Okay, that was our security tech—"

"Whoa, no Wonder Boy, or Tech Kid or—"

Her lips curled upward from his attempt at conjuring a nickname. "Sure, we can call him anyone of those."

"You're telling me you don't have one for him?"

She snapped her fingers. "You're missing the point. Devries found more footage on Tux and you're not going to believe this."

"You're using his real name?"

"You want me to tell you my news?"

"I'm waiting, but you keep talking about nicknames," Clinton said sarcastically.

She narrowed her eyes. "The guy should be a detective. He ran the footage forward and back. And while forward led to a dead end—"

"A dead end?"

"Looks like Tux left out the back door. No cameras out there but he showed leading up to it."

"That sounds professional and planned."

"Anyway, Tux was here on Friday. And—" She held up a hand to make sure he didn't interject. "—he went inside of the Governor's room that day too. He wore a tux that day as well."

"He knew where she would be staying and was familiarizing himself with the surroundings. He wanted to blend in. If people did look at him, he'd come across as distinguished."

"Yep. I'd wager on the fact he placed surveillance bugs in the room too. I mean, why not, right?"

"He swiped a copy of the all-access key," Clinton said.

Wingham nodded. "Cameras have him raiding a maid's cart. Likely a cover for the swipe. He disposed of the toiletries in the garbage of the public restroom. Just a tad wasteful but I guess it wasn't on his list of priorities. Anyway, according to the front desk Behler checked in about ten thirty. When she did, Lanky stood behind her while she took care of the paperwork."

"So, obviously, the killer knew about her bodyguard and wasn't sure if she'd enter the suite alone."

Wingham shrugged. "Sometimes it seems that Lanky and Tux were in on it together, the way they were outside the door, and other times it doesn't seem like they were."

"I agree except for the part to do with her phone. Why take it? How did this third party, Tux, know about it and take it?"

"You're assuming he, and not the missing bodyguard, took the phone."

More questions that required settlement. Clinton thought back on the video. "Lanky's got to be in on it with Tux. He never barred entrance. We need to speak to the people at the front desk, see if they have more to offer, get over to the Governor—" Both of their cell phones rang.

"I've got a bad feeling about this." Wingham lifted her cell to an ear at the same time as Clinton.

Seconds after hanging up, neither spoke. Their eyes communicated everything. They were no longer investigating an attempted assassination. There had been a successful one.

CHAPTER TWENTY-EIGHT

I pulled back from the scope slowly.

Job complete.

There was no satisfaction, nor any guilt. It wasn't personal. It was necessary. My watch showed it was just after noon. Seventeen hours of the deadline leftover.

I dissembled the rifle and worked at fitting it back inside the case. My movements stopped when I heard footsteps in the hallway. My breathing took pause. A key was inserted into the lock.

Time to move!

One last clasp on the case…I stuck my head out the window and eyed the fire escape which was inconveniently placed outside of another window. I bent over and picked up the shell casing, tucked it into a pant pocket.

I heard the tumblers turn.

Shit!

My heart sped up with an adrenaline rush—realizing everything was at stake. If I ended up in prison, Christian would kill my family. He might anyway given the fact I had initially failed him. This could be an elaborate scheme to make me think I had some control of the situation when really I had none.

The handle turned, but I was already down the hall. Expletives were streaming from the tenant's mouth as he pushed the door, but it wouldn't give any more than a few inches. I prayed the chain I put across would hold.

The guy's bedroom was worse than the rest of the place. I nearly slipped flat on my back when a shirt found its way under my footing.

"What the fuck!" The man was yelling in the apartment hallway.

He would be drawing way too much attention. I needed to move. I recovered my balance and made it to the window. An empty beer bottle sat on the sill along with a condom wrapper. I couldn't imagine a woman making it through the rest of the apartment to the bedroom. Maybe the guy deserved props because he must have been a smooth talker.

"Get out of my apartment. Fuck!" The guy was kicking on the door. "I'll kill you if you stole my laptop, you fucking shit!"

Charmer.

Ironic how in a moment of intense anxiety, which could decide between confinement and freedom, I found any amusement in this loser.

The window opened without a hassle, and I slipped out onto the escape just as I heard the chain hardware tear from the doorframe.

"Where you are?"

I heard his raised voice as I made my way down the fire escape stairs. My breath labored as my heart pumped from infused adrenaline mixed with the fear of getting caught and losing everything. I pressed against the outside of the building, around the bend and out of sight from the angered tenant.

"If I find you, I'll kill you!" The window slammed shut.

I had stood there for only a few seconds before I spotted my ride to the bus station.

CHAPTER TWENTY-NINE

"This case has been reassigned to the FBI." The agent speaking held an air about him that communicated he thought himself above all men and only a peg lower than a Greater Being.

They stood in a meeting room at the hospital. The agent's name was Tony Leone. When Clinton and Wingham showed up, they were shuffled off into a room and not allowed near where the Governor had been pronounced dead at quarter past twelve.

Clinton held no respect for a man who projected a narcissistic ego. And there was no way Clinton would be backing down. "We've been on this case from the start. It happened in the city of Niagara Falls, New York. Local law enforcement was originally called in. It falls under our jurisdiction." *You're only showing up for the credit.* At least that's what he wanted to add.

"In your great city of Niagara Falls, the Governor of Michigan had her life taken essentially twice. Excellent job."

Apparently the man only knew one way of speaking—sardonically. "The Governor herself had come under your care, your protective custody. Maybe one of your men did it." Clinton shot back the accusation, and the agent's eyes burned with an intensity that would have melted the polar ice caps. If the goal had been to intimidate Clinton, it would take a lot more than that. "We have information, suspects you don't have."

"And you'll be passing that information along to us. You shouldn't have been holding it back in the first place." Leone pointed to another agent who came over to his side and looked at him as a young child does to a parent for direction. "I need to get all their investigative reports so far." He directed his next statement to Clinton. "Make sure we're going to get all the forensic results from the hotel scene as well."

"You fail to assume any responsibility for any of this, Agent Leone?" Clinton asked. Seconds passed without an answer. Wingham seemed to have lost her voice. Clinton would have to change tactics, soften a little, but he told himself it in no way meant his character had weakened. "Listen, there's no evidence the killer crossed state lines and with that consideration, the case should remain that of the Niagara Falls Police

Department." He noticed Wingham's eyes flicker in his direction. She didn't approve of what he had just said. He knew it may be a stretch of the truth because the missing bodyguard would have come from Michigan. But he could live with it right now. "Unless it can be proven that the killer—"

"We have an assassin who knew right where to find her—both times. The FBI considers the direct assault on a US Governor to be a matter for them to handle. Must I also point out the Governor herself had crossed state lines?"

Clinton disregarded the agent's last statement. "Yet you allowed us this time to gather the evidence in the case, round up suspects."

"Consider it a professional courtesy. Nothing more."

"Nothing more?" Clinton paused and stared at the agent. *Special agent, my ass.* "You've come in to claim the benefits of our investigation, our labor, our time. How do you think the taxpayers of New York State will feel about this?"

Agent Leone seemed to be chewing on his tongue as his jaw slid side to side in a teeth-grinding movement. He seemed to be giving pause and consideration to his next words, his ego taking a plunge for the cause. "The people of New York would be proud of the efforts put into a case of such prominence. And the people should be—"

The door flung open, and the Mayor of Niagara Falls walked in with the Governor of New York. All eyes in the room went to them. Clinton noticed the junior agent take a few steps back.

"Sir." The Special Agent Leone had to swallow pride to address the dignitary.

"Gentlemen."

In person the Governor of New York exuded confidence one would expect from a man in charge. He wore the position with a dignified honor expected of those in the public eye. Clinton nodded at him. The media and hype that surrounded him would have the naïve viewing him as a caped crusader, yet he was simply a man of flesh and blood. But there was something about the way the man's eyes moved around the room as if he were nervous and taking everything in, and considering everyone a threat.

The Governor took a seat, and the Mayor sticking close sat beside him. The Governor tapped the flats of his hands on the table. His hands appeared older than his sixty-three years and were marked by age spots and wrinkles.

The room's silence held a tactile quality before the Governor spoke. "The death of my respected colleague and esteemed friend has placed a smudge on the sanctity of this city. I know that you are probably in the middle of a turf war right now." Talbot paused to survey the room. "Yes, just as I suspected." He turned to the Mayor. "Perfect timing on our behalf. I would like to make the request that this case stay in the hands of the local police department."

Agent Leone pulled out on his collar and straightened his tie. "With all due respect, sir—"

"Maybe I never made myself clear enough. This isn't so much a request as it is an order."

"The FBI does not report to—"

"But it does report to Director Abram, and he and I are very close friends."

Clinton had to fight the victory he felt surging through his veins. Agent Leone looked like a snake that had swallowed too large a rodent. It would take him time to digest the news delivered to him.

"Detective Clinton," Governor Talbot turned to face him.

"Yes." Clinton found himself sitting up straighter, holding up his chest and sucking in his gut.

"I want you to head up the investigation. However, you will work in coordination with the FBI. This has also been discussed with your Chief. I want whoever did this to pay with the utmost severity the law allows. Do you understand me?"

"Of course, sir." The man had the ability to extract sweet talk from Clinton who swore he'd cower to no one.

"But one further thing. You have until the six o'clock news tomorrow evening to solve this thing. I want there to be answers to provide the public when this comes out. Until then, I want what happened kept from the media—"

"Governor." Agent Leone must have thought he held some sort of bargaining chip.

"As far as the rest of the world is concerned, Governor Behler is still in critical condition," Governor Talbot said. "Can you men adhere to that?" He paused for a moment, his gaze passing over everyone in the room. "Good then." Seemingly satisfied that things would proceed as stipulated, Governor Talbot rose from the table. He gave another quick glance toward Clinton who didn't miss the unspoken implication, *screw this up, and your career is over.*

He and the mayor exited the room in unison strides, both projecting the united front that stood fast in the face of an unknown assassin. Clinton was suddenly thankful for his position in life. With a higher rank came prestige and wealth, but it also painted a target on your back.

CHAPTER THIRTY

Niagara Falls, New York
Sunday, June 13th, 1:00 PM
16 Hours From The Deadline

I stood in the middle of the crowded bus terminal, a man renewed and ready to put an end to this nightmare. Every breath I took turned into a laborious effort. My heart hurt and my head throbbed. My family needed me now.

People moved around me, paying little or no attention. To them, I was simply a stranger, a visitor to the city, one of the numerous tourists eager to the see the Falls. They had no idea I was the man who had just taken out the Governor of Michigan.

I pressed the speed dial and lifted the cell to my ear. Two rings followed by silence. I knew Christian was on the other end, breathing and waiting for me to speak, maybe even possibly trying to intimidate me. I was beyond that. "It's done."

"Tsk. Tsk."

"What the fuck do you want?" There was hysteria in my voice as emotions rose to the surface.

He laughed on the other end.

I lowered my voice, my eyes watching people move past. My words were deliberate and held promise. "I will kill you."

"You will kill me? It takes you two bullets these days. You'll be dead before the first leaves your gun. And you seem to forget that I have your family, Hunter." He was composed and calm. He feared nothing or no one.

"You will not harm them."

"How do you know I haven't?"

"Enough games. It's done. We're done. This is finished. Where can I pick up my family? And I want that thing out of my house." In the last five hours or so I gave no thought to the bloody mess in my bed. The concept of returning home made it a necessity to be dealt with.

The line fell silent.

"Christian, my family."

"You come back. We need to talk."

"This was my last job."

"And Hunter? The clock's still ticking because until I know she's dead for myself, well, I can't control what may happen."

If there had been a wall to punch a fist through, there would be a hole. "Greyhound bus station, the corner of Porter and Williams Road. Send someone now." I terminated the call.

. . .

Clinton led the way out of the room behind the Governor and Mayor. He spoke over his shoulder to his trailing partner. "We have to speak to the hotel staff. Find out what Tux was up to the day before."

Wingham hurried in front of him and spun around to face him. Her hands were on her hips. "You lied to a federal agent."

"No nickname?" He let out a small grunt and continued walking.

Wingham followed. "This isn't a joke, David. This is our careers we're messing with. My career—"

"I didn't lie."

"You're missing the point. By omission I did. I could have spoken up."

"And that wouldn't have benefited you. That's why you feel guilty. To your conscience your consent with the lie meant you might as well have told it."

"Not everyone is driven by headlines." Wingham brushed past him into the Governor's hospital room.

Clinton shrugged off her attitude. It was unwarranted. Really, he wasn't even sure if he told a lie. He allowed them to believe the evidence in the case didn't conclude a killer from out of state; it led to that assumption, but therein his conscience relieved him of any guilt.

Stepping into the hospital room, Clinton prepared himself for a messy scene but in contrast it was somewhat serene.

The Governor's eyes were open. The bullet had entered the side of her head. It was a keyhole wound, making it more oblong than a perfect circle, likely due to the tumble of the bullet caused by impact with the glass. Very little blood splattered from the wound, leaving the scene somewhat pristine. The bullet would still be inside her head as there was no exit wound.

Crime Scene had photographed and combed the room while the Feds tried to bully them around only to lose control based on the New York Governor's connections with the FBI Director.

Clinton studied the room and was certain about one thing. This would be the case of his career…once it was allowed to get out.

CHAPTER THIRTY-ONE

Niagara Falls, New York
Sunday, June 13th, 1:30 PM
Less Than 16 Hours Until the Deadline

The sun was being crowded out by gray clouds and the news report had changed to one calling for showers. It served as a poetic goodbye to a man who had replaced life with death, light with darkness.

I stood under the overhang at the front of the bus station and waited for my ride to show up. I had retrieved my belongings from the locker and rearmed myself with the holster and the .44.

With the incoming precipitation, a type of melancholy seized me. I wasn't used to experiencing emotion with a kill. Maybe it had to do with carrying it out twice? For some reason, my mind wanted to rehash those last moments in the hotel room—the way her eyes had enlarged and her last words. There were things that still didn't make any sense. How had the Governor survived a direct shot to the front of her head?

I opened up the Internet app on my phone and Googled Governor Behler. I knew it was stupid and careless to do such a thing, but I also realized it would take a lot more than a browsing history to tie me to her murder. I clicked on the first link which read like a brief biography. I scrolled down, reading facts that I had been told first hand.

She had served with the FBI back in her late twenties and early thirties. She retired from the service due to a desire to better serve the people.

My finger stopped scrolling down. Maybe she hadn't been completely honest with me.

Agent Leone walked into the hospital room resembling a dog with its tail tucked between its legs. Despite the straight back and protruding chest, his facial expression belied his veneer of confidence.

Wingham shot a glance at her partner as if requesting a confessional.

That wouldn't happen in this lifetime, Clinton thought. Besides, there was a line between an implied assumption and a blatant lie. "There are some answers we don't have."

The agent's face read, *whoopty-doo*.

Clinton had just accepted the Governor surviving the first attempt on her life as an anomaly he had been willing to overlook. At least, that was the case until now. Of course, he was also told clearance on that ranked over his head. "If we're going to solve this, we need full disclosure too."

"By all means." Snide sarcasm saturated every word as gasoline-drenched rags—a potential fire hazard. Leone paced around the room, the clack of his dress shoes marrying with the tiled floor. "She served as an FBI agent back when she was younger."

It was Clinton's turn to convey the expression, *whoopty-doo*, but he kept his composure.

"There was a case she worked. A shooting. Her skull was compromised," Leone said.

"This poor woman's head was shot twice before the third bullet killed her. Unbelievable," Wingham said.

Agent Leone disregarded her interjection. "They had to install a steel plate—"

"The assassin wasn't aware of that." That took away the theory of someone knowing her well. The evidence seemed contradictory now. The killer knew her enough to know how to reach her, took her phone, but wasn't aware of the plate?

"Shit." The word verbalized as I read the real reason the Governor had left the FBI. My legs lost their power, and I felt my knees buckle as I fought to regain my stance. My incompetence, my hurry to get the job over with, cost my family what they were experiencing now.

All I wanted was to get the job done, the first time around. But one week was such little time to gather all the intel required to effectively pull something like this off—especially of this scale. I should have known I was ill-prepared.

The Town Car pulled to a stop in front of me. The driver got out, but before he made it around to open the door, I was in with my bags and had slammed the door behind me. I noticed his hands flail in the air from frustration.

We drove in silence to the privately owned airfield. I popped in ear buds and watched the proof of life video on my phone again. With each scan of the camera and close-up shots of my family, it wrenched at my heart. Yvonne's screams pierced and resonated in my chest.

I had a bad feeling about all of this when I left Detroit and Christian's hesitant response to releasing them made my stomach churn. There was nothing we needed to discuss. The business transaction had been concluded, had it not? I would never return to being his gun for hire— ever. I would kill him and the entire Russo Family before that would happen. My hand went to my holster as if needing reassurance the .44 was still latched there. I envisioned putting one of the bullets right into his chest and then between his eyes. He wouldn't have a face left for identification.

The dark thoughts stalled when I heard something in the background of the video that I hadn't heard before. I rewound the video, turned it up, and replayed it. There was the sound of engines in the background, but it wasn't a car or vehicle. I still wasn't sure and rewound to listen to it again. It was a plane's engines.

My head lifted quickly to look out and study the fields around me. We were getting close to the tarmac and the plane that would return me to Detroit. Could it be that my family was at the private airport back home?

I replayed the video several times and the only distinct characteristics I pulled were the concrete floor and the sound of plane engines.

. . .

Unknown Location

"Please, please don't touch me." Yvonne's lips quivered. She did her best to control her emotions, but at times they burst through the fractures of a weakened spirit. The man mostly ran his hands across her skin; his fingers were rough.

She hadn't eaten since last night and the man only provided her a glass of water, but for that she had to let him touch her. Her skin still prickled from the recollection of selling her soul for water. Would her mother ever forgive her?

"You're beautiful." The man who whistled like a bird leaned into her ear and softly nibbled on a lobe.

The bile rose up into her throat again bringing with it a burning sensation as she swallowed it. "Please…don't."

He swept her hair back, holding it in a ponytail with his hands.

The door flung open with such force the back of it hit the wall with a tremendous thud. The man who had huddled in beside her, jumped from the bed as if she had leprosy.

"Out now!"

She would have considered the Italian man handsome under any other circumstances. He had an olive complexion and dark features. His jaw was cut at perfected lines sought after by modeling agencies, and he smelled of nice cologne. It lingered in the air behind him in wisps. It sure beat the smell of cow manure that threatened to saturate her sinuses.

"Out!" He yelled again at the man who whistled and would forever be a part of her nightmares.

As the two men left, Yvonne shivered into the corner feeling more violated than ever and only wishing for one scrap of covering. She still wore a bra and underwear, but she dreamt of simply pulling a sheet over her head and retreating to a place where these men couldn't reach her.

CHAPTER THIRTY-TWO

Christian snapped his fingers. It wasn't a move that came naturally to him and he had worked to perfect the mannerism over time. Now he could do it with both hands. Yet his father never considered him to be a disciplined person. He based the conclusion on the fact he couldn't choose one killing method. Christian accepted this as a form of dexterity. He wasn't limited to guns or knives. He rather enjoyed experimentation. He would teach the old man something about focus and improvising.

Berto hurried toward Ingo with a speed one wouldn't expect from a man his size. The man was careful to provide an ample girth to Gabriel and Adolfo, Christian's pit bulls. Gabriel's name meant able-bodied one of God and Adolfo stood for noble wolf. They were his girls and the only bitches who were ever loyal. Christian only hoped to instill as much fear as did his canine friends. He realized he was well on his way.

As Christian watched Berto corner Ingo, it infused Christian with pride for choosing him and confirmed the fact one could never presume anything from an outward appearance. Ingo had pleased him well over the years, but this sin…this sin could not be forgiven.

"No…please." Ingo waved his hands in front of his chest and he kept backing up.

Weakness.

Berto pulled the smaller man to the wooden chair and pushed him down onto it.

"No." Ingo's eyes steadied on the dogs who were snarling with their teeth bared, and their jowls salivating over their human treat. They were hungry. And who was Christian to deny them some pleasures in life. After all, he preferred them to most humans, save the pleasures of the flesh with a female companion. He didn't remember crying at any other funeral except for the one held for Mitchell, the bitches' predecessor.

Christian let go of their short leather leashes and snapped his fingers. Both dogs sat.

Christian walked around the room slowly, as Berto made fast work of tying his counterpart to a wooden chair. Christian couldn't help but draw contrast knowing that in the neighboring room, Mrs. Hunter was in the same position. "Be happy I didn't strip you naked." Spittle sprayed across Ingo's face. "You make me sick."

"Boss, I didn't rape her."

Christian stopped walking, bent down in front of Ingo silently studying the eyes, watching his pupils widen. Christian swiped the back of his hand across Ingo's face and felt the cartilage of his nose give way.

Ingo let out a sharp cry. His hands opened and lifted from the arms of the chair the amount the restraints would allow. "You son of a bitch!"

He was brave on the outside, Christian gave him that. He snapped his fingers. Berto came over and punched Ingo in the gut. The man hunched forward. Blood poured from his nose, and the cries of pain made Christian sick from the presence of weakness. Ingo's face contorted with fear and panic.

Unattractive.

"You dare call me a son of a bitch." Christian spit into Ingo's face again. "You be thankful I don't break both your knees—"

"Boss, I didn't rape her! Boss—"

Christian snapped his fingers again, and Berto retrieved a nine iron from a golf bag and handed the club to his boss. "Is this what you want?" Christian swung back, letting it go with force, right into Ingo's shins.

The released scream could have reached into the city. Christian exercised patience. His dogs were well trained and sat there watching. He felt pity for them.

Not long now, girls.

Christian tapped the iron in his one hand as he circled around Ingo like a vulture hovers above their prey. Ingo's outcries dissipated to sobs; blood mixed with tears. He had learned a lesson. But it would be too late to benefit him. Christian attempted to test it by making Ingo look at him. Ingo's eyes quickly diverted to the floor. The man had been broken.

"You must think I'm stupid." Christian took small steps around the chair.

Ingo shook his head, blood dripping onto the concrete from the motion.

Christian leaned over and spoke in his ear. "You think I'm stupid."

"No…no, Boss."

Christian snapped his fingers again and the two pit bulls, his joy in life, came over. They sat in front of Ingo eyeing him like a delicacy. Christian smiled. They never let him down. They never gave cause for disappointment.

"Because of you, everything is fucked up! Because of you!" Christian turned his back on the man who would never leave this room.

"No! Help!"

The dogs snarled. Christian's girls were hungry. A smirk grazed Christian's lips. He would have found more pleasure if it had been Ray in the chair, but give it time.

Berto followed, but Christian gestured for the man to leave before him. Christian stopped in the doorway without looking back. "You messed up, and for that, I can't forgive you." Christian snapped his fingers again and closed the door behind him. The screams resonated through the walls and were heard for minutes before they were rendered mute.

I'll give you focus, Pops. Ingo was one of my best men.

CHAPTER THIRTY-THREE

Niagara Falls, New York
Sunday, June 13th, 2:00 PM

Clinton found amusement in the fact the egotistical FBI Special Agent Leone had to babysit an empty hospital room for pretense while Wingham and he were doing real work.

Wingham pulled ahead of him through the doors into the lobby of The Grandeur. "You really should wipe that grin off your face."

"Come on, why can't a man have a little happiness?"

"Anyone ever tell you you're a real jerk sometimes."

"You know you like me." Clinton came to a stop in the hallway and put two hands on his chest. She kept walking at a good clip toward the elevators. He let out a large sigh.

Wingham was determined to go back to the suite to see if there was anything to be found in the way of bugs or other recording devices. There was also a request to have the phone in room 836 tested for prints. It might get them closer to the identity of Behler's bodyguard.

Clinton would be speaking to the hotel clerk—a Lauren Chapman—the lady from the front desk on Friday, June eleventh when Tux had made his way into the Governor's suite. He had lost the penny toss. Not that a literal penny was involved, but when his partner got her attitude set, she became the Alpha dog. He complied simply because it wasn't worth the antacids he'd have to pop from an argument with her. Let her have the suite. Crime Scene had been all over it.

The lady behind the counter wore a low-cut blouse and a pleasant smile. "Welcome to The Gra—"

Clinton thought she looked familiar from the video feed. Her name tag confirmed it. He held up his badge. "You're Lauren Chapman?"

"Yep."

"I'm Detective Clinton with the Niagara Falls PD."

She picked at the tip of a French-manicured nail. His first wife had thrown hundreds away on spa trips.

"You're here about the shooting," Lauren said.

No one could say she wasn't a smart one.

"This man." Clinton held up a picture of Tux. Wayne Devries from security had forwarded a printout to them. His face averted the camera, and he wore sunglasses, but the girl may be able to offer something.

"I recognize him." She went back to picking at the nail.

"Tell me about him."

A shoulder lifted and fell. "You think he did it?"

"You let me worry about that." Clinton didn't possess the patience to banter back and forth.

"He was handsome. Pleasant face, but he was tense."

Clinton leaned on the higher portion of the counter. If he had been a stereotypical male, he would have put the vantage point to good use. His eyes wanted to drift to her cleavage. "Tense?" He would need something more than that.

"Well, yeah and strange." The nail went to her mouth.

"Tell me about your entire interaction—" The lobby door opened and a handsome couple came through, more money than God. She toted a large designer purse and had on a pair of oversized sunglasses. She looped her arm through her male companion's. A concierge was loaded down with luggage behind them.

"Welcome to The Grandeur." The pleasant smile extended Clinton seemed dull compared to the one offered now. The clerk loved money, but then again who didn't?

Clinton stepped to the side and watched as the woman handled the transaction at the counter. Things had changed a lot in his fifty-two years. Women were the new Donald Trumps of the world. It's like they finally realized how by combining their brains and beauty, they could conquer corporate America.

With them heading toward the elevators, Clinton perched back where he was before.

The clerk let out an audible exhale. The phone rang on her desk. She passed a glance at Clinton before answering. "Good morning, The Grandeur. May I book a suite for you?"

Clinton's fingers tapped an uneven rhythm on the counter.

The clerk settled into the phone call for a few seconds. "Thank you and have a wonderful day." She slowly hung up the receiver.

"I won't take up much more of your time."

She went back to picking at the nail.

"When Tux—," Clinton paused and corrected himself. "—when the man in the tuxedo came in here, did he give you a name, have any outstanding features?"

"You mean besides his ass?" The balls of her cheeks lifted when she smiled. "He was hot…I mean for an old guy."

"An old guy?"

"Well, he must have been in his forties or near to it. To me, that's old."

Y'ouch. Clinton shook it off. "So he came up to you and said what?"

"He asked if his friend arrived yet."

"And that was the Governor?"

"Yes. But he called her Marian Behler."

"Then what?"

"He asked if I would call up to her room." She stopped picking at the nail. "But this is the strange part. He never left a message."

Clinton's eyes moved to the phone. This perspective provided a clear view. He tapped the counter, thanked her for her help, and dialed his partner on his cell. "Tux had the clerk call up to the suite—"

"So he got her room number from watching her dial it."

"Why did you do that?"

"What?"

"You stole my thunder." The line went quiet. Wingham was still mad. "You find anything?" Clinton asked.

"Not really, but I never expected to."

That response surprised him.

"The killer was definitely a professional. We know that now."

A shot from over five hundred yards away had cinched that. Clinton kept his sarcastic thought to himself.

"There would be no reason for him to go into that suite unless it was to plant a recording device. But there's no sign of one."

"He took them with him."

"Yeah."

"Detective." The voice came closer. "Detective." A hand went on Clinton's shoulder causing him to turn around. It was the concierge.

"Wingham, gotta go." He hung up on his partner, cutting her off in the middle of a word. *If she wasn't happy with me before...*

The man extended his hand. "Miles Prevost, Hotel Concierge."

"Detective Clinton of the—"

"Please, I know who you are. Please, come this way." The man walked with a head that turned left and right, taking in the room. The way his head was constantly in motion it made Clinton think of a Bobblehead. And, in further analysis of the man's proportions his head was larger than the rest of his frame.

They went into a compact office off the front lobby. Everything was a gleaming white, including the top of the desk which only held a computer monitor and a tray with a quarter inch of neatly stacked paper.

Miles took a seat behind the desk and gestured for Clinton to take the one in front of it.

"I know you're investigating the shooting of Ms. Behler."

Clinton found it interesting he didn't use her title but dismissed it as Miles being a personable individual. He also made the observation that his summation statement served as merely a delay tactic for what he really had to say.

"This may not even help you, but I must tell you. We value our guests, Mr. Clinton, Detective," he added. "Our guests' privacy and confidentiality is of high importance."

"If you have something that can help us find her shooter." The word killer almost slipped out. "Then you need to help us."

"Maybe this was a bad idea."

Clinton had managed to silence another possible source of information. "My apologies." He choked on the words. But he wanted those headlines. "It's just you obviously wanted to speak with me or you wouldn't have come after me."

Miles swallowed hard as Clinton watched his Adam's apple bob. "I know where she had her last meal."

CHAPTER THIRTY-FOUR

I realized I had left my family two hundred and forty miles behind me. But to know that I could have been so close to them, that they could be at the hangar near Detroit—that would be another thing altogether. I remember making the observation of the doors and how I had concluded they were offices. They could be doorways that led to hallways and more rooms.

If I had been driving this Town Car, I would have flattened my foot to the accelerator a while ago and kept it there until I got out to the hangar. I pressed the button on my phone to see the time.

At least I had completed the job before the mandated twenty-four hours. Surely Christian would have confirmed the hit by now, but I still hadn't heard from him and the uneasiness that came with that twisted my gut in a knot. And his words about needing to talk when I returned weren't reassuring. There would be nothing to talk about other than where my wife and children were. I would never return to working for him.

The car's tires crunched gravel and its body rolled slightly, as it headed down the third-class road toward the private airport.

With my other kills confirmation that the deal had been completed had proven easy. Most times Russo's men came in to take care of the cleanup, or I was to stage the kill as an unfortunate accident that law enforcement would spin their wheels on. Some of the murders would make the news. With this situation, it should have been guaranteed—this involved the life of a high-profile dignitary.

"Turn on the radio. Local news." I made the request of the driver as I went on to the Internet to see if any reports about the Governor's assassination had made it there yet.

The driver complied but shot a look through the rear view that communicated, *we're almost there now.*

For the time of day, there should be a news update with the Governor as the top news story.

"In local news…"

"Turn it up."

There was a soft sigh from the driver, but again, he followed my directions.

"…a twelve-year-old boy has been found after having been missing for twenty-four hours. The search concluded—"

"You can turn it off." I must have missed the report. The leading story must have already been given.

Shit.

It would have been nice to receive audible confirmation of the Governor's death. Not hearing it left a bad feeling that proved hard to shake.

"…and in other news—"

"Stop." I leaned over the seat. The driver's hand was almost to the power. His eyes bounced up to the rear view mirror and back to the road in front of him. He pulled his hand back. He turned into the driveway for the hangar.

"…and an update on the Governor of Michigan tells us she is doing just fine. They have moved her from critical care to serious."

"What the—" The words came out, and the driver looked at me over his shoulder. He put the car in park and sat there watching me.

How was that even possible? I saw the bullet burrow into her head. There was no way she was still alive, let alone on the mend. Someone out there must have had one sick sense of humor. They'd better pray that I'd never find them.

I got out of the car and walked toward the plane, dismissing any efforts of the hired driver to assist with my belongings. As I went up the stairs to the private jet, my legs were like iron re-enforcement bars, heavy and planted with each step. This flight would be the longest ninety minutes of my life. If Christian heard the same report, my family would be dead before the plane touched down.

CHAPTER THIRTY-FIVE

Niagara Falls, New York
Sunday, June 13th, 3:00 PM

Clinton held up a badge to the maître d' of Casa Grande. "We're here to ask a few questions. Would a manager be available?"

Wingham stood beside Clinton, her attitude clearing up as the sky after a bout of rain clouds.

The maître d's features were small, his lips the thinnest Clinton had seen. Even his hands were bony despite being overweight. Most of his investment was carried out front. His eyes were sunken as if housed in two small caves. He stood there blinking as if Clinton's words weren't penetrating.

"Is there a manager?" Clinton raised his voice, hoping the volume would increase the chance of breaking through.

"I heard what you said."

Okay, then what's the problem?

"It's about the Governor, yes?"

"It is," Clinton said.

"She was here that night." The maître d's eyes met Clinton's.

"That night?"

"Yes, the night she got shot—Saturday."

"Do you know if she was with anyone?" Clinton asked.

He started shaking, and his eyelids seemed heavy. Wingham put a hand on his elbow and directed him to a chair at a nearby table. The late lunch crowd at Casa Grande was light. Based on the menu Clinton had scanned he understood why. People could justify spending thirty bucks on an entree for dinner, but most wouldn't for lunch.

Clinton noticed a man coming toward them. His shoulders were broad, his physique likely the result of a regular gym regimen. "Is there a problem here?" His voice was deep.

Clinton and Wingham lifted their badges in sync.

The man waved a hand to brush them aside. "No need to be flashing those in here." He gave a quick glance over to the few who could afford to eat lunch here. They were more absorbed in their early cocktails and pricey meals to pay the front door any attention. "I'm the manager here. Name's Joe Needham." He extended a hand to Clinton. "Come this way."

The maître d' made a move to follow them. "No, Ian, you stay." The manager gestured toward the front door.

"Actually, I believe he knows something that can help us," Wingham said, putting her charming etiquette to work with an appealing tone.

The man lifted both arms. "One moment." He held up a single finger.

Not long later, Needham returned with an Asian woman in her early twenties. Her features and stature were small as most of that culture, and Clinton felt Wingham's energy shift beside him. She would get on a tangent periodically about needing to shed a few extra pounds, but the resolve lasted until the first temptation. Clinton didn't see what she was concerned about.

The Asian introduced herself; her smile weak from nerves. "I'm Jenny."

Clinton's guess was she normally worked in the back away from the customers' view.

"No time for chit chat, Jenny. I need you to cover the front while Ian comes back with me. Okay?"

She nodded.

The manager spoke to the rest of them, "All right, come this way now." He led the three of them to a back office.

This one was a far contrast from the concierge's at The Grandeur. Papers were scattered across the surface of the desk as if a fan had blown them. Clinton looked around the room—no fan.

"Sorry, there's not enough seating for everyone." Needham sat behind his desk.

Clinton gestured for his partner and Ian to take a chair, while he remained standing. "We're here about Governor Behler."

"Sure, if we can help." Needham opened his hands to invite them to commence with their questioning.

"She was in your restaurant for dinner last night."

He clasped his hands on the desk and leaned forward. "We have a lot of high profile people in our restaurant. We respect their privacy—"

He stopped talking when Ian held up one pointed finger in the air as if asking to be called on in a school classroom.

Needham rolled his eyes. "Yes, Ian."

"Have you not heard the news? She was shot," he said.

Needham looked at Wingham. "She's dead?"

Now, let's see if she stretches the truth, Clinton thought. *She wouldn't want to be telling any lies*. He rested an elbow on a four-drawer filing cabinet, leaning against it. His attention was on his partner; her eyes were on Needham.

"She was shot…last night." She passed a glance to Clinton.

The manager noticed. "Why do you keep looking at him when you speak?"

Wingham bit on a bottom lip. She was insulted by the man's observation. "You notice a lot of things, Mr. Needham. Did you notice if Governor Behler had a friend with her last night?" She shifted her position crossing her arms, pushing up on her bosom as she tightened her arms.

He leaned forward, broadcasting a smile that likely lit many a bedroom. "You're a sly one." He turned then to Clinton. "Honestly, I don't know. I heard a rumor that she was here, but I never looked for myself. Along with the genuine articles, you get celebrity look-alikes. Saturdays are our busiest night and the washer broke down."

Wingham turned to Ian. "But you remember her?"

He took a deep breath and requested consent from his boss who nodded. He still seemed hesitant to speak.

Clinton stood straight. "Did anyone else join her?"

Ian looked at him nervously but didn't say a word. He must have sensed their thought process. The shooter had been here. His eyes misted and rapidly blinked.

"A name?" Clinton went out on a hunch it was someone he could ID with a name. Ian glanced at his employer.

"I'm not sure if I should tell them," Ian said.

Before Needham could answer, Clinton interjected, "If you know something that can help this investigation, you have the responsibility to say—"

Needham rose to his feet. "Don't pressure him into this—"

"Mr. Needham, this isn't a thug who got whacked, this is a state Governor, who had an attempt made on her life." Clinton gestured for the man to retake his seat. He did so reluctantly.

"This news can't get out. If people find out, we disclose our customers' identities—"

"This isn't a lawyer's office or confessional booth. It's a restaurant."

"The finest in the area." Needham tugged out on his jacket.

Clinton placed a hand on Ian's shoulder. "Who was it?"

"Governor Talbot." He latched his hands in his lap and crossed at his ankles. He let out a sigh. "She joined him at his table."

Clinton and his partner shared a look.

"You're certain it was the Governor of New York?" Wingham asked as she stood up and took out her cell phone. She didn't seem to listen for his answer; she read the screen and texted something.

"Absolutely." Ian's eyes brandished up to Clinton, then quickly downward.

Clinton took the seat Wingham had freed up, and the four of them continued to discuss last night. Ian related how, in fact, the Governor had two men at her table at the time of appetizers, but Talbot had left before the main entree. The other man, described as handsome, possibly in his forties, and wearing a flashy tuxedo, remained at her table until the bill came.

"She picked it up. They shared some laughs. I think they might have left together." After speaking for about fifteen minutes or so, Ian's tongue had loosened up. "But I don't think the Governor of New York was having a good time."

"Why's that?"

"Well, the three of them were at the table, but his eyes drifted around the room. You know, like when you really don't want to be somewhere. He had two double Scotches once she joined him but also had one before she arrived."

Interesting.

An hour after entering the manager's room, Clinton and Wingham walked out.

"More questions than answers," she said.

"But, we did get some answers. Ian mentioned the man who ended up joining their table had been seated at a private table for one originally."

"And he wore a Tux."

CHAPTER THIRTY-SIX

Outskirts of Detroit, Michigan
Sunday, June 13th, 3:30 PM
Less Than 14 Hours Until the Deadline

This time I was awake when the wheels hit the runway. The aching in my chest intensified from the fear of having no control over what Christian did to my family, or possibly would still do. If he heard the news, they'd be dead already, and I would be returning to a fight for my life. But if they were gone, I'd have nothing to live for.

My hand went to the .44 in my holster, and I spoke a silent prayer for help to make it through with my family. I realized the irony in praying to a God of life and goodness when what I asked for was worldly restitution. But I needed something to hold on to other than merely a hope that things would work out according to plan. In the last few days, I should have learned at least that—life didn't follow a set course.

My body weighed heavily from fatigue, but as the door on the plane opened my physical issues muted to the background, superseded by the facts I held in my defense. I had shot the Governor. She was dead. I would accept no other statements. I would not go back for her head to serve it to Christian. He would have to accept the truth.

Christian stood at the bottom of the stairs. "How nice of you to join us."

It almost took more self-control than I possessed not to shoot him where he stood. My hand steadied over my gun. "Where's my family?"

His dimples creased with a broad smile. His eyes took in the positioning of my hand. "Oh, you feel threatened." Christian laughed.

"Did you kill them?" I closed the distance between us.

"I think the real question is, did you take care of your end?" He snapped both fingers and turned his back on me.

I followed him to the back of the hangar, my heart beating fast from adrenaline. I would give him no indication of fear. It would only fuel him and provide him with more power. I wished and hoped he was leading me to my living family, but my gut said differently. Something was wrong.

I noticed the large form come from behind. A beefy hand was placed on my shoulder.

This was not good. At all.

I clenched my jaw and passed him a glance that told him to get his hand off me. The silent death threat must have worked as he slowly removed it.

Christian went through a door off the hangar into a mechanics storage bay. Tools, extra parts, and lubricants for the airplanes were neatly arranged on steel shelving. Maybe I had been wrong about a series of hallways and my family being kept in offshoot rooms. But wherever they were, they were near planes and the floor was concrete.

"You've come here wanting to fight." Christian gestured toward my gun. "I doubt you shot her with that."

"I came prepared."

He assessed me. "Sit." He pointed to a chair in the middle of the room.

"I'll stand."

"You'll sit." The large shadow had a voice and he spoke bent over to reach my ear. I estimated the big guy to be six-six, maybe taller.

"The Governor, is she dead?" Christian paced slowly around the chair.

"Job is done." Where was my family?

"Tsk. Tsk."

"Whatever you heard on the news is wrong."

"Where's my verification? I give you back your family, you walk away?" He kept moving around me with slow, deliberate steps. "I will make a deal with you."

His Italian accent made my stomach churn. Big Guy watched me as if he was ready to act. I hated the fact I was sitting. It made me vulnerable. And with the holster and gun, it was a tight fit between the arms of the chair.

"Aren't you going to say, what deal, Christian? Hunter, you disappoint me." Fire sparked in the man's eyes with enough heat to bring a building down. He stopped walking and crouched down on his knees in front of me. He studied my eyes. A few seconds later, he stood to full height and waved his man to take a few steps back. "No trust between us anymore."

"I killed her." My family's faces flashed through my mind. The touch of my wife's skin, the smell of her hair, the way she and Yvonne would fight, the debates I'd have with Max over NASCAR. I wanted my life back.

"You're starting to bore me with what they say…" He rolled his hands to summon the words. "—Broken record." He continued to study my face.

I believe he wanted to bore a hole through my head and take control of my brain. The thought transported images from the past when he had taken a drill bit to a man's skull. Sweat dripped down my back.

"When I have verification she is dead, from the media, I will release them to you."

Big Guy stepped forward. Christian waved him back again and swore at him in Italian.

"He wants to kill you. Part of me…part of me, wants to let him."

At this angle, I noticed the spots of dark red on Christian's sleeve—dry blood. Was it from my family?

"You killed them." My eyes fell to the floor without thought. For a moment, I lost all fighting power. If they were gone, I had nothing to live for.

"As I said to you before. I owe them nothing."

I jumped to my feet. "You son of a bitch!" I had Christian against the wall and held by the collar of his shirt before he could react. The barrel of a gun shoved into my side.

Christian started laughing. "You're still stealth-like, Hunter."

I continued to hold onto him. The big guy pressed the gun further into my side.

"All I have to say is pleasant dreams, Hunter." Christian remained calm even held in a death grip.

My hands were locked in a clenching position on his collar. My breath carried on deep exhales. I matched eyes with him before backing up. "Let them go."

Christian stepped away from the wall and straightened his shirt. Big Guy kept the gun pointed at me.

"You're only who you are because of me. Did you really think you could leave The Family for good?" Christian laughed. "We own you. We always will. Do you think it was a coincidence that you ended up with Governor Behler as a client? We wanted to keep tabs on you. And we never knew when we could use your services. You're stubborn and wild like a stallion. But we will break you." He snapped his fingers on both hands. Big Guy tucked his gun into the back of his pants.

"Do you hear what I'm telling you, Hunter? Do you understand?"

My outlook turned from three-dimensional to omniscient. With his words, I had been granted insight. It all made sense now. The pride I had taken in setting up and keeping a business going was extinguished like the flame of a candle that had been snuffed out.

"Aw, you think you did this on your own. How naïve of you."

He laughed again. The sound threatened to weaken the hardened stance I had and reduce it to dust.

Big Guy watched from the back of the room. The way his eyes were trained on me, I questioned whether I would make it out of here alive. Christian was unpredictable, carried by emotions of the moment. And he had always failed to see the larger picture. Pleading for my family did little for moving this forward.

"Why did you want her dead?" I asked.

"You ask a lot of questions, Hunter. Perhaps at some other time." He snapped his fingers, and Big Guy opened the door to the room.

Did this mean I was free to go? What about my family?

"Dad!"

My head snapped to the doorway. Max came running toward me. He stopped shy of contact when he noticed Christian. I reached for my son, pulled him in, and held him as I would never again. Part of me didn't know if I would ever get this opportunity. It could have been a sick tactic of Christian to instill hope when there was none.

Max lifted back from the embrace. "What's going on?" His hand felt the gun on my waist, his eyes enlarged.

Tears stung the corners of my eyes, and I let them fall. It felt so damn good to hold my boy. I pulled him in again.

"Enough." Christian snapped his fingers.

Another man who must have accompanied Max to the door tore him from me. I stretched to reach Max. A solid hand pulled on my shoulder, hard enough it jarred my back. "Max!"

"Dad!" Max's face was blotchy. Tears poured down his cheeks. He struggled against the man who held him.

I would kill the son of a bitch! All of them!

"Take him out of here. Now." Christian gave the orders.

They started to walk away. I wanted to follow them, but the hand held me back. "I love you!"

Max turned his head. His eyes were scarred by his experience here; the darkened crescents I saw in the video must have just been shadows. More tears fell and he said nothing.

My eyes went back to Christian. The pulse in my cheeks swelled with such intensity, I felt their throbbing. My earlobes must have been a burning red for the heat that manifested itself there. "I will kill you."

Christian didn't laugh like I had expected him to. Instead his eyes went vacant. "You are free to go—"

"My family—"

"Are not. They will stay with me until news reports verify your kill."

"Trust me."

"First you say you will kill me, then you say trust me?" Christian cocked his head to the side. "You, too, must think I'm stupid." He snapped his fingers. "Now, go."

Big Guy hovered until I reached my car. He stood there with his meaty hooks clasped together in front; his legs braced shoulder-width apart.

Simply putting the keys into the ignition sliced at my soul. I brushed a tear that fell with the back of a hand. It would be the last one I let fall. They would be sorry for getting me and my family involved with their matters.

CHAPTER THIRTY-SEVEN

A Half Hour Earlier...
Niagara Falls, New York
Sunday, June 13th, 3:00 PM

Clinton still found the rouse of telling the media the Governor was on the mend to be a brilliant move. It would shuffle the power from assassin to law enforcement. Wingham and he were on the sidewalk out front of Casa Grande. She was pecking at the keyboard on her cell.

"What is it?" Clinton asked.

"Prints came back on the phone in room 836. His name is Rick Carson. He has a record. Just minor B & E." She kept texting.

"So we've got him then?"

"We have his last known address and phone number. Both tie back to Detroit."

Clinton let out a deep breath. All he was thinking about was the slipping headlines. This confirmed the killer crossed state lines. "Wonderful."

"Okay, you're going to love me." She glanced up for a second.

"You know I don't buy into that." He smiled.

"I have a friend in Detroit. He's not a cop, but he's a PI."

Clinton liked where this was headed. A private investigator would fit the bill. There was no way they could disclose their position just yet. The FBI would scoop in and claim the credit for what wasn't their right. He knew they would be getting copied on the report, but by the time they acted, Clinton would already have the answers. And the Michigan State Police would be even further behind them.

"I have him going by to check his place out. He'll secure Carson if he can. He said he'd do it for me right away."

"Did you have to sleep with him?"

Wingham narrowed her eyes. "You seriously didn't have to go there."

Clinton suspected from the way she blushed he was an ex-lover she hadn't quite been cured of.

"And you told a lie in there." He hitched a thumb toward the restaurant. He referred to her denial that the Governor was dead.

"I did not." Her eyes went to slits. "I simply diverted."

Clinton shrugged. "Omission is a lie. At least someone tried to tell me that once."

"Mine was implication. I said she was shot. She was." Wingham's phone rang and she answered. Clinton tried to read her facial expression to determine the caller and their message. She turned her back on him. Her voice carried the manifestation of a smile. "Thanks… you take care too…oh, okay. Bye."

"Are you sure you don't mean, later sweetheart? We'll meet up and sip on fine wine."

"I said what I meant." Her earlier playfulness had disappeared. "He went to the address we have on file for him. It was an abandoned warehouse."

"He was squatting." Clinton shook his head.

"We're missing a much larger picture here. We have a dead Governor, who took a stand-in bodyguard to Niagara Falls. Why? We have a meeting between her and the Governor of New York. And then we have this third party, Tux. How does it all fit together?"

Wingham walked toward the car and Clinton followed. "And how does Tux, who shows up at the restaurant, end up with her back at the hotel?"

"The restaurant staff said they seemed surprised to run into each other."

Clinton stopped walking. "They've all got to be connected somehow."

"It's the somehow that's eluding me." Seconds had passed in silence before Wingham spoke again, "Well, you know there's only one person we can contact right now."

"Talbot." Clinton let out a heavy exhale. "I was just hoping we didn't have to go down that route."

Wingham pressed her lips. "It's the only way."

"Sonya?"

"Yeah." Wingham turned around.

"How did your guy respond so quickly? You know, to driving by Carson's address?"

Wingham smiled and got into the car. "I got the text about the prints an hour ago when we were in with Ian and Needham."

CHAPTER THIRTY-EIGHT

I wasn't the type of person to back down. I also couldn't accept that all I had worked hard to accomplish was an allowance by another individual. I had made it on my own terms, regardless of what Christian tried to make me believe. Behler was one of my largest clients.

One other thing I knew for certain—my family would be coming home with me and we would all resume our normal lives. I imagined the events of the last few days would forever be etched in our psyches, but at least we would be there for each other.

I drove back to the city of Detroit like Max's favorite NASCAR driver—quick yet aware of his surroundings. I assessed the distance between my front bumper and the rear ends of other vehicles and made my moves. I had somewhere to get to—a score to settle. If Christian wasn't going to respect my mission as complete, I would make his Pops see it my way.

My foot lifted off the accelerator only minutely as I realized the stupidity and naivety of my thinking to presume that I could affect The Detroit Partnership by impacting the Russo Family. I wasn't even an integral part of their organization. I was an outside contractor with everything to lose. Disposable. Honestly, I was surprised that I had survived the encounter with Christian. I wasn't even sure why he had let me go. Why not hold me there until he received his confirmation of Behler's death? Was it simply to toy with me and make me feel there was hope when there was none?

His words played as a chant in my mind, repeating in an endless stream, *you're only who you are because of me.*

He said that the Governor was my client because it made it possible to keep an eye on me. By extension that would mean she was connected with them. But that was nonsense and didn't make sense. Behler spoke out against organized crime.

But then again maybe it held more logic than I first gave the thought credit for. I remembered the man with the Rolex, her bodyguard; he must have been put in place by the Russos. Otherwise, why would he have known my name and touched me the way he had? He was expecting me and not simply because the Governor had notified him a visitor would be coming. The connection was further made apparent due to his murder.

The Governor's words just as I pulled the trigger—*I was one of.* Had she tried to tell me she worked along with the Russos?

I shook my head and kept driving, weaving in and out of the lazy Sunday drivers that all appeared to be sitting still next to me.

Why would a Governor align herself with them? Money was the first thing that came to my mind but was quickly replaced by another thought. Behler had money; she had sold her soul for political advantage. As long as she kept police from narrowing in on the Russos, they would ensure her candidacy. It was a symbiotic relationship. So what went wrong?

My inquiries turned to the personal when I felt heaviness in my chest. My family was in danger, and the longer they were left with Christian and his men, the higher the likelihood something really bad would happen.

The way my thoughts escalated, I really didn't see any other option than the path I was taking now. I had killed the Governor, twice really, in my opinion. Because the result hadn't been death originally didn't mean that I hadn't killed her—in my mind I had. With Christian merely being a pawn and spokesman for his father, I would pay a visit to the head of the serpent and get my family back—even if it cost my life in exchange for theirs.

The best place to find Pietro Russo at most times on any given day was the back room of the racetrack bar. It was likely suicide attempting what I had planned, but there was no other choice. Again, Christian had placed me in a corner and I needed to fight my way out. If Christian couldn't accept that I had killed the Governor, and use one of his many resources to verify this fact, there would be no winning for me. It was a game he had stacked for me to lose.

I thought of the dead man in my bed. He had been Christian's contact. Why did they kill him?

I knew the likely answer to the question as it formed in my mind. The rat-like man was put in place to ensure Behler was killed. He had fled the scene before confirming she was. He had let Christian down.

I swerved the car to the side of the road. A car went by with a blaring horn. I didn't pay the driver any attention. Leaning over the back seat, I rifled through my bag looking for the one thing that might provide answers to everything.

Why was Governor Behler in Niagara Falls to begin with? It wasn't official business, yet she had met with the Governor of New York.

He didn't look too happy to be sharing her company, the way his eyes kept going to his drink, and the way he held the glass as if it were his means of escape.

Where the hell was that thing?

I kept working through the bag, my hands touching everything but what I was looking for. I finally gave up and got out of the car and went to the back seat. I found it right away—the Governor's phone. I powered it up and made my way back to the driver's seat.

The sky had darkened and a few raindrops hit the windshield. The wipers went up, making a noise against the glass. It wasn't quite wet enough. I found myself jumping slightly. I blamed it on my exhaustion and imagination.

There was something larger going on here. For them to take down the Governor of Michigan, assuming she was one of theirs, would involve a huge betrayal.

Maybe she had been there reaching out to Talbot for help in getting out? Yet she said they never saw eye to eye.

The phone seemed to be taking forever to power up all the apps. I pulled out mine and searched the Internet for a connection between the Governors. The only results showed them attending similar conferences in the past. There was nothing beyond that to indicate a personal relationship.

Had she sought out Talbot for help? Maybe she knew they were on to her. But if that had been the case, and she had been placed to keep an eye on me, why wouldn't she recoil at the sight of me? Instead, she invited me into her company. She had asked me to join them. She even invited me back to her suite. She either felt no fear or had no idea that the Russos were going to exact revenge for something.

With her phone powered up, I went to her text messages first. Nothing beyond taking-care-of-business texts. There was still one sent from me a couple weeks ago trying to arrange a time to get together about her taxes. It had been left unread.

I touched the screen to bring up a list of all data and photo files. The names were nondescript and likely for a reason. I worked my way through them and came to a file entitled, NYF. When I tried to open it, a message window came on the screen: ENTER PASSWORD.

This was definitely the file she was showing the Governor. At least, I felt it was in the pit of my stomach. I wiped a hand down my face and set out trying a series of entries hoping to break into the file.

In the middle of another attempt, the phone's screen lit up and vibrated in my hand. A pop-up box read, YOU HAVE 1 NEW MESSAGE. It dated back to Saturday night.

My heart cinched as I opened it and noticed its sender.

CHAPTER THIRTY-NINE

For Sunday afternoon, there were a decent number of patrons at the Thoroughbred Bar. Televisions mounted on every wall that normally covered the live races from the outside track, broadcasted past races and some poker tournaments. The bartender was one I recognized from nearly two decades ago. It was his eyes that gave him away. Otherwise, the passage of time hadn't treated him kindly. I believe there was recognition in his eyes as well. When he greeted me, it was confirmed.

"Ray? Well, I'll be damned." A huge grin lit his face. He was clean shaven and baby-faced except for the deep creases etched from a hard life. He used to have a mustache and a goatee.

I slipped onto a bar stool, a few down from a woman in her mid-fifties. She smiled at me and drowned the greeting with a pressed glass to her lips. Her blonde hair was shoulder length and salon cut. Her nails were manicured. She was a stereotypical cougar, but the pickings must have been slim if she narrowed in on me. I felt like shit and probably looked like it. My eyes burned more than they had before, as if the tears shared with Max had compounded the effects of exhaustion.

"I need to speak with Pietro."

The grin disappeared. The light that had been present in his eyes flickered to darkness. "You know I can't let you." He leaned in toward me. "And it wouldn't be a good idea."

"It wasn't a question Stan." Our eyes locked. The older man did his best to intimidate me. I put a hand on my hip and lifted my shirt to expose the gun.

Stan laughed. "You come in here what, fourteen years—"

"Fifteen."

"Fifteen years later and expect me to answer to you." Stan turned his back on me and walked away. He spoke over his shoulder, "Not happening in this lifetime, boy."

A door behind the bar opened and three men came out. Stan must have pushed the button underneath the bar that called for Pietro's soldiers.

"Do we have a problem here?" A man in his mid-twenties, who was between the other two men, spoke the question.

I pulled the shirt down over the gun. "I need to talk with Pietro."

"It's not going to happen."

"Tell him I have information he'll want to hear."

"Don't think so. You have something for him. You tell me, I'll pass it along." I could read the unspoken threat in his eyes, *we might even let you walk out alive if you leave now.*

Faced with three men who eyed me as an appetizer for their sadistic pleasure of torture and murder reminded me why I had left in the first place. I didn't want this life to consume me to the point where I lost my identity. I had reclaimed my soul from the Devil although he kept trying to take it back.

"It's about Governor Behler."

All of their faces dropped, and they glanced at each other.

"He will want to hear what I have to say." I reiterated my earlier words.

The guy to the middle man's left, walked toward the back room. I went to follow but had a large palm splayed in the middle of my chest. "You stay here."

Time passed, possibly minutes of standing there, before the back door opened.

"He will not see you." His hand went to his piece. His eyes were on me as he went back to where he had been standing before.

Honestly, I hadn't expected it to be easy to gain access to the Don, but I thought mention of the Governor would get me into the room.

I took a quick glance around the restaurant, surveying the number of people in the room, and the potential collateral damage. I really didn't want to do this, but I had no other choice. I pulled the .44 from my holster, aimed it at the man in the middle. Three guns came out, all pointed at my head.

I said, "Rule one, never underestimate your opponent."

"Rule one?" The middle guy smiled. "Look around. Numbers aren't in your favor."

"If I have to kill every one of you to get to Pietro, I will."

"Tough shot, old man—"

Before his sentence left his mouth, I spun and roundhouse kicked the man on the right. My foot impacted him in the solar plexus. He dropped to ground, rolling around and groping at his abdomen. The butt of my .44 came in direct contact with the temple area of the middle guy. He fell to the ground unconscious. The third one backed up. His gun shook in his hands. I cocked my .44 and stared him down. The entire attack took less than twenty seconds.

"Don't be stupid."

"Holy shit, old man." His hands weren't the only thing shaking. His voice quivered when he spoke.

"Turn around. Take me to him."

"He'll kill me."

"Your options aren't looking very good either way." I gestured with a small nod toward the door. My gun readied in my hand. One wrong move and this guy would no longer have a face.

He took a deep breath. His eyes dropped from my face to my gun where they fixed. He lowered his gun and put it back in place. He bit his lip hard enough I expected to see blood. "This way."

Deep green leather furniture was arranged around a large screen television. It was at least an eighty inch. A recorded horse race filled the screen. An older man sat on a sofa facing the television. Three men were posted around the room for his protection, one stood at each end of the couch. One man stood sipping a drink at the bar in the corner of the room. He held a drink and he had a gold ring on each of his fingers. I felt his eyes on me, even though he tried to cover the fact he was watching.

Number three who escorted me in said, "Boss."

The element of submission to the Don that manifested in his address, tone of voice and demeanor, shot me to my past, these men's present.   Young,   influential—weak—men flocked to the Russo Family searching for direction and purpose in their lives. They wanted to belong to something larger than themselves. What they failed to realize is the very thing they sought, that illusion, would eat them like rot from the inside. Taking an innocent man and turning him into something unspeakable.

The race continued to play out for a few more seconds before Pietro gestured toward one of his men who paused the playback. Pietro kept his face forward. The young man who led me into the room looked like he had shit his pants the way his face distorted and his legs planted to the floor.

"He said it's about the Governor."

Silence.

"It's Hunter." I spoke the words.

Pietro slowly rose to his feet and turned to face me. "You come into my house after..." His face scrunched up. "You left The Family. Get out before I kill you!" He signaled to his men who all advanced toward me—except the man at the bar.

"The Governor is dead." The words burst from my mouth.

His men stopped moving.

"How do you know this?" The man represented pure evil, but unlike his son, his decisions were always calculated.

"I killed her."

One look from Pietro, guns from every corner of the room pointed at me.

"Your son hired me for a job."

"Bullshit!"

I raised my hands in surrender. "I have proof."

"Why should I listen to you? You turned your back on me."

"I saved your son's life."

He scoffed. "That will only take you so far." Pietro came toward me. His men's guns remained on me until he came to a stop inches in front of me. "Why must I believe you over my own son?"

I proceeded with caution to a pant pocket and pulled out the compact recorder. It held the conversation that had taken place at Christian's house the night I accepted the job.

Pietro's face hardened and went a bright red as he listened to the recording. "*Che cazzo!*" What the fuck!

One man's revolver clicked as he cocked the hammer. Time was running out.

"I know now the job didn't come from you."

Pietro's hands balled into fists. "We don't kill dignitaries."

"It draws too much attention, I know." After the confession came out I worried how he would twist it.

"Then why do this?"

"You heard the recording. Christian said the order came from you."

Pietro clapped his hands together; the noise they made like thunder in the small room. One of the guys from the back of the room came toward the one who had led me in here.

"Please…no." He pulled him by the arm and escorted into a room that was an offshoot to this one. The torture chamber as Christian had dubbed it in the past. The walls were soundproof.

Pietro's eyes snapped to mine. A hand slapped my face hard and fast, causing my neck to crank to the right.

"How dare you blame my son!" He stared in my eyes, and it was like facing the Devil in person. "You killed her! Her blood is on your hands, not mine! And for this, you will pay!" Spittle misted the air with the force of his words.

"Christian has my family."

"And you think I should care about this?" Pietro laughed, looking around the room. His men echoed his amusement. He pointed to the recorder. "How do I know this is Christian and not, what you say, a setup."

I moved slowly, not wanting to startle anyone into pulling back on a trigger. I requested permission to continue the playback with a submissive energy, yet careful not to solidify direct eye contact. Pietro gave a slight nod.

I told him about my recent confrontation with Christian and how he said I owed everything to him and that the Governor was placed in my life for a reason.

Pietro said nothing and went back to the sofa. His men's guns remained trained on me. "*Basta!*" Enough. "Put your guns down."

It wasn't my right to speak as the Don had turned away. It would be an utmost demonstration of disrespect, worthy of death. All I envisioned was my family. I had to take the risk. "He will kill them."

What felt like minutes of silence…

Pietro rose to his feet. "Get out now and live."

"Pops."

The old man sprung across the room as if he were in his youth. He slapped my face. The skin still burned from the first impact, and a kink in my neck throbbed from the torque of the assaults.

"Don't you ever." Pietro spit in my face.

"You were close with the Governor. I know now the orders never would have come from you. For that I greatly apologize." The pain in my face and neck were more than I had felt in the last fifteen years.

He remained quiet as he studied me from the top of my head to my feet. On the way back up, his eyes stopped on the .44 in my holster. "You came here to start a war."

I had to think through my next few words if I was going to make it out of here alive. Maybe silence was the better option.

"You tell me my son ordered this hit."

I remained silent. There was no need to reiterate that he used Pietro's name to authorize it. He heard the recording.

He ordered one of his men, "Take his gun."

I wanted to fight against his advances to remove my weapon but didn't have an option. I had to surrender it.

"You come here and tell me lies, falsify recordings—"

"You know what's happening—"

His eyelids lowered slowly, reopened. "You plead for your family's lives as if I should care. I cannot accept the word of a traitor from years ago." He waved his hands in dismissal. Two of his men hurried toward me. Each of them grabbed an arm and dragged me into the torture room.

. . .

Niagara Falls, New York

Based on vantage point and trajectory, the shooter's perch would have been elevated. Forensics provided Clinton with the address of a secured apartment building a few blocks away, which would align with those parameters. Wingham and he were on the way there now. Talbot would have to wait.

Wingham held her Starbucks as if sucking it for life force. "Do you think the same guy is involved in both shootings?"

"I believe so."

She took a sip but made a slurping sound as the department-issued Crown Vic hit a dip in the road. "But why would a professional screw up the first time?"

"Simple. He didn't know about the plate in her head."

"Simple? Aren't trained assassins supposed to gather intel before acting? And how do you explain two different killing methods—one shot at close range, the other at a distance?"

"Maybe he was running out of time? Or he wanted to get it over with? Or the beefed-up security?" He glanced just for an instant to his partner and eyed her Starbucks.

She shrugged a shoulder. Her cheeks were flushed a shade paler than a Coca-Cola can, exposing her exhaustion. Something as simple as that gave Clinton a revelation.

"Our shooter's got to be getting tired." His attention was already back on the road. "That means he'll be making mistakes. And that also means he'll be easier to find."

"Well, we better hope so. It's been over twelve hours and our leads are mostly at a dead end. We've got Tux and Rolex—"

"Rolex?"

He glanced over at her.

She said, "I didn't like the nickname Lanky anymore." She flashed a small smile.

"Or we could just call him Carson." He found it interesting how she sometimes stuck to nicknames even when she had the legitimate ones. "Still no ID on Tux."

"The two of them must have been working together. It's the only thing that makes sense."

"Not really. Professional assassins work alone. And why did Tux hide his face from the cameras while Rolex flaunted his?"

"He feared nothing."

"I don't know. I just don't like any of this."

Still more questions than answers.

CHAPTER FORTY

Detroit, Michigan
Sunday, June 13th, 5:00 PM
12 Hours Until the Deadline

The lighting in the room was dull. Their faces were covered by shadows. Two men had taken me into the torture room, but only one stayed by my side. There was no sign of the other man who had allowed me access to the Don's quarters. It didn't leave me with a very good feeling about my future. The only thing I found comfort and hope in was the fact Pietro never kissed me on the cheek. If he had, I'd know my fate.

Valuable time was being wasted. An hour possibly went by as the man standing watch, shifted his position as if his hip or leg hurt from standing for so long. I had presented the only tangible proof I had of Christian's directive, and the Don had dismissed the evidence. Maybe he was having a hard time accepting the fact his son had double-crossed him.

The text message on the Governor's phone revealed everything. My thought process paused as the door opened. I straightened as Pietro walked toward me. He gestured for his man to back up.

"The news says attempts were made on the Governor's life, but her health has improved." He paced around me. "The Hunter I knew didn't miss."

"I didn't—"

A hand rose to silence me. "Prove to me she is dead, as you say."

I went to reach into a pocket. Two of his men advanced. Pietro called out something in Italian and they stepped back. I extended the Governor's phone to him.

"You hand me a phone in exchange for your life?"

"It's Behler's."

"Doesn't mean she's dead."

"Based on what's on that phone, it does. She wouldn't have let it out of her sight." This play on my part was risky, yet I saw no other way. I still didn't know exactly what the phone contained. All I knew was the reaction it received from the New York Governor when Behler showed it to him and the most recent message received. I solidified eye contact with Pietro to prove the honesty of my words.

"We don't kill dignitaries," he said.

"Yes, I know."

"Yet you followed orders to do so on my behalf?"

"Why would I doubt your son?"

Pietro stopped walking. The energy in the room shifted, and again I feared for my life.

"I've done some thinking." His words were riddled with the pain of betrayal yet fueled with a need to exact revenge. "You say he has your family?"

I nodded. *There was a time to speak and a time to remain silent,* a passage from Scripture my mother loved to quote.

"I'll get your family back. Family is everything. Without it we have nothing in this life." A tangible dark aura radiated from the man of five-foot-five. "You will kill my son."

. . .

Niagara Falls, New York

Special Agent Leone stood outside the apartment building waiting for Clinton and Wingham. He didn't look impressed to be on the outside of the investigation. His eyes revealed contempt for the local police with most of it specifically directed toward Clinton. It was as if he threatened him in some way. It was apparent Leone didn't want to share the headlines with

PD. For now the man's uneasiness served to amuse Clinton.

"So, what have you got?" Leone looked up.

"The gun was a custom job. Land and groove impressions on the bullet were not a match to any particular make of gun. They didn't come back in any database as a match to previous crimes. So all we're left with is a 6mm bullet. Factoring in velocity, trajectory would indicate he would have chosen an apartment on the third to the fifth floor," Clinton said.

"You're giving us a range of three floors."

"Unless you're hard of hearing." Both men stared off, challenging each other to a figurative measuring contest.

Wingham brushed by both men. "The building is a secured one. You need a key to get in."

"A building's only as secure as the tenants allow it to be," Leone said, not taking his eyes off Clinton.

"Tells me Tux fits in just fine no matter where he goes." Wingham let the nickname slip; Leone was quick to catch it.

Leone kept focused on Clinton. "You have a suspect you haven't shared with the FBI, Detective Clinton?"

Clinton could have pummeled his partner for the slip-up. There was still too much in the way of gray areas, and until evidence solidified speculation, he preferred to keep a case tight. "Nothing's for certain."

The reflection in his eyes disclosed Leone wasn't buying it. "If you withhold a suspect from a case, you could be deemed an accessory."

"You come down here from your fancy headquarters and try to project a machismo that just isn't you. Your low self-esteem—"

Leone moved in close. He extended his arm, his hand balled into a fist. He dropped it to his side before making contact with Clinton. "You're not worth it."

"If we're finished here..." Clinton walked away.

. . .

Detroit, Michigan

"You want me to kill your son?" *Did I hear him correctly?*

Pietro gestured for his men to leave the room. "You will if you want your family back."

I didn't want to get involved in the middle of a blood feud for supremacy. The way the Don looked at me, I really didn't have a choice.

"I want him to know it's from me. But," he said, accompanying his words with a pointed index finger. "You will make it appear as an accident to police. You will also make it clear that he killed the Governor. He acted alone."

The overall directive came across as complicated. I had to mentally break it down into components and go from there. However, with the blame directed to Christian, I would be in the clear and my family would be returned to me.

"I want this taken care of by first thing tomorrow morning."

His words made a grown man want to cry. My eyes were burning from exhaustion, and my limbs were dragging. Basically, I remained on the same twenty-four-hour deadline Christian had imposed upon me.

"I can tell you are tired. You have that half-mast thing." Pietro rolled his hand. The door opened as if on cue. One of his men walked in with a glass of cloudy water.

"You drink," Pietro said.

There was one thing I had learned early on. The Don tells you to do something, if you valued your life, you'd do it. I reached for the glass.

"All of it."

I drained the liquid. The texture was chalky. I handed the glass back to the man who had delivered it to me. His nose sat crooked on his face as if it had once been broken yet never reset.

"Now you will wake up." Pietro paced a few steps, a smile pursing his lips. "You have much work to do."

Crooked Nose went to the door and held it open.

My time in front of the Don had expired.

I tested my limits. "There's one more thing…" I hadn't trusted that Christian took care of it. "I need your help with something."

CHAPTER FORTY-ONE

Niagara Falls, New York
Sunday, June 13th, 5:00 PM

Clinton resented the fact he had to take part in the door-to-door canvassing. He'd rather be in company with the Governor of New York finding out why he and Behler had met at Casa Grande—whether it was for business or pleasure.

Clinton had gut feelings about the entire situation, and it told him there was something larger going on. Of course, he had nothing tangible to prove his theories besides an increasing stack of speculation and coincidences.

They had obtained entry from the manager of the apartment complex, a ruddy man in his late forties. He was more than enthusiastic to help with the investigation of a home invasion—a lie told to cover up the real purpose—although the way he watched them, Clinton suspected his imagination had run off. His expression clearly read, *a little overkill for a B & E.* He pranced around their feet like an eager puppy working for adoption.

"You can go back to your apartment now. We'll call you if we need anything," the junior FBI agent said, as he put a hand on the man's back gently attempting to prod him into submission. This was the same agent who was in the room at the hospital, taking direction from Leone.

"Sure." The building manager's shoulders sagged as he left them.

"I didn't think the leech would ever leave us to do our job," Agent Leone said.

For once Clinton smiled as the result of the man. Maybe he wasn't that bad after all?

"I say we all split up. Wingham, why don't you take the fifth floor, Clinton the fourth, and Bakker and I will share the third." Agent Leone spewed the directions as if he was in charge.

Clinton let him have this one moment and consented with a nod. He noticed the sideways glance from his partner who seemed shocked that he didn't protest. She lifted her eyebrows when Clinton remained silent.

"Okay then." Wingham was the first to break away from the group.

. . .

Detroit, Michigan
12 Hours Until the Deadline

My legs and arms were energized with a slight tingling sensation. I worked through it and made it back to the car where I momentarily stared across the massive parking lot of the racetrack.

Pietro had commissioned me to kill his son, the one man whose life I had saved many years ago. If only I had let him die then everything would have been different. The great irony presented itself as a stinging slap across the face.

Speaking of which…a hand went to my cheek where Pietro had struck me twice. The reflection in the rearview mirror disclosed a blotchy, flushed cheek. I rubbed it as if it would somehow reverse time and the predicament I was in.

Pretty much the same deadline. Another mission.

As the pins and needles sensation worked through my system, I felt more alert. Even my burning eyes were better. Whatever it was that Pietro had given me, I could use some at tax season when there were too many clients for the amount of time.

My business…Tomorrow was Monday, and I wouldn't be in. Not that I needed to make excuses when I was the boss, but Serena would likely be getting curious about my whereabouts. I never took more than a day off since I opened the doors fourteen years ago.

Christian's words came to the forefront, you would be nothing without me. I made you who you are.

The hell he did! I studied hard for a year to obtain my accountant license, a feat that would take most years to accomplish.

Had he sent me all my clients? I highly doubted that. But he had confessed to one of my largest accounts—that of Rose Buds—Behler's business.

My heart sank as I thought once again of my family, not that I ever actually forgot about them. But the only way I could function was to allow those thoughts to seep into the background so I could deal with the present and get them back safely.

Before I left, I watched Pietro slip out a back door with the Governor's phone clenched in his hand. An unmistakable scowl marred his expression, and he spoke in mumbled Italian. He would leave to grieve his son. Betrayal equated death. And soon enough he would have a body to accompany the philosophy.

I reached into the glove box and pulled out a small plastic container for a memory card. I held it up to the afternoon sunlight. I smiled at the irony. My bargaining chip had been a chip. The phone Pietro had from the Governor contained everything this chip did. I wasn't stupid enough to give the man nothing, but from the text message I had received before going into see the Don himself, it provided me a form of protection.

I slipped the card into the slot on my phone and re-read the text, even though its message was clearly etched in my mind.

"Is the Bluebird going to nest with the Robin?"

Maybe to most people this wouldn't mean anything, but I knew something was going on. It was only further confirmed by the sender's name—Lorenzo Ferrero. Pietro was an avid fan of Ferrero's opera composition. And Pietro always mentioned *Rimbaud, ou le fils du Soleil* from 1978. The name of the opera meant Son of the Sun.

As for the rest of the cryptic message, I did a quick Google search for state birds. Bluebird represented the state of New York, while the Robin, Michigan. It didn't take long to piece it together. Pietro was conspiring with Governor Behler to work at getting the Governor of New York, Talbot, on board with something. And as soon I figured out the password to the file, I might be closer to figuring out what.

I placed the phone down in the console. As I did, my hand brushed the gun in my holster. Pietro's men had returned it to me before I left. I put the car into gear.

Whatever was about to go down, it wouldn't be pretty.

CHAPTER FORTY-TWO

Niagara Falls, New York
Sunday, June 13th, 5:45 PM

And this is why Clinton hated door-to-door canvassing. It reaffirmed the craziness of the human race. Not that anyone could really define normal, however, most people never approached the wavy line.

The fourth floor held nothing but a lot of dead ends because mostly no one was at home. There used to be a time when people went to church Sunday morning and then stayed home in the afternoon and evening.

Clinton lifted a hand to knock on the last door. The door had opened before his arm dropped back to his side. The woman on the other side wore a plain black shirt with a gray-pleated skirt. She assessed him from his scuffed shoes to the slacks and jacket he wore. She smiled. "I have religion."

He found it interesting that was her first reaction. "I'm not here about that—"

"Why not? Everybody needs something to believe in."

How old was this woman anyway? She only appeared to be in her mid-to-late thirties, but her words spoke of antiquated tradition. The Bible and religion were for older people weren't they?

Clinton pulled his badge. "We're here—"

"We?" The woman tucked out into the hall and did a quick look. "I only see you."

"Detective Clinton." He paused assuming she'd cut in with something to say. Surprisingly she didn't. "We're investigating a break-in. Did you see anyone in the building you never saw before?"

She tucked an escaped strand of strawberry-blonde hair behind an ear. "I don't let anyone in this building."

Clinton picked up on her awkward mannerisms, the shifting on her feet, the fidgeting with her hair, topped off by a defensive statement. He needed her to keep speaking. He contemplated how Wingham would approach this. Empathize. "Ah, someone looks trustworthy, you open the front door. People don't know all their neighbors these days."

Her eyes shifted. She conceded with a nod.

"So you know what I'm talking about?"

"I never knew someone's place would be broken into."

Oh, it was a lot worse than that. Clinton needed to tighten his jaw to avoid saying his thought aloud.

"He looked like a Bible-thumper," she said.

It had been a long time since he'd heard that phrase. Clinton studied the woman before him. If anything she would fit that description.

"I let him in."

"What did he look like?"

She seemed surprised that he didn't react differently. Clinton thought she looked like she expected chastisement.

"I don't know…that was around noon."

Bingo!

"What time?"

"I was heading to an afternoon Bible study group."

"Did you see what floor he went to?"

"No, I was already down the sidewalk when he went through the door."

"And you don't remember what he looked like?"

The woman crossed her arms. Clinton noticed the defensive body language. This woman held a lot of guilt but was it truly deserved or self-inflicted from religion? At least that's how he viewed things. He grew up a devout Christian but couldn't stomach feeling bad about things all the time. His parents believed in confessing all sins no matter how small. And for imperfect beings that tally would go on indefinitely.

"He was rather attractive. Dressed nice in khakis and a Polo shirt."

"Did you notice a Rolex watch?" Clinton asked.

"No, I don't think so. As I said, I thought he was here about the Bible. And people in this building need that, Lord knows. The drugs and loud parties—"

"Was he tall, thin, short, overweight?" Clinton redirected back to the investigation.

"I didn't do anything wrong."

Clinton took a deep breath. "I'm not saying you did. I just need your help right now."

"Average height, relatively attractive. He filled out the jacket nicely—"

Clinton's cell phone rang, and he debated whether to answer it. Little Miss Religion just seemed to be opening up. He held up a finger, but she slunk back into her apartment a few inches at a time. By the time he got his phone off the clip, she was behind her door with it cracked open only a few inches.

"Remember God. He hasn't forgotten you." She closed the door on him leaving him in an empty hallway.

Clinton ground a heel into the floor. "Shit!"

"That's one helluva way to answer your phone." It was Wingham.

"I was this close…" He held his fingers pinched to within three-eighths of an inch as if she could see. "To getting an ID."

"Well, I'll trump that. Get up to the fifth floor. I've got the shooter's apartment."

CHAPTER FORTY-THREE

Christian hated how berto skulked around like a man who had lost his dog. Ingo had been a valuable asset at one point, but his usefulness had expired. Christian didn't owe an explanation to anyone as to why he had him executed by the girls. He had directed Berto to clean them up and put them in new chokers. His countenance shook but Christian convinced him the girls would still be full. He would be safe.

Nothing on the news indicated the death of the Governor, only reports to the contrary about how she was on the mend. He hated thinking about that traitorous, hypocritical bitch clinging to life. Her nine lives should have been exhausted by now. Surely, she knew her time would come. One never associated on the fringe of The Family for long before being cut off as a useless tentacle.

He didn't understand how Pops couldn't see the grander picture. His vision was archaic while Christian foresaw the future. They didn't need dignitaries or authorities to dictate how they ran their operations. They didn't need the government absorbing their profits in taxes. And they most certainly did not require an outside liaison to take care of business. He could have handled that himself. Why send the servant when the master would have much more impact?

One strength of those in the public eye, however, was they were accustomed to structure and being provided with direction. They just had to remember where the power came from—yet they often forgot.

Christian leaned against the wall of the wash bay watching the pink water flush down a floor drain. Berto wiped an arm across his forehead and continued scrubbing the dogs. He refused to look at his boss.

Christian respected that aspect of the man. He never confronted him or questioned any directives. He jumped like a seal for a fish any time a situation required it. Almost as loyal as a dog, but less intelligent.

The clock moved at too fast a pace for Christian's liking. His contacts in Niagara Falls were limited. And he didn't need to be involving his New York connections until everything had worked out. When the timing was right, he'd call for them. Right now, he had other things to take care of. And thanks to Ingo, Hunter would have likely figured out his family was being held at this airport through the proof of life video. Christian realized the irony of the situation and it caused him to smile. Maybe Ingo never had to die, as Christian himself exposed the location by bringing out the boy.

Oh well…

He had many more Ingos waiting for recruitment. Eager men seeking to find some sort of redemption always found their way to him. There would be a new era and Christian would be the ruler. The ones who didn't bow to him would be eradicated.

CHAPTER FORTY-FOUR

Detroit, Michigan
Sunday, June 13th, 5:45 PM
Less Than 12 Hours Until the Deadline

The concept of Behler working with the Russos didn't make sense to me at first. But as I drove, recent events composed a picture. Behler was in New York to make Talbot see the benefits of aligning with the Mafia, possibly through blackmail. Maybe they were using threats against his family too.

Talbot's face had read of discomfort being in Behler's company. He avoided eye contact and withdrew. When I had pulled my chair in, I remembered him moving back; the legs of the chair had made noise against the hardwood. It wasn't until right now, I realized my slip-up.

Shit!

I pounded the steering wheel. Governor Behler had introduced me by name. By now I was certain Talbot knew the town I was from. He could have shared this information with the police or Feds investigating the shooting. My thoughts whirled and melded. *How could I have screwed up this badly?*

I tried to convince myself that I had planned on taking care of it the first time, but the fact that I hadn't affected my ego. If only I had managed to put this behind me with one bullet, instead of two. Would that have made a difference?

Before leaving the parking lot, I had turned on the radio, but no news reports came on. As far as the rest of the world was concerned, the Governor was on the mend. And, unfortunately, that world included Christian.

A job that had presented itself as a one-time-handle-it-and-be-done-with-it had turned into the worst possible nightmare.

If Christian knew his old man had planned a meeting between the Governors, using Behler to manipulate Talbot by some means, he must have pissed himself with glee when I picked the date and location for the hit. It was obvious Christian wanted to take over as the head of The Family, but why wasn't he going about it directly and killing Pietro? I knew the answer. He wanted to feel in control, a director of events, a master of ceremonies.

I swerved the car into my driveway and walked through the front door expecting the smell of decomp to plaster my sinuses. Instead, a strong chemical odor filled the air. Pietro had things taken care of, and it would have been handled discreetly by his men who were specialized in this area.

I dropped my bags on the sofa on the way through to the office and keyed in the name Governor Talbot into a search engine on the Internet.

I knew I shouldn't care about why the Governor had to die, but if I was going to gain any insight into my next mark, I had to start with a connection to his last. And with father and son pitted against each other and me playing monkey-in-the-middle, I needed to know the rules.

After clicking on numerous sites and reading about the man, I knew that Talbot had an honorable service record—possibly too clean for a man of politics. His official site boasted of his success against street gangs and how the level of violence against innocents had taken a nose dive. It also bragged of cleaning up the streets by coming down hard on the drug trade, prostitutes, and the weapons trade.

> *It may not happen in our lifetime,*
> *but the impact it will have on future*
> *generations will be immeasurable.*

This man had high ambitions, even for a politician. No one, let alone a man of office, was this righteous. Maybe the Russos had found the chink in his armor and threatened to expose it.

I kept reading and the image gained shape.

*Organized crime must be severed
one limb at a time until rendered
a defenseless torso at which time
the perfect opportunity to strike the
heart will be exposed.*

I opened another browser page and confirmed my suspicions. The amount of time I had spent with the Russos, I knew the Italian Mafia spread across borders. Families dictated local Dons, but collectively the Italians were more powerful than people realized. They weren't the spotlight in a Hollywood movie. They were real people who got themselves involved with unsavory things. Yet at the same time, they held dignity among themselves. Their actions were justified and measured. They weren't compulsive and guided by emotion. As a group they were referred to as The Commission. If need be, they will help each other, involving themselves in a brother's affairs.

Flipping back to Talbot's website, my stomach sank as I looked at the picture of the man who had also shared Behler's table. He stood behind a podium, his one hand braced on the edge, the other raised in the air as the American flag rippled in a breeze behind him—the typical backdrop for an eager politician.

The mission Pietro had placed upon Behler was for the brotherhood. With its failure, Pietro risked exposure as a traitor, punishable by death. And if The Commission knew about him, it wouldn't take them long and they'd know about me too.

. . .

Niagara Falls, New York

"I came home and the chain was across. How the hell does that happen when I'm not inside? That's how I knew someone was here." The tenant, Dean Holmstead, was in his early twenties. His hair was a dark brown and greased back. His eyes were large in proportion to the rest of his face.

Clinton left him standing there and went around the apartment sniffing in to find the source of a moldy cheese smell, even though he wasn't quite sure if he wanted to.

"Whatcha doing there?" Holmstead followed Clinton. He carried a laptop tucked under his arm. "Careful what you touch."

How could someone live like this? For a moment, Clinton experienced empathy for an assassin who had to resign himself to this dump.

"Did you see this person?" Clinton asked.

"No, like I said, he was inside, I was out." The other hand went over to touch the laptop then dropped back to his side.

Clinton shared a look with his partner. She took over.

"Once you got inside did you see anything?"

"I was yelling for them to get out." He turned to Wingham. "I didn't even know it was a guy. I'd just assumed."

You assumed correctly.

Clinton walked toward the window and noticed the third floor of County General in plain view. He counted across windows to what would have been the Governor's room. The curtains were now closed. If one could see that clearly with the natural eye, it would be in complete focus with a scope.

Clinton put a hand to his jaw. His face was no longer smooth but could use a shave. The stubble made a noise against his rough hand as he rubbed over it. He turned toward the tenant. "You sure you never saw anything?"

"No, I swear to you." An arm jolted out straight and pointed toward the hallway. "He went down the fire escape before I could get to him."

"Huh." Clinton faced back to the window, but he took in more than the view. His attention was on the window sill. He thought of fingerprints, but a man of the killer's caliber wouldn't make that mistake. Although, he did miss killing her the first time.

"Why do you say that like you don't believe me?" Holmstead asked.

"Was anything stolen?"

The amped up tenant stepped toward Clinton. Wingham put a hand on his shoulder and pulled him back.

The apartment door opened and Agent Leone came through. "What's going on in here?"

Apparently a party.

Leone came toward Clinton with large strides and little attention to the apartment as if attempting to win a speed walking competition.

"Oh shit," Holmstead said. Everyone's eyes went to him. He set his laptop down on a coffee table and looked at them as if to say, *touch it and I'll take on your guns.*

"He moved my stuff." He bounced in front of his media area, which consisted of a modest stand about two-feet high and a flat screen of about thirty-two inches. "Now it's not center in the room." He went to move it back and six hands went to him.

"Don't touch anything," Leone said. He addressed Wingham. "Get him out of here."

Clinton watched as his partner first looked to him. The diplomatic side in her eyes said, *I don't report to you.* Yet the fire in them said, *Fuck you.* To keep the peace, she moved toward the kid.

"Come on Gamer." Wingham put a hand on his shoulder and directed him to the apartment hallway. Holmstead pulled out from under her hold and scooped his laptop on the way by.

With the door closed behind them, Leone and Clinton stared at each other.

A finger stabbed downward, accompanying Leone's words, "You are to keep me informed."

Clinton never said anything. He didn't need to justify his stand. He never called Leone to advise they found the apartment, but that didn't prove he wasn't going to. Sometimes silence was more powerful than a raised voice.

"This case should belong to the FBI in the first damn place. A Governor of State is assassinated and you city apes are put in charge because of some connection."

"City apes? You come down here in your pressed suit thinking everyone should bend at the knees with respect. Me, well, I don't have the best knees. And I'm not wasting them on you."

Leone cocked his head to the side; his eyes narrowed.

"Now a beautiful woman, that's a different story." Clinton looked back to the window sill. Most times he was eager for the next confrontation. Right now, he didn't report to this man. In fact, he was given the lead by the Governor of New York.

"You know who the killer is," Leone said.

"We have the leads we shared with you."

"Bullshit! You know who did this followed the Governor from Michigan. Your friend might be friends with the Director, but you know what, he also has a boss."

Clinton found it interesting that he referred to the New York Governor as a friend. Why would he make that assumption? Just because the case was assigned to local PD?

"You start sharing this case with me, or I'll blow it wide open. Maybe even lock you up as an accessory after the fact." Leone glared at Clinton, driving home the intent of his words. "We know about the meeting between the Governors. We know that they were together the night before the first assassination attempt. We also know they weren't together for business reasons."

"How do you—"

"See, we Special Agents, we know more than we're given credit for." Leone pulled out on the lapels of his suit jacket.

"So you followed us."

Leone laughed. "You have an answer for everything."

Clinton didn't say a word. His anger would only have jumbled the words that would spew from his mouth. As for Mr. Special Agent, there were things he didn't know. Knowing about the dinner between the Governors could be explained by tailing him and Wingham, or tipping off the concierge at The Grandeur. And it probably wouldn't even have taken that.

"You know who the killer is," Leone repeated his earlier words still hoping for a bite.

"We need to get Crime Scene down here." Clinton heard the agent exhale loudly and his footsteps move toward the door. It had opened before he reached it.

"What's going on?" It was the junior agent. Leone never answered him but kept walking.

Clinton looked out the window, Leone's question repeating in his mind, *do you know who the killer is?*

Clinton was pretty certain he did. The lady in the apartment had described Tux perfectly—attractive and filling out a jacket nicely. Coincidence? Possibly. But when they all started stacking up, it crossed from coincidence to evidence. Now he just had to find him before time ran out and Mr. Special Agent went running up the power ladder.

CHAPTER FORTY-FIVE

Outskirts of Detroit, Michigan
Sunday, June 13th, 5:45 PM

Yvonne tucked further into the corner of the room. Her hands had been removed from her constraints, but she was too afraid to move. She felt so cold; she was aware of her bone structure. She rubbed at her arms to get the blood flowing. But the sinew-tearing screams continued to slice through her. They had stopped a while ago now, but they replayed in her mind as if still taking place.

Canary Man hadn't been back, and she had the feeling he never would be. Just the way fear for his life had flashed through his eyes when he left her. He knew he wouldn't be returning.

The handsome Italian was the one in charge—and deadly. That only meant one thing. They needed to get out of here before his anger turned on them. She had given a lot of thought to the entire situation in the hours that had passed. They weren't told why they were kidnaped and held hostage, and it wasn't like her dad was a wealthy man who could compensate with a ransom. What did these men want?

Tremors from being chilled ran through her again. She was so hungry; she found her eyes heavy with fatigue. At least, the pains in her stomach had stopped a while back.

She willed herself to move and felt faint as she rose to her feet. There was a window that ran the length of the room and was about two feet high. It had been painted black to keep out the light. But the problem was its location. It was at the top of the wall—a good five feet above her extended reach from the floor. The bed only provided a few feet of elevation. Even on it tiptoed she couldn't reach the sill—she had tried. She even jumped to get a grip on it.

She scanned the room. There was nothing else that could lift her higher.

The door opened; the distinctive click as the seal gave way.

"Well, looky here." A large man stood in her doorway for only an instant before lunging toward her.

Yvonne screamed, but he had his hand over her mouth before it became satisfied. The flat of his hand exposed her only means of possible escape. She shook her head. His hand moved with her and secured in place. But his hand slid down—just enough. She sunk her teeth into his flesh. She tasted the metallic flavor of blood. It didn't stop her. She bit down harder until it filled her mouth.

The large man released her and threw her to the ground. He cradled his hand, swearing in another language. When he finished, he came to her. "You little bitch!"

The last thing she remembered after that was her eyes closing.

. . .

Detroit, Michigan
Just Over 11 Hours Until the Deadline

I was in my home office. My hand rested on the mouse, and my attention was on the screen in front of me and the numerous browser windows. For once, I wasn't really certain what my next step would be. All I knew was I wanted my family back, and if that meant going after them, freeing them, and running to the other end of the earth to hide, so be it.

While I wanted to kill Christian for personal reasons, I really didn't owe anything to Pietro. I knew the thought process was harmful. I would be a targeted and sought after man for the rest of my life. This would also include my family.

With Max being at the hangar, I felt that's definitely where Christian had all of them locked up. If freeing them resulted in a gun fight, so be it. I would make it look like Christian's men had turned on him. It would appear as nothing more than a shift in the heads of the Russo Family. But I knew I couldn't have it carried out that way. Pietro specified it was to look like an accident. If a firefight went down, it would reflect back on him as if he had cleaned house. He wanted this fight far from his front door.

First, I had some preparation to do. I brought up Google Earth and went to the area of the hangar. I hoped to study the structure and determine the best angles in and out. I would utilize my memories of the layout and go from there. A hand went to the .44 still in my holster. I wished I could shut off the other part of my mind that wanted to know what was in that file on Behler's phone. Yet I had convinced myself that if I got the answer to that, I might be better able to know exactly what was going on here. Why had Christian wanted her dead? Was it simply a power move?

I knew who could help me.

CHAPTER FORTY-SIX

Keith Buxton worked out of his townhouse. He had security cameras and motion sensors rigged around the perimeter of his home. He once told me when people stepped within a thousand feet of his property, he knew about it.

I waved to the camera and kept moving to his back door. I didn't even need to knock. The door slid open.

"Ray?" Keith Buxton was about four inches shy of six feet. He was the smartest person I knew and had the IQ of a genius. The only reason he was shut up in a suburban townhouse was because of poor life decisions. His inventions and advancements in technology were made while he was employed for a salaried wage. The patents for everything belonged to the companies he worked for. From what I knew he had retired early and was in his mid-fifties. He carried extra weight on his frame and was soft from inactivity. His hair had turned a dark gray, but his eyes sparkled with life. He wore small round glasses with silver frames. They were perched on the end of his nose; he looked over them.

"Keith." I held up the chip I had replicated from Behler's cell phone. "I need your help."

A large grin filled his face. The expression balled his cheeks and had me thinking of Santa Claus. "Well, come on in then." He went to take the chip from my fingers, but I pulled my hand back.

"It doesn't leave my sight."

Keith extended his hand for the chip again. This time I let him take it.

"It must be real important stuff on here."

Despite Keith's intelligence, he spoke like an average person making it hard for anyone to suspect what he housed in that skull of his.

"You keeping out of trouble these days?" Keith spoke as he led me through the tight confines of his home. Computers and monitors were everywhere, chirping and humming. It was surprising that he didn't have cancer with all the invisible signals bouncing around the place.

I never answered his question, and I hoped he didn't really want a response. But he stopped in front of a bank of computers and stared at me. He repeated his question. "You staying out of trouble?"

"You don't want me to answer that."

"But you have a family now, don't you?" His eyes were no longer on me, but I sensed the passing of judgment from his energy and the tone of his voice. He stuck the chip into the side of a laptop.

"Yeah, a girl and a boy."

"A million dollar family." Keith looked over his shoulder, a huge smile on his face, and he nodded for me to sit on a task chair.

Keith sat beside me in another one and pecked some keys on the keyboard. "How long has it been anyway?"

"Fifteen years." My wavelength was on how long my affiliation with the Mafia dated back. Keith knew I was involved with them, yet he never knew to what extent. I don't think he ever would have helped me if he knew I had been a killer.

"No, it hasn't been that long." He stared at me from over the rim of his glasses. "You last came to me, what ten years ago. You had an accounting business and were doing a software change. How's that going?"

I forgot how many questions Keith asked. Maybe that was his excessive intelligence that hungered for facts. But today, he wouldn't be getting any more than necessary. I disregarded his personal inquiry. "I need to access a locked file on there." I nodded toward the screen. "It's password protected."

"And you forgot what it was?" Keith shook his head, a smile on his lips. I was starting to wonder if he had an unhappy expression.

Keith continued, "People do that all the time. That's why I tell 'em to make notes on this sort of thing. And I'm talking about the old fashioned way—pen and paper."

"Surprised you'd give that advice to anyone." I returned the smile relieved he allowed me the pass.

Keith took his eyes off the monitor. "I know. Maybe my old age is changing me."

"Ah, I doubt that." I glanced around at all the banks of computers and monitors. The man didn't have regular furniture save a sofa chair in the living room. Books were piled on a side table and a reading light was behind it. It looked like something you'd see in a movie. Keith had always been as much a reader as he was a computer hacker and inventor.

"Okay, here's the coding for the file. I'm looking for—" Keith stopped talking, a finger pressed to the monitor and dragged downward. "There it is."

"Just like that?"

"Well, we're not in yet." He jabbed at some keys, and the document started filling in the screen.

"Keith, if you don't—"

"What is this Ray?"

A spreadsheet with a lot of tabs filled the screen. They were named as dates followed by Talbot's name.

"Is that Governor Talbot?" Keith looked at me. "What are you involved with?" There were a few seconds of eye contact. "This isn't your file is it? That's why you didn't know the password."

There was no point in lying. I remained silent.

"Am I an accessory now? Did you involve me in something illegal? I thought you stopped those ways a long time ago."

To hear him talk to me in this manner felt like a lecture from my old man. My father had always expected nothing but perfection and purity. He also assumed that I would carry on in the family religion. It wasn't for me. I held more interest in guns than God.

Keith made a note on a piece of paper, the tip of the pen moving wildly. He ripped the section off and handed it to me. "I don't want to know what it is."

"They have my family." The words escaped.

"Who does?" The pen dropped on the desk; he raised his eyebrows, the odd long hair extending from them. "The Mafia?"

My eyes went to the piece of paper, *Bluebird*. I should have known to try that password.

Keith exhaled loudly and handed me the chip. "You just be careful Ray. You don't know what you're involved with."

Was he making a blanket assessment or did he know something I didn't? I left his townhouse feeling uneasy about trusting him. It had something to do with the way he looked at me with condemnation in his eyes. I never suspected the old man of copying my files before. But this time, I wasn't so sure.

Please mind your own business one last time, old friend.

CHAPTER FORTY-SEVEN

Clinton stood back as he oversaw the Crime Scene techs work over every square inch of Gamer's apartment. They probably wished they had brought in the hazmat suits.

Leone had left the apartment building after their confrontation and wasn't answering his cell phone. Not that Clinton cared, but the junior agent had been bitching about it for a while now.

Clinton said, "Maybe he took a last minute vacation."

The agent, a man who remained unnamed simply based on Clinton's estimation of his importance, rolled his head to the side.

"You don't think so?" Clinton put a hand on the man's shoulder. Maybe it would help if he had a name. Actually come to think of it, Leone mentioned it before—Bakker or Bernard—it didn't really matter. He'd be free of him soon enough.

"This isn't doing us any good hanging around here waiting for something to be found." Wingham crossed her arms. "They've got your number. When they find something—"

Clinton's ringing cell phone interrupted her. It resulted in her raising her arms and turning her back on him. He spoke on the phone. "Talk to me…yeah…hey, Murray…all right." Murray Hamilton was another Major Crimes Detective. Wingham faced Clinton again, and they matched eyes. "We'll be right there."

"I'm going to get a coffee." Junior brushed by Clinton, nudging him in the torso on the way out.

"Hey, watch yourself!"

"Whatever!" The agent waved a hand over his head and kept walking.

Clinton addressed his partner, "Murray's found us a lead."

. . .

Detroit, Michigan
7:30 PM
Just Over 9 Hours Until the Deadline

The files from Behler's cell phone were loaded with financial information. Bank statements showed withdrawals and deposits. Some of the information pertained to Talbot's personal while other sheets were tagged State of New York.

I scrolled through the file, analyzing all the numbers and was thankful that I had become an accountant. I started noticing discrepancies in the books. Nothing reconciled.

Governor Talbot wasn't squeaky clean. Not that I ever believed a politician could be.

. . .

Niagara Falls, New York

Clinton drove; Wingham rode shotgun. They pulled into the parking lot of The Oasis motel and noticed Murray standing outside of room 11.

"He's in there?" Clinton nodded toward the door.

"Yep."

Clinton didn't wait for another word but pushed past his colleague. He had a lot to ask the son of a bitch. His feet became grounded once he made it through the doorway. He stopped so abruptly Wingham went into his back and Murray into hers.

"He's dead," Clinton said, snapping his head in Murray's direction.

"I said I found Rick Carson. I never said he was alive. You were so quick to get off the phone."

Clinton looked at the figure on the bed. The bodyguard who had been scrawny and unattractive in a grainy video was a model in contrast to his current condition.

Wingham put a hand over her mouth but moved closer to the body. She mumbled something.

"What did you say? Couldn't make it out for the hand." Clinton shot her a look.

Her eyes narrowed. She slowly dropped her arm. "He didn't die here. There's no blood pool. The wounds aren't fresh."

"I've already called in the coroner. They should be here soon," Murray said. He kept back toward the door, his attention on the parking lot.

"The guy's been tortured. His ears, his nose…" Wingham's hand lifted but lowered when Clinton looked at her. "His fingers. Some of them are gone." She surveyed the room. "And they're not here either. None of his missing parts are."

"There's something larger going on than an assassination of a dignitary," Clinton said. "This guy comes all the way from Michigan and gets off'd like this after Behler. It's not adding up to a day of roses and pony rides." The headlines were flashing through his mind as stock exchange ticker boards, and in every one he held the main caption. Niagara Falls Detective Clinton Brings down the Governor's Assassin and Uncovers an Organized Crime Ring Behind It.

"The only people who do this sort of thing—"

"Is the Mafia." Wingham finished his sentence.

It was one thing to think it and yet another to verbalize the speculation with conviction. All Clinton could do was nod in response.

Wingham continued, speaking her thoughts aloud, "His background didn't show anything major."

Clinton shook his head. "Just something's not adding up with this." His words stalled as he took in the man on the bed.

Rolex, or Rick Carson, was splayed on the double-sized mattress, legs spread eagle, arms extended. In a way, he resembled a sick sort of snow angel suspended in mid-flight. He wore a pair of blue jeans, tattered at the knees, and a white shirt stained with blood. There was a large slash to his neck and likely what killed him. And there was something about the way his shirt was pressed against his chest.

"I don't think he was wearing this at the time he died," Clinton said and looked over his shoulder to Murray whose back was to him. The man's arms were crossed.

Clinton's eyes went back to the body and the darkened mass under the shirt. He took a step toward the body and had a hand braced above it just about to pull open the shirt.

"Stop! Right there!" A woman's voice called from the doorway. "Don't you dare touch that body. I don't care if you were the President of the United States himself, you hear me?"

She was beautiful. Clinton took a few steps back and admired her as she seemed to glide across the motel room. Her presence made him feel patriotic. An eight-inch salute formed in his trousers.

When she reached the bed, she stopped in front of Clinton—inches away. If only they were closer and naked, he would really show his respect.

"I'm Paulina Thompson." She didn't make an effort to extend a hand. Her complexion was smooth, and for a lack of clear thinking, he'd describe her as melted chocolate. If he had a moment to step back and analyze, maybe he'd come up with an even better analogy.

Clinton couldn't get a word to come out.

"We're detectives Wingham and Clinton." Wingham's eyes narrowed and her head moved on an angle as she matched eyes with her partner.

"If you could please step away." Thompson held out a hand gesturing for Clinton to move backward. She took photographs of the body careful to capture every angle.

Clinton watched as her body moved.

Wingham slapped his arm. She whispered, "What do you think you're doing?"

"Working."

"Uh huh." Wingham left the room and stepped outside. Clinton lingered around a bit longer. When Thompson finished with the photographs, her gloved hands, her slender fingers, worked over the dead man. For a moment, Clinton was jealous of the deceased.

"He's coming out of full rigor. TOD is estimated at over twelve hours ago."

That time of death wasn't long after the first assassination attempt. Was he killed because he had failed?

"Can you help me?" Thompson addressed him, speaking over her shoulder as she leaned over the body. "In the box there." She nodded toward her case. "There's evidence bags. We need to bag his hands...at least what's left of them."

"Sure." Clinton was proud to have found his voice. Even if it was one word. He was coming back around, breaking free of her spell. He handed her the bags. They made contact. Fireworks—Fourth of July!

When she finished wrapping up his hands, Clinton mustered strength to speak more than one syllable. "Cause of death the neck slash?"

Thompson lifted up the front of the man's shirt which peeled from blood-tacky flesh. Her finger traced above the flesh, right to left. "The words TSK TSK appeared to have been sliced into his torso by a knife." Thompson's brow lines pointed downward as she lifted the shirt higher. "Hmm, interesting." She left the shirt up and went for her camera. She snapped a picture and pulled the man's shirt back down. "I'll take more pics back at the morgue, catalog everything of course, and finalize my ruling on the cause of death."

"I really think we already have." Clinton walked away from her relieved that he finally had his independent strength back. Murray and Wingham were outside the room laughing. "Is there a joke I'm missing? Forgive me if I'm mistaken, but a man's mutilated body is feet away and you're both laughing like it's prom night."

Wingham's head snapped to her partner. "Interesting that's where your mind is freshman."

He disregarded her dig. "Who called it in?"

"Motel manager came by to make sure everything was okay," Murray began. "Said that a guy checked in earlier today and had left. But he heard some noise and came down to check things out."

"A guy?" Clinton asked.

"Yeah, he's certain our DB isn't the man who checked in."

"Manager's name?"

"Edwin Taylor. No priors, clean background. Originally from Canada," Murray said.

"Yeah, that says it all."

"Someone's cranky."

"Someone's frustrated." Wingham defended her partner, braced both hands on her hips, and challenged Murray with eye contact.

"I want to talk to the guy," Clinton moved toward the motel office.

"The guy's pretty shook up. Ronny's in there with him now, keeping him company." That was really code for making sure a suspect or witness didn't get away.

Wingham performed a half skip to catch up to Clinton. "What are you thinking?"

"What am I thinking?" Clinton stopped walking. "We're in the middle of a damn mess. We've got a dead Governor, a mutilated lead, and another suspect in the wind. The only thing connecting any dots is the Governor of New York. But until I have a few more facts, well, we're stuck with the Canadian." He moved again.

"Hey, they're not that bad. They're just like the rest of us, only they're buried in snow, love hockey, apologize a lot, and say eh."

CHAPTER FORTY-EIGHT

The documents confirmed my suspicions—Governor Talbot was skimming from State funds. Trips abroad, vacation villas in Thailand, drinks and dinners in fancy restaurants. Deposits made into his personal bank accounts never matched exactly but were always within a few hundred of the funds withdrawn from the State's money. And it was taken in small values, on a regular basis. If my math was correct, and it always was, the Governor had defrauded the State of New York two point five million since his term in office.

I opened up a search window to get a complete picture of his biography. His family was wealthy until his father lost all their money in an unwise business investment and took an overdose. This left behind Talbot's mother to raise two young children.

Talbot who was already accustomed to the finer things in life, worked hard to climb the corporate ladder—eventually it paid off. Today, they all lived in Manhattan estates and owned secondary houses on Rhode Island.

I closed the browser and sat there thinking. If Behler had been meeting with the Governor and had this on her phone, their meeting wasn't simply a conversation. It was coercion with the most expensive thing at stake—Talbot's term in office and exploitation of the family's name and money.

Pietro's message, *Is the bluebird going to nest with the Robin*, replayed in my mind. Behler was there presenting the facts. As long as Talbot saw things the way of The Commission, aka, the Italian Mafia, and laid off his quest to squash them, he would remain in office and continue to have access to the government's money like his own personal piggy bank. If he didn't cooperate, well, he stood to lose everything and face fraud and embezzlement charges. For a man of Talbot's history, that would be enough to warrant a barrel in the mouth.

CHAPTER FORTY-NINE

Time was running out. Pietro expected that Christian would die of some accident before morning; I planned on getting this taken care of by Christian's first imposed deadline.

I had considered Christian's death from many possible angles. One method that kept reoccurring to me was to sabotage his plane somehow. Yet it would involve a knowledge of planes, which I had little of, and a need for Christian to get on one.

I thought about making it look like a revolt, that his own people turned against him. But that wasn't really an accident either, and it would paint a large target on everyone. The spotlight would shine on Pietro Russo, which would clear him with The Commission including the Mafia Families in New York. But it definitely wouldn't free him of a police investigation and the allegations of house cleaning. Of course, direct evidence would be impossible to obtain.

This stipulation and cause and effect made the option of staging a coup, implausible. All I knew for certain; I was going to get my family back. Tonight. From there, the future was unwritten. I realized I still had to take care of the job given me, or we'd never rest from the chase, but one thing at a time.

Honestly, I was surprised by how effective the stimulant was that Pietro had given me. My eyes, despite being scratchy from being open for so long, were relatively at ease. The burning sensation that had willed them shut before had muted to the background.

I needed to push aside everything related to my discoveries about the Governors. To my cause, it didn't really matter. One way or another, my family had been put in the crosshairs of some very dangerous men. And if The Commission came to Pietro and figured out the assassination had been played out on the whim of a child who felt he was a born leader…well, suffice it to conclude, my family needed to be far away when the gunfire broke out. And so did I.

...

Niagara Falls, New York

Agent Leone had to keep his distance from Clinton before he acted on his impulse to pound on him until his eyes closed for the last time. He had already envisioned it more times than was healthy—reliving the fantasy and dwelling on it. But he had more important things to take care of right now.

He entered the bookstore off a side street, avoiding the main entrance security cameras and crowds. He hated crowds, but sometimes it was necessary to blend in.

Inside, the smell of paperbacks and binding glue mingled with fresh baked goods and coffee. Even he wasn't immune to the bear claws and donuts displayed behind glass. He turned to look and caught the eye of the lady behind the counter. She smiled at him. He returned the smile with a wink.

He always had a way with women. Getting them wasn't the problem, keeping them around, and not becoming bored with their cramping in on him was. For some reason, he normally attracted the needy, high maintenance variety. And while entertaining for a short while, their self-absorbed nature that helped draw him in quickly constricted around his neck making it necessary to cut them loose.

Any other time, Leone would have gone after the barista and shown her a night in a luxury hotel suite. But this was no other time. He had work to do and needed to remain focused, or risk his entire world combusting to ash.

Running a hand through his hair, and pulling down on his suit jacket, he took a seat at a far table. He straightened his tie, a few hundred dollar silk number, against his shirt.

He watched his visitor approach. The man walked with more arrogance than Leone recalled from past meetings. He held his head high, making it easy to trip over an extended leg or an undone shoelace. If Leone had been closer and not known the man, maybe he would have taken the chance to test his theory.

"What? No beverage? I thought you Americans lived for pleasuring yourselves while making twenty decisions on how to take your caffeine."

Leone observed how the man attempted to elevate himself above the rest of the country. A major contrasting irony as the man was born in the United States and only a fraction Italian; his mother had been a street whore. He only made it into the Don's world because he was his only son.

"Didn't need any stimulus this evening." Leone gestured for his guest to sit across from him. "Please." The words went dry on his lips as he caught a glimpse of the man's backup—he could have played as a linebacker. He pretended to be interested in travel mugs and stainless steel water bottles but noticed Leone's glance and latched eyes with him.

His Italian friend, who had paid him well over the years, maybe extravagantly well, leaned back in his wooden chair. It moaned with the movement; it had nothing to do with the man's size.

"What do you have for me?"

"The investigation's fucked up." Leone leaned forward, clasping his hands. He learned a long time ago the young Italian preferred to be talked to like a friend, yet respected as the President.

"Tony, it's up to you to un-fuck it." His dark brown eyes were like pits or black holes in space.

"I don't think they have any clue what's up or down." Few dared to speak to the man this way, but Leone needed his attention. "Then the Bluebird gets his nose involved in something that doesn't concern him, assigns the lead to some media hungry detective. This case should be FBI."

"Tsk. Tsk." Nothing more was said. Nothing more needed to be. Leone had proven himself a disappointment.

"I'm on them to keep me informed, but this Clinton guy is a real piece of work."

"You are one of my best informants, and you're letting some detective bully you around. This isn't grade school."

"I'm doing the best I can."

The Italian leaned forward. "You must do better than that. Find the evidence; make the evidence, whatever you need to do. You report to me. Speaking of which." He paused while reaching inside his jacket. Leone prepared for the sight of a gun barrel. Instead, the man came out with a box. He set it on the table between them. "For you." He nudged it a few inches forward.

This was the one downfall of the Italian. He felt he could buy anyone with lavish gifts and obscene bonuses. And, for the most part, his tactic worked.

"What you're not even going to open it?" He asked.

Leone noticed the homicidal rage flash through the Italian's eyes when he feared being rejected.

"I'm sure you shouldn't have." Leone scooped it off the table and put it in his jacket pocket as if disinterested. "This could cause me my career."

"Huh, I give you a fifteen thousand dollar Rolex, and you stuff it in a pocket like a used tissue." He sat back, crossed his arms. His attention was fully on Leone.

"If I pawn it in, it wouldn't cover my lease for six months." Leone knew he stepped out of line when the Italian balled a fist on the table.

"You disrespect me; you won't ever have to worry about that." His voice remained calm despite the potency of the message.

Leone conceded. "My apologies—"

"You apologize? Not good enough. You take care of this…this mess."

"Yes, Boss."

"Don't call me that. That's my old man." One corner of his mouth lifted. Both of his hands went to the table and he rose.

The big man, who had given up on stainless steel water bottles, had buried his thick fingers in a magazine. He looked up as the Italian came toward him. Leone sat there observing and taking mental notes as they left the bookstore.

Leone pulled out the Rolex and sat it on the table. Probably a little much for a tip. Leone shrugged his shoulders and left. Maybe it would have made a great gift for the barista? Too bad it wasn't any other time, or he'd find out the depth of her appreciation.

CHAPTER FIFTY

Detroit, Michigan
Sunday, June 13th, 8:00 PM
9 Hours Until the Deadline

I gave a lot of thought to how to kill a man and make it look like an accident. For the most part, it wouldn't be a huge deal—if that target weren't the son of a mafia Don. Christian would have men surrounding him who would know his intentions of taking over The Family business. These men would be loyal to him at the risk of their own lives. Christian would settle for no less.

In my days with the Russos, it hadn't proved to be much of a challenge to stage a murder to look like something other than what it really was—a hit. I needed to figure out how I would spin the truth this time.

The murder, or death of the Don's son, would be high profile news. The rumors and gossip would spread like gangrene infecting the country with meaningless speculation. I could ill afford reflection being cast on the Don himself. He would have to stay far removed from any reproach or the casting of guilt.

Myself, I needed to remain invisible while killing the man whose life I had saved so many years ago. The simple irony of it made me breathless. If only there were a way to travel back in time and right wrongs.

But would things have worked out as they had if that moment in time had gone differently? Would I ever have met Brenda, got married, and had a family, if I never realized how valuable those things really were? And why did I need to experience the worst this life had to offer before appreciating the best it had to extend?

Brenda had come into the club that night, and it wasn't love at first sight, but I knew there was something between us. I had grown up in a family with a mother and father who truly loved each other—who had the perfect marriage. I originally turned my back on the predictability that came with latching your soul to another's.

I was guarding the door to the back room that sheltered Pietro from the rest of the world—a promotion, he had termed it. Long behind me were the days of carding underage patrons and turning away the wannabes. My job, on top of being a hitman for the Russos, was at times to be a protector of the Don himself. For a while, I took great pride in the advancement. At least until life seemed to have other plans for me.

Brenda had stumbled down the hallway, more than a little intoxicated. Her steps were uncertain, her hands reached for the wall. A finger pointed to the room I stood in front of.

"You guard the lady's room?" She smiled at me. At that moment, something inside switched over. But the reaction was relatively subtle. Her eyes were a piercing green and seemed to refract the light as intoxication danced in them.

"Are you going to move? I really have to... go." She started bouncing. The laugh faded and transformed into a heart stalling smile.

"Washrooms are around the corner. There." I pointed and clasped my hands in front. The woman didn't seem to pose any threat.

She didn't move. Instead, she heaved over, doubled in half, and vomited on my shoes. Now for most men that would seal the deal. Any feelings that may have started to stir would be finished with that action. For me, well, I was a different person. I was used to bodily fluids, mainly blood, being spilled in my presence. A little bile wasn't too much of a deterrent. But the smell—that took my composure.

"I'm so sorry." She held a hand over her mouth as she spoke. Flirtation paraded in her eyes.

I nodded toward another man who stepped in to guard the door. I placed a hand on her arm. She felt so fragile under my touch. For some strange reason, at that moment, I knew I wanted to get to know her.

"You have a gun." She pointed at the .22 in my holster.

"Come on." I kept moving, trying to convince her to start up again. Her feet remained grounded.

"Why do you need a gun to guard a bathroom?" She smiled sheepishly, and I wondered if she knew more than she was letting on. For an instant, I feared for the safety of the Don. She could have been sent in as a diversion tactic.

"I hate guns, but you're cute—"

"Brenda!"

We almost made it to the women's washroom when a lady with thick glasses and a bob cut came hurrying toward her. "You all right?" She eyed me suspiciously and took her friend out of my reach. I let go reluctantly.

"She'll be all right now." I pointed behind us to the vomit on the floor.

Brenda nodded. "He's right." She looked at me for the last time that night. Her smile slightly askew, but nonetheless, perfect.

Something else inside triggered. Maybe I'd had this lifestyle for long enough. It was possible for this line of work to eat one alive and spit out nothing but a corpse. I would go out on my terms. I spent the next few months trying to hunt Brenda down and I never regretted it.

Coming back to the present, my heart ached that she was with Christian and his men. They better not have laid one hand on her. Lifting my cell to an ear, I listened to her message again. Despite the hurt and anger that registered in her voice, in some way it drew her back to me.

Christian would die. He would pay for his sins. And he wouldn't see it coming.

CHAPTER FIFTY-ONE

Chimes sounded when Clinton opened the door to the motel office. Ronny, who pretty much just graduated the academy, sat beside Edwin Taylor, The Oasis's manager. Taylor held on to a paper coffee cup and stared into the brew.

"Detectives." Ronny stood and approached Clinton and Wingham. He hoisted up on his pants as if they were a few sizes too large.

Clinton self-consciously placed one hand on his stomach thinking he could lose a few pounds. It had been a while since he had to pull up on any clothing. Maybe it was an adolescent reaction to hormonal levels jacked through his body from his having been in heat over a woman who likely wouldn't pass him a second glance. He had two ex-wives, and they were enough to prove love and he didn't mix.

Clinton pointed to the side at what served as a lobby. The business name might conjure up a luxurious hotel in Las Vegas, but this dive was far from it. A sofa, which likely dated back to the sixties, sat across from a pale laminate counter. A bell sat on it in the case the door chimes hadn't been enough to notify the working clerk he had a guest. The plastic fern in a corner pot catered a solid layer of dust.

Clinton asked Ronny, "What's he telling you?"

"He came by to check on the guy. Said he left in a taxi and then he heard a noise. Thought he'd check it out—"

"It wasn't the guy!" The raised voice came from Taylor. He sat down the cup; his beady eyes danced over the three of them.

Wingham dropped her notepad to the height of her thigh but lifted it when Clinton motioned for her to continue taking notes. Clinton walked over to the manager.

"What do you mean it wasn't him?" Clinton remembered Murray had mentioned something about that. He placed his hands on his hips, latching a thumb on the waistband.

"Just as I said. It wasn't him." His hand went back for the cup, but when he noticed it was empty, he placed it on the counter. "The man who checked in two days ago." He paused, shook his head. "Heck, he was here from Friday to Saturday, checked out, and then came back this morning. I hardly had time to know he had checked out before he was back."

Clinton and Wingham shared a look. Clinton didn't know what Wingham was thinking, but his mind went to Tux. He was at The Grandeur on Friday—coincidence?

The door chimed when Ronny stepped outside to join Murray.

"Let me get this straight. The man who was here this morning was here Friday and Saturday but had also checked out before showing up again this morning?"

The man nodded. "He had a gun too. I saw it on his waist. Never saw one in person before today. Can't say I liked it much."

This could be the guy they were looking for. Clinton motioned for Wingham to take out a picture of Tux, courtesy of The Grandeur security cameras. "He look familiar to you?" Clinton knew it would be a stretch with the man avoiding the camera head on. But even if the manager could relate to similarities in size and stature between his guest and the unidentified man it would give them something.

Taylor barely acknowledged the photo. His eyes lifted and his face scrunched. "This guy ain't got no face, eh."

"Do you have a name for us?" It seemed like an obvious question, but Clinton didn't put too much weight on it. No assassin worth his weight would disclose his real name—yet most professional assassins never missed with the first bullet.

"He paid cash up front. I'm sorry." He stopped talking; his eyes widened. "Actually, I do have a name. Peter Williams, I think it was. Yes, that's it." Taylor rambled and spoke low as if he was having a conversation with himself.

Wingham scribbled the name down in her lined pad and nodded to Clinton that she got it.

"So this guy, Peter Williams—" Clinton rolled a hand, "—checked in, checked out, and then checked back in again. This time with a gun."

"Yeah, I found it strange. I didn't get his name the first time like I said. He paid cash." Taylor paused, seemingly hesitant whether to continue. "Someone else paid for his room today. Said it was important to have room 11. That was the room Peter was in on Friday and Saturday. The person who booked it today said it was for a friend."

"Can you describe this person for us?"

Taylor shook his head. "Just an average guy. Nothing that stood out. Brown hair, brown eyes. He paid cash too."

"Anything else you can tell us? Did Peter Williams register a car with you at any point?"

"I don't care about getting that info from people, but I watch. He did have a car. It was a rental. It had green stickers on the back window and on the bumper."

"License plate? Name of the rental company?"

"Didn't get the plate, but it was Streamline Rentals. It was a modern silver sedan. I'm not up on all my vehicles."

Clinton turned to Wingham. "Streamline's main location is at the airport. My guess is he swapped his ride for a new one. He probably did it when he got in on Friday."

"On it." She took out her phone.

"Anything else you can tell us?" Clinton asked Taylor.

"Well, that was on Friday. Today, he showed up in this fancy Town Car. A Lincoln, I believe. I know what they look like. But he left in a taxi. Been seeing some strange things lately."

"Strange things?"

"You mean besides that? Well, he wasn't here long before he called the taxi. That idiot almost run me over. Was standing right there." The manager moved forward and pointed out the window toward the doorway to room 11.

"He took all his luggage with him. I mean who checks into the same motel, out, and back into the same room all within, what, thirty-six hours? And then, when he comes back, leaves within an hour. Doesn't make sense."

Clinton shook his head. "It doesn't at all." At least that's what he said aloud. Internally, it made relative sense. In Clinton's mind Tux, or Peter Williams, was the hired assassin they were looking for. But it still didn't explain why he'd return. Clinton compiled the possibilities, each of them stacking on top of each other and melding together. It only took a fraction of time before he realized something. The assassin had returned to finish the job, or he would be the one to pay for the failure.

I'll be damned.

Wingham hung up her phone and addressed Clinton, "Can I talk to you for a minute out—?"

The door chimed.

"Keeping me out of the loop again I see," Agent Leone said.

"This discovery stays out of the media, understand?"

Leone rolled his eyes.

Clinton noticed there was something different about the man. Just the way he carried himself and stood there with his back straighter than before. With his jaw locked and his head slightly cocked to the side, Clinton wondered if he went and paid a twenty dollar hooker to bolster his self-esteem and feed his narcissistic ego.

Something about the man, Clinton just didn't trust.

CHAPTER FIFTY-TWO

"I reached Streamline Rentals and the name came back to Peter Williams. The address matches the one on file for Rick Carson," Wingham said.

Clinton let out a sigh. "The abandoned warehouse."

"Well, at least it tells us they are connected even if in a roundabout way."

They were standing outside of The Oasis motel office. Edwin Taylor, the ex-Canadian manager, had poured himself another cup of muddy brew from a carafe before they excused themselves. Leone came outside with them but stood there like an ape in Clinton's opinion. His arms were crossed; his eyes were glazed over as if he wished to be someplace else.

"Maybe you want to come back to the crime scene," Clinton said.

Leone's eyes dragged across the parking lot and slowly aligned with Clinton's eyes. "You want input from me now?"

Clinton sighed and rolled his eyes. He knew the action was dramatic, but nonetheless it was the honest reaction to how he felt about the man—Special Agent Leone was a toddler in a suit.

"Have you even stopped to ask yourself some questions?" Leone tapped a hand to his shirt pocket and then to his pants' pockets. He mustn't have found what he was looking for based on the deepened frown lines. "For example, why Behler was targeted in the first place. Why she was here meeting with Talbot. Why the first assassination attempt failed."

"Of course—"

"Why a body suddenly appears that is tied to your case."

Clinton noticed the disdain tagged to *your case*.

"What you're looking at detectives is something outside of your pay grade." The patting down of pockets stopped, and Leone pulled out a pack of cigarettes. He popped one out of the sleeve. He perched it in his lips, letting it bob there as he continued, "We're looking at organized crime."

"Organized crime?" Clinton intended it to sound as if he was shocked by the agent's assessment. Instead his tone betrayed him.

"You were leaning that way?" Leone paused, lighting the cigarette with such a deep drag that his cheeks concaved. "Impressive."

"They don't normally touch dignitaries. It goes against everything they stand for."

Leone laughed while tapping the cigarette ash to the ground. "You think you have it all figured out."

"Well, the Mafia slant would explain a lot of things," Wingham said. Both men turned to her, and she shrugged. Clinton noticed excitement flash in Leone's eyes. "The killer knew she had something on her phone. She was here to meet with Talbot, unofficial business. So we assume otherwise, that the phone didn't hold anything important, why would the killer take it?"

Leone exhaled a cloud of white pollution in Clinton's direction.

Clinton waved it out of his face. "If you would kindly blow the other way."

Leone put special effort into the next exhale, directing it toward Clinton intentionally, letting it out in a slow, even flow.

"Would you guys focus? Please." Wingham had reached her patience threshold. "If you guys put as much effort into the case as pissing each other off we'd have found the assassin already."

Clinton locked eyes with Leone. "The body in that motel room had the words TSK TSK carved into the chest. The blood around it indicates the guy was alive when they created their artwork. I don't think we're dealing with the same killer who shot the Governor."

Leone continued taking slow drags on the cigarette, but without another reaction from Clinton, blew the smoke to the side.

The attitude coming off Leone told Clinton he hated being at a dive like this motel and that he had high standards. Clinton looked down at Leone's shoes and noticed there wasn't one scruff mark on the black leather. They shined as if they were just polished. Clinton's shoes were beige loafers, a purchase from two years ago.

"I don't think the guy—Tux you call him—killed the guy in that motel room. But I do believe he was involved somehow with the assassination of the Governor." Leone took one deep inhale before tossing the cigarette to the concrete and extinguishing it with a twist of his shoe. "And normal criminals don't hack off fingers and ears, let alone the nose. The brutality of the crime tells me this guy pissed someone off—"

"No shit Sherlock."

The comeback surprised Clinton. He turned to Wingham, who spoke the words. Determination crackled in her eyes. She continued, "Maybe our DB was the first assassin—the attempt that failed? Then this other guy was called in to finish the job."

"I don't know—" Clinton was going to add that he didn't buy that assessment. He felt both men were involved, but that Tux was the one who pulled the trigger, both times.

Leone said, "Figure out the why, you'll get the killer."

"Normally we work the other way, Agent," Clinton added a tone when he threw out the man's title. "We go after the bad guy. If the motivation fills in along the way so be it, but it's not the case." Clinton left Leone and went back in with the manager. Wingham followed.

Edwin Taylor was sitting on the sofa staring at the wall.

"Mr. Taylor." Clinton sat beside him.

His head turned slowly in acknowledgment of his name.

"We have more questions for you."

The older man sat up straighter. "Can I call my wife first? Let her know what's going on."

Clinton shook his head. "There will be plenty of time for that later. Right now we need you to tell us if you know anything else. You mentioned a taxi almost hit you."

His head went up, then down.

"Did you notice the number on the cab, a license plate, anything?"

"The driver wasn't Indian."

Clinton's eyes blinked hard, a headache setting in on the back side of them.

"You know how that's the stereotype, eh?" He took a sip, his teeth forming a perfect mold on the paper cup.

Clinton dragged a hand down his face, doing his best to conjure patience, but there was nothing to tap into. "Anything else?" He knew he sounded exasperated. He was. He didn't care if the Canadian picked up on it.

The man's head stayed straight forward and for a moment, Clinton wondered if he was still breathing, but he noticed the rise and fall of the man's shoulders.

"I smacked his hood—of the taxi. I think the number was 623."

"Do you know what company?" Clinton asked.

Taylor scrunched his face. "Falls Taxi, I believe."

Clinton looked at Wingham who already had a phone to her ear. He looked back at Taylor after passing a glance outside. Clinton moved to get a better view. Agent Leone had left again. Maybe he had gone back to the room. The first time the man came out after seeing the body, his expression was stoic. It could have been how he operated—keeping himself at an emotional distance to do the job.

That's how Clinton had started out originally, but he found it ate him from the inside out like cancer. Anyone in public service had to find a way to suppress their human emotions in a traumatic situation while balancing them with action, or it could come back to haunt you later.

For Leone, Clinton believed it was something else. Exactly what that was escaped his understanding, yet the man showed more alarm over the dead Governor than a mutilated body. That wasn't a normal human response.

Wingham cupped her phone and spoke to Clinton, "We've got him. The taxi's in the garage."

Clinton noticed the brief panic on Taylor's face as if to say, *I didn't do any damage to it.*

She must have picked up on the look too. "For maintenance. But we have the driver's name and address."

Clinton pressed his hands to his thighs as he rose from the sofa. He hated how small things such as bending or getting up from a seated position made his joints bark. Some days he felt his fifty-two years more than others.

"Detectives," Taylor called out to them in a weak voice.

Both of them stopped at the door.

"The Town Car. It was black, dark tint. I didn't catch the driver or pay much attention anyhow. He wasn't the one who nearly hit me. But I did notice the lettering on the back window. It was swirly and kind of hard to read."

Clinton's foot started tapping.

"It said Professional Car Service."

CHAPTER FIFTY-THREE

Detroit, Michigan
Sunday, June 13th, 10:00 PM
7 Hours Until the Deadline

Over the last couple of hours, I studied the private hangar from the Google maps and my memory, drafting out an approach plan onto paper.

In concept, killing Christian was simple. It was the other stipulations that complicated everything. I kept glancing over at the reports from the file that had been on Behler's phone. I knew that if I utilized some of that knowledge, I should be well on my way to handling the situation. If I could pin the assassination directly on Christian, make it clear he was acting separately from his father, I'd have the golden solution. My mind, maybe blame it on the lack of sleep, wasn't firing at full capacity.

In my fantasy version of the situation, I would go in with guns blazing and rescue my family. No one but us would survive the hail of bullets.

Right now, I was hoping that in Niagara Falls, New York, a body was being discovered at The Oasis motel. Pietro had been more than willing to respond to my request and stipulations. His face lit into a sinister smile when I told him where I wanted the body. He said he'd arrange for it immediately. With the inscription on the torso, past cases would eventually lead detectives straight to Christian.

I held no fear of being tracked down from prints or DNA as I cleaned down the place each time before leaving. At least, my logic told me that I had no need to worry. The other part kept drowning in the what ifs. What if I had left my prints behind either at the motel or at the apartment?

When time came to a pause, it had a way of making one rehash everything. They would find no trace of me and only find what they were intended to—proof to use against Christian.

. . .

Niagara Falls, New York

The taxi driver was a man named Mario Downe. The three of them, Clinton, Wingham, and Leone tracked him down at his house where his curious wife hovered over them. Clinton could tell she controlled her husband, wanting to know his every word and movement. Just another reason Clinton would never remarry. Once a woman knew she was chosen, she latched on with a death grip. He swore he still had lesions on his back from the last one.

Mario told them that his fare directed him to the bus station. "He had a lot of luggage. But he wouldn't let me help him. Oh." His eyes enlarged. "And he had a huge gun on his waist. I asked him if he was a hunter."

Clinton and Wingham shared a glance. The man was potentially a hunter but not the kind Mario had in mind.

The couple sat on the couch with Clinton and Wingham sitting on a facing one, while Leone paced the modest living room, touching framed photos. The wife kept an eye on him.

"Did he tell you where he was going?" Clinton asked.

"No, he wasn't the chatty kind. Sometimes it's hard to get a fare to shut up. This guy didn't want to say a word. He didn't seem to like the attention so I didn't push."

Clinton wouldn't want attention if he were the assassin. It was a matter of being as discreet as possible, slinking through crowds undetected.

CHAPTER FIFTY-FOUR

I parked the car three-quarters of a mile away from the hangar. The dash read ten thirty and for a June evening, the sun had fully set about nine. Six and a half hours remained on Christian's original deadline.

The drink Pietro Russo had given me continued to provide energy. Any light-headedness, or tingling in my arms and legs, had long subsided. My eyes were finally accepting they wouldn't be closing for a while. It meant my life. It meant my family's lives. While the passing thought of sleeping for an hour had occurred to me, there was too much to organize and prepare for.

I had placed my .44 in a chest holster and covered it with a lightweight jacket. The bulge was noticeable, making it appear that I had gained an extra ten pounds. Yet the night air was damp and chilly. A light fog hung over the fields and the ominous call of a screech owl carried overhead. It reassured my decision to bring the jacket and the larger gun.

On my waist, I wore a double holster, a .22 secured on each side. Over the years, I had worked on perfecting my aim with both hands. In fact, I could accurately shoot on target, firing a .22 in each hand, and have them meet at the board. I also had an ankle holster strapped to my leg with a .22 there as well.

I took one last look at the car before I walked down into the ditch and started through a cornfield. The stalks were only a foot high—nowhere near enough to provide cover. But that's why I also dressed entirely in black and waited until nightfall.

While I had never served in the military, I knew how to approach undercover without being spotted. After all that was part of the job for the Russos—to be invisible. To survive until now that had been a requirement. A quarter of the men I had been hired to take out were armed men themselves.

The field was uneven and the dirt was loose. My ankle gave way for an instant and threw off my stride. I had a GPS on me and a small flashlight that I used to guide me in the right direction.

The car had been placed in a concealed area that wouldn't draw any attention from law enforcement if one happened to drive by.

Everything was taken care of so why did I feel hesitant and find my feet planting in the dirt? I braced over like a man winded and in need of catching his breath. Both my hands gripped my thighs, and I stayed there willing myself to garner strength. My family was in that building, and I was their only hope.

Thinking of them only weighed me down further instead of propelling me into action. What if they were already gone? I had failed as far as Christian was concerned. News reports continued to say the Governor was on the mend.

Taking a deep breath, I made myself move. Nothing would change by my standing here. Pietro Russo had made it clear Christian must die, and I must be the one to do it. I still didn't hold any trust in the fact he would restore my family to me when it was all over, even though the man had said he would. Normally the word of the Italians was as good as fulfilled. Lately, I believed nothing. I had to take care of everything myself.

Until I could prove Behler was dead, Christian would hold my family for leverage. I had to trust in the fact that despite the man being unpredictable, he loved to have the power. He would allow my family to live if only to manipulate me.

As I went through the field, I watched my breath exhale as wisps of white. The night was quiet in the country and dark, unlike the city where the street lights overpowered the moon. Out here only the strobe of my small flashlight weaved among the corn, and a partial moon lit the field. There weren't even any stars on display tonight. The sky was overcast, and the air felt damp and spoke of impending rain.

There was a faint ringing and I dug into a pocket for my cell. The lit LCD screen was almost blinding in contrast to the darkened field. The caller identity read CR. Maybe I didn't need to go through with any of this. Maybe the news had finally come out with the truth—Behler was dead. Christian could want to arrange the return of my family. I pressed the accept button yet said nothing.

"Now you want to play games?" His Italian accent carried heavily. An amusement-type quality lingered in his voice. He enjoyed being the one with the power. Little did he know his reign would be short-lived.

I didn't know what he referred to by his reference to my playing games. Had he found out about the body at The Oasis somehow?

"Where is my family?"

Christian laughed. "We're back to that again, are we? You amuse me, Hunter. But you always have."

"Why are you calling?" I could picture him held up in the private hangar, a knife waving erratically in his hand as if he was bored. He sought me for entertainment. I was tired of being the jester.

"Maybe I know something now," he said.

I stopped walking.

"Let them go." My left hand went to the bulge of the .44. I knew it was overkill, but I would bask in blowing a hole in the man's head.

"There's one more thing you must do for me."

My teeth clenched; my grip on the cell phone tightened. "I'm not doing this anymore."

Christian let out a laugh as if it was a joke I told that he found funny. "You do what I tell you to do. You report to me; I have your family."

I held my cell away from my ear and looked at the time counter. If Christian had any intentions of tracing this call, I had twenty-five seconds left.

"What do you want from me?"

"We meet. Now."

A cool breeze moved through the field. The small cornstalks swayed and the sliver of the moon went behind a cloud.

I said, "In an hour."

Christian remained silent on the other end.

"One hour," I repeated the stipulation. If my plan went according to schedule, I'd have my family back and be meeting with Christian to put a bullet in his head.

Dogs snarled and screams riddled the air. The voice was a woman's—Brenda's. My stomach curdled.

They are here!

"What did I just hear, Hunter?"

Shit! He heard the sound come back to him through my phone.

"You don't boss me, Hunter. Half hour at the hangar."

"Christian!" The connection lost, my word fell to an empty line.

Any fear of not succeeding, of being played a fool, of losing my family to a madman was eradicated. The screams of my wife served to embitter me, to fuel the indignation that rose like fissures in the earth's crust. Christian had picked the wrong man to pull out of retirement.

CHAPTER FIFTY-FIVE

The three of them stood in the bus station without any new leads. None of the staff members at the ticket counters recognized the figure in the grainy photo or acknowledged seeing a man loaded down with baggage and a large gun holstered on his waist.

Wingham hit a vending machine and popped opened a bag of Doritos and offered the men some.

"You're serious? At a time like this?" Clinton was always amazed by the contrast between his partner's appetite and her waist size. Most women would hate her for the ability to eat whatever she wished while remaining a size ten.

"I'm hungry…at a time like this." She stuffed a few in her mouth and forged a smile with bulging cheeks.

"So what do we know?" Clinton asked.

"You're one of those."

Clinton looked to Leone. "Is there something else you'd rather be doing?"

"Listen, we know who's involved. The Italians. Chasing down this guy who wore a tux—oh, huge crime, punishable by law, by the way—is a waste of our man hours."

"Is there something you should be telling us?"

Leone patted his jacket pocket and came out with his pack of cigarettes. He put one in his lips but never lit it. In Clinton's view, it served as a soother does to a baby.

"I've seen it before." The cigarette bobbed up and down as he spoke. "Tsk tsk."

"And you're telling us now?" Wingham scrunched up the emptied bag of chips.

"I tried to tell you before but you guys didn't want to listen to me. It's like I have nothing to offer."

Clinton improvised sniffles at the end of Leone's statement. Suck back on the soother a little harder.

Leone took the cigarette out of his mouth and held it in his fingers as if it were lit. "There was a family in Detroit. Fifteen years ago, give or take. Dad worked at a law firm, nothing luxurious, just a clerk working his way up, but he had a betting habit. He owed the wrong people."

"The Mafia," Wingham filled in.

Leone disregarded Wingham and glanced to Clinton. "No one survived. Two kids, ten and sixteen. The kids were shot; the wife was raped and then shot. The father was found in an apartment he kept just for entertaining other women, with knife wounds like the ones on the man in that motel room. The words TSK TSK were carved into his flesh. He was then fed a bullet for good measure."

"They never caught the guy?" Wingham was determined to stay involved regardless of whether Leone gave her any merit. Clinton respected her attitude.

"The guy who did it was the Don's son, think The Godfather." Leone kept his eyes on Clinton who got his point, the Don, or Mob Boss. "You don't find proof when it's someone like that. Of course, we went as far as the investigation would allow us, but the roadblocks were sky high."

"He got away with four murders." Wingham's voice was low.

Leone's head snapped to her. "I assure you the body count is much higher than that."

Wingham rebutted, "It still doesn't make much sense. The Mafia typically leaves dignitaries alone. Aren't they more likely to buy them off than kill them?"

"It's not unheard of. But, Christian Russo, that's the Don's son, has been wanting his father's power for a long time. Rumor is the Don, Pietro is his name, has no intention of passing his power on anytime soon. And when he does go, he already has a successor chosen."

"Not his son," Clinton said.

Leone shook his head.

"Sounds like motive if we could figure out exactly how Behler fits in."

"Uh huh. But I didn't think you cared about the why." Leone slapped Clinton with his words from earlier in the day.

"You know a lot about the Russo family," Clinton said.

"Yes, and The Detroit Partnership. There are a few Italian families in the Michigan area. They all work together." Leone's eyes matched with Clinton's. "Yes, I know this assassin crosses state borders. But so does the Italian Mafia. They adhere to what they term The Commission. They help each other out when needed."

Clinton did his best to read the agent's eyes, yet they were deep and withheld more than he was willing to grant access to. As Clinton studied him, Leone did likewise.

If Leone knew the crime crossed state borders, what made him hold back from going up the power ladder? And why did Governor Talbot want the investigation to remain on a local level? If Clinton was the state Governor where the assassination happened, and the murder was of a colleague, he would stop at nothing to get the killer found. Yet Governor Talbot had been brief and direct with his comments.

Clinton thought back to their first meeting at the hospital. He was even possibly a little scared. But scared of what? While some answers were filling in with pencil, even more remained as blank underscores. There would be no more putting it off. They needed to speak with Talbot.

. . .

Outskirts of Detroit, Michigan
6 Hours Until the Deadline

Brenda and I had always told the kids that there's no such thing as the bogeyman. While Brenda was convinced she told our kids the truth, my life history had taught me otherwise. There was such a thing. In fact, he was even worse than the monster from the closet or under the bed.

The recent screams from Brenda and the proof of life video blurred together. My steps quickened as I made large strides through the uneven rows of dirt, pushing aside fledgling stalks of corn. The night air clung and hung over the field like a suffocating blanket. The humidity kept the fog at chest level. I was thankful for the added cover.

The approach I had chosen was from the side of the hangar. I hoped there would be less security and vigilance if I came in from the side opposite the house and driveway. I anticipated there would be men guarding the front of the hangar at night, especially with Christian on the premises. I expected they would conduct occasional sweeps to the sides. And thanks to Google Earth, I saw cameras mounted on the front of the building.

My flashlight danced on the cornstalks. Looking back, I could no longer see where I had parked. Faint lights ahead indicated I was getting closer to the hangar. The time had come to get my family back.

I crouched low and traveled the remaining distance like a marine carrying out a special ops mission. In a sense, this was mine. While I was no marine, I had an objective, and I would carry it out. And to do so would require intellect and patience.

CHAPTER FIFTY-SIX

"You believe the son of a mob boss carried out the assassination?" Clinton directed the question to Leone.

"Directly, or indirectly—moot point. You can bet he was involved." Leone flipped a lighter out of his pocket. Wingham placed a hand over the agent's to stop him from raising his arm.

"Not here you don't." She locked her hazel eyes with Leone, who dropped his arm.

"The man in the photograph, is he this Christian you mentioned?" Clinton asked.

Leone's eyes ignited with a flame of intense heat. "When you're the Don's son, you don't have to do anything yourself. You have people to take care of things for you. If Christian does something, it's simply for his pleasure. He's more into torture than snuffing life. He has a means of overpowering people. Making them see his way, if you know what I mean. Manipulation may be the better word."

"Bribery." The word came off Wingham's tongue.

"Possible. The promise of harm to a family member, or to the killer himself. He also has an unlimited means of money at his disposal. If we go to him, we'll get the answers," Leone said.

"And you expect to waltz in and be granted free access?" Clinton scoffed. "This is ludicrous. You're rushing an investigation in one direction when all the facts haven't even been gathered. Crime Scene hasn't even fully processed the forensic evidence from the motel. And there's still Gamer's apartment—"

"If you wish to spend a lifetime on this, then that is your choice. However, I can't see your boss being really happy about it." Leone flicked the lighter and headed in the direction of the doors.

"Oh, that man infuriates me. He thinks he knows everything," Wingham said.

"Maybe he knows more than we're giving him credit for."

"What do you mean?"

"What I mean is." Clinton took a pause. "Why hasn't he gone up the ladder, got the case reassigned to the FBI? At first he seemed eager to make that happen. Now, well, he's back in the deep end of the pool with both feet and his swimming trunks."

Wingham's eyelashes fluttered, and Clinton noticed her sigh.

"It's just a word picture."

"Well, don't give up your day job." She smiled. "Continue."

"I realize there's new evidence in the case with Carson being mutilated, which may have been the cause of this—" Clinton rolled his hand while he searched for the right word. It escaped him. "This change of direction with Leone. But he's been different since he left us at the apartment and came back."

"You don't trust him? He's FBI."

"Yes, I know *what* he is, but I don't know *who* he is. Get me?"

"Not exactly. No." Wingham gave him the face she would when she was lost for what to say, or when she wanted to understand but couldn't. Her eyebrows sagged like a tired hound and her mouth turned slightly downward.

Clinton exhaled a rushed breath. "Never mind then. We still have a case to solve." He took a look around at people as they waited for their bus to come. Most of them appeared exhausted.

A mother with a young child sat on a nearby bench. She couldn't get him to sit beside her. When she reached for him, he let out a wail.

Observations like this made Clinton satisfied with his decision not to have any children. Some would view the choice as selfish. To him, he felt it representative of the opposite. To bring a child into the world where they wouldn't be adequately cared for was a greater sin.

"Before Captain America—"

"Would you stop that? He could hear you." Wingham glanced to where Leone stood outside sucking on the cancer stick like it would save his life, not end it prematurely.

"And how could he hear me?"

Wingham shrugged.

"As I was saying. We know our guy didn't board a bus or buy a ticket, so why take a taxi to a bus station. It doesn't make any sense."

"He could have done it to throw the investigation off his tail. Say if he assumed we'd get this far, it wouldn't make sense for him to take the taxi from The Oasis straight to the hospital, or the apartment where he did the shooting."

"Slight detour."

"Exactly." Wingham smiled as if she solved the case. "He likely took another cab from here and good luck tracking that down."

"Taxi." Clinton let the one word sit there and marinate. "The taxi driver mentioned the fare had baggage. He wouldn't want to go hauling that all over—"

The child screamed again, sending instant irritation through Clinton's bloodstream. The mother yanked on the child's arm and placed him on the bench. A wildly pointed finger wagged in front of his face. As Clinton watched the mother discipline the boy, his attention on them blurred when he noticed what was behind them.

CHAPTER FIFTY-SEVEN

Outskirts of Detroit, Michigan
Sunday, June 13th, 11:15 PM
Just Under 6 Hours Until the Deadline

Darkness changed perception. In the day, the hangar appeared large yet somehow more vulnerable. At night, lights from the building cast an eerie glow as it mingled with the haze that covered the fields around it. It made me think of horror movies where teenagers rent a cabin on a lake and a fog hovers over the water. It was all about surroundings and setting to make the scene just right. The fact that my present circumstances made me think of hack-em-and-sack-em movies wasn't reassuring. I would do my best not to have any of that come to fruition.

I remembered my foolish assumption that Brenda would never find out and that neither she nor the kids be affected. How wrong I had been.

They were in that building. Not only had Brenda's scream disclosed that, but I could feel they were close in the depth of my being. They say that it's possible to feel the pain of a loved one, how those really connected can feel when their loved one has passed. In my soul, I felt they were all alive. Yet with that came the intense pain in my chest that told me they were suffering. My wife both physically and mentally—she likely wondered who her husband was.

I believed the screams were a ploy for me, a manipulation tactic to help realign me, and remind me that Christian was in charge. I was simply a pawn on his chessboard. The video that showed my daughter and wife being ogled by a man was also a tactic to weaken me and to keep me in line. I had never been one to play by the rules.

Even as an only child in a religious family, I couldn't bring myself to bring my parents joy. My ideals in life didn't align with theirs, despite my attempts to see things from their angle. I had a hard time accepting that prayer and a Greater Being could be the answer to our problems. Yet at a time like this, I almost considered a small prayer—not that I would know where to start. I realized the hypocrisy of it. How could I pray for the safe return of my family and myself when I wouldn't hesitate to take life? I would kill everyone if it were necessary.

I lowered to the ground and since the fog hovered above it about two to three feet, it afforded me a clear view between it and the top of the stalks. Two figures were outlined against the front of the building. I recognized the larger stature of the one. He had been outside Christian's house the night I had let myself inside. If I remembered correctly, the one from the front had called him Carlos. I was surprised he was still on this side of the ground. He must have been a tremendous asset to Christian—gullible and malleable.

The other man paced around. He said something to Carlos; I heard the voice but couldn't discern what was said.

I closed the distance another ten yards. Neither man looked in my direction. The lights were bright on the building and cast a glare over the fields. The men were little more than silhouettes. But I could make out that both of them were carrying. Based on shadows only, they were AK-47s.

"I just got to go. Nothing's happening." His words carried across the field this time.

"We're not to move. That's the rules," Carlos said.

He was definitely an asset to Christian. He always valued those who bent at the knee and followed every command.

"I just have to fuckin' pee!"

"Piss your pants! I don't care! You don't move!" An arm jabbed downward.

"Fuck you." The guy walked away.

"Get back here now!"

The smaller silhouette kept moving and went around the other side of the hangar.

My attention went to the back end of the building. My hope was that with so much attention being paid to the front side, the back would lay exposed. The plan was to sweep out far enough in the field and then work my way down the side.

A pain bit in my lower back, seizing me motionless. I had to straighten out or risk becoming locked in this position. If I stood up, I risked something worse—being spotted. But I didn't have much of an option. The body wasn't what it used to be. Years had taxed the joints and bones, only reaffirming the fact I was no longer in my twenties.

Carlos's back was to me. I placed two hands on my lower back and talked myself through the process of straightening up.

With a sharp spasm threatening to stop me, I discounted it and headed toward the hangar. I had to close the rest of the distance. My family was in there; I could feel it even more so the nearer I got.

My breath heaved when I reached the side of the building. A plane was on the tarmac and I could hear voices. I couldn't see anyone. That was a dangerous combination. I pressed flat against the aluminum exterior of the building; the metal was cool through my light jacket yet soothing to the ache in my back.

The conversation continued among a few men. The words that made it through to me were, *he, Niagara Falls*, and *he just got back.* I couldn't be certain as I received the discussion piecemeal, but the inflection in their voices made me assume the he they referred to was Christian. But the rest of it didn't make a lot of sense. Why would he have gone to Niagara Falls?

A wave of a relief blanketed over me. I knew it was a premature, irrational response to an emotional journey I had been subjected to, but maybe he went to determine that the Governor was, in fact, dead. Or was there more to it? Why not just call a contact there?

Maybe he wanted to restore my family to me. The elation crashed with the recollection of his words, *there's one more thing you must do for me.*

CHAPTER FIFTY-EIGHT

"Bingo!" Clinton clapped his hands together.

Wingham followed his gaze to the row of lockers.

"Think about it for a moment. Tux had baggage, he couldn't take it with him. It makes perfect sense." Clinton felt the burning start at the base of his stomach and work its way through him.

"We need in those lockers," she said.

Clinton's back was already to her, his large strides stopping in front of a customer service counter.

"We can't let you in the lockers. That's a violation of human rights." The night manager locked his arms in front of his chest. An average-sized man with small lips whom Clinton guessed was normally mild natured. "If you can get a warrant, some sort of court order—"

"There's no time for one," Clinton said.

"Then, I'm sorry, but I can't help you. It's not rational, or ethical, for us to go along breaking off the locks." He stopped talking, his eyes saying, *how do I even know you're real cops.*

They didn't have time for this. The longer the killer walked, the colder the trail. The real news about the Governor would be hitting the news tomorrow night. Clinton received the call earlier in the evening from the Police Chief. It was a reminder of the deadline and that if he didn't have a solid lead or the case solved by then, he might as well hand in his gun for a desk job.

Leone walked up to them. "What's going on?"

The manager looked at him as if to say, *now who is this?*

Clinton introduced him to speed things along.

"As I was telling him," the manager started.

Clinton picked up on the underlying degradation. Now that the manager had an official FBI agent in front of him, a major crimes detective wasn't near as exciting.

"We can't start opening lockers."

"Detective Clinton, can we talk a minute?" Leone came close to placing a hand on Clinton's shoulder but obviously thought better of it. The smell of cigarette smoke clung to his clothing as a saturated stick of incense.

Clinton placed a hand over his holster, the thought of killing the Mr. Special Agent flitting through his mind. He jacked a thumb back toward the counter. "You better have one damned good reason—"

"He would have come back for his belongings."

"And what makes you such an expert on everything?"

"Think about it. Why haul stuff around if it wasn't important?"

The simple logic stole Clinton's words. Maybe he was more exhausted than he realized.

"I've told you what our next best lead is."

"I'm not giving up on this case because of some hunch you have."

"It's not a hunch. It's based on fact and calculation. This is organized crime. Whether you wish to accept this fact or not, doesn't change the truth—"

Clinton's cell phone rang. The two men held eye contact as Clinton answered. He kept his face expressionless as the news being relayed to him came from the forensics lab. He glanced at Wingham, who had remained with the manager. They were talking about something that was more pleasing to the man as he had a smile and was laughing. Clinton even detected a slight reddish hue on the man's cheeks.

About forty seconds later, he hung up.

"What was all that about?" Leone asked.

"Wingham," Clinton called for his partner who excused herself and came over. "I just got a call from the lab. The room at The Oasis has been processed. Zero prints."

"Not sure why you expected any. The guy's a professional," Leone said.

"All of this is definitely connected. We need to find out more about this Rolex guy, Rick Carson, dig into his life." Clinton passed a glance to Leone. He knew he could call Detroit PD, but wanted to limit the reach of the case as much as possible. "Maybe you and Junior could take a flight to Michigan and get those details worked out."

Leone's jaw tightened. "Could. But I'd be traveling alone."

Clinton didn't care; anything to get the man out of his sight. Clinton looked at Wingham. "As for you and me, we need to track down this car service, the one that serviced Tux. We need to know who paid the bill."

"I can already tell you what you'll find," Leone intervened.

"If you know everything, make the arrest." Clinton and Leone matched eyes, everything brewing near the surface, their intense hatred for each other evident.

CHAPTER FIFTY-NINE

Most people would have been driven to the point of insanity. Considering the circumstances, I felt I remained relatively calm and focused. But there were times when irrational reasoning attempted to take precedence over common sense. I envisioned going in *hot* like they do in movies. I would dodge the hail of bullets fired at me, crouching, rolling, and moving at just the right time. I would hide behind some sort of cover and take them out one at a time—but I knew this wasn't fiction. Things in real life never worked out like that. An attempt to relive a scene of Hollywood would end up with me resembling Swiss cheese.

The men inside the hangar continued to talk. Based on their footfalls and their breathing, in my estimation, they were moving boxes or something. Their voices would come close and then drone in the distance.

I looked overhead to the corner of the building—no camera here, just a light that shone over the field. I tucked my flashlight into a pocket and strained to listen to the men.

"…why do we….it seems…need more money for this…"

The other voice: "…this is hard work…shit!"

"What the fuck do you think you're doing?" A third voice overpowered the end of the hangar. The Italian accent combined with the enclosed arrogance—this third person was Christian.

Any movement stopped except for one set of footfalls. The soles made soft pats on the concrete floor. Christian loved his Burluti leather shoes.

"I told you how I wanted them stored. Fix it now!"

"Yes, Boss, yes."

"Get it done." He snapped his fingers and dogs snarled. I heard chains chink against the concrete as they moved against their restraints. "Quiet!" Two more snaps of the fingers and the dogs went silent.

They would be Christian's replacement killers. Mitchell would have long since been retired—dogs don't live forever, especially on a diet high in human flesh. The thought sent nausea through me. As the reality of the situation weighed in on me, I felt my courage slip.

I stared out at the cornfield, my back still pressed flat against the exterior of the hangar. My senses remained poised on full alert, yet I knew my eyes had glazed over. My heart seemed to take pause as I struggled to realign my thoughts on what needed to be done. I didn't have time to give in to emotions. Emotions compromised success.

The screams of my family replayed, their vulnerability, their fear for their lives, their not knowing why they were even here or involved. All I wanted was time to hold them even once more, tell them how much I loved them, and explain to them how none of this was their fault—yet the blame rested all on me. I felt my eyes moisten with tears. What if I didn't have what it took to pull this off, and instead of saving my family, they died because of me?

CHAPTER SIXTY

Niagara Falls, New York
Sunday, June 13th, 11:45 PM

Professional Car Service had an office on 88th Street. Wingham had called and got a hold of an after-hours answering service who assured her the message would get through before morning.

The woman had said, "That's all I can promise. I can't make people check their messages or return calls."

Wingham didn't care for the snarky tone of the lady's response. "This is highly important."

"Yes, I have marked it as such. Anything else?" The not so hidden implication coming across, *you're driving me; gotta go.*

Wingham hung up without another word. If her partner could function in life with minimal etiquette and concern over other people's feelings, so could she. Sometimes, it seemed she was left to do all the work, the sniffing and digging through the scraps of clues they'd get. Yet she didn't report to Clinton. She rested her arm on the car door and bent it so she could rest her forehead in her hand. Her eyes were on the passing blurs of color even though Clinton drove like an old man taking a leisurely Sunday drive; her eyes were too tired to focus.

She was in such a miserable mood, a corner of her mouth lifted at the agitation of it. The bag of chips was long gone. She needed real food. Her stomach growled, and she was tired, worn out. She knew Clinton lived for the chase, the long hours, the overtime, the lack of sleep, and the functioning on adrenaline. She was dreaming of a hot shower and of sipping on a glass of red while reading a good novel, and slipping off to sleep. But that wasn't an option so her fantasy bubble popped with a loud noise like a balloon poked with a needle.

Clinton had it in his head that they would pay Governor Talbot a visit at the hotel he was staying at. Normally the man lived in New York City but he had decided to hang around while the investigation was in progress. Wingham knew about the imposed deadline, and the pressure it put on Clinton, but he operated best that way. She didn't understand why he didn't know that. Instead, he'd bitch about it and somehow make it her problem.

"I don't really think he'll be happy to see us this time of night," she said. She referred to Governor Talbot.

"I've called ahead. He knows we're coming."

Wow, he actually made a call without directing me to. She didn't verbalize her thought.

Wingham glanced over at her partner. He watched the road. He slowed down at the yellow light but didn't stop; the signal ticked off as he made a right-hand turn.

She studied his profile briefly, not that she was really assessing his looks. She had always considered him handsome in a friend sort of way. She didn't feel any attraction otherwise. Then, of course, at this point, it would be like kissing a brother—incest.

"What?" He glanced at her. His left hand still on the wheel tapped to his own beat. "You're staring."

"Nothing." The word was relatively simple— eight letters. Yet they were loaded with more innuendo for those who cared to pick up on them. Rarely did the word nothing ever mean that.

His attention had gone back to the road, hers out the window. Her thoughts traced to Agent Leone. Clinton didn't trust the man nor care for him; this much was evident and even stated more than once.

She had run a background on Leone only to find an impeccable service record. He graduated from a military college at the age of seventeen. He was intelligent and the government pursued him. He had no family connections. His parents had died in a house fire and he had no siblings— an only child.

He had spent time overseas and was awarded the Medal of Honor for his service. The man was highly decorated to simply serve as an FBI field agent. That was what Wingham mistrusted. And that was what motivated her to keep digging.

Research was something she excelled in. She pulled up his financials, normally something that required a warrant. Yet she knew her way through the system, around the system, and above the system.

Twenty years ago, Leone had lost everything. He had returned a military hero, but the bank had reclaimed his house and his accounts were frozen. He had sacrificed all for his country. He was forced to claim bankruptcy. But five years after that, luck turned around for him.

The file now had his primary address near Madison Avenue in New York City. It would be worth millions. And there were also two other properties, one in Paris, and another in Florence.

How does an FBI agent turn his life around from begging for shelter to basking in the high life? Until she had the answer to that, Wingham would continue to unearth truths that Leone wanted to remain buried. For those reasons, she sided with her partner. She didn't trust Leone either.

CHAPTER SIXTY-ONE

Outskirts of Detroit, Michigan
Monday, June 14th, Midnight
5 Hours Until the Deadline

I braced myself for the worst scenario possible. I pictured them bleeding, decapitated, carved up, eaten by dogs. Somehow, I convinced myself that by conjuring up those images, real life would pale the nightmare, make things more bearable. A portion of me feared that I may not be in touch with my family as much as I thought I was. They were dead and I didn't feel it even potentially a few yards away.

Max had looked so fearful when they brought him to me. When I called out and told him I loved him, he never said a word in response. The silence stung like rubbing alcohol to an open wound, but I had to analyze his reaction. It wasn't out of spite or malice. The boy was ten years old. What did he know about such things? But I sensed from his eyes and his energy, he was pained and afraid. He had given thought as to why they were taken here, held against their will, and treated as prisoners.

As my eyes burned with the tears that filled them, I reflected on how exhausted I truly was, and that the only reason I was vertical was due to chemical alteration. My family didn't have anything to help carry them through. How I hoped to God they were given food and water.

"Get this shit outta here!" Christian bellowed another request inside of the hangar. I heard the snapping of fingers after his outburst, and the dogs barked.

The noise made my body tense up, the feeling that someone could come around the corner at any time without my foreknowledge weighed heavily on my list of concerns. I stared toward the end of the building, a hand to my waist ready to pull a .22 from the holster.

After several minutes had passed, no one came around the corner. The dogs had stopped barking, and all I heard were the hustled movements of shoes and boots shuffling along the floor.

I pressed my eyes shut tight to abate the moisture and salve the burning. With them closed, my other senses peaked; my hearing more attuned, I discerned the one man walked with a dragging heel. And, if at all possible, I felt the energy of my family stronger now. They were here. Now came the tough part. I had to wait it out until all noise had stopped, and I felt it was safe to round the bend. If that took hours, then I had all night.

CHAPTER SIXTY-TWO

Talbot's bodyguard stood outside the suite, eyeing their badges as if they picked them up from a costume shop. He compared their faces to a printout he had on each of them and eventually nodded his consent and unlocked the door.

"Good evening, Detectives," he said.

Good evening, my ass. Clinton clipped his badge back on his waist. He hated being looked upon as a suspect and treated like a regular citizen. He had put years into having a position of trust and responsibility. He shouldn't be scrutinized further. And if they were that much of a threat, take their guns. After all, police can be dirty too. They could be there to off Talbot. Clinton rolled his eyes at the absurdity, despite that a fraction of him gave merit to the concept. He imagined the headlines: LAW ENFORCEMENT OFFICERS ASSASSINATE GOVERNOR IN HIS SUITE.

"Detective Wingham, just as beautiful as the last time I saw you." Governor Talbot extended a hand to her. "Detective Clinton." His shake with Clinton didn't linger as long as it had with Wingham. "If you two would please join me in the sitting area."

Talbot was ironically staying at The Grandeur. His room was laid out differently than Behler's. He had a full sofa and two chairs. He had a kitchenette off to the one side.

Another bodyguard stood near the counter, both hands clasped in front of him.

Clinton noticed his chest enlarge and his shoulders go taut. He put on a good show for his employer. With all this talk about the Mafia and knowing their connections, Clinton eyed every one as a potential suspect.

"This is Henry. He's been with me for about five years now." Talbot must have read the expression in Clinton's eyes. "Please sit." Talbot gestured to the sofa chairs as he dropped onto the couch.

Henry remained unaffected by his employer's introduction. Clinton pried his eyes from the bodyguard.

A rocks glass with an amber liquid sat on a nearby coffee table. Talbot reached for it. "It's late. You could almost say early." He passed a wandering glance to Wingham, who had taken a seat and crossed one of her legs toward him.

"We have a new direction in the case," Wingham started.

"What she's trying to say is we know you were with Behler the night when the first attempt on her life took place."

Talbot wasn't amused. His jaw tightened. The energy in the room shifted to one full of defense as if two mountain lions were about to face off for survival. "Are you saying I killed her?"

"Absolutely not, sir," Wingham interjected. "Detective Clinton may come across the wrong way at times—"

"Yes, accusatory."

Clinton felt the chastisement in the Governor's eyes. Talbot's faith in his original choice to assign the case to him was wavering.

After seconds of silent discipline, Talbot dragged his attention from Clinton to Wingham.

Wingham said, "We're just hoping you can help us."

"I sure hope so."

Clinton heard the man's words, but something in the eyes glazed over; his grip on the rocks glass tightened, his knuckles went white.

"Are you thirsty, Detective? You're watching my drink like a baby does its mother's breast."

Clinton heard Wingham swallow loudly, an automatic response from the candor of the Governor's comment. Her legs uncrossed.

"No, I'm fine," Clinton said.

"Good, then, back to business. Detective, you were saying." Talbot faced Wingham.

Maybe it was advantageous he paid such attention to his female partner. It allowed Clinton time to make observations. There were always small tell-tale signs in people who spoke mistruth. Even if one believed the lie they spoke as gospel, there was always something there, even if it was as subtle as a drippy nose, an itchy ear, a developing twitch. At this junction, Talbot displayed none of them, but they were just getting started.

Wingham leaned forward, a small notepad in her hands. Clinton had noticed when they first arrived at The Grandeur about twenty-four hours ago her nails were painted with a bright red polish. At this point, chips of it were missing.

"Were you and Governor Behler friends?" Wingham's tone was soft, the hint of a smile on her lips.

Was she flirting with the Governor? Clinton leaned back and watched the show. He patted his hands on the arms of the chair softly enough not to cause a distraction.

"You're really asking if we were more than friends." Talbot raised his glass, swirled the remaining liquid, and drank it back. As his lips released the glass, they curled upward into a smirk one could imagine a wolf flashing its prey before lunging for the jugular. But Talbot's hunger wasn't for a badge or for power; it was for Wingham's neckline.

Clinton watched as the Governor's eyes passed over her. Talbot never even tried to conceal his attentions. The directness of his approach made Clinton watch his partner too, not with hungry eyes, but from an objective, distant point of view.

The woman was attractive, slim figure—the kind that you could wrap one arm around. She had a long neck that would beg many men to kiss and nuzzle into it and lose a few nights' sleep over. She wore black dress pants with these boots she insisted were her favorite. They had scuffed heels from overuse but added a couple inches to her height. The shirt she wore under her blazer had the top few buttons undone, and as she sat there leaned forward, the mounds of her breasts peeked over the edge of the fabric.

Wingham's cheeks flushed. Her eyes darted to her partner and narrowed.

Crap, she had noticed him.

As if pulling from Clinton's thoughts, Talbot cleared his throat and took a pause from his lecherous glances. He massaged his right temple with his thumb and index finger for a few seconds. "We were friends in the sense of our jobs, Behler and I. I am a married man, have been for twenty-five years now."

He passed a somewhat guilty glance to Clinton but didn't really allow any conviction to set into his features.

Always the politician—speak on behalf of everything, commit to nothing.

Wingham leaned her body into the side of the chair. She took her time re-crossing her leg toward the dignitary. Clinton saw the look in her eyes, the one that spoke of determination despite the costs.

"I didn't mean to imply anything improper," she said.

"No, darling, I'm sure you didn't." He reached for the glass he had set on the table. When he was reminded it was empty, he turned to Henry. "Refill."

The bodyguard weaved through the room without causing much disturbance.

Talbot shifted his weight and moved to the end of the couch to be closer to Wingham. She buckled minutely. He seemed to pick up on it and pulled back. His hand went to the collar of his shirt, loosened his necktie, and undid the top three buttons. "It's been a long couple of days."

With his words, concern showed in his eyes, the source of which Clinton had a hard time pinning down. Clinton even swore he picked up on some fear. It was the same look he had witnessed in the room at the hospital after Behler had been assassinated.

Henry placed the refreshed drink on a coaster; Talbot dismissed him with a wave of the hand. "She wanted to discuss some things. Politics."

The way he said *politics* implied they wouldn't understand if he elaborated. It was too complicated for their simple minds to comprehend.

"When did you meet?" Clinton asked. He was the intrusive waiter; Wingham was the gourmet meal.

Talbot ran his tongue along his top teeth as he slowly turned his head. "We met years ago, back in Governor College." Seconds of awkward silence. "That was supposed to be a joke." Talbot didn't even seem amused. "No, we've known each other for years. We first met at a budget meeting. She saw things differently than I did. She always did." He reached for his drink.

Clinton didn't break the silence, and neither did Wingham. He felt that more was forthcoming, and in instances like that he could find the strength to be patient.

Talbot's gaze shifted around the room. The effects of the alcohol were imprinted on his eyes giving them a glossy, dazed look. They also read of gratification while hinting at discontent. When he seemed to realize neither of them was going to speak, he pulled his lips from the glass. He didn't place it on the table but kept it in his hands. "I'm not really sure what you two are looking for from me."

"There was a third man at the table that night." Clinton leaned forward bracing his elbows on his knees. He clasped his hands. "The restaurant staff said that you left not long after he showed up. Who was he?"

"I don't remember his name."

Enough time had been spent dancing around the perimeter, but Clinton hardly viewed this visit a waste of time. Talbot revealed more than he realized he had. Again, it was in the small things, the sideways glances, the uncharacteristic tilt of the mouth when he spoke. It was insightful. The subject of Governor Behler made him uncomfortable, an otherwise confident politician reduced to an alcoholic reaching for his fix.

Clinton picked up on the subtle shake of Talbot's hand as he pressed the glass back to his lips.

CHAPTER SIXTY-THREE

I crouched down with my back pressed against the metal of the hangar. The fog had settled in; it seemed more encompassing than when I left the car over an hour ago. There was a substance to it, a dense quality that gave it the sensation that eyes were watching. This feeling made my stomach tighten and I straightened out. I held a hand over the .22 on my right hip, my preferred shooting arm if I had a choice.

The illumination cast from the building over the field revealed nothing but a hazed beam of light in the darkness. The footsteps continued in the hangar for a while but then petered out into silence. The voices faded into a low mumble. The back of the hangar remained open. If they chose to pull the plane in, my position would be compromised.

I slowly made my way to the edge of the building, straining to listen while trying to envision where the voices were coming from and what they were saying.

Taking a deep breath and placing a hand on my .22, I rounded the corner. Collateral damage was an acceptable option should it become necessary.

I heard the tingle of chains and surmised it was the dogs lying down on the concrete. They could be my downfall.

Dogs had highly attuned senses. They could sense impending storms; they could feel a stranger in the vicinity, typically they could smell fear. I had to take the fact they laid down, at least by the sound of it, that my estimation of them exceeded the laws of their natural confines.

I kept moving, one painfully slow step forward at a time. I huddled close to the building and pulled out the .22. I held it braced in my hand, readied to fire. More tinkling of chains and it stalled my breath for an instant. But the sound was of another lying down. They must have been relatively close to the inside of the hangar.

How the hell was I going to get past them?

The answer was pure and simple—I wouldn't. The second my shadow graced the doorway they would be snarling and disclose my position. They may even pick up on my scent before that. Men would seep from the shadows, bullets would hurl through the air.

I went into my jacket pocket and pulled out the silencer. Screwing it over the barrel of the .22, I knew what I would likely have to do. I kept moving until I reached the edge of the door. Taking a deep breath, I centered myself, readied to fire, and quickly turned my head inside.

I took less than five seconds to make an assessment. There were, in fact, two dogs—pit bulls. They were chained to a rod on the wall. Both of them were lying down and looked sated.

Another five-second glance, and I took in more of the hangar. Two men were coming off another plane that was inside. Christian stood at the end of it with a woman—Landen. She let out a deep-throated laugh, and as her head rolled back, Christian went to it. I remembered her words from the first time I met her, *this here is my hangar, my planes.*

I pulled back around, my eyes on nothing but field. But as I stood there calculating my next step, I noticed a darkened shadow in the field to the left. It looked like a utility shed of some sort.

More laughter filtered from the hangar into the night. The dense air seemed to draw it like a sponge absorbs fluid.

A ten-second glance. The gun in my hand grew ready to fire, eager to pull back on the trigger. Firing guns burned in me like an insatiable hunger. When I didn't have them in my hand, I dreamt of the firing range, of the euphoria and rush that came with the release of the bullet as it left the barrel. Having one in my hand, without the ability to ease back on the trigger and feel the recoil brought with it a melancholy slump.

Christian and Landen pulled out of an embrace. They were pointing fingers and directing two men to do something. I couldn't discern their words. Christian and the woman came toward me.

I pulled back around. My heart thundered in my chest like a wild piston. I held the gun as tight to my chest as the .44 would allow. I felt the gun press into my chest, and I shifted from the discomfort.

Fingers snapped. I heard the chains as the dogs stood up. They let out snarls.

"*Basta!*" Stop.

"*Silenzio!*" Quiet.

The dogs complied. More footsteps and they were so close to me now that I feared they could hear my breathing. I knew the fear was unjustified. They were still a good sixteen yards away.

The chains were undone and I heard Christian's shoes tapping on the concrete, the accompanying heels of the woman's boots beside him. They were walking away and taking the dogs with them.

I moved to the doorway, tucked my head around the bend. They were heading to the front of the hangar. I couldn't see the other two men who were there a moment ago. They must have left for something else that Christian had directed them to do.

My intended ten-second glance extended as I took the time to study the hangar and the doorways. A quick look behind me and no one was on the tarmac, no chance of someone coming up on me. As the front door to the hangar opened and Christian and Landen left, I took my first few steps inside. I was going to do this. I would get my family back. And I would kill Christian, not for Pietro, but for getting back into my life.

CHAPTER SIXTY-FOUR

"So you shared drinks with him and don't remember his name?" Clinton laced his fingers tighter.

Governor Talbot's eyes burned with fire. "Why so accusatory? Do you think I killed her?" He lifted his arm up, the one with the drink; it sloshed a little over the side of the glass. He pulled it back down and licked his hand. "Why would I? Can you answer that?"

Clinton's thoughts needed to be cataloged before he would allow himself to verbalize them. He thought of Rolex, Carson, and the Mafia connection with his mutilation and murder. He had been Behler's stand-in bodyguard. An intelligent woman of her position would have conducted some sort of background check to know who she put in place to protect her.

"What was the purpose of your dinner?"

"She had some concerns."

"Specifically?"

"How to handle organized crime." Talbot's eyes shifted when he spoke the words *organized crime*. "If you know anything about me at all, Detective, I am a strong advocate against them."

Clinton chose ignorance. "Them?"

Talbot rolled a hand. "Street gangs, the Chinese, the Italian, the Russians—you pick a flavor. Anyone who thinks they own the streets of my state." Passion and conviction saturated his expression. A pointed finger jabbed down into the arm of the couch. "I will not tolerate their sort of justice."

"And Behler?"

Silence for a few seconds.

"I think you should leave. Surely you have some work to do. Find the person who did this," Talbot said.

"Do you think it's organized crime, Governor?" Clinton stood with his attention on Talbot. The man shifted uncomfortably as a guilty suspect does in the interrogation room.

Henry stepped toward Clinton and put a hand on Clinton's arm, pulling on him in the direction of the door.

Clinton walked a few steps. He stopped and turned back. "Do you think it's the Italian Mafia?"

"Why don't you tell me?" Talbot swigged back on his drink and set the glass heavily on the side table.

Henry tugged harder on Clinton's arm. "Come on, it's time to go."

Clinton looked at the man's grip and up to the bodyguard's eyes. He shrugged free. "What are you hiding, Governor?"

Talbot's aura went cold, yet a flash of fear pranced across his features. "Get out!"

. . .

Niagara Falls, New York

"I'm headed out on the red-eye. And the best part? It was the detective's idea." Leone spoke into his untraceable phone. The line was as secure as the President's in the White House. Leone should know as he had been privy to private meetings with the President on occasion.

"Bravo." The Italian-accented voice belonged to Roman Agostino, the Consigliere, or advisor, to the Boss of the New York Caparelli Family. Leone had never met the man in person, but sometimes you had to cross sides and go with the higher offer. He received a call from him after the first assassination attempt. They were taking the attack as a personal affront. And for cash Leone was always willing to not only turn the other way, but to get involved.

"You know what you must do," Agostino said.

"But of course. When it's complete, I will provide proof."

"No need. I will know. Grazie!"

Leone envisioned a wide smile on the face of the Italian. He would have good news to report to the Don. The job would be carried out and unlike the Behler assassin he would get it right the first time around. There wasn't room for failure in Leone's world. Failure meant the difference between life and death, poverty and wealth.

Leone stuffed his cell into a pocket and did his best to get comfortable in the hard chairs of the airport waiting room. He had an hour to kill.

CHAPTER SIXTY-FIVE

Outskirts of Detroit, Michigan
Monday, June 14th, 12:15 AM
Less Than 5 Hours Until the Deadline

There wasn't a sound coming from inside the hangar. I would almost swear they shut down for the night except for the opened back side and the million dollar plane just sitting on the tarmac, not that one could just walk off with it. I knew men would still be posted at the front, their guns readied to fire at any unfamiliar figure. One misstep and they would be alerted to my presence. They were likely told to do a perimeter sweep at certain intervals, even though I had yet to see them deviate far from their front post.

There were a bunch of wooden crates against the wall. I moved closer to them and in the direction of where the dogs had been lying. I ran a hand over one of the crates, but my eyes were on the door to the right.

When I was here after Niagara Falls, Christian had me taken to the room a few doors down from this one. My heart clung to the entry as if it would provide meaning and return order to my life. My family was behind that door. There would be a hallway with rooms, and they would be there. I felt the emotion rise in my chest, the burning sensation in the back of my eyes from fresh tears that formed. I swallowed hard. I would not release them. I had to stay vigilant and aware.

I extended a hand to the doorknob and twisted. It moved. It was unlocked. I kept turning it but stopped when my cell rang.

Shit!

I ducked behind the crate while frantically reaching for my phone. If anyone heard it…

CR name came up on the display. I pressed ignore to the call and changed it to silent. As I went to move it back to my pocket, the screen lit up. It was Christian again. Again, I hit ignore. This time I stuffed it into my pocket before I had a chance to know if he tried a third time. It didn't matter. I had my own agenda now. I didn't report to him. I didn't report to Pietro. I reported to myself.

I stayed crouched down behind the crate, listening but still heard nothing. I moved toward the door again. As it released, I pushed on it expecting to find a hallway with doorways. But things rarely go how you expect.

. . .

Niagara Falls, New York

Clinton and Wingham loaded onto the elevator. She had been unusually quiet since they left Talbot's room. Even though the room was only feet behind them, Wingham normally always had something to say.

"What did you make of that?" Clinton asked as he pressed the button for the main floor.

"What?" Her eyebrows lifted in irritation. "The fact that you blatantly accused the Governor of New York of murder, or the fact the Mafia may be involved?"

"The latter." He knew not to push her too much when her mood was like this. He could go for hours without sleep, without stopping. She was more fragile.

As for him blatantly accusing the Governor, Clinton withheld his true feelings. She didn't appreciate the restraint he had used. He realized the difference between suspicion and speculation. Despite being defined similarly, they were worlds apart.

Suspicion was based on something substantive, something remotely evidence, whereas speculation equated a gut feeling with nothing conclusive. If Leone was right about the Italian Mafia and this Christian guy being involved, there had to be a deeper connection with Rolex and the Governor besides him serving as a bodyguard. She knew what he represented and she was okay with it. Her loyalty to the post was compromised. He hated speaking ill of the dead, but most times it was only with death that the mistruths, the misconceptions, came to light.

By extension, making the speculation that Behler was involved with the Mafia, maybe she was here with Talbot to make him see her way. But what would motivate her to approach a clean politician to see her worldly ways? Clinton knew the answer; Wingham wouldn't like it.

"What if Behler had something on Talbot?"

She rubbed a hand on her forehead, letting it run the full length of her face. "What if there's a leprechaun at the end of the rainbow?"

Her rhetorical snapback silenced him.

She continued, "We don't have proof of anything, David. We know he met with her, he's obviously hiding something—"

"So you noticed—" Her glaring eyes stopped his words.

"Yeah, it didn't escape me." She crossed her arms. She was now tired, insulted, and angry.

"Maybe we should break for a few hours, get some sleep, come back fresh."

"That's the most intelligent thing I've heard you say in hours."

Clinton turned and realized Wingham was smiling.

"You know I get cranky when I don't sleep."

Clinton smiled. "Five hours."

"Six, then I'm all yours." She shut her eyes and leaned against the side of the elevator until it chimed their arrival.

CHAPTER SIXTY-SIX

The door opened to an empty store room. I could have pounded the walls in frustration. I had felt they were here; I was wrong. I feared what else I may be wrong about. What if they were already dead and I didn't sense it? So close, yet so far away.

I moved back to the door I had shut behind me and pressed an ear against it. No sound from the main hangar. I slowly twisted the knob and squeezed my head through the opening. I couldn't see anyone.

I worked my way along the wall lined with the wooden crates to the next doorway. A man's voice called out. It sounded like it came from around the front of the plane. I crouched down and saw the bottom of his legs. He walked back to the other side of the hangar. I hurried to the next doorway and was thankful it was also unlocked. I slipped inside, the .22 in my hand, readied to fire. My feet moved out of instinct, being willed by my heart. They were here. I felt it.

Four doors came from the hallway, three on the right, and one on the left. I hurried to the first and noticed the scrap of material at the base of the door. I picked it up. It had NAS on it. That was part of the NASCAR logo from Max's pajamas.

My hands went to the handle, but it was locked. I shook it rapidly. No sounds came from inside.

Where were they?

"Max. Max." I yelled in the form of a whisper, as loud as I could without drawing Christian's men.

There was no response. I went to the next room on the right. There was a small window in the door. I peered inside and saw the cot from the proof of life video. I saw the restraint bar on the wall, the cuffs that dangled from them. This was Yvonne's room. I jiggled the handle. It was also locked. I put a fist to the glass and hammered it. I hoped she was in a part of the room I couldn't see.

"Yvonne."

Silence.

A sickly kind of dread compressed my chest.

I hurried to the third room. I pulled on the door handle; it opened. I wished it hadn't.

Blood stained the concrete floor. I dropped to my knees. My family had been executed by the madman. My face fell into my hands as I sat there doubled over, a man destroyed. As the tears fell, and anger stormed within me, my eyes opened.

This would not go unpunished. This meant war. I rose to my feet with an adrenaline rush of a Roman warrior. Blood pulsed under my skin. There would be retribution.

Fueled by vengeance and nothing else to lose, I went to storm out of the room. Only something caught my eye and made my steps come to a standstill.

Bile rose in my throat, the acidic flavor coating my tongue. Swallowing hard, I forced it back down. It came up again threatening to be expunged. I swallowed and held my breath for a few seconds.

The hair in the corner of the room was attached to a head. The mental images I had conjured up earlier, to prepare myself for a nightmare, the ones I never thought I'd have to experience in reality, flashed in front of me now.

The hair was dark and short, like Brenda's. My heart lurched forward while my legs were weighed motionless. I had to know if this was her. Something inside of me, a primal urge that needed to know what happened, compelled me to move. Each step painfully executed until I was near it. I watched my footsteps doing my best to avoid the pool of blood on the floor. I blinked my eyes shut. I willed myself to recall the nightmarish pictures—the ones I had fabricated. Inside this room, the actuality of them singed on my psyche. When I opened my eyes, my prayers were answered. This was not Brenda.

The vomit rose in the back of my throat and expelled without any chance of swallowing it.

CHAPTER SIXTY-SEVEN

Clinton grabbed a beer from his fridge and dropped himself in front of his computer. Snapping the cap off on the corner of the desk, he lifted the opened bottle to his mouth, draining back half of it in a few swallows. He was tired, but it wasn't a choice for him to give in. As long as he had answers to address, his mind wouldn't let him rest.

He knew himself well enough to know there would be no point in lying down. He would stare at the ceiling and toss and turn until his neck and hips ached. Why not make better use of his time, get some answers, and come out of it without back pain?

He didn't have the ability like most people to go to bed at a predestined time, sleep their eight hours, and get up ready to go. He didn't function like that. For him to sleep his body would have to give out on him. And when it did, he was down for a while.

He sat the bottle on the desk and brought up an Internet browser. His intentions were clear the moment he dropped Wingham off at her apartment. She mumbled something indiscernible as she got out of the car. The only thing that made it through was six hours.

Clinton smiled about it now, a light buzz from his beer already affecting him due to lack of sleep and an empty stomach. He dialed for pizza and ordered an extra cheese and pepperoni. Any other topping was ruining something good.

He sipped on the bottle and held it as he pecked with one finger on the keyboard. The question he would endeavor to get an answer to was why Behler met with Talbot. Given the assumption Behler worked with the mob—Clinton paused with the thought, amused. He still found it hard to believe. It seemed more of what Hollywood was comprised of.

He pulled up Governor Talbot's page and read the captions. Talbot was a strong advocate against organized crime. The quotes from the man himself potently exposed his viewpoint. Clinton shook his neck to release some tension. He kept scrolling and clicking before sitting back. His speculation could be getting some momentum.

He opened another browser window and brought up Behler's page. Hers mostly centered on the economy and how they would rebuild and renew a crumbling automotive industry. It spoke of developing jobs.

As Clinton worked his way through the site, there was one small area that mentioned her promise to work with the fine people of Michigan State to decrease crime. Her page then boasted of less violent crimes in the last few years.

Clinton searched the page for the word organized. The findings weren't related to crime but rather *organized to make a difference.*

He went back to Talbot's page which blatantly boasted about bringing down organized crime, in none too subtle terms. In fact, the terminology was aggressive and defiant.

What if—and this was a large what if—Governor Behler did work with the Italian Mafia and she had come to meet with Talbot to see her way? It wouldn't be the first time a politician got into bed with powerful allies. The Italians would be able to ensure her post, feed her money to keep her mouth shut, and turn the other way in exchange for loyalty.

Clinton researched the arrest rates in the last year of Talbot's term and there it was in black and white. His one speculation had just graduated to suspicion. Talbot took the responsibility for bringing down a part of a New York Italian Mafia family.

In fact, six of the Don's Caporegime, or Captains, were now awaiting trial and facing multiple life sentences. Talbot stood behind a move that brought NYPD Swat to the front door of the Italians' operations. They seized millions in cocaine and an equal amount in illegal weapons. Also uncovered in the search was evidence that implicated their involvement with several murders.

Clinton leaned back in the chair and rubbed the back of his neck. He stared at the screen as he drank the rest of his beer.

The words of Governor Talbot streaming through his mind. She wanted me to see things her way, but we've always seen things differently.

If Behler did work with the Mafia and was sent to tell Talbot to back off it would explain a lot of things. It would clarify why Talbot wanted to keep the investigation localized, and the reflection of fear in his eyes and unwillingness to elaborate on his meeting with Behler. And for Behler to approach Talbot, Clinton was almost certain it would involve bribery that would include blackmail. Most politicians had some sort of past wrongdoing to disclose and bring to light. He was certain Talbot would be no different. If he could figure that out, he'd be that much closer to understanding what got Behler assassinated.

The buzzer for the door sounded. The pizza was here already; the hour and the fact that the pizzeria was across the street didn't hurt.

He moved slowly toward the door, his thoughts weighing him down. What if Talbot was the one behind the assassination of Behler?

He opened the door to a freckle-faced teenager holding out a pizza box toward him.

"That will be twenty-five dollars."

Clinton paid him including a two dollar tip and then refreshed his beer. As he dropped onto the sofa and turned on the TV, he knew one thing with clarity. All this speculation had made him hungry.

CHAPTER SIXTY-EIGHT

Outskirts of Detroit, Michigan
Monday, June 14th, 1:00 AM
4 Hours Until the Deadline

It wasn't the amount of blood or the sight of a decapitated head that did me in. From my line of work before Brenda, before my family, before the best life I had ever known, blood was a common sight. It was like flour to a baker, a torch to a welder, mail to the postman—blood was part of the job and a necessary aspect of getting the job done.

Maybe I had been witness to enough death that most corpses were not even human to me anymore. The body was a carcass that held the essence of the individual. But no matter how much I had witnessed or had a role in playing out, I didn't care for the decapitated head in the corner of this room.

I moved in closer, despite an inner voice telling me to flee and to get on with getting my family out of here. The other part insisted on seeing if I recognized the man.

Another wash of bile projected up my throat carrying with it the sour reminder of the vomit I had on the floor—not that I needed the reminder, it saturated my sinuses.

The man's nose and face were mangled and there were punctures all over it—dental impressions. The teeth had sliced through the flesh leaving behind holes. This man had been eaten by the dogs.

I looked around the room. Blood spray lined the back wall. He had been alive when they took him down.

My human compassion over what he would have gone through caused me to peer back down at him. Yet I was thankful this wasn't a family member. And I was appreciative it wasn't me.

I had to convince myself this man had done something unforgivable that deserved death. Regardless that the means of execution was excessive at least his experience was over now.

As I tried to dismiss it, I found myself battling with re-living what his last moments must have been like. The absolute terror and pain he would have endured to this point.

The man's head had been severed by a sharp knife, possibly a Samurai sword. The cut was clean.

So first Christian fed him to the dogs, and then decapitated the head and offered it up as a dessert platter? The man whose life I had saved so many years ago was an animal, not one who had been worthy of saving. He deserved to die. He deserved to suffer. I would make sure he would.

Brenda was aware of the smell before anything else. Her head was in a foggy haze; her eyes unwilling to open. It was like before. The headache would be coming shortly.

Who were these people? What did they want from her, from her children?

"Let them go." She remembered the words cutting from her dry mouth. She tried to fight the large man, but he overpowered her like a hurricane wind to a twig. She didn't stand a chance. The cloth had been pressed against her face.

Before that she remembered the screams. They were immortal, etched into her memory for life. They were the sounds of a man being killed. She knew this because she sensed the fear and the absolute horror encased in the sound. He knew he was going to die.

She willed her eyelids open. They wouldn't move. They were heavy and seemed welded shut.

She needed to know her children were okay. Somehow she sensed they were near and as crazy as it would sound to her when she came out of the daze, she felt Ray was too.

She rocked her head side to side, hoping to cut through the drug-induced haze. She knew she lay on something hard. She put her arms to the side, her fingers stretching out and feeling the surface. She felt springs through a thin mattress—another cot?

Why did they move her? Did they move the kids too?

Her hands went to her body. She wasn't covered with a sheet, but she could feel the fabric of clothing. They had redressed her in the pajamas she had worn to bed the night before— the night they kidnaped them. Something about feeling the silk transported her back to the security of her home, the way it used to be. She felt warmth run over her. She remembered Ray's touch. Yet the memory transported the tarnish he had placed on their relationship. Had another woman been feeling her husband's caress while they lay suffering here?

Tears ran down her face, her sinuses stuffing up from crying while lying on her back. The smell of the room still penetrated that barrier. She felt the dampness and the scent was that of mustiness mingled with sweetness—mice.

The thought was enough to force her eyes open. She sat up and felt light-headedness roll her mind around like a spinning top. When her focus came back, she saw them. Yvonne and Max were in the room with her. How she wanted to run to them, but her legs wouldn't move.

CHAPTER SIXTY-NINE

Outskirts of Detroit, Michigan
Monday, June 14th, 1:15 AM
Less Than 4 Hours Until the Deadline

Enough time had passed. Enough had been wasted standing here. The time had come to seek out my family and get them out of here. I headed for the door and heard voices coming from the hangar. I went back inside the room. The voices dulled and then disappeared.

I crept toward the door, my faith in the fact my family was still alive and that I would be their only chance of survival, forcing my steps. Turning the door slowly, I listened. I heard nothing. I peeked out and saw no one.

All I could do now was follow my heart. If Christian wanted to ensure my family's capture was secured, he'd hold them close to himself. He had left through the front door with Landen, the woman who owned the property, the same woman who sipped from a mug when I came the first time.

My family was inside the main house. The burning realization carried me to the back side of the hangar where I paused, pressed against the aluminum of the hangar. This time I was on the left side of the bay door, closer to the house.

I twisted around the corner to look down the side of the building. The voices of the two men from the front carried in the fog. As I took a few steps to the side, I saw the silhouette of a man's back as he moved to the side and then back to the front, behind the building.

Six feet from the hangar, a row of bushes lined the driveway. About halfway up, the bushes came to an end. I calculated the distance at about fifteen yards. I needed to make it there, cut through, and get to the house.

I tucked behind the hangar, my eyes going to the shed I had noticed earlier. It was made of fieldstone to match the main house.

There was no break in the bushes to the back side of the property. I had one option—forward.

As I moved back around the side of the hangar, the man at the front was now out of vision. The men's voices carried in the night air, yet it was still hard to discern exactly what they were saying.

I took the fact they were in conversation as a bonus. Hopefully, it would keep them occupied and allow me to do what I needed to. I crept up the side of the building with a hand on my holster, vigilant, and ready to draw the weapon should the need arise.

The house had a front porch that swept the width. Lights shone on the back deck. I checked the eaves of the building for security cameras and didn't see any.

"Do you really think I care if steak is on sale?"

The random sentence traveled through the fog from the front.

Another voice, "It's good stuff. I'm just sayin'."

I pressed against the hangar as I studied the house. Three upstairs windows were on this side with two main level ones. I could go up the wall like I had at Christian's yet there would be too much risk of exposure. A hand went to my chest—and hard to carry out with the bulk of the .44 under my jacket.

Part of me also felt if they were in that house, they would be in the basement, more discreet, isolated, less chance of escape. If I made it to an upstairs window, I'd have to somehow get through an entire house without being spotted. The possibility also came to me that with old houses basements were sometimes only accessible from the outside.

Then I saw it in the garden bed on the side of the house—a cement abutment with a wooden door, disclosed a point of entry. My heart seized thinking that if my family were in there, there should be a man posted outside— unless Christian had underestimated me or overestimated himself.

Random sentences kept filtering from the front. This would be my chance. With every footstep across the graveled driveway, I held my breath as if it would somehow make me lighter, quieter.

The door's latch was unlocked and flipped open. I lifted the door, slowly, with caution. Its hinges creaked. Someone with a gun aimed at my head could be inside ready to fire. No one was on the other side. Only darkness greeted me. I slipped behind the door and beneath the ground.

I fished my flashlight out of a pocket and cast the weak light across the surface and down the hallway. More offshoots of rooms. Dirt served as the floor. I walked slowly tweaking the direction of the light.

There were closed doors on each side. Had I found my family?

"Brenda. Yvonne. Max." I kept moving. My words were exhaled as loud whispers. I couldn't yell and risk being exposed, but it took control not to allow the devastation I felt at this moment to saturate this century-old home's walls. To be aware I was so close to my family, yet powerless to reach them…

I put a hand on the first door handle and twisted it. It cooperated. I pulled a .22 out with one hand and held the flashlight cocked over it with the other. I crept inside.

More crates and boxes filled the room. These were smaller than the ones in the hangar. I knew I should back away, leave now, go to the next room, but my curiosity sank me. A lid sat askew on one of them.

Taking a ten-second pause, I closed my eyes and strained to see if I could hear anything. Nothing.

I walked over to the crate and placed my .22 back in the holster when I reached it. I told myself it didn't matter what was inside. I had come for one main reason—the rescue of my family.

With the lid the rest of the way off the crate, I flashed the light into the darkness. My hand ran over them—artillery of all shapes and sizes— illegal weapons. I needed to leave now. I put the top back on as it had been.

There was no way you'd leave a stash like this unattended. Someone would be coming back to guard the stairwell, to check in on inventory. Realizing the implications, I felt trapped.

Hurrying to the next room, I called out my family's names again. Hoping for an answer, yet praying there wouldn't be any. If they were down here, I feared I would never get them out alive.

I turned the handles on the next couple rooms. Inside them were more crates.

My family wasn't here. The sinking feeling in my chest told me something was wrong. It was too quiet. Yet I knew they were nearby—I could sense it.

The outside door to the basement opened. My breath caught and I slinked further into the room. I turned the flashlight off and stood there in absolute darkness listening to the irregular rhythm of my heartbeat and the accompanying jagged breaths.

I worked at closing the door to encase me inside the room. It creaked on the hinges.

Shit!

"Did you hear that?"

A light turned on in the hallway.

"Ssh." Footsteps on the dirt floor came down the hallway and stopped right outside of the door. Two men. I could see the shadows of their shoes.

My eyes closed for just a second. I weighed my options. There were two of them, one of me. If I went out, guns high, there would be a lot of muzzle flashes and a cleanup crew required to scrape brain matter off the walls. If I stayed here, they would find me, and I would be a weak target. Christian's men were trained to kill if someone posed a direct threat to the Don's life. Any other kill was to be approved of by the Don or Christian himself. The chink in that theory was everything had changed.

Christian aligned himself as the replacement Don. The man was unpredictable. His men might run on a different, refined set of parameters. I really didn't want to find out.

I concentrated on my breathing and steadying it.

"You're just hearing things," one of them said.

"I'm telling you I heard something."

"Anything to get out of work." One set of footsteps walked away.

Seconds later, the other man walked away too. The light went off and the outside doorway closed.

I would wait them out. A few minutes of silence and inactivity passed. I turned on the flashlight and stepped into the dark hallway.

The cold end of a gun barrel pressed against my temple.

CHAPTER SEVENTY

Outskirts of Detroit, Michigan
Monday, June 14th, 1:30 AM
Deadline Reached Early

My mother had always taught me to place my mind somewhere else when I experienced something I didn't enjoy. For example, the dentist or even getting a haircut—I never trusted a man with a drill or scissors. She told me to picture something I loved, and the experience would be over before I knew it. My father used to back her up by telling me the mind is stronger than all else. Even at the ages of eight, ten, fifteen, I put faith in his words. And now a grown man of thirty-nine, I knew they were the truth.

Some things in life were out of control, unavoidable, but if you had a strong mind, you could make it through to the other side. I used to picture hiding out in my friend's clubhouse to mentally escape. It was there I had availability to hunting magazines and their articles on guns. In a strange way transporting there provided me the reprieve to make it through almost anything—even the day I fell out of that tree house and broke a leg and the doctor had to reset it. It actually turned out to be the best summer ever. Casts got the sympathy of girls.

As Christian's men dragged me into the hangar, I wasn't really envisioning any of this, but it was the cycle my mind used to prepare itself for a bad situation. And running into Christian this way would top the list. Never mind a drill and a pair of scissors—this man would use a knife, if I were lucky, and fillet me like a fish.

His men's hands went up and down my body. They took my cell phone and all my guns. A man with a chest built like a barrel pushed a hand into my jacket pocket and came out with the flashlight. He passed a glance at the other man of average proportions, but who dragged a heel when he walked.

"What are you going to do? Kill us by flashlight?" He tossed it on the table with the rest of my weapons. "Sit!"

Before I could oblige, they pushed me backward onto a hard chair. My arms were yanked and tied to the arms. I put up a pitiable struggle to make them feel like they were in control. I knew there was no point in fighting; I would lose. The power ratio wasn't in my favor. I glanced at my flashlight.

They had me set up in the middle of the hangar. There was a table in front of me about six feet away.

The barrel of an AK-47 was slid down my cheek by Limpy. Most people might buckle under this, but for me it told me two things about the men in front of me. They were weak and resorted to scare tactics. They held no real power to make one step without Christian's approval.

"Why don't we kill you right now?" As he leaned in close, I noticed the sliver-line scar that ran the length of his cheek.

"Nice beauty mark," I said.

His expression died. "You think you're funny shit?" He turned to the large guy who had backed up a few steps. "He thinks he funny shit."

I never even saw the fist coming, but as it connected with my face, I felt bone shift. The radiating pain brought with it a light-headedness. It was time to put myself someplace other than here. I transported back to Sunday mornings with the family. We missed our brunch yesterday. We would have had eggs, pancakes—I could smell the bacon.

Through my imaginings, I felt the heat of blood rushing from my nose down my face. I let my head fall slightly forward to ride the endorphins racing through my bloodstream. Blood dripped to my lap.

"Look at me funny shit." Limpy Scarface bounced in front of me, waving the AK-47 as a child's toy. To him, this was all a joke. He held no respect for the weapon or the power it provided him. People like that were naïve, weak-minded.

"Leave him alone Dominic." Barrel Chest directed his counterpart.

The fire in the man's eyes extinguished as he was doused by the counseling words of the larger man. The gun didn't seem secure in his hands now. He seemed to have lost resolve.

"We should kill him. Prove our loyalty—"

"He doesn't ask for us to make the rules. Back down." The warning was given with a few steps of forward movement.

Limpy Scarface held up his hands in surrender. The AK-47 hung on an angle at the front of his torso as he raised his arms.

The front door opened and I turned to look. The large man slapped me hard across the face. Blood sprayed as my head was forced to the left.

"*Basta!*" Christian snapped both his fingers. The two pit bulls came in behind with Landen, who handled their leashes. In the past, no one touched Christian's dogs—Mitchell had been the man's sole property and was to remain untouchable by anyone other than himself. The dogs snarled, lips curling, mucus dripping from their jowls to the concrete floor. Whoever this woman was to Christian, they were close.

The barrel-chested man jumped back. "I found him, Boss."

Christian looked to the table full of my guns, his eyes taking in every inch of space. He pulled his attention from there to me.

It would be easier to mentally transport myself somewhere else but now was not the time. I would have to endure whatever pain was coming my way and stand up to Christian, let him witness the defiance in my eyes. To do anything less would be construed as a weakness. If I was ever going to get my family back, this was the last thing I could afford to reveal.

Christian touched my weapons. His hands stopped on the flashlight. "You come in here dressed like Rambo."

The men in the room snickered until Christian silenced them with a glare.

"You're just missing grenades." His hands retracted, and he stepped toward me. "You come in here like this after I have a job for you—"

"I don't want—"

"Rarely do we get what we want in life, Hunter." He took a few steps around me. His tactic was one of intimidation, and it would work on most people. In this regard, I found myself among the majority. Christian was as unpredictable as a snow squall.

"What are you doing here?" He asked. "I doubt the snooping was en route to our meeting."

The fact blood flowed from my nose didn't even seem to impact him. His eyes skimmed over my face, barely acknowledging any difference there from the last time he saw me.

"You want to be White Knight, rescue your family?" Christian clasped his hands behind his back as he walked.

The woman kept her distance with the pit bulls. She exuded confidence, which kept her chest out, a look that most men would find themselves attracted to.

"Why are you not looking at me when I talk?"

I continued to refuse eye contact. "Where is my family?"

"Where is my family? Where is my family?" Christian mocked me. "You sound like parrot. Squawk, squawk."

His people apparently found his sense of humor amusing as snickers filled the hangar—laughter paid for with fears and money.

"You don't want to play by the rules." Christian came to a standstill in front of me. "Rules are put in place to protect us, to direct us."

"Governor Behler is dead." The final word cut through gritted teeth.

He turned around looking at the other two men and the woman, who shrugged her shoulders.

"The media say she's alive," Christian said.

"That's shit!" Blood and spittle sprayed from my mouth. Christian jumped back. My anger propelled me upward. The restraints limiting my movements; my legs lifting the legs of the chair off the floor. Barrel Chest pressed me backward until the chair leveled out again.

A smirk spread on Christian's lips the way I would imagine gangrene spreading across flesh, eating away at it slowly yet steadily until it claimed its victim. "I know she's dead, Hunter."

"Then, what the fuck—"

"You know things, too many things." Christian snapped his fingers and everyone left the hangar except for the woman. She stayed and held the leashes of the dogs. He spoke something to her in Italian I didn't understand. She nodded, walked down, and tied the dogs where they were before.

There was only one thing keeping me alive until this point—the fact that I had once saved the man's life. I feared how long it would be before the benefits of that favor expired.

"I know nothing," I said.

"You lie." He stood there watching me as if he anticipated my making a move.

My eyes drifted to the table where my guns and flashlight were. They were only feet away but might as well have been left in my house back in the city.

"By now you likely figured out everything." He paused. "I have an agenda, plans of my own. You're not the only one with ambitions, Hunter."

I remained silent. My mind projected beyond the pain that relentlessly came in waves, varying from intense to mild, to the murder of the man before me. There would be a correcting of an earlier misjudgment that happened eighteen years ago.

"Your eyes deceive you." Christian bent down in front of my face. "He sent you to kill me, didn't he?"

CHAPTER SEVENTY-ONE

Niagara Falls, New York
Monday, June 14th, 2:00 AM

Clinton didn't know why he even bothered trying to sleep. The pizza was heavy in his stomach and the couple beers he had made him feel bloated. He watched the ceiling of his bedroom counting the imperfections in the plaster, the dips and curves, the cracks—easily fifteen that he could determine in the relative darkness.

His bedroom faced the main street and the lights filtered through the thin, black curtains. He had thought of getting darkening shades or something to cut out the light but never put value in the investment given the fact he rarely slept. When his body did finally give out on him, it wouldn't matter if he were in a dorm room with partying college students. Maybe his bad relationship with rest had started early in life. He just always felt there were more exciting things to do than sleep. He'd push himself by his fleshly inclination. When his body ached for sleep, he'd stay up a while longer. In a way, he had programmed and conditioned himself for a career that would benefit from his sleep regimen or lack thereof.

One name stamped in his head as he watched the ceiling with intense scrutiny. Leone. He was a man Clinton just couldn't find himself trusting. He had been eager and egotistical from their first meeting. Not that this necessarily weighed into it. A lot of people walked around the city with a superior sense of self. Narcissism was the catch word of the twenty-first century. Everyone had a slice of it embedded in their fibers. No longer frowned upon, it was deemed a defense mechanism. It erected boundaries of restraint that would dictate what they were willing and unwilling to do, what was considered beneath them and what was acceptable.

It was none of these things that raised suspicion on Leone. It was his adamant stance on committing to the fact the Mafia carried out the hit and assassination. How could he know this with absolute certainty?

Clinton didn't think of himself as a difficult person, or one who would contradict the grain of the world just simply for the fight, but he wanted more proof than they had. Leone could simply be the type of person who fueled his suspicions from the pit of his stomach. Clinton respected a level of that in any decent cop, but Leone went over the top with it.

In recap, they had a dead Governor and her mutilated bodyguard. Clinton wasn't naïve enough to believe the two weren't connected. He also wasn't stupid enough to dismiss the possibility of the Mafia's—or another type of organized crime's— involvement. But Leone had a name.

Christian Russo was the son of the Don, Pietro Russo. Clinton had confirmed this fact online prior to dragging himself down the hall to his bedroom. The names and their positions agreed with what Leone had mentioned.

It was then Clinton remembered the family Leone had brought up. A father was murdered after his wife and children were. Where did Leone say that was again?

Clinton narrowed in on a large chip of plaster that had curled back due to being painted. Didn't people know they weren't supposed to paint plaster ceilings? With his disjointed observation, he had his answer—Detroit, Michigan.

He said that Christian had been a suspect in the case, but the charges against him were dismissed. Leone never elaborated on why they were. Clinton didn't really need the details— the Mafia had power and money. This he knew drawing from Hollywood's portrayal and very little from real life.

Surprising as a cop and detective for twenty-two years, he never had a case that led him to their front door. Maybe he should consider himself fortunate that he didn't have the run-in. Right now, he considered it a negative, something that made him ill prepared for this case.

More than heartburn churned in Clinton. The questions about what happened to the old case couldn't be ignored. If they had strong evidence, where did it go? None of Clinton's guesses cast good light on Leone.

Clinton bounded from the bed, giving himself over to the fact that he wasn't going to sleep. When his mind demanded answers, it compelled him to find them.

He flicked on the computer monitor. He squinted and averted his eyes from its brightness as they adjusted to the light. Moving the mouse around and watching the screen with one eye open, he noticed the flying cursor approach the taskbar.

He yawned as he took a seat. Again, his mind had betrayed his body's sleep requirements. Maybe he could fall asleep if he actually gave himself over to the idea. Instead, his hands splayed on the keyboard. He fumbled over the keys, backspacing and cursing until finally he had the results he was looking for—the Detroit newspaper. He went to the archives and was thankful they kept the last twenty years available for free viewing; he only needed to go back fifteen.

> *Robert Riley, father of two, was murdered in a city apartment after his wife and children were killed in the family home. No leads in the case yet, although the police department is leaning toward mafia involvement.*

Clinton continued working his way through the updates on the story.

> *The FBI has been called in to handle the case of the four murders, involving a man and his family. Last week the woman and two children were found in their suburban home. The husband was found in a downtown apartment.*

Clinton scanned the article.

> *...Special Agent Leone is heading up the investigation but working with Detroit PD. When asked for information, he declined comment.*

"I bet he did," Clinton said aloud as he leaned back into the chair. His body was starting to sag with fatigue.

Clinton worked his way through a series of articles on the investigation and ended with the last one.

Evidence in the case has been inconclusive," FBI Special Agent Leone said outside of the Detroit Police Station. "There is no further need to continue casting light on an organization that already has enough speculation placed upon it." Leone walked away as we tried to obtain more answers. His last words being, "No further comment."

Clinton stared at the last three words. They were the words that founded America's lies that replaced darkness for light, mistruths for gospel. Behind those three words, the ultimate truth lie buried.

CHAPTER SEVENTY-TWO

Outskirts of Detroit, Michigan
Monday, June 14th, 2:00 AM

The twinges of pain held a predictable rhythm in Brenda's head. Her legs were barely willing to move as she did her best to conjure up the strength to make it to her children. To be able to see them across the room in the same place with her, gave her a sense of hope. Even if the feeling remained unfounded and based on nothing more, she had to clench onto anything tangible she had.

She had maneuvered her way down the cot she had been lying on, but the remaining distance seemed unattainable. As if in a nightmare where you needed to run but your legs wouldn't move, she sat there watching her children.

Her eyes went to their chests, to determine rise and fall, breathing. Max was curled on his right side with his legs tucked up. He always slept in such strange positions at the best of times. Yvonne was lying on her back. As Brenda strained to verify life, she heard her daughter's soft snores and saw the slight movement of her son's shoulder as he breathed.

A rush of air left her lungs—they would be okay. A jab of pain seized Brenda's forehead, this time at an irregular interval, and it tightened more than the rest. A hand instinctively went to her forehead. As she talked herself through the pain, she felt such hatred for the bastards who did this to them. She worried that they used the same dosage on the children as they had her. If she felt this way, how did they make it through the last time?

She wanted to tell herself that they would have adjusted the dosage, giving them a lesser amount. But nothing in this place could be given a positive spin. To be humiliated, stripped of her clothes and tied to a chair, to be leered at by men, and her body caressed by a stranger. They were bereft of human compassion.

She found thankfulness in the fact they hadn't raped her. The thought of such a violation made Brenda's eyes settle on her daughter. She needed to wake her and make sure they didn't do anything to her, to her angel.

Brenda looked at her legs and willed them to move. She gave herself a pep talk about the fact she was a woman meant for childbirth—a woman who had experienced and survived that pain twice. She could move if she wanted to. Harnessing one's true strength required an exercise of mental power.

If they touched one part of Yvonne, she would kill the men responsible for their capture and their violation of human rights. She had differences with her daughter, most mother and daughter relationships were wrought with them. It didn't mean their importance to each other was strained irreparably. Instead, Brenda took some sort of satisfaction from the fact the two of them did have differences of opinion. Maybe before now, before all this, she never would have admitted enjoying the arguments, the debates over boyfriends and curfews. But now, here in this prison cell, the fight she saw in her daughter made her proud. Ray and she had groomed Yvonne to be an independent person and if the reward for that stipulated differences in opinion, it was well worth it. Independence was a necessity in this world.

Brenda swallowed back the latter thought. Independence. That single word stole her breath, a portion of her soul. She thought of Ray and their promises, of their marriage commitment. She swallowed a well of emotion that would unquestionably receive power and seize her if she allowed her thoughts to continue. Yet she was only human. Sometimes it was near impossible to muster strength.

A few tears fell as she thought of the man she sacrificed her life for, the same man who took off on a last minute trip and ordered a tux to be picked up at the destination. No one required a tuxedo for a tax seminar. She hated herself for being gullible enough to believe him.

Her legs started to respond to direction and moved over the edge of the cot. She was able to wiggle her toes. A feeling of control swept over her. She went to stand, but her legs gave out beneath her. She fell hard to the dirt floor. She moaned and cried from the pain, more from heartbreak than the physical discomfort.

As she lay there, the words she had screamed out to her captor repeated. "Why are you doing this?" She remembered the way she felt when she had asked—so desperate, so confused, and drained of emotion.

"Talk to your husband lady." The man's boots had scuffed along the floor and then the door had shut heavily behind him.

His response didn't make any sense, even now. Ray was an accountant. They were careful about their spending and sticking to a savings budget. Brenda had seen enough movies where a gambling debt or such got someone killed… but they normally didn't come after the entire family. And something told her these people weren't bookies.

Brenda wondered if she knew her husband at all.

CHAPTER SEVENTY-THREE

Clinton didn't even remember shutting his eyes, but he remembered a series of dreams—segments and snippets that revolved around the case. Inserted within the layers of strange images were underlying suspicions that played out. In his mind, Leone was more of a bad guy than a good guy. Not that Clinton had anything to base his gut feeling on.

Clinton rubbed at his eyes—the sockets tender from exhaustion as he willed them open. The monitor flashed the screen saver and the Windows logo danced across the screen. It felt like he had been asleep for hours. He moved the mouse and realized he had been out for about thirty minutes. According to the clock, in the bottom right-hand corner, it was two-forty-five.

The newspaper site was still up. Clinton's eyes went right to the name—Leone. If he were going to find out anything about this guy, he'd have to delve into his past. With the current case the scale of this one, he found it hard to justify this side mission. What did it really matter if the guy wasn't a saint? How many people in this world were anyhow?

But there was that nagging tug on Clinton's intuition, as if by finding out who Leone really was it would somehow bring him to the assassin.

It had been his idea to send the man on a plane to Michigan. He could justify the trip. They needed to know more about Rolex, or Carson, to find out what was really going on.

From his research on Behler he knew she kept mostly to herself. She owned a chain of florist stores by the name of Rose Buds. It had started out in one location but had flourished into a profitable entity.

It seemed like a lot of what Behler touched turned to gold. Was it merely good fortune or did she have the backing of people who could culture diamonds from stone?

Clinton had the phone in his hand and pressed the numbers before he considered the possible repercussions.

"Detroit Police Department." Based on her tone, the woman who answered would rather be at home in bed.

"I need to speak with Detective Sergeant Kyle Unger." He was the one in charge when the murders happened.

"You mean the Chief?"

The lack of sleep mingled with a bit of rest had made Clinton's mind fuzzy. He had never even given consideration to fact the man could have advanced his rank. "Yes."

"He's not in at this hour, sir. Is this an emergency? Should I page him?"

Clinton gave his response little thought. If he roused him from his sleep at this time of night, he would be less likely to cooperate. He was certain the fact he was from Niagara Falls PD would be enough to warrant a call back. "Please just leave a message for him."

A yawn encompassed his face, and he knew it was time to listen to his body. In just over four hours, he'd be meeting up with Wingham.

CHAPTER SEVENTY-FOUR

Outskirts of Detroit, Michigan
Monday, June 14th, 2:45 AM

There were things in my life i wished i could retract, do over, mulligan as my golfing friends would say. But in real life, we don't get a second chance to reset a lapse in judgment, do something differently. As the man paced in front of me, around me, watching me as intently as I was him, I would exchange this for a time eighteen years ago. But unlike most things in life, I did have the opportunity to right a wrong, reset.

We latched eyes as if in a battle of wills, but I saw more there. He knew I was sent to kill him. How? Was the report of that man's body aired on the news, or did he have an inside source? Is that what he referred to earlier when he said he didn't want to play games? Had he connected it to the Don?

"Release my family," I said.

The blood from the blow to my face had congealed and stopped a while ago; the blood caked to my flesh.

"You won't answer me. I have ways to make you talk." Christian snapped both fingers, and the pit bulls growled from where they were chained.

If the man was trying to instill fear, he failed. I only feared one thing at this point—the safety of my family. I didn't have the luxury of kneeling to fear, submitting to it. They needed me to free them. I was their only hope. My mind replayed the message from my wife. The anger and betrayal that had filled her voice. How I wished that she could forgive me. I was tired of the lies, the deceit, hiding who I had been. It was time for her to know. Yet there would be some things I would withhold.

"Why are you doing this?" I asked.

Christian stopped walking. He was behind me. With his shoes no longer tapping on the concrete floor, it left an uncomfortable silence. Part of me feared the quiet more than the noise. The fall of footsteps could be calculated, held a rhythm, a precise increment—predictability. Silence couldn't be gauged. While it could be sensed, even hold a tangible quality, it was unpredictable. Volatile.

"I did as you asked me to. She's dead." For some reason, I felt compelled to fill the empty space.

Slicing through the stillness, I heard the gun being pulled from the waist of Christian's pants, the metal scrapping over the belt he wore. The barrel pressed into my skull.

"I'm the one who asks the questions."

Fear and adrenaline mixed together, infusing me with a high like no other. While the adrenaline gave me a sense of empowerment, the fear tamped it down bringing logic back into focus.

"I could shoot you right now." He pressed the barrel harder into my head.

"Do it." The words escaped, and I wished I could reel them in. Stupid to call a man's bluff, especially when that man was Christian.

The gun dropped and the footsteps started. He walked around to face me. He waved the gun in his hand as he spoke. "I hold a gun to you. You say shoot?" A laugh hurled upward from his gut. "I could you know. I'd feel no guilt."

For a minute instant, I saw betrayal reflect in his eyes. "You didn't want to let me go," I said, referring to fifteen years ago when I had turned my back on The Family in pursuit of a life of my own.

His lips pressed together.

"You put yourself into my life so you could call back on me when you needed to."

"You're only who you are because of me!" He spat in my face. I shut my eyes just before impact. The slime of his mouth dripped down my face and mingled with the dry blood.

"You let me go because of Pops."

"Don't call him that! He never was to you!"

"He was."

He slapped me hard. The burning that had finally subsided came back with a vengeful intensity.

"How can you know family, Hunter?" The gun waved as he gestured empathically. "You turned your back on yours. Your parents, Bible-thumpers. You love violence." His arm extended and showcased the length of the table littered with my weapons. "You don't know family."

He attacked me at my most vulnerable point of impact—family. It was everything to me and always had been. The fact I didn't want to follow the course of my parents shouldn't be held against me and attested to at every turn. We all have to make our own choices in life; I had made mine when I was seventeen.

"You wield guns like Rambo. Walk around like a type of god." Christian mocked me. "But," he paused, holding up a finger. "Then you met me. I gave you a place where you belonged."

"We knew it wouldn't last—"

"Correction you thought it wouldn't." He replaced the gun back into the waistband of his pants. "Once you become one of us, you are one of us for life."

"You could have killed me before."

My statement was responded to by another laugh. "Why would I do that?"

Another reflection flashed through his eyes, one of a disappointed child who receives a gift they never wanted but are forced to play with.

"He wouldn't let you," I said.

"Ridiculous—"

"He told you to let me go."

"Absurd. I will not listen to—"

"I saved your life; he extended me mine."

"Stop talking."

"Or what? You will kill me like you wanted to years ago?"

Christian let out a wail of anger. He tugged on his hair. "You don't know him."

"I know you. You want to be in control. The Boss."

This statement met with a physical lashing out, another hand across my face. He couldn't silence me. I spit blood. "You could have killed me by now. Why haven't you?"

He drew the gun to my face. I could smell the gunfire from the tip of the barrel. This gun had been fired recently. I feared it might be again.

CHAPTER SEVENTY-FIVE

Detroit, Michigan
Monday, June 14th, 2:50 AM

Commuter flights were meant for the commoner, not for someone like Leone. People pressed in on his shoulders from the left and right while he jealously observed nearby seats that remained empty. Yet flight personnel had directed him to stay put. Seats were assigned on flights for a reason.

Leone knew the reason was to identify them in the case of a plane crash. He hated planes but had found a way to overcome his fear of flying. Fear for his life was a powerful motivator. He was more afraid of displeasing powerful allies than facing the ground in a ball of fire.

But all of that risk was now behind him. He had landed on Michigan soil twenty minutes ago. As he unloaded, he pulled down on his FBI issued windbreaker. He looked out over the automotive city of Detroit with disdain. It had never been a pretty city to him by any set of standards. The air was thick with pollution and everything was so industrialized, bland. A city of steel and concrete. He preferred the colors and cultural flare of a larger city.

He had called ahead. The plans were in place. Pietro Russo had been thrilled to hear from him—despite the hour. He said things would finally be set right.

Pietro directed him to his residence. Classified a house, but it was not much smaller than some castles. Leone pulled up to the front gate.

"I must verify your arrival."

The guard was armed with a machine gun. He would be one of The Russo Family's soldiers, the lowest in the Mafia pecking order. The way he seemed aware of the weapon with each movement of his body told Leone he was new to all of this.

He watched him saunter off into the gatehouse and pick up a phone. He studied his facial reaction as Leone's presence was verified. His cheeks flushed as he hung up. He nodded toward Leone and lifted the gate.

Leone didn't reciprocate with a nod but continued through the gate. Young and impressionable—weak. He never considered himself to have been that insecure.

"How nice of you to come, Tony." Pietro held out an arm and braced a hand on Leone's shoulder. Due to the man's height, the reach had his arm on an upward forty-five-degree angle.

"Sit, Special Agent." Pietro gestured to a pairing of leather chairs that sat on top of an exquisite Persian carpet. Leone knew from past meetings the Italian had paid nearly two hundred thousand for it.

Leone took a seat and glanced at the fireplace beside him, which boasted a fire for mid-June.

Another man stood in the back of the study, leaning against a large picture window, mindlessly gazing out of it periodically. Leone wasn't sure what he'd be looking at as it was dark out. The man directed a gentle nod toward Leone when he had walked past.

"How is the investigation?" Pietro asked.

"Everything is going according to plan." Leone smiled at Pietro who returned it with wide smile.

"I love that about you. You are obedient. A gift for you." Pietro extended an envelope across the table to Leone. "For your loyalty." He sank back into his chair. "Now, why have you come?"

"The investigation has led us to your son." Leone studied the Don's expression and body language. The man didn't seem surprised by the allegation. He continued, "We believe he may have killed the Governor." Still another brave statement when confronting a man who had the power to eliminate you with the utterance of a one-word command.

"What leads you to him?"

Leone noticed the underlying rage that wanted to surge to the surface. It rang through the Don's tone of voice, the arch of his brow, and the way he refused eye contact.

Leone extended the photograph of Carson from the motel. "He was one of Behler's men. But he also had some sort of connection with your son."

"I recognize him." Pietro kept staring at the photograph.

"Now it could be explained away that your son killed him, and it was unrelated to the assassination of Governor Behler."

"How does this tie back to my son?"

Leone noticed the pulse in Pietro's cheek, an unrestrained sign of anger.

"The markings on him. TSK TSK. This is similar to fifteen years ago."

Pietro tossed the photo onto the table. His attention was on the fire that burned wildly in the fireplace. "Why are you telling me this?"

"As you mentioned. I am loyal." Pietro remained silent; Leone felt wrath permeate the air between them. The aura was powerful enough to strangle.

"We don't touch dignitaries. It is a rule," Pietro said.

Leone bit back his initial reaction. He wanted to say something to the effect of dignitaries were easily bought and paid for. Instead, he said, "Well, that's what I thought." Leone scooped up the photograph and placed it back in his shirt pocket. He went to stand up and Pietro followed his lead.

The man near the window averted his eyes to outside. Leone had noticed him glance over periodically as he spoke to Pietro.

"Sorry to have disturbed you," Leone said with an extended hand.

Pietro's jaw tightened and a pulsing twitch tapped in his cheek. He gestured toward the door.

"Actually, one more thing," Leone said.

Pietro's eyes met with Leone's and enlarged when he saw the gun pointed at him. Seconds later, he lay dead and bleeding on his rare and expensive carpet.

Leone shrugged. He never did like the rug.

CHAPTER SEVENTY-SIX

Outskirts of Detroit, Michigan
Monday, June 14th, 3:00 AM

"You did all of this to prove yourself." For some reason, I found myself provoking Christian, taunting him as a schoolyard bully. I may be the one tied to a chair, captive, by all standards, vulnerable, yet I possessed something Christian never had—mental strength. If a man could be overpowered in mind, he was the weakest sort. Why I felt the need to prove my theory with a gun pointed on me, I didn't really know.

"Ah!" Christian let out a wail and retracted the gun. His hand went into a pocket and he pulled out a knife. "*Basta!*"

With his lash out of anger, I remembered the man who stood at the corner bar in Pietro's back room. His rings were oversized for his fingers, and his eyes were darkened in shadow. "He was going to leave everything to someone else."

The knife tore into my flesh with relative ease, right through my clothing and into the meat of my thigh. I focused on another place, another time, than the now.

"What? You think you're so smart." He thrust the knife into my open wound, the blade biting further into my flesh.

The pain sent shivers down my legs and up my torso. The sting bit inside my chest. I dropped my head.

"Finally, you show weakness, Hunter."

It took everything from within to lift up my head. The throbbing pain threatened to deplete all my strength, physically as well as mentally. I needed to keep talking so I wouldn't blackout. "Why did you want her dead?"

"She…" The knife motioned in erratic movements in the air; the steel stained crimson. My other leg instinctively prepared itself for impact with the blade. He never executed on my suspicion.

Unpredictable.

"I don't answer to you, Hunter. I answer to no one."

"So it's the truth. Everything was just out of reach for you. Power, money, happiness."

"Basta!"

"That's how you deal with it. You scream enough, you wave a gun, cut with knives. You're a coward!" The pain had seized control, rendering me a man gone mad.

"How dare you?" Christian's hands gripped at the collar of my jacket. He spoke inches from my face, spittle projecting with each syllable. "You don't know me."

"I do—more than you like."

Christian released me. His eyes fell downcast, and I felt sadness in the air. "He sent you to kill me."

"I want my family back."

"But he sent you to kill me in exchange for them!"

I didn't say another word—there would be no advantage.

. . .

Detroit, Michigan

"Bravo!" Hands clapped, and the man at the picture window stepped toward Leone.

He knew that voice, the exaltation. Agostino? Leone had suspected that the mysterious man at the window had his back. Leone handed the envelope Pietro had given him over to the Consigliere for the Caparelli Family.

"You keep. You earned it." He shoved it back toward Leone. "Now you must finish things."

Leone nodded his allegiance to this man. He had originally questioned why they had chosen him to take care of their *house cleaning* and had concluded it was a matter of deciding who was trustworthy. Their trust had been betrayed by the Russos and that was unacceptable. Leone made the perfect candidate as they would have known he had access to both Pietro and Christian. They knew Leone could be bought.

The door opened and another Italian walked in, darkened crescents highlighted his deeply set eyes. He laced his fingers together, oversized rings on most of them, including both pinkies. He passed a glance to Roman and then extended a hand to Leone. "Welcome to Detroit."

Leone smiled and bowed his head slightly to display respect. The man he shook hands with would become Pietro's successor as the new Don.

. . .

Outskirts of Detroit, Michigan

Yvonne felt eyes on her and the shiver that ran through her core shook her awake. She bolted straight upward. It took a while for her eyes to focus. She saw her mother on the floor near another cot. "Mom." Her word came out not much stronger than a whisper.

"Mom."

Yvonne looked to her side and noticed her brother lying there. She could hear his breathing and knew he would be okay. She wondered if she would ever see her family again yet here they were, all alive—at least for now.

"Mom!" Finally, her voice came back with some strength.

"Yvonne, my baby." Her mother opened her eyes and crawled along the ground, moving in between her and her brother. "You all right?"

Yvonne nodded, but the tears flowed. She wrapped her arms around her mother. "I'm sorry…for everything." She spoke through sobs as her chest heaved for a solid breath.

"Don't be, sweetheart. I'm sorry too." Her mother held her tighter than she had ever remembered. Even as a little girl with a scraped knee, her mother's embrace never communicated as much love as it did now.

She had always considered her father her favorite parent, even though she knew something wasn't right about choosing one over the other. Maybe most teenage girls went through the stage where their mothers knew nothing about what it was like. They had forgotten about the boys and the desire to be pretty and fit in. Somehow they gave that up in exchange when they became mothers.

"Why are they doing this?" Yvonne asked. In response, her mother grouped her daughter's hair with both hands and then let it fan against her shoulders.

What wasn't her mother saying? Her mother was never quiet.

. . .

Christian leaned over me with the knife swaying erratically. He went to my wrists and I shivered backward in fear. This man was an unpredictable missile that would take on another target with a newly appearing heat signature.

"Don't!" I felt the pain; I lived it as if he had sliced my wrist. I envisioned the blood spraying as the knife slit through the artery. My thoughts went to my family, how they would be without a father, searching for answers, and yet never getting them satisfied.

Christian didn't say a word as the knife moved closer to my wrists. He cut the ropes that tied me to the chair.

"Get up!"

He refused to look at me, and I rose. The throbbing in my leg bit, and rendered me temporarily immobile.

"Move it!"

My attention went to the table with my weapons. My interest on the flashlight.

Christian shoved the butt of the gun between my shoulder blades. Each step shot fiery twinges through my entire body. My mind blurred. All my senses were encompassed with pain. I had to think about something else. I exaggerated a jab in my lower back and moved closer to the table. I lost the strength in my legs and caught myself on the edge of it. I struggled to get up and as I did slid the flashlight from the table into a pocket.

"Move!" Christian pulled up on my arm and forced me to my feet. I wondered if he was going to kill me. His energy spoke of homicidal rage, yet there was something about him that I couldn't read.

He dragged me down the hangar like a bird with a wounded wing. I could barely move or keep pace with the knife gash in my upper thigh. He hauled me through the doorway I had opened earlier in search of my family. It was the hallway that led to the room filled with blood and the decapitated head.

"Think about what you're doing." The plea fell weak, pathetic to my own ears. He was playing with my mind, instilling hope when my fate had likely been sealed.

He unlocked the door to the first room where I had found a swatch of Max's pajamas. "In there!"

Maybe it meant I would be spared?

With the door opened, he pushed me hard enough that I lost my balance between the momentum and my busted leg. I crumpled to the ground. My back was to him. I prepared for the sound of a firing gun and the impact of a bullet. Instead, the door closed with a loud thud.

"Christian!" My yell fell on the empty room and the four walls that encased me—my prison cell.

I went to spring upward, for an instance forgetting the wound to my leg and quickly fell back down. I willed myself to move. Crawling along, dragging my injured leg, I finally reached the door. Inching up I put a hand on the knob, and my fear had been confirmed. Christian had locked me in. As my arm came down the door, the dire reality of the situation set in.

Blood had left a trail a foot wide as I had shimmied across the floor. The bleeding needed to be stopped. Coaxing myself up with my back to the door for support, I worked at tearing off my jacket.

The pain bit with razor-sharp teeth as I leaned forward to undrape the jacket from behind my back. I held it up and assessed the length of the sleeve. When I determined it would work just fine, I ripped it off and wrapped it around the wound. I applied pressure and bit down on the other sleeve as a means of preventing the pain from becoming audible.

The sleeve was just long enough to wrap and tie it into a tight knot. With the pressure on the wound, the blood would congeal and the bleeding would eventually stop. The pressure brought its own source of pain, yet comfort at the same time. My mind knew this needed to be done in order to survive.

I slid a hand into the pocket with the flashlight and pulled it out. Inside the jacket was a hidden pocket where Christian's men had searched but left alone. They came out with the single .22 bullet and had put it back in.

"What's he gonna do with this when we have all his guns?" The smaller man, Limpy Scarface, had a good laugh over stripping me down.

I looked down at the flashlight in my hands. When Christian came back, I'd be ready for him.

CHAPTER SEVENTY-SEVEN

Hours had passed and Leone knew time was running out. Daylight would be here soon enough and he preferred the cover of night. He knew Clinton would be expecting answers come mid-morning about his findings on the Rolex guy—Rick Carson. But Leone had another agenda, and it paid a lot more than some Federal job.

Christian's house was empty when Leone had shown up after popping off Daddy Dearest. The kill had embedded an adrenaline rush in his bloodstream and had filled him with hunger to kill again. He was disappointed to meet with an empty bedroom. The bed was made and the house had been tidied. In fact, Christian's house didn't even appear to have been lived in for at least a couple days.

He rooted through the nightstand and office. The entire time he wondered why the house of a Don's son would be left unattended.

The scenario blanketed him with a sense of uneasiness.

There was a safe in his den, a predictable, stereotypical type. Fireproof with a large combination dial on the front of it. Leone viewed it as a waste of effort to even try to open it. And he knew even if he got inside, there likely wouldn't be any information there that would help him determine Christian's location.

He had stood there, in the middle of the room for a while, hand to his chin contemplating his next step. As he did, he imagined the clock ticking off the seconds.

He thought long and hard about any possible place the man could be, knowing that anything he came up with would be best guess and founded on nothing substantial.

When he came up to meet with Pietro Russo the first time, fifteen years ago, he had been offered a flight to anywhere in the world. He had taken him up on that and went to St. Lucia. It was a beautiful island matched only by the women who lined the shore in bikinis. Many of them were topless. It had been a terrific vacation. But he didn't leave from the regular airport on a commuter flight. Pietro had sent him on a private jet.

It was a long time ago now, but Leone bet he could still find the place. He fished a cigarette out of his pocket, lit up, and was on the move.

. . .

Niagara Falls, New York

The cell phone rang on his nightstand and dragged Clinton from a good dream he was having. He could only recall sketchy details even fractions of a second later when he reached to answer. It involved the beautiful ME that much he knew.

"Hey."

There was a few seconds' pause on the other end.

"Detective Clinton?"

It was a man's voice and one he didn't recognize. His head was still in a foggy trancelike state. "This is."

"This is Chief Unger from Detroit PD. You find out more about the Governor?"

Clinton sat up, sliding up the wall and bumped his head in the process on the bottom of a picture frame that hung over his bed. He rubbed his head. What time was it anyhow? The clock read five thirty. He fought off a yawn.

"I just have some questions," Clinton said.

"You have questions, but you can't answer how the investigation is coming along with the Governor of Michigan?"

Too many departments wanted to have control. Now it was the Detroit PD. "It's coming along."

"Well, that couldn't get any more vague."

"With all due respect, we don't have time for that. And this is regarding another case. The Riley murders from fifteen years ago. You worked on the case with the FBI."

The line went silent. It told Clinton the man on the other end wasn't sure whether to discuss the case or not. He probably wondered what his old case had to do with this current one.

Clinton continued, "We believe the same person involved with those murders may have had something to do with the assassination attempt." Clinton was certain the Detroit PD hadn't been informed of the successful assassination. It was to be contained as much as possible.

"You believe the Mafia is involved?" Unger asked.

"The investigation is leaning that way."

"The Mafia doesn't hit dignitaries. They make a public spectacle of honoring them."

Or of buying them off. It was time to redirect the conversation where Clinton desired it to go. "What happened to the Riley case?"

"Well, four murders. The motive, the knife wounds on the husband, were all tied back to the Mafia from Detroit. But nothing on the bullet."

"Specifically Christian of the Russo family," Clinton said.

"You've been doing your research."

"The same markings have shown up here in Niagara Falls, New York and there's a connection between that and Behler's case. Why was the case against the man dismissed?" Silence again. Clinton felt he may have pressed his luck too hard.

"Maybe we shouldn't be talking."

"What aren't you saying Chief?"

Another delayed pause. Unger broke the silence. "All the evidence against him was proven inadmissible as everything had been obtained without the proper warrants. And the knife went missing from lockup."

"But all the evidence had pointed to him. Robert Riley owed the Russo family thousands in gambling debts."

"The law doesn't always account for the evidence as past generations would have. These days they like to see the forensic proof align as well. We didn't have that. Combine that with unlawful search and seizure..." Unger let his words trail off.

"So a guilty man walks."

"I guess." Unger went quiet again. Clinton wondered if he was thinking what he was: someone in charge was bought off to make the evidence inadmissible.

Clinton could also relate to the Chief's distaste for the modern way requiring forensic evidence to catch a killer. What happened to the good ol' days when detectives did their legwork, held interrogations, and established motives, and built on lack of alibis? If it walks like a duck, talks like a duck, it's a duck. But that line of reasoning didn't fly these days. They'd need a sample of its blood to check the DNA coding.

"Do you remember FBI Special Agent Leone?" Clinton asked.

"Well, of course. We had called in the FBI for help with the murders. Your research should have told you that."

The mention of Leone's name established another facet to the Chief's tone of voice. He didn't care for the man either.

"He was given the lead on the case," Clinton said.

"That's correct, yes. Why?"

"I'm just confirming my research."

"Does your research also show the number of good men who lost their jobs due to that man?"

Well, that was easy.

"Agent Leone wasn't so much an asset to the Detroit PD as he was a detriment."

Clinton wanted to dig into Unger's comment but kept it simple. "Why?"

"He moved in to make the arrest. But he didn't do it by the book. He went in on his own, no backup."

"Not too smart especially when dealing with those types of people."

"I have to believe in the good in people, but with that man…" Unger's words fell off. "He went in and confronted the Don directly."

Obviously Leone had always been a cocky, self-assured, son of a bitch.

"Not long later, it seemed the case fell apart."

"You're saying they bought him off?" Clinton asked.

"I'm not saying anything." There was anger in the Chief's voice now. "I must be going. Good luck with your investigation."

"Thank—" The rest of Clinton's statement of gratitude fell to a dead line.

CHAPTER SEVENTY-EIGHT

Outskirts of Detroit, Michigan
Monday, June 14th, 5:30 AM

When a man is alone, this is when he's the strongest. Dreams become not only concepts but realities. Inventions are born and improvised. For me the silence of this room holds nothing but hope unrealized, yet soon to be fulfilled. I would find my family if I had to crawl along the ground beside them.

I knew hours must have passed by, and that I had drifted in and out of broken sleep. My family's faces formed a collage in my mind. My leg felt cold and numb. The bleeding stopped, but the memory of the impact and the pain remained.

Howling dogs broke my line of thought.

Were they coming closer?

A deep breath released as I heard them move farther away. But there were footsteps in the hallway; someone was out there. I tightened my grip on the flashlight proud of myself for thinking ahead. The flashlight was really another type of zip gun ordered from a specialty online catalog.

One bullet, that's all it should take.

With that thought, my failure in the initial assassination attempt chastised me. It taunted me with a harsh, unrelenting light that threatened to showcase my weakness. I blamed the lack of preparation time as being the reason behind it. This time I would not fail. Christian didn't have a plate in his head, but I wouldn't be shooting at his forehead.

I thought of my family and all they would have been through in the last twenty-four hours. I gripped at the cot I sat on, dwelling on Max as if the bedding would somehow bring me closer to him. Just knowing that I am where he laid bound hours earlier fueled me with determined purpose. Christian would not get away with this.

And Pietro's directive to kill his son in exchange for the freedom of my family, I didn't want anything to do with it.

My mind went to the man who had sat at the bar when I went to meet with Pietro. The way his eyes watched everything yet gave the impression of not seeing. Christian had reacted with intense rage when I brought up the need of proving himself. It had been a stab in the dark that must have revealed the light of truth. Christian wasn't the only man with his eye on the Don's power. And now with the assassination of Governor Behler, New York Mafia Families would be after Pietro as well—yet not for his power. They would view it as a mockery that she was sent there in the first place. To give the impression that Pietro was cooperating, and yet had the woman killed on their soil, would be unforgivable, only redeemed by Biblical standards—a soul for a soul.

Pietro Russo might not even be alive by the time I made it out of here. I stretched out my neck and tried to calculate everything starting with why Christian had wanted the Governor dead. He seemed very pleased when I picked Niagara Falls and now I knew why. The act would reflect on his father, making him a target. He would have failed The Commission. It would have communicated a lack of adherence to their brotherhood. It would have told them that Pietro Russo wanted to run things his own way.

For some reason, I was getting the feeling I was in the middle of something much more serious than a father and son pitted against each other. My family and I were right in the midst of a mafia power struggle.

CHAPTER SEVENTY-NINE

Niagara Falls, New York
Monday, June 14th, 6:00 AM

"What the hell are you doing here?" Wingham answered the door barefoot and wearing a fuzzy robe. Her feet were dry and scuffed along the floorboards of her apartment as she retreated inside. "You said six hours. I have another hour."

She left the door open behind her so Clinton took that as a good sign and followed her. Her hair was tousled and grouped back into a clip. Wild, random curls sprung from her head. Clinton knew better than to say she looked like shit—the words would be a lie and his tone would disclose that.

"We have a case to solve."

"D'uh." She looked at him blankly and rubbed her fingers in a circular motion on her left temple. "I have a headache. I'm exhausted. I'm cranky."

"Leone isn't who we think he is."

"Oh God, this is how the day's going to start out? Another dick measuring contest?"

She dropped onto the sofa and cat hair fluffed up in its wake. She batted it down but didn't seem embarrassed by the unkemptness of her apartment.

"It's not that." He paused expecting to be interrupted, but instead she stayed quiet, her facial expression reading, *then what would it be.* Clinton continued, "He had a case way back. Remember the one—"

"Yes, the murdered family."

"The case was sealed tight, but everything fell apart. Leone was involved."

"So you're saying he threw the investigation."

"What I'm saying is the Mafia bought him off," Clinton said.

Her reaction wasn't what Clinton had expected. He assumed she'd look studious, as she analyzed what he had said; instead she let out a laugh.

"The Mafia bought him off?" She picked at the edge of her robe where it wrapped around her legs. She suddenly seemed aware of her attire and became self-conscious.

"Well, let's just say I spoke with someone from the Detroit PD."

"Did you even sleep?" Wingham let out a yawn.

Clinton batted a hand toward her. "Doesn't matter. This guy confirmed everything went in the tank after they sent Leone in. I believe Leone when he mentioned the cuts being the same as the ones found on Carson."

"So you believe that but have no faith in the man." Wingham didn't speak it as a question.

"Well, we know that Behler met with the New York Governor to discuss something off the books. It wasn't a scheduled meeting for their jobs or some conference. We know there was something important on her cell phone, or why would it be missing—"

"Could be a coincidence."

Clinton shrugged. "Carson was her part-time bodyguard—"

"That's right. She chose to work with him."

"Whatever. You're not listening to me. There's something larger going on here."

"Larger than a Governor's assassination?"

Hearing it come from her lips, it sounded absurd, but... "Yes."

Clinton had been married before. He knew when a woman left the room and said, *just give me five minutes*, she'd return in closer to thirty. Wingham didn't disappoint. She came back twenty minutes later. Her wild curls had been tamed and sleeked straight through the flat bars of an iron. She wore makeup and her nails were redone. Her blue jeans hugged her curves in all the right places, and she wore a white, collared shirt.

"Don't look at me like that." She walked around the apartment, gathering some things. "If you say I look good, I'll drop you to the floor faster than you could say another word."

Clinton held up both hands in mock surrender. His eyes must have betrayed him, because at the moment she came around the bend of the hallway, the sight of her made his breath catch—just a little. "I wouldn't even think of saying that."

"Jerk." She smiled at him as she fastened her holster and slid a chain that held her badge over her head.

"So we've got a busy day ahead of us," Clinton said trying to cover over any awkwardness.

"And don't forget the imposed deadline before the truth about the Governor hits the news."

As if Clinton needed reminding of that ultimatum—solve the case before the six o'clock news or risk being a desk jockey for the rest of his life.

She picked up keys from her kitchen table and they jingled as she lifted them. "But before we get started—coffee."

. . .

Outskirts of Detroit, Michigan
6:33 AM

Leone was certain he could get used to this type of lifestyle—the money, the connections, the power. He only had to take care of one more thing to truly be taken seriously. With Christian out of the picture along with his father, he would be in. Agostino would make sure his loyalties were repaid and assign him the finer things in life. As great as the daydream felt, reality kept coming back in disappointing waves. Could he ever really belong to them, or would he be knocked off once his usefulness had been utilized?

If Leone had his wish, he would be able to continue on with the Mafia and leave his job with the FBI. But he knew one thing for certain. The Italians would never let him leave his day job. With him in the position of Special Agent, he would prove useful repeatedly—better than a good luck charm.

He drove out to the hangar he remembered from years ago. The distance out of the city seemed further away, but it could have simply been his eagerness to kill again. Shooting Pietro brought back the hunger.

In his work as an FBI agent most firing of a gun was done on the range for recertification. And if you did fire your weapon in the line of duty, you were looking at piles of paperwork. In this line of work, there was so much freedom. He could shoot and kill without consequence. In fact, instead of being questioned and judged, he had the ability to play God Himself.

He tapped the cigarette butt in the ashtray of the car, extinguishing it with a small push and twist. He looked over the fields and smelled the manure. Both were sensory reminders of how close he was. As he rounded a bend in the road, his headlights caught and refracted off metal. Probably just a kid's bicycle; they were stolen and ditched in the country all the time. But as he slowed down, he realized it wasn't a bike.

. . .

Niagara Falls, New York
6:45 AM

Clinton noticed how tight Wingham's grip was on her Starbucks cup. Her knuckles were white, and when she lifted it up to take a draw, he could imagine the sides of the cup sucking in. He smiled because they were truly opposites, but for whatever reason, their partnership worked. He got himself a coffee as well but had finished it in a few large mouthfuls and dumped the cup in the garbage.

They were standing outside of interview room one, watching Dean Holmstead through the one-way glass.

"Do you think Gamer's really involved?" Wingham asked the question before pressing her lips to the cup again.

Clinton answered her with his eyes on the kid who looked like he hadn't slept in hours. Lockup wasn't a friend to most people. It wasn't just the uncertainty of their future, but a bench in a roomful of rowdy drunks wasn't conducive to a good night's sleep.

"Nope," Clinton said.

"Then why are we doing this?"

"To make sure of it." Clinton brushed by her and went into the room. "Dean Holmstead." He opened a file folder on the table. He had filled it with sheets, most of it meaningless gibberish, but the forms and typestyle looked official. He didn't have a record and seemed to stick to himself. His largest crime was the way he kept his apartment. "Listen, we need to know something."

"I don't know who was in my apartment, okay? We went through this yesterday. Before you made me stay here—" His arms crossed and his brows pressed downward. "I don't know why you guys are so interested in me. Someone broke into my apartment. Shouldn't you be out looking for them?"

Clinton watched confusion cloud Holmstead's eyes. If he only realized that a professional assassin had graced the inside of his apartment and had taken down the Governor of Michigan from his window sill.

"So you came home and your door was locked?" Clinton detected the feebleness of his attempts to corner the guy. He didn't seem to have a clue but he had been closer to the killer than anyone.

Holmstead nodded.

"Yet nothing was stolen."

"I told you—"

"If it was a robbery, don't you think they would have taken things?"

An ear went to a raised shoulder. He rubbed it there as if wishing his current situation away.

"You don't have a smart answer for that?" Clinton asked.

"I just want my laptop back. I want to go home. Sleep in my bed."

The desperation in his eyes made Clinton realize Holmstead was close to tears. Normally, this type of reaction wouldn't elicit any feelings in Clinton, but this time he found himself actually feeling sorry for the kid. Circumstance had placed him in a situation where he was a suspect in a Federal investigation whether he wanted to be or not.

Clinton's cell rang, and he lifted it to see the caller identity. He felt Holmstead's eyes watching him the entire time.

"Can I go?"

Clinton nodded and waved in officers from the observation room to get Holmstead out of there as he answered his phone.

. . .

Outskirts of Detroit, Michigan

The sun was up, and Leone would have killed someone else if it would have stalled its rising. He didn't have a plan of attack, and the closer he got to the hangar, the more he realized the stupidity in his course of action.

He knew there would be others coming after Christian. The fact that the Russo Family was a traitor of The Commission branded the target on their heads. Leone knew that Behler was in Niagara Falls to help Governor Talbot see her side of things. Leone surmised this would involve coercion and manipulation. What politician had an entirely clean record? None that he knew. There were most certainly none found in DC. And he knew enough of them personally to be a good judge of this.

He parked his car beside the other one he found in the ditch. Was it even possible that the driver of this car had nothing to do with Christian Russo and the claim on his life? Leone highly doubted it.

. . .

Niagara Falls, New York
7:00 AM

Clinton walked out of the interrogation room and approached Wingham. "I just got a call from Paulina."

"The coroner." She smiled.

He disregarded the underlying implication of her expression. "She found a hair in the wound track and was able to extract DNA. There was a match. We have a name."

CHAPTER EIGHTY

Outskirts of Detroit, Michigan
Monday, June 14th, 7:00 AM

The four walls of my prison did their best to hinder my resolve. It's not that I would ever give up on getting my family out of here alive, but I wondered now more than ever how I was going to turn my plan into a reality.

There hadn't been any noise in the hangar for hours now. The feeling that someone was in the hallway had left me a while ago. I attributed that to a form of paranoia. At this point, I believed I had imagined the presence of someone else, the noise, and any sensations being conjured from an overactive imagination that sought meaning in my present circumstances.

I sat on the cot, leaning my head against the wall wishing for the opportunity to hold my family just one more time before Christian killed me. I felt remorse for being such a weak character that I even got involved with the Mafia in the first place. And yet, with that realization,

I knew I had never sought them out, but had simply been in the wrong place at the wrong time.

Time and unforeseen circumstances befall us all.

I remembered my parents quoting that from scripture when I was young. I remembered the talks from the platform of their church telling us that *vengeance too is the Lord's and He shall repay*.

Maybe if I had a little more spirituality, I wouldn't be in this situation in the first place. Maybe my family and I would be safe and getting ready to go about our regular Monday routines.

Leone could see the hangar. Two men guarded the front of the building and were armed with AK-47s. Did Christian know he was coming? Or was he already aware that his father had been murdered?

Fear did its best to override his logic, but he had to get things under control. He was trained to deal with intense circumstances, negotiate with terrorists. How was the Italian Mafia any different? They may not have been a threat to the average citizen yet they had the power to execute their own justice. They had their own standards as to right and wrong.

. . .

Niagara Falls, New York

If clinton never saw The Grandeur hotel again, he'd be all right with it.

"You make an appointment with the Governor?" Talbot's bodyguard stood in front of the suite door with his hands laced together. He didn't view them as a threat this morning.

"Tell him we're here. Detectives Wingham and Clinton."

Clinton watched as he visibly swallowed, the bob heaving his Adam's apple, before he turned on them and slipped into the suite. Clinton forced his way in behind him. Wingham followed her partner.

"What are you doing? Stop there—"

The bodyguard's words stopped when Governor Talbot came out of the bedroom, adjusting his necktie. Politicians and those in power always rose early. They had a lot of fires to put out, and the day started at 5:00 AM, if not earlier. If the Governor were just waking up now, he would have slept in.

"Sorry, sir. I told them to wait in the hall—"

Talbot silenced his man with a wave of the hand. "Back in the hall."

"Yes, sir. Again, sorry, sir." The bodyguard cast a glare in Clinton's direction that could spark a forest fire.

When he left the room, Talbot motioned them into the sitting area. "What are you doing here Detectives and it better be good."

"We have a name."

"You've found the assassin?" He twisted his wrist and looked at his watch. "Very impressive. In just over twenty-four hours."

Wingham dropped herself into the same chair from last night. Clinton remained standing.

"Does the name Brenda Hunter mean anything to you? The hair pulled from the body came back a DNA match to her."

He shook his head. "Should it?"

"We don't have time for this Governor."

"What do you expect me to say?" He crossed one leg over the other.

Clinton looked at Wingham directing her in silent eye communication that it was time for her to excuse herself. They had discussed the possibility of this happening. If there were repercussions from what was going to be said, Clinton would take the heat alone.

Talbot watched nervously as she left the room.

Clinton sat on a sofa across from the Governor. "What are you afraid of?"

"What—"

"I know that Governor Behler was discussing things with you. Things you don't want coming to light."

He uncrossed his legs, leaned forward, and clasped his hands. His expression saying, *what do you think you know?*

"Behler had a connection with the Italian Mafia—"

"Ludicrous! I won't stand for this besmirching of a murdered, respected colleague." He glanced at Wingham.

"Because you're afraid—"

"Watch your allegations, Detective."

"She came to you with them backing her."

"Insane. You must have spent the night dreaming and fabricating these lies."

"I know you stand hard against organized crime—"

"Damn right I do. Have you looked at my track record?"

"That's part of the problem. Clean."

Talbot appeared confused.

"What Governor or politician has a clean history? Name one."

"This is ludicrous."

"What's ludicrous is your hindrance in this investigation. And I don't care why, that's not my issue. But the man who joined you and Governor Behler for dinner Saturday night at Casa Grande, what was his name?" Clinton knew he was acting on a hunch, a speculation, not a suspicion, as it was grounded on nothing but a gut feeling.

"I told you last night. I don't remember."

"But the name Hunter, it sounded familiar to you."

He shrugged a shoulder. "I've heard the name before—"

"So—"

"But I hear lots of names in my line of work. Surely you understand that."

Clinton sat back, exasperated. Talbot was a politician through to his sinew. A minute of silence passed.

"I know you're afraid, and if the Mafia had Behler killed, well, then it's quite plausible you could be next." Clinton watched as the Governor pulled out on his necktie and then undid it. "We could protect you."

"Like you did her?" Talbot's jaw tightened, but then he continued, "The man that night. His name was Hunter."

"She knew him?"

"Yes. She introduced him as her accountant."

Since when are things ever straightforward? Clinton stepped into the hallway to meet back up with Wingham. He filled her in on what he found out about the man named Hunter.

"So he followed her from Detroit to here?" Wingham analyzed the information aloud. "He must have a connection to the Mafia. But he's got a wife and two children."

The background report they pulled on Brenda led them to the name of Raymond Hunter, her husband.

"Lots of men keep secrets from their wives."

"Yeah, other women and hidden Playboys in the attic, not their second career as an Italian Mafia hitman. Besides, the guy's an accountant. Aren't they supposed to lead boring lives?"

"Well, apparently this one doesn't."

"Forensics has her hair, though, not his."

"It's just like the duck theory."

"The what?"

Clinton thought he had explained this to her before. But he went about doing it again. "Just because forensics could put Brenda Hunter's hair near the body, doesn't mean she is the killer. It doesn't even mean she physically came into contact with the body." That's where DNA failed.

"I think you're going to have to come up to this century, Clinton. Forensics have kept a lot of innocent people from going to prison—"

"But how many more has it sent there?"

Clinton dialed the number for Leone's cell phone a few times, but there was no answer. It didn't leave him with a good feeling. He needed him to go over and pick up Raymond Hunter. Finally on his fourth attempt and the fifth ring, there was an answer.

"Hello." Leone picked up as if there were no hurry in life, no concerns that weighed him down.

Arrogant bastard. Hearing the man's voice only reaffirmed the value of distance between them. Clinton relayed the findings in the investigation including that of Raymond Hunter.

"I've actually come across a potentially good lead myself. There's a power shift going on within the Italian Mafia," Leone said.

"How would you know—"

"Just trust me."

Not a chance.

"I went to go through Carson's things at his house. There was a car in the driveway."

Interesting. Didn't Wingham's PI friend say that the address on file was for an abandoned warehouse?

Clinton played along. "Was the man killed there?"

"I looked in the window and it didn't show any sign of a struggle or a break-in."

"The car?"

"I have a plate for you. I was hoping you could do a quick check. Let me know who I'm looking at."

Clinton typed in the digits as Leone fed them to him. "Raymond Hunter."

"That's quite the coincidence."

"I don't believe in coincidences." Clinton hung up the phone. It left him wondering where Leone got the plate number. And how did it pull in Raymond Hunter? Something was about to go down, and there would be a rogue FBI agent right in the heat of it.

. . .

Outskirts of Detroit, Michigan

Leone had a hard time suppressing the smile that wanted to engulf his entire face. Here he was headed into a combat field with nothing but determination and the plan of blaze of glory, yet he felt confident. Clinton had no idea what was going on here in Detroit. Leone only fed him what felt safe. Next time Clinton called, he wouldn't get an answer.

Leone pitched his cell phone into the field behind him and kept walking toward the hangar. He would be killing more than just Christian Russo. He would take out his competition.

CHAPTER EIGHTY-ONE

Outskirts of Detroit, Michigan
Monday, June 14th, 7:00 AM

Everyone has a point in their life when it's time to own up to what one's done. Sometimes coming to face that truth isn't easy. Sharing it with loved ones may even be harder. But if given the choice between holding it in any longer, and breaking free of its rein over your conscience, at what point do you say enough is enough?

The four walls of this room hadn't provided me with the answers to those questions, or the dilemma I'll face when I get out of here—and I will get out of here.

For the last while, I traced the walls of the room looking for any sort of secret opening or means of escape. I found nothing. My only hope of getting out of here was someone opening the door. And when they did, they would die.

Leone continued through the field wishing that the cornstalks were taller and provided coverage. This entire situation was insane if he let himself really dwell on it. Who goes after a member of an Italian Mafia Family alone? It was ludicrous really.

Even knowing that Agostino directed his moves with the backing of The Commission, Leone still felt vulnerable. Christian Russo didn't make it to where he was simply because he was Pietro's blood and flesh. The man was a killer in his heart. Leone had witnessed it firsthand in Detroit years ago. And what kind of a sick man must you be to exact justice on a ten-year-old child?

Even the sixteen-year-old teenager was raped prior to being murdered. To simply imagine carrying out such a crime didn't do anything for Leone. He preferred the real thing—a full grown woman in stilettos, experienced in the ways of pleasing a man. He couldn't even imagine conjuring an erection for a child. The idea was disgusting and revolting on many levels.

Leone pulled out a Glock 22. Not his favorite weapon of choice, but still deadly. The naïve marksmen always thought in terms of Hollywood. It was as if they believed numerous bullets were required for a kill shot. Leone knew it only took one.

He crouched down further into the mounded dirt of the cornfield. Of the two men guarding the front of the hangar, one had a larger build than the other, but one thing working in Leone's favor was neither of them seemed to be very alert. They had probably been stationed there most of the night and not called upon to take care of anything. The AK-47s they held were likely cool from the night air and not kissed with the heat of gunfire.

Leone thought of Hunter. If the man was here to execute some sort of justice, why? Leone remembered from what Clinton told him that the man was an accountant. How did he get mixed up in this situation? He must have had a prior connection to Christian and been the man hired to assassinate Behler. The thought actually brought a smile to his lips. The man had failed the first time. If he took aim at Leone, maybe he would fail again. Leone didn't make room for failure. The accountant would die.

Hunter was likely Tux, the term both of the detectives used for him. Such a childish way of going through life—assigning nicknames to people around you. But Leone supposed that was the way a lot of people functioned. He just wasn't one of them.

He lifted the Glock preparing to take fire. He would have to seek shelter the minute he popped the guy on this side. His partner would likely be more than trigger happy just to get the chance to do something other than stare over empty cornfields.

Leone moved closer to the building. He would take the shot, roll and hide behind the side of the hangar. Gunfire would ring out over the field in the direction of the deadly shot, but Leone wouldn't be there to receive payback.

As he neared the edge of the building, his heart beat rapidly and he noticed the white wisps of his breath rise in the cool morning air.

He braced down, his Glock readied and took aim on the man who never had a clue his life was about to end. Leone squeezed back on the trigger and executed the rest of his plan.

Yvonne sensed fear in her mother and the sudden pullback from their embrace only confirmed it.

"Mom?"

Her mother shook her brother aggressively. "Wake up! Wake up now!"

"Mom?" Yvonne watched her mother with large eyes.

"Max!" She huddled over him and dropped her head to his chest. "He's not breathing."

Tears streamed down Yvonne's face, her heart racing faster than when Jamie stepped into home class.

"What do you mean...he's not breathing?" Yvonne moved over to her brother, her eyes on his chest. It no longer moved up and down.

"Mom, what was that noise?"

Her mother kept working on Max trying to make him come to. Yvonne's extremities were frozen in place. Even willing herself to move an arm, to stir her brother, was impossible.

"Mom?"

Her mother's body sagged as she sat back from Max. Both hands went to her face. Yvonne had never seen her mother so heartbroken.

"He's probably just sleeping really deep." The words sounded weak to her ears, but she had to help her mother through this. She wouldn't give up on her brother.

Her mother went back to rest her head on Max's chest.

Yvonne shook his shoulder, finally able to move. Her mother kept avoiding the other question about the noise they just heard, but she didn't need her to confirm what it was. She had watched enough movies to know what gunfire sounded like. It wasn't exactly like the movies, more like a cross between a firecracker and a car backfiring, but she knew it was unmistakably a gun. She started shaking her brother vigorously.

CHAPTER EIGHTY-TWO

Niagara Falls, New York
Monday, June 14th, 7:15 AM

Clinton looked to Wingham who was sucking back on a new Starbucks. "We have no choice but to involve Detroit PD." He said the statement and sensed the sulking nature in his voice. There went his headlines. Maybe he could salvage it by being the one involved with pointing the investigation in the right direction.

"I don't think we do." The way she watched him, he sensed she was analyzing him, trying to read his mind.

"We're still the ones who got the investigation to this point."

"That's right."

Not that it felt like much of a consolation prize.

"So you're sure that this guy Hunter is the one who did it? I mean it was his wife's DNA on the body. Maybe she's the killer," she paused. "And I don't want to hear anything more about your dang duck theory."

He smiled briefly. She could be such a smart ass. Maybe that's why they made great partners. "Statistically, assassins are men," he said.

Wingham lowered the cup and gestured with her one hand. "Again, the twenty-first century calls out to you, Dave. Women are equally as brutal these days."

As if she needed to point that out to him. His last wife did the cheating. So much for the advancement of womankind. They were empowered with putting on a business suit and with it took balls in their own hands—sometimes literally. Anything was then free game, including retribution on past generations of men who discounted women's contributions and value to society.

"It's the guy," he said.

"You can be so stubborn. You saw her background too." Wingham put the cup back to her lips. She looked like she was about to say something when her cell rang.

Clinton watched the seriousness in Wingham's eyes transform to enlightenment. She thanked her caller and smiled as she hung up.

"That was the car service. They have a name for us as to who rented the Town Car." She held up her hand as she noticed he was about to interrupt her. "And they have a place where Tux was picked up before going to The Oasis motel."

"We're still calling him Tux now we know his name?"

Wingham shrugged her shoulders. "Sometimes the nicknames are better than their real ones. Anyway, he was picked up from a private hangar outside of Niagara Falls."

. . .

Outskirts of Detroit, Michigan

The noise was unmistakable. The report that saturated the air made its way inside my prison cell. I sat up using the support of the concrete wall. The abrupt movement shot pain from my leg through my entire body.

All I could think about was the safety of my family. I needed out of here now. I stumbled to the entrance of the room and pounded my fists on the metal door.

"Christian!" I didn't know what to yell or what to say. But I needed to create a ruckus and make myself a large enough nuisance so that someone would come to silence me.

And now, there was one.

Blood was expelled from the man's head, and Leone watched as his body crumpled to the ground like a rag doll. Leone rolled across the mounds of dirt and pressed against the aluminum exterior wall of the hangar.

"Rocco!"

Leone heard the panicked outcries of the other man. He knew he was alone now and a target.

"Shit! Rocco!" The voice got closer to the edge of the building.

Leone pictured the larger guy hunched over his fallen comrade.

Instead of feeling fear, Leone had been infused with adrenaline.

Deafening reports of the AK-47—sporadic and uncontrolled.

The man let out wails that accompanied the steady hail of bullets. Leone sensed the heat from the weapon. The man was close. Too close. As soon as he had a chance, Leone would round the bend.

Then there would be none.

My fists ached from the repetitive drumming on the metal door. With each impact, they bit a little more, the pain in my leg now a dull ache.

"Let me out!"

I screamed out random words hoping that someone would hear and that someone would come. Minutes passed.

"Max!"

Brenda's words fell flat against the confines of the room. She noticed the panic sweep over her daughter's face when there was no response from her brother. Somehow she had to dig within herself and find the strength to be strong for her daughter.

Brenda's arms went still as she dropped herself down to her son's chest. If there was a heartbeat, it was so faint she couldn't hear it. Had she lost her son in this place? If she had been alone without the fawn eyes of her daughter, she would have screamed and let out a wail that would permeate the walls and reach the city.

"Mom?"

Her daughter kept repeating herself. She was scared too. They needed each other to get through this and get out of here.

More loud reports littered the air. Brenda knew exactly what they were. Maybe she should tell her daughter.

And she would have, but Max coughed and struggled to sit up.

"Max!" Tears fell down Brenda's cheeks, and both mother and daughter hugged him tightly. Brenda was the first to pull back. He would be okay—thank god! But she needed to get her family out of here—now.

She rose to her feet, leaving her children to comfort each other and banged on the wooden door.

"Let us out!"

"My boy!"

"Help!"

Her kids might actually find out something about their mother today. She wasn't as innocent and fragile as she tried to project.

. . .

Niagara Falls, New York

The name given to Wingham for the company that hired the car service was one Grugger's Waste Management from New York, New York.

According to the Internet, it was a large corporate company that specialized in the removal of garbage and recyclables from businesses. People paid thousands a month just to have the crap hauled away.

"Ironic it's waste management," Wingham said it with a smile, and Clinton picked up on the connotation.

The Mafia operated profitable business fronts in areas such as construction, waste management, casinos, and restaurants. "I don't believe in coincidences."

"I know you don't. So what do New York Mafias have to do with our case?"

"I'm not exactly sure yet. Let's talk this out. You've got this guy from Detroit, a Don's son. He wants the power," Clinton said.

Wingham nodded, following along so far.

"He doesn't just want to take out his father— too easy. Maybe not enough of a challenge."

"Okay, but it still doesn't explain New York Mafias."

"Patience." Clinton smiled at her. "Say if, for some reason, Christian knew he'd never have the power within the Russo Family."

"His father, the Don, Pietro was going to leave the legacy to someone else. Yeah, that would piss me off."

"So he makes it look like Pietro betrayed the New York Families. At a meeting set up to make the New York Governor submit to mafia direction, their spokesperson is taken out. Then Christian will swoop in, look like a good guy, replace his father." Clinton shrugged. "It could work like that. It's still speculation."

"I wonder if they knew of Christian's elaborate scheme."

"Hard to say."

"They're normally loyal, aren't they?" Wingham held the cup near her face as if about to take another mouthful but didn't.

"Normally, but if they sense a conflict in direction, they will eat their own."

"So, Christian hired a guy, Tux, Raymond Hunter, to kill the Governor, the same weekend she's there to convince Talbot to see the power of the dark side."

Clinton rolled his eyes at her reference to Star Wars.

"It says to them that Christian's serious about this. He and his father are working on bringing the New York Governor into the fold, as it were. But with the hit, it makes the New York Families think the Russos have betrayed all of them. At the same time, it tips off Pietro Russo. He knows something's been set up." Wingham put her cup down.

"I wonder if the guy's still alive."

Silence passed between the two of them for a few seconds.

"This is going to be a bloodbath before it's over," Clinton said.

Wingham nodded. "We've got to get to the private hangar and find out about the flight Hunter came in on. Find out where his origin was, more specifically than Detroit."

"How much do you want to bet it's another private hangar?"

"Not a gambling woman, but I'd say there's a dang good chance."

. . .

Outskirts of Detroit, Michigan

Leone counted off the rounds. Fifteen. The magazine was empty; it must have been standard stock issue. There was a pause, but he sensed movement. The guy was getting ready to insert a fresh magazine. This would be Leone's only chance.

He rounded the corner. The man didn't even have a chance to yell before his brains splattered onto the metal of the hangar.

CHAPTER EIGHTY-THREE

Clinton and Wingham drove to the private hangar where the Town Car had picked up Raymond Hunter. Wingham had finally dropped his nickname in exchange for his given one. They were now past generics and had adopted Hunter as their assassin.

His DMV photo was a close match to the grainy video from The Grandeur. And they had Murray go back to visit the former Canadian, living the American dream as a motel manager. He confirmed the man in the DMV photo was, in fact, the man who had stayed at The Oasis.

"So Hunter gets on a private plane, comes here and kills Behler. Do you think he was the one who originally failed? Or do you think it was Rick Carson?" Wingham slipped a hand under her chin and delicately scratched it with her painted nails.

"Well, I don't believe in coincidences remember? Hunter was on the security video. He went into the suite with Behler. He was also the one who checked into The Oasis motel twice."

She let out a deep yawn. "Yeah you're right. Blame it my lack of sleep."

"Well, then let's get this thing wrapped up, shall we?"

She gestured to the road in front of her. "You turn right here."

Clinton passed her a glare. He was better at following directions—when it came to destinations—than she was.

The private airport hangar was on the outskirts of Niagara Falls. There was nothing but crop fields around it.

The gravel crunched under the tires of the department-issued Crown Vic as Clinton pulled into the drive.

"Hopefully, someone's home."

"Well, it's still early." Wingham let out another yawn.

"Am I keeping you up?"

"Ah, yeah." She reached for the door handle and got out.

From first observations, it didn't look like anyone was around. All the doors on the hangar were closed. Clinton went for the handle on the front door and found it unlocked.

There was a plane inside, but no one they could see. A piece of metal hit the concrete floor and rang out through the hull of the building.

"In the back," Clinton said, and they both approached where the noise came from.

More metal hit the ground, and they had their room. Extra parts for planes were stored there with the tools to fix them. Wrenches lay on the ground scattered as if the person was looking for the right one.

"Niagara Falls PD." Wingham showed her badge to the man who came around from the back side of the room.

"Holy shit!" A hand went to the guy's chest. "Never even heard anyone come in."

The guy was easily mid-to-late forties wearing stained mechanics coveralls. His rounded torso fought with the straps for control. He stood there gasping to catch his breath.

"What…do…you…want?"   He   spoke through exhales.

"We need to know the origin of a man who flew in here yesterday."

"Nope." His head shook and along with it his thick neck.

He could be a preventative poster candidate representing the benefits of a healthy diet and exercise. Do it, or look like this.

"I'll need to see a warrant." He bent over and picked up the wrenches, one at a time.

"There shouldn't be a reason for that. It's just a simple favor we're asking," Wingham said.

"People fly from here, and to here, because of confidentiality. I'd lose my job."

You have a lot more than a job to lose, Clinton thought, realizing how shallow he could be at times.

Wingham splayed a hand on her hip and bucked it slightly to the right. "You sure? Just one location."

"Listen, lady, if you're trying to pick me up, you've come to the wrong place. Monty's Bar is down the road."

Wingham straightened and her jaw tightened. She gave him a definite glance over. "If you relish not going to jail, I suggest you cooperate with us—"

"You can't make me do something without a war—"

"People do it all the time. It's termed cooperating with law enforcement," Wingham said.

"It's called the unemployment line." He picked up a wrench and stood back, a hand resting on his rounded belly.

"Think of it this way, when was the last time something exciting happened to you?"

Wingham could be impressive. Clinton remained quiet.

"I don't need excitement in my life. I have to get through it."

Clinton stepped forward. "We don't have time for this—"

"Nobody has time."

"There was a man who left here in a Town Car yesterday. We know this for a fact. We also know his name, for a fact. We need to confirm his origin."

The mechanic remained quiet.

"I'll make it real simple for you. Yesterday morning. Early. Did you have any flights come in?"

"Maybe, maybe not."

"Okay, we'll go with maybe. Did this *maybe* flight come in from Detroit?"

The man passed glances between the two of them deciding whether to acknowledge Clinton's question. After seconds of silence, he bobbed his head.

"Now, was that so hard?"

"Now, this *maybe* flight, where in Detroit did it originate from?"

"Oh, no."

"We're just talking in maybes." Clinton smiled at the mechanic.

"Another private hangar. But that's all I'm telling you."

Back in the car, Wingham snapped her belt up with a hasty click.

"Something wrong?"

"How could he not find me attractive?"

"Honestly? I don't think it was that." Her head snapped to face her partner. "I don't think he's seen his pecker in years and it's dead."

"Yeah, you might be right." She laughed. "And there's nothing like feeding him the answers."

Clinton shrugged. "Hey, we do what we've got to do. The next step would have been threatening to actually get a property search warrant. Guessing his employer would appreciate that even less."

CHAPTER EIGHTY-FOUR

Leone knew he had a clear line into the building now. He watched the farmhouse intently, expecting a door to open, for a shot to ring out—nothing but silence. He hated silence; in fact, he preferred chaos at any point in time.

Maybe he should have relished the moment a little longer though. A door opened, one he didn't see, and before he could turn around, something hard hit him in the back of the head. His legs buckled beneath him and he fell to the ground.

I cradled my knuckles into my chest. They burned like fire from the repetitive beating on the door. Panic mingled with pain, and a sense of hopelessness threatened to diminish all my power. But the only thing that kept me moving forward was knowing that my family needed me. I would be their only saving power from this place that they had known for over twenty-four hours now.

The hail of bullets that rang out in the morning air had sliced through silence, and with their demise an eerie calm had returned. But something inside told me they were all right. I had to believe we were all going to come out of this alive.

I set to banging on the door again and screaming whatever random words spewed from my mouth.

Christian paced around Leone. Two other men, one with a large build and one with a scar that ran the length of his face, must have dragged him inside the hangar. Leone kept drifting into unconsciousness. His head throbbed like it had been busted open. His vision was fuzzy and faint. It hurt to breathe.

"There's been so much disappointment these days." Christian took the butt of a pistol and jabbed it into the meat of Leone's upper thigh.

The pain ricocheted through him, but Leone refused to give in to the cry that balled in his throat.

"You can take pain?" Christian replaced his gun in the waist of his pants and withdrew a knife. He laid it carefully in his hand, seemingly admiring the blade. His face went from an expression of peace to one contorted with anger as he brandished the blade downward into Leone's thigh.

Leone could no longer fight against the intense pain. He let out a wail that echoed off the walls of the hangar and back to his own ears.

"Oh, now we're getting somewhere." Christian paced a few steps. "Every man has a pain tolerance threshold. We'll find out where yours really is." Another downward jab with the blade. As it tore through his flesh on the other thigh, Leone felt dizzy and faint. The pain was overtaking his mental powers and his other sensory functions. He would die here.

"You killed my men—" Christian stopped talking and kept still. "What the fuck is that?" He turned around to look at the two other men who seemed to be nothing more than spectators waiting to watch justice be meted out.

The man with the scar said something, but to Leone's ears the words were faded and jumbled; they seemed to be spoken miles away. Leone had to fight to remain conscious.

"Go! Shut him up!" Christian snapped both fingers and dogs snarled.

Leone couldn't see the dogs, but he heard them. They sounded even further away than the man's voice had been. He made out faint footsteps as one of them walked away on Christian's command.

Christian looked back to the knife in his hand. With his eyes on the bloody blade, he said, "Tell me why I shouldn't kill you."

I continued pounding until i heard the door in the hangar open. Someone was in the hallway for certain. I screamed out, "Come here!"

I watched the handle turn and the door opened cautiously. Limpy Scarface came in.

"Shut up!"

He went to shut the door again. I moved quickly and grabbed his wrist. I bent it backward and felt the bones snap under the pressure. He reeled back and cried out. He lashed back out of instinct, coming at me with the determination of a locomotive, yet weak in strength. My fist met his nose and I returned the favor that he had bestowed on me earlier. Vengeance in my hands felt redeeming and more rewarding than waiting for someone else to step in, whether it be a Greater Power or another person.

"You son of a bitch!" Spittle flew, and blood streamed from his face. A man truly gone mad, his eyes raged a wildfire. This man would leave me no choice.

He lunged at me, with his arms flailing as if an epileptic and unable to control his movements. "I will kill you!"

I jumped backward. The pain in my leg bit. I stumbled while trying to redeem ground but lost the battle. I fell to the concrete floor; the man continued to come at me with fury and speed. He kicked at my ribs and I spewed blood.

I refuse to die in this place.

I curled down on the floor in a fetal position, the pain in my torso sapping my sanity. He kicked me again; this time in my back. For a moment, I envisioned just falling asleep. But then my family's faces paraded in my mind. I saw them clearly, felt them. I was their only hope.

CHAPTER EIGHTY-FIVE

Outskirts of Niagara Falls, New York
Monday, June 14th, 8:00 AM

Clinton and Wingham drove back to the station with the lights on, flying through intersections in the city as if in a car chase.

Wingham said, "All right, I guess the call has to be made. Leone still isn't answering his phone." She had repeatedly tried to reach him as Clinton drove and they made their way through the morning commuter traffic.

"I think it's pretty obvious he's not one of the good guys by now."

"But the guy got a medal. That should mean something," Wingham said.

Clinton found it amusing after all her years as a cop and detective, having witnessed all the horrible things she had, that she still sought to see the best in people. He had lost that ability a long time ago.

"Maybe at the time it did." Clinton shrugged. And maybe it didn't.

He pulled the Crown Vic into the parking lot and parked on a wild angle. They both bounded from the car and hurried up to the Chief's office. They needed the Detroit PD's full involvement.

. . .

Outskirts of Detroit, Michigan

"What the fuck? What…the hell is going… there now?"

"Want me to…out Boss?"

The words were only making it through to Leone's ears in broken segments. He expected to feel shivers and chills just before his last breath, yet he was experiencing the opposite effect—warmth. Maybe he would survive this, though he highly doubted it. His eyes wanted to close and he feared that if he allowed them to, they would never open again.

He heard faint screams coming from another part of the hangar, even over the racket of barking dogs.

"*Basta!*" Christian shouted out in Italian and Leone assumed from the little he knew that meant enough or shut up.

Leone pulled up on his arms, but they were tightly bound to the chair he sat on. He willed his legs to move, but they weren't responding.

He looked down at the gashes Christian had inflicted on him. He would need rehabilitation at minimum. Blood leeched out of the wounds and soaked the jeans he wore.

Christian turned back to Leone and based on the intent in his eyes, Leone knew he was on borrowed time. "You killed two of my men." He placed the blade in front of Leone's face. "They were good men. Faithful men." He bent over and kissed Leone's cheek—the Italian Mafia kiss of death.

The feeling of warmth was overtaken by a chill that made Leone's skin prickle.

Christian dropped the knife to the floor and pulled out the pistol from the back of his pants.

Please make it quick. Leone closed his eyes.

He heard the bullet leave the chamber. It was as if time had slowed down and he could distinguish everything. His hearing was clear now. He opened his eyes to face his death, but the bullet kissed a shoulder.

Christian started laughing. "I will not let you off that easy."

The sound of the man's laughter froze Leone further. He watched Christian raise the gun again, readied to fire on him.

Smoke filled the hangar. Screams from another room.

"What the—" Christian ran off in the direction of the smoky haze, and Leone knew he had only a few more minutes to live. The question was would it be by a bullet or by fire. Not that any means of death would be pleasant but of the two neither option was very welcoming.

There were not words to describe the level of pain that coursed through my body. But knowing that I was my family's only hope, I had to get up. I couldn't allow myself to be defeated.

As Limpy Scarface retracted his leg readying to kick me again, I rolled and extended my leg beneath him. It hit him directly in the shin, and due to his balance being mostly on the one leg as he drew back the other, he came crashing to the floor beside me.

He shuffled and wormed along the floor trying to get further away from me. I followed after him. My breathing clipped. I must have at least one broken rib.

For an instant, he stopped moving, and the determination in his eyes flickered again. He moved back toward me. I reached into my jacket pocket ready to use the one bullet I had reserved for Christian. Instead, my hand came out with a package of matches. I didn't even remember how they got in there—at least at first. Then I remembered how only days ago, I had barbecued for my family and needed to light it.

The man must have noticed my find as he came at me across the concrete. He reached my arm, and the matches went flying across the room. I crawled across the floor, my back to him. He pulled on my shirt, dragging me to him. Another fist met with my face. I let myself go into the backward dive and rolled coming out the other side of him. The matchbox lay on the floor behind him.

I struggled to my feet. He came at me as a football player tackles his opponent. I was thrown into the wall. The impact jostled all the bones in my body. It hurt like hell to breathe.

He took another jab at me, but I ducked out of the way. My fist met with his torso. He doubled over. I kneed him in the chin with my good leg and his head snapped back. I drew back my fist and came into contact with the soft cartilage of his face. The bones shifted. I had for certain broken his nose this time.

He cradled his face and stood there gasping for breath. I took the opportunity and pushed him aside. He fell to the floor in the corner of the room. I dashed toward the matchbook and opened it. One match.

Shit!

No room for error. I could do this. I struck it across the lighting strip. Nothing.

Shit!

I tried it again and a small flame ignited.

"No!" The man came at me from across the room to stop my toss.

The lit match came into contact with the cot and it caught fire.

He went to move past me. I had pulled him back before he had a chance to stamp out the flames.

"Son of a bitch!" He yelled again, repeating the same words. His eyes reflected pain and the back of his arm swiped beneath his bleeding nose. "I will kill you!"

I saw the spark in his eyes, which disclosed his next move. He hurried toward the door, but I beat him to it. I closed it and held it shut until smoke filled the room and I didn't hear him anymore.

Christian followed Berto to the side door. The smoke was dense and made him cough.

"You go find out what this is," Christian commanded.

Berto looked at him but would never question him, at least not with words. The man sometimes had a way of doing so in silence, but he would never dare verbalize them. He knew Christian didn't tolerate insubordination. Even though easily double his weight, Berto followed orders and went down the hallway.

Christian heard his man let out a yelp and then there was silence.

The big guy when down heavily. It took everything not to cough, but I crouched low to the floor and made my way steadily to the doorway of the hangar. I made out the shadow of a man I recognized as Christian standing there. I held my jacket over my mouth to help cut out some of the smoke.

I reached into my pocket for the flashlight.

Leone squirmed in the chair doing his best to free himself. He realized in little time the constraints were expertly put in place likely from years of experience. The blood pouring from his leg wounds made him faint and he feared that another possibility was he might die from blood loss. That option of falling asleep and not waking up, in some ways, felt like a better one than the others presented to him.

The smoke gathered in the hangar, lingering at the ceiling. This was one thing Leone was thankful for. Maybe, somehow, he could break free and get the hell out of here before the smoke and flames filled the entire building.

His scheming stopped when he swore he heard car doors slam shut.

CHAPTER EIGHTY-SIX

Outskirts of Detroit, Michigan
Monday, June 14th, 8:10 AM

The moment of truth had come. The time of redemption and the executing of vengeance. I couldn't stay in this hallway any longer. Before I got lower, I noticed through the window in the door that the flames were ceiling high in the room I had been in.

I shimmied along the floor and lined myself up. I wouldn't be targeting Christian's forehead. And I had decided the kill shot wouldn't be to the heart. There were too many variables, and I wanted to ensure when I shot this man, he would fall down dead.

In fact, I viewed it as my job—not as directed by Pietro Russo—but as commissioned by myself. It was something I should have allowed to happen eighteen years ago.

I took aim at his left eye and pulled the trigger.

Leone heard the shot and his head snapped toward Christian. The man fell backward, flat out onto the concrete. Out of the smoke, came a man he recognized before now only in a grainy video photo. And with the smoke gathered around him, he resembled the quality perfectly. That was Raymond Hunter, and he had just taken down Christian Russo.

Now, as soon as Leone got free, he'd take him down.

Maybe i should feel bad for the taking of a life. When I had first started into the Mafia lifestyle, there were times I felt regret, guilt, possibly even a type of melancholy knowing that I had killed someone. But as I looked down at Christian's body, I only saw poetic justice.

I needed my guns if I was going to get out of here with my family. My footsteps went slower as I noticed the man tied to the chair that I had been in. Both his legs were cut, a bullet wound to his shoulder. I looked at the table; I was relieved my guns were still there.

The man watched me approach. His jeans were stained a deep red on both thighs. Blood pooled beneath him. But he wasn't my problem. I was no white knight. Even when it came to my family, I had failed them—just putting them in such a position to be here, to be like this now.

"Hey." The guy called out to me.

I ignored him as I put on my holsters and guns.

"Let me out of here."

I kept my hands moving over my guns, collecting them.

"Raymond Hunter, right?"

I stopped moving but didn't turn around.

"I came to save you. FBI."

The FBI never acted alone. Where were the rest of them? I turned quickly and went over to him. I saw his jacket on the floor, the white capital letters on the back of it. My eyes went from it to him.

"You've been caught in the middle of a mafia war," he said.

He had my attention. His eyes rolled backward as he seemed to fight for consciousness. He had lost a lot of blood.

"You were in the wrong place at the wrong time."

He kept speaking as I ripped the sleeves off his jacket.

"You were likely coerced into cooperating. That's how they work."

Did this man know about my family? About the fact I'm the one who killed the Governor?

"What do you know?" I continued working on the sleeves. When one broke free, I fed it under one of his legs and tied it tight. He winced. I went for the other sleeve.

"I know that Christian was trying to gain power from his father, Pietro Russo. He hired you to kill the Governor."

I fished the other sleeve under the second leg and tied it even tighter than the first one. The smoke was getting thicker. It was time to move. Either I left him here to die, or I had to untie him. I noticed the bloody knife on the floor beside him.

But I couldn't go to prison. If I left him here, I would have killed a Federal agent—a life sentence guaranteed. If I let him go and he charged me with Behler's assassination, I would be serving a life sentence. There wasn't much in it for me either way.

"Are you here to arrest me?" I asked.

He shook his head, but it more or less rolled, pivoting on his neck. "I'm here to save you."

"But you know I killed her?"

"There's no proof on you. Only circumstantial at best. Easy to dismiss."

I held eye contact for a moment, thinking and debating whether to buy into his lines. But I couldn't allow a man to die who didn't need to.

I picked up the knife and went toward his wrists. I heard his breath catch as I undid the ropes that had held them in place.

The man rubbed at his wrists. "Name's Tony Leone."

Something in his tone of voice changed. I didn't like it. I saw his eyes dive to the table with the guns. I didn't have all of them on me yet.

He rose from the chair and buckled down, but not all the way to the floor. The man had an intense capacity for pain suppression. He stood straight and held out a hand.

His eyes were jumpy and kept diverting to the table of weapons. He took a few quick steps forward and then stopped all movement.

He must have heard me pull a .22 from the holster.

He turned to face me. Anger filled his expression, even above the level of pain he must have been feeling.

"Who are you really?" I asked.

"I told you, FBI Agent Leone." He paused as a cough compressed his body. The smoke was getting worse. "Special Agent."

I stepped closer to him and coughed myself. "Why are you here?"

"To save you. I told you."

"Try again."

We both coughed some more. I directed him, "Get down!" He complied as I was the one with the gun pointed at his head. "You came to kill Christian."

"What does it matter? He's dead now." Another cough. "Thanks to you."

"You're not FBI."

"You saw the jacket."

"The jacket doesn't make an agent. You were bought off by a New York Mafia Family. You came here to clean house. That would include me."

He said nothing.

"When Pietro Russo sent Behler in to talk to Talbot in New York, and she was assassinated on their soil, it was like shitting in their front yard. It was like saying they were on their own to deal with the Governor and his vendetta against them."

Still no response. His eyes kept rolling up into his head and returning.

"You were hired by them," I said.

He laughed and winced from the pain. I gripped at my chest. My ribs hurt and my breath kept catching. It would become a matter of mind over body. I nudged the gun toward him. "Who hired you?"

"You're stupid. You don't have a clue."

The front door swung open and a number of uniformed officers stormed through.

"Gun down! Now!"

Assault rifles were pointed at our heads. They were more than willing to take fire and end this right now—no questions asked.

I raised my gun and the other arm in the air as a sign of surrender and bent to place the gun on the ground in front of me.

The bullet whizzed through the air, slicing through the smoke. Leone fell to the floor along with one of my .22 handguns that he must have held behind his back.

An officer hurried toward us and kicked the guns from our reach. One leaned over Leone and checked for a pulse. He looked back to the man in charge and shook his head.

"Everyone out! Now!"

Firemen headed in as two cops pulled on me. Cuffs had been slapped onto my wrists, but I bucked against them. "My family is in there!"

A firm hand was placed on my shoulder. "It will all be fine."

"You don't understand! They were kidnaped." My eyes were full of tears; I made eye contact with the one officer. "Please, you have to—"

"We'll find them."

I'm not sure why, but something in his eyes told me he meant it. Exhaustion buckled my legs and the officers lifted me and supported me out of the building.

A while later, a fireman came out with a few more trailing behind him. He reported to a man who stood by a red SUV; it had Fire Chief written on the side.

Three black bags were carried out. One was for a man who had introduced himself as Special Agent Leone, and another was for Christian's man who I had burned alive in that room. But the third would have contained the body of a man I had known and loved like a brother fifteen years ago. There would be no tears shed over the loss. These bags were placed beside two others on the ground in front of the hangar.

Paramedics came out with the large man who I had knocked to the ground. They had an oxygen mask on his face.

A decorated officer stepped away from his SUV; this one was with Detroit PD. He pushed off the frame of the vehicle with his foot and make quick time toward me. "Raymond Hunter?"

I nodded.

"You've got a lot of answering to do."

His breath smelled of onion bagel and coffee. It's ironic how at a time like this I made that type of observation.

The man spoke to a nearby officer, "We'll need him downtown. But first, escort him to the hospital."

"Yes, Chief.". The officer who kept a hold on my cuffs led me toward an ambulance. The city of Detroit had come prepared for everything.

We passed a squad car. Landen sat in the backseat, her face wrinkled up. She hurled spit at the window as I walked by.

Two paramedics came toward me.

"They'll take you to the hospital, Mr. Hunter. I'll escort you."

My legs wouldn't move. I stood looking at the building, thinking about the nightmare and how it had all started. I wanted to be left alone but hadn't been granted that wish. "My family… Christian had my family. I know they're here. I couldn't get to them before he—"

"You have my promise." The officer put his hand on my shoulder again. "We'll be doing an entire sweep of the property.

"Please, let me go. I know where they are."

The paramedic came to help me into the ambulance.

"Please. Listen to me!"

Somehow between the cop and the paramedic they got me into the vehicle. They shut the door, and I watched as we drove away. My heart and soul tore from being pulled away from my family. I knew they were in that shed. They just had to be.

CHAPTER EIGHTY-SEVEN

Niagara Falls, New York
Monday, June 14th, 10:00 AM

The chief called Clinton and Wingham into his office. Governor Talbot was standing in the corner of the room.

"It seems this is all behind us now," the Chief said. "Detroit PD moved in and found the rogue agent. He was busted up pretty good. They also had no choice but to execute him when he didn't heed their warning."

Governor Talbot moved forward and extended a handshake to both detectives. "And thanks to you a colleague has justice."

"And we also have something to tell the public. Did you ever figure out everything that went on?" The Chief looked at Clinton.

Clinton passed a glance at Talbot and answered the Chief. "There's some questions you never get answers to. Other times, you get answers you don't like." The Governor averted eye contact. "And sometimes the answers never really mattered in the first place."

"Oh, please, that's your official statement, David?" Wingham turned to face her partner. Hope lit in the Governor's eyes.

The Chief smiled at her. "You have something to say?"

"Dang right I do. Detective Clinton should be promoted."

Clinton turned to face her.

"He followed the clues in this case; he exposed a corrupt FBI agent. I naively assumed since the man had a medal, well, he was a saint. My own issues, I need to sort out. I mean, I didn't really care for him, was kind of suspicious—"

"Point, Detective." The Chief still smiled.

"He found your assassin. Guess that's all that matters." She crossed her legs and laced her hands on a knee.

The Chief exhaled in satisfaction and excused them.

Down the hall, Governor Talbot called out to Clinton. "Do you have a minute? I know you're a busy man. You'll have some press conferences to do."

Clinton looked to Wingham, who shrugged. "I'll meet up with you down at the television station," he said.

"Sure."

Clinton walked back the few steps to Talbot.

"Thank you for what you did in there."

"Just doing my job."

"If you're interested I could use a good man like you on payroll. It would pay double your current salary, but you'd have to willing to lose sleep, stay up all hours of the night. And be at my beck and call," Talbot said.

"Operating without sleep is what I'm good at, sir. But, with all due respect, I'm rather happy where I am right now."

Talbot nodded. "You have my number."

Clinton could have hit himself hard in the head. Isn't that what he wanted? Money, glory, dominance, and acknowledgment. The Governor offered him all of that, but he turned it down? He wasn't sure if he liked the person he was becoming.

. . .

Detroit, Michigan

Hospitals held the smell of death. Even though they should be a place where one feels safe and has a chance to heal, the disinfectant cleaners spoke of covering over the stench of decomposition.

Officers stood outside my room keeping guard over me to make sure I didn't run off with my three broken ribs, displaced nose, and wounded thigh. They said the knife just missed the femoral artery.

I sank my head heavily into the pillow wondering if they found my family yet. I hurt so badly, not from the physical pain, but from the uncertainty of not knowing they were okay.

"Let me in to see him now!" I heard the woman's voice firing in the hallway.

"Ma'am, I'm going to have to ask you to back off."

"I will beat you with this thing!"

"Ma'am!"

"Hell with it!"

Brenda stormed through the doorway, and Yvonne and Max followed her. She was hooked up to a mobile feeder. An IV tube ran from a bag into her hand.

I wanted to smile, to jump up, and embrace all of them in a group hug. But I held back afraid of how she would react to me, to what I had put our family through.

The three of them came to my bedside and stood there watching me as if I were a stranger. An officer graced the inside of the doorway but stepped back out.

I put a hand to my wife's cheek first. Tears fell and she smiled at me.

"I thought you were dead." She spoke through sobs that shook her body.

I pulled her into me and overlooked the pain that singed through me. My family had never looked so good to me. I held Brenda tight and breathed in her hair, her skin. "Are you okay?"

"We're all fine. My sugars are a little low so they have me hooked up to this thing. Apparently kids bounce back faster."

Yvonne moved in closer and so did Max. We stood there hugging and crying for minutes. I'm not even sure for how long. I just knew I never wanted to let them go. Never.

Max pulled out of the hug. "Dad."

"Yeah, Champ." I put a hand on his head and tousled his hair affectionately.

"I love you, too." Tears fell from his small eyes. The innocence of a child who had no idea why he was put through what he had been, yet he was willing to forgive. I hoped Brenda would be.

"All right that's enough." The Chief walked into the room with another man beside him.

I held my family tighter. These men would be taking me to prison, and not long from now, I'd be wearing an orange jumper at the penitentiary.

"Come on kids, out," I said.

Yvonne and Max squeezed me tighter. I didn't want Brenda to witness this. I tightened my grip on her hand and released it. It took everything inside to do so.

"You're not getting rid of me. I'm staying." When that level of defiance showed up in those green eyes of hers, there was no option but compliance.

"You might not like what you hear."

She took my hand back in hers. "We will work through whatever it is—together."

"Mr. Hunter," the Chief began, gesturing the man beside him. "This is a Detective Lieutenant Royce with the Michigan State Police. You are being investigated for the murder of Marian Behler, Governor of Michigan."

My eyes weren't on him but on Brenda. She licked her lips and looked away from me. Her hand fell limp in mine. I squeezed it, but she didn't reciprocate.

"You have a connection with the Italian Mafia, and they hired you as a hitman," Royce said.

I remained silent. All I could think about was losing Brenda and the kids forever. Emotion bottled in my throat.

"You killed Christian Russo with a .22 to the head. The same type of bullet that first went into Behler."

If the Lieutenant were fishing for a reaction, he wouldn't get one.

"The second bullet that went into her came from a customized rifle. The barrel's rifling, land and groove impressions, don't match anything in our databases."

He paused as if expecting my conscience to win out and provide him with information. My conscience had been sacrificed years ago. I remained silent.

I also knew they wouldn't find my customized rifle even if they searched my property. After seeing Pietro Russo, I had put it in a storage rental unit that I had taken out years ago under an assumed identity. It wouldn't be tied back to me. When things died down, I'd retrieve it and return it to my gun storage room where it belonged.

Royce continued, "We will be conducting a search of your property." He turned to face Brenda. Her head cocked to the side.

"Your DNA was found on another dead body. Behler's hired bodyguard."

I adjusted my position and studied my wife. "How is that even—"

"A hair in one of his wounds."

It took a moment, but I realized Brenda must have had secrets of her own, otherwise how would they have her DNA to match? I fought back a smile.

"But all of this." The Lieutenant made a circular motion with his hands. "None of it matters because at the end of the day we cannot prove you are the one who pulled the trigger." He turned back to Brenda. "And we cannot prove that you are the one who killed her bodyguard."

Was he saying that I'm free to go?

He must have read the expression on my face. "That's right." He pressed his lips and anger and frustration flashed in his eyes. "I can't charge you with anything. I mean, maybe the murder of Christian Russo, but from what I see you'd have too strong a case for self-defense. Of course, you'll need to answer a lot of questions about everything. Get some rest and we'll talk."

. . .

Niagara Falls, New York
1:00 PM

Wingham sat behind the table Clinton and she were directed to. Their announcement to the world would be broadcasting live in five minutes.

Clinton told her about Talbot's offer and that he shot it down.

"Wow, you do have a heart after all."

"Don't tell anyone."

"God no, it would ruin your cover as the tough cop." She laughed.

Clinton was proud of himself. He found out about Hunter's family, and he knew there was likely more under the surface. Nothing was a coincidence and Christian wouldn't have gone to him if there wasn't a past connection. But that didn't concern him. He had a case to solve—the assassination of a dignitary—and he had. As far as the public would know a man by the name of

Christian Russo had her taken out. They would also be informed of how the power struggle among the Mafia families resulted in his death.

There was nothing that could increase his speculation to evidence when it came to Governor Talbot either. If he had done something to warrant bribery to cover his tracks, there was nothing to prove it. They never did find Behler's cell phone. It's like it disappeared.

EPILOGUE

When one has a lot of time to think, the answers usually present themselves. They morph out of images, compilations, and blend with facts. It was only a week ago my family and I escaped from Christian Russo, but in a lot of ways the experience felt like another lifetime.

For me, it sought to be filed in the category of my past and I wished it to be buried there. As for the replica of Behler's phone chip, I had ensured it would never be found along with my original cell on which I did some Internet searches about her, and the recorder that contained the job offer from Christian. That could be the evidence that would make me see inside the walls of a government prison, not just a makeshift cell of a crazy man with dreams of grandeur.

At this point, I think I had it all figured out. Christian had always wanted the power, the recognition. This entire scheme was nothing more than an elaborate way of accomplishing all that. News reports told how Pietro Russo had been taken down by a bullet to the head on private property. The reporter concluded, *"It appears as nothing more than an elaborate shift in mafia power."*

They would never hear of the FBI agent or the Governor who pocketed public funds.

But I couldn't help thinking about the other man who had sat silently in the corner of Pietro's private quarters in the room at the racetrack bar. Christian couldn't have the power so he set things up so that his father would be taken out. But what he didn't count on was the fact Pietro's right-hand man was just as hungry for the power. When contacted by a New York Italian family, the man would have been more than eager to set matters right. And if that included taking out both father and son, that was a sacrifice for peace he would have been willing to make. FBI Agent Leone hadn't been sent to save me. He had been sent to kill Christian and realized I was in the way.

I walked down the hallway after my morning shower and joined my family at the breakfast table. "I forgot how great your pancakes were." I washed a mouthful down with a gulp of milk.

"Mom's are the best." Yvonne smiled at her mother.

Max was busy trying to get a slice of bacon and a chunk of pancake loaded onto his fork.

Brenda held eye contact with me, and I knew in that instant there was no other place I'd ever want to be. We had been fortunate, lucky, if one believed in that sort of thing, to be where we were today.

"You sound as if you haven't eaten them in forever." Brenda took a swig back on her coffee.

"Well, we missed last week." I spoke the words and the table went silent.

"We agreed not to ever bring it up again," Brenda said.

"I don't know. Dad's pretty cool."

Everyone looked at Max, who hadn't said much all brunch. He was too busy pushing food into his mouth.

"Well, he is. He's a gunman." He grinned, syrup running down his chin.

"Gross," Yvonne moaned.

"Wipe that Max." Brenda handed him a napkin. "It's not cool. It's dangerous." She passed a glance in my direction. I heard her words yet sensed attraction.

She had accepted my explanation of the murder of the Governor—I did it for the safety of my family—but it was never to be spoken of again. When she found out about how much money our family was really worth, I got a shot in my arm and was told she was quitting her day job.

"You'll have to teach me how to fire a gun, Dad."

"Max," Brenda attempted to correct him again.

"Maybe someday, Champ."

"Oh." Brenda's eyes got large, and she threw a dish towel at me. I caught it and went after her as fast as my injuries would allow. She left the table and ran down the hall toward our bedroom.

"Gross!" Yvonne yelled from the kitchen. "Close the door! We can hear you!"

Brenda fell onto the bed with me on top of her. The force on my ribs made me wince; I would not allow her to see it. We were both laughing but stopped as we looked into each other's eyes. She would never know about the man who had been murdered in our bed. She never pressed about the hair being found on him either, or discussed the fact police had her DNA on file.

My cell phone rang on the nightstand, and I reached for it.

"Is this Raymond Hunter?" The man's voice held a thick Italian accent.

My heart beat sped up. I closed my cell phone.

"Who was that?"

"Wrong number." Maybe it was time to move and get as far away from Detroit and my past as possible. "Brenda."

"Yes." Her eyes narrowed to slits.

"I have a question for you."

"Uh huh."

"Why is your DNA on record?"

Her smile faded but was reborn. "And what, I can't have any mystery about me?"

Maybe it was at that moment, or maybe I had known this for a long time, but she was my perfect match. And our children, well, they were the offspring of their parents, so they were okay too. I smiled as I leaned down to kiss her.

There is no getting around it: reviews are important and so is word of mouth.

With all the books on the market today, readers need to know what's worth their time and what's not. This is where you come into play.

If you enjoyed *Assassination of a Dignitary* please help others find it by posting a brief, honest review on the retailer site where you purchased this book and recommend it to family and friends.

Also, Carolyn loves to hear from her readers, and you can reach her at Carolyn@CarolynArnold.net.

Upon receipt of your e-mail, you will be added to her newsletter mailing unless you express your desire otherwise.

Keep on reading for a sample of *Eleven*, book 1 in the Brandon Fisher FBI series.

If you love Assassination of a Dignitary, you'll love my Brandon Fisher FBI series.

Find out what happens when rookie FBI Agent Brandon Fisher takes on his first investigation, and the serial killer turns their sights on him.

CHAPTER ONE

Nothing in the twenty weeks at Quantico had prepared me for this.

A crime scene investigator, who had identified himself as Earl Royster when we'd first arrived, addressed my boss, FBI Supervisory Special Agent Jack Harper, "All of the victims were buried—" He held up a finger, his eyes squeezed shut, and he sneezed. "Sorry 'bout that. My allergies don't like it down here. They were all buried the same way."

This was my first case with the FBI Behavioral Analysis Unit, and it had brought me and the three other members of my team to Salt Lick, Kentucky. The discovery was made this morning, and we were briefed and flown in from Quantico to the Louisville field office where we picked up a couple of SUVs. We drove from there and arrived in Salt Lick at about four in the afternoon.

We were in an underground bunker illuminated by portable lights brought in by the local investigative team. The space was eleven feet beneath the cellar of a house that was the size of a mobile trailer. We stood in a central hub from which four tunnels spread out like a root system. The space was fifteen feet by seven and a half feet and six and a half feet tall.

The walls were packed dirt, and an electrical cord ran along the ceiling and down the tunnels with pigtail light fixtures dangling every few feet. The bulbs cut into the height of the tunnels by eight inches.

I pulled on my shirt collar wishing for a smaller frame than my six foot two inches. As it was, the three of us could have reached out and touched each other if we were so inclined. The tunnels were even narrower at three feet wide.

"It's believed each victim had the same cuts inflicted," Royster began, "although most of the remains are skeletal, so it's not as easy to know for sure, but based on burial method alone, this guy obviously adhered to some sort of ritual. The most recent victim is only a few years old and was preserved by the soil. The oldest remains are estimated to date back twenty-five to thirty years. Bingham moved in twenty-six years ago."

Lance Bingham was the property owner, age sixty-two, and was currently serving three to five years in a correctional facility for killing two cows and assaulting a neighbor. If he had moved in twenty-six years ago, that would put

Bingham at thirty-six years old at the time. The statistical age for a serial killer to start out is early to mid-thirties.

The CSI continued to relay more information about how the tunnels branched out in various directions, likely extending beneath a neighboring cornfield, and the ends came to bulbous tips, like subterranean cul-de-sacs.

"There are eleven rooms and only ten bodies," Jack summarized with impatience and pulled a cigarette out of a shirt pocket. He didn't light up, but his mouth was clamped down on it as if it were a lifeline.

Royster's gaze went from the cigarette to Jack's eyes. "Yes. There's one tunnel that leads to a dead end, and there's one empty grave."

Jack turned to me. "What do you make of it?" he asked, the cigarette bobbing on his lips as he spoke.

Everyone looked at me expectantly. "Of the empty grave?" I squeaked out.

Jack squinted and removed the cigarette from his mouth. "That and the latest victim."

"Well…" My collar felt tighter, and I cleared my throat, then continued. "Bingham had been in prison for the last three years. The elaborate tunnel system he had going would have taken years to plan and dig, and it would have taken a lot of strength. My guess would be that Bingham wasn't working alone. He had help and, after he went to prison, someone followed in his footsteps."

Jack perched the unlit smoke back between his lips. "Hmm."

I wasn't sure how to read *Hmm*, but the way his gaze scrutinized me, I was thinking he wasn't necessarily impressed.

"Anyway, you'll want to see it for yourself." Royster gestured down one of the tunnels and took a step toward it. "I know I haven't seen anything like—" Royster didn't catch his sneeze in time, and snot sprayed through the air.

Ick. I stepped back.

More sniffles. "Again, sorry 'bout that. Anyway, this way."

Jack motioned for me to follow behind Royster, ahead of him.

I took a deep breath, anticipating the tight quarters of the tunnel.

Sweat dripped down my back, and I pulled on my collar again.

"Go ahead, Kid," Jack directed.

He'd adopted the pet name for me from the moment we'd met, and I wished he'd just call me by my name.

Both Jack and the CSI were watching me.

The CSI said, "We'll look at the most recent victim first. Now, as you know, the victims alternated male and female. The tenth victim was female so we believe the next is going to be—"

"Let me guess, male," Jack interrupted him.

"Yeah." Royster took off down the third tunnel that fed off from the bottom right of the hub.

I followed behind him, tracing the walls with my hands. My heart palpitated. I ducked to miss the bulbs just as I knew I'd have to and worked at focusing on the positive. Above ground, the humidity sucked air from the lungs; in the tunnels, the air was cool but still suffocating.

I counted my paces—five, six. The further we went, the heavier my chest became, making the next breath less taken for granted.

Despite my extreme discomfort, this was my first case, and I had to be strong. The rumor was you either survived Jack and the two years of probationary service and became a certified special agent or your next job would be security detail at a mall.

Five more paces and we entered an offshoot from the main tunnel. According to Royster, three burial chambers were in this tunnel. He described these as branches on a tree. Each branch came off the main trunk for the length of about ten feet and ended in a circular space of about eleven feet in diameter. The idea of more space seemed welcoming until we reached it.

A circular grave took up most of the space and was a couple of feet deep. Chicken wire rimmed the grave to help it retain its shape. With her wrists and ankles tied to metal stakes, her arms and legs formed the human equivalent of a star. As her body had dried from decomposition, the constraints had kept her positioned in the manner the killer had intended.

"And what made them dig?" Jack asked the CSI.

Jack was searching for specifics. We knew Bingham had entrusted his financials to his sister, but when she passed away a year ago, the back taxes had built up, and the county had come to reclaim the property.

Royster answered, "X marked the spot." Neither Jack nor I displayed any amusement. The CSI continued. "He etched into the dirt, probably with a stick."

"Why assume a stick?" Jack asked the question, and it resulted in an awkward silence.

My eyes settled on the body of the female who was estimated to be in her early twenties. It's not that I had an aversion to a dead body, but looking at her made my stomach toss. She still had flesh on her bones. As the CSI had said, *Preserved by the soil.*

Her torso had eleven incisions. They were marked in the linear way to keep count. Two sets of four vertical cuts with one diagonal slash through each of them. The eleventh cut was the largest and was above the belly button.

"You realize the number eleven is believed to be a sign of purity?" Zach's voice seemed to strike me from thin air, and my chest compressed further, knowing another person was going to share the limited space.

Zachery Miles was a member of our team, but unlike Jack's reputation, Zach's hadn't preceded him. Any information I had, I'd gathered from his file that showed a flawless service record and the IQ of a genius. It also disclosed that he was thirty-seven, eight years older than I was.

Jack stuck the cigarette he had been sucking on back into his shirt pocket. "Purity, huh?"

I looked down at the body of the woman in the shallow grave beside me. Nothing seemed too pure about any of this.

"I'm going to go," Royster excused himself.

"That's if you really dig into the numerology and spiritualistic meaning of the number," Zachery said, disregarding the CSI entirely.

Jack stretched his neck side to side and looked at me. "I hate it when he gets into that shit." He pointed a bony index finger at me. "Don't let me catch you talking about it either."

I just nodded. I felt I had just been admonished as if I were his child—not that he needed to zero in on me like that. Sure, I believed in the existence of God and angels, despite the evil in the world, but I didn't have any avid interest in the unseen.

Zachery continued, "The primary understanding is the number one is that of new beginnings and purity. This is emphasized with the existence of two ones."

My eyes scanned Zachery's face. While his intelligence scoring revealed a genius, physically, he was of average looks. If anything, he was slightly taller than Jack and I, probably coming in at about six foot four. His hair was dark and trimmed short. He had a high brow line and brown eyes.

"Zachery here reads something once—" Jack tapped his head "—it's there."

Jack and I spent the next few hours making our way to every room where Jack insisted on standing beside all the bodies. He studied each of them carefully, even if only part of their remains had been uncovered. I'd pass him glances, but he seemed oblivious to my presence. We ended up back beside the most recent victim where we stayed for twenty minutes, not moving, not talking, just standing.

I understood what he saw. There was a different feel to this room, nothing quantifiable, but it was discernible. The killer had a lot to say. He was organized and immaculate. He was precise and disciplined. He acted with a purpose, and, like most killers, he had a message to relay. We were looking for a controlled, highly intelligent unsub.

The intestines had been removed from nine of the victims, but Harold Jones, the coroner— who also came backed with a doctorate unlike most of his profession—wouldn't conclude it as the cause of death before conducting more tests. The last victim's intestines were intact, and, even though the cause of death needed confirmation, the talk that permeated the corridors of the bunker was that the men who did this were scary sons of bitches.

Zachery entered the room. "I find it fascinating he would bury his victims in circular graves."

Fascinating?

I looked up at Jack, and he flicked his lighter.

He held out his hands as if to say he wouldn't light up inside the burial chamber. His craving was getting desperate, though, which meant he'd be getting cranky. He said, "Continue, Zachery, by all means. The kid wants to hear."

"By combining both the number eleven and the circle, it makes me think of the coinherence symbol. Even the way the victims are laid out."

"Elaborate," Jack directed.

"It's a circle which combines a total of eleven inner points to complete it. As eleven means purity, so the coinherence symbol is related to religious traditions—at minimum thirteen, but some people can discern more, and each symbol is understood in different ways. The circle itself stands for completion and can symbolize eternity."

I cocked my head to the side. Zachery noticed.

"We have a skeptic here, Jack."

Jack faced me and spoke with the unlit cigarette having resumed its perch between his lips. "What do you make of it?"

Is this a trap? "You want to know what I think?"

"By all means, Slingshot."

There it was, the other dreaded nickname, no doubt his way of reminding me that I didn't score perfectly on handguns at the academy. "Makes me think of the medical symbol. Maybe our guy has a background in medicine. It could explain the incisions being deep enough to inflict pain but not deep enough to cause them to bleed out. It would explain how he managed to take out their intestines."

Was this what I signed up for?

"Hmm," Jack mumbled. Zachery remained silent. Seconds later, Jack said, "You're assuming they didn't bleed out. Continue."

"The murders happened over a period of time. This one—" I gestured to the woman, and for a moment, realized how this job transformed the life of a person into an object "—she's recent. Bingham's been in prison for about three years now."

Jack flicked the lighter again. "So you're saying he had an apprentice?"

Zachery's lips lifted upward, and his eyes read, *Like* Star Wars.

I got it. I was the youngest on the team, twenty-nine this August, next month, and I was the new guy, but I didn't make it through four years of university studying mechanics and endure twenty weeks of the academy, coming out at the top of the class, to be treated like a child. "Not like an apprentice."

"Like what then—"

"Jack, the sheriff wants to speak with you." Paige Dawson, another member of our team, came into the burial chamber. She had come to Quantico from the New York field office claiming she wanted out of the big city. I met her when she was an instructor at the FBI Academy.

I pulled on my collar. Four of us were in here now. Dust caused me to cough and warranted a judgmental glare from Jack.

"How did you make out with the guy who discovered everything?"

"He's clean. I mean we had his background already, and he lives up to it. I really don't think he's involved at all."

Jack nodded and left the room.

I turned to Zachery. "I think he hates me."

"If he hated you, you'd know it." Zachery followed behind Jack.

CHAPTER TWO

Salt Lick, Kentucky was right in the middle of nowhere and had a population shy of three hundred and fifty. Just as the town's name implied, underground mineral deposits were the craving of livestock, and due to this, it had originally attracted farmers to the area. I was surprised the village was large enough to boast a Journey's End Lodge and a Frosty Freeze.

I stepped into the main hub to see Jack in a heated conversation with Sheriff Harris. From an earlier meeting with him, I knew he covered all of Bath County which included three municipalities and a combined population of about twelve thousand.

"Ah, I'm doing the best I can, Agent, but, um, we've never seen the likes of this before." A born and raised Kentucky man, the sheriff was in his mid-fifties, had a bald head and carried about an extra sixty pounds that came to rest on his front. Both of his hands were braced on his hips, a stance of confidence, but the flicking up and down of his right index finger gave his insecurities away.

"It has nothing to do with what you've seen before, Sheriff. What matters is catching the unsub."

"Well, the property owner is in p-pri-prison," the Kentucky accent broke through.

"The bodies date back two to three decades with the newest one being within the last few years."

Harris's face brightened a reddish hue as he took a deep breath and exhaled loud enough to be heard.

Jack had the ability to make a lot of people nervous. His dark hair, which was dusted with silver at the sideburns, gave him a look of distinction, but deeply-etched creases in his face exposed his trying past.

Harris shook his head. "So much violence, and it's tourist season 'round here." Harris paused. His eyes said, *You city folks wouldn't understand.* "Cave Run Lake is manmade but set in the middle of nature. People love coming here to get away. Word gets out about this, there go the tourists."

"Ten people have been murdered, and you're worried about tourists?"

"Course not, but—"

"It sounds like you were."

"Then you misunderstood, Agent. Besides, the counties around here are peaceful, law-abidin' citizens."

"Churchgoers?" Zachery came up from a tunnel.

"Well, ah, I wouldn't necessarily say that. There are probably about thirty churches or so throughout the county, and right here in Salt Lick there are three."

"That's quite a few considering the population here."

"S'pose so."

"Sheriff." A deputy came up to the group of them and pulled up his pants.

"Yes, White."

The deputy's face was the shade of his name. "The in-investigators found somethin' you should see." He passed glances among all of us.

Jack held out a hand as if to say, *By all means.*

We followed the deputy up the ramp that led to the cellar. With each step taking me closer to the surface, my chest allowed for more satisfying breaths. Jack glanced over at me. I guessed he was wondering if I was going to make it.

"This way, sir."

The deputy spoke from the front of the line, as he kept moving. His boots hit the wooden stairs that joined the cellar to the first floor.

I inhaled deeply as I came through the opening into the confined space Bingham had at one time called home. Sunlight made its way through tattered sheets that served as curtains, even though the time of day was now seven, and the sun would be sinking in the sky.

The deputy led us to Bingham's bedroom where there were two CSIs. I heard footsteps behind me: Paige. She smiled at me, but it quickly faded.

"They found it in the closet," the deputy said, pointing our focus in its direction.

The investigators moved aside, exposing an empty space. A shelf that ran the width of the closet sat perched at a forty-five-degree angle. The inside had been painted white at one time but now resembled an antiqued paint pattern the modern age went for. It was what I saw when my eyes followed the walls to the floor that held more interest.

Jack stepped in front of me; Zachery came up behind him and gave me a look that said, *Pull up the rear, Pending*. Pending being the nickname Zach had saddled me with to remind me of my twenty-four-month probationary period—as if I'd forget.

"We found it when we noticed the loose floorboard," one of the CSIs said. He held a clipboard wedged between an arm and his chest. The other hand held a pen which he clicked repeatedly. Jack looked at it, and the man stopped. The CSI went on. "Really, it's what's inside that's, well, what nightmares are made of."

I didn't know the man. In fact, I had never seen him before, but the reflection in his eyes told me he had witnessed something that even paled the gruesome find in the bunkers.

"You first, Kid." Jack stepped back.

Floorboards were hinged back and exposed a hole about two and a half feet square. My stomach tossed thinking of the CSI's words, *what nightmares are made of.*

"Come on, Brandon. I'll follow behind you." Paige's soft voice of encouragement was accompanied by a strategically placed hand on my right shoulder.

I glanced at her. I could do this. *God, I hated small spaces.* But I had wanted to be an FBI special agent and, well, that wish had been granted. Maybe the saying, *Be careful what you wish for, it might come true,* held merit.

I hunched over and looked into the hole. A wooden ladder went down at least twenty feet. The space below was lit.

Maybe if I just took it one step at a time.

"What are you waiting for, Pending?" Zachery taunted me. I didn't look at him but picked up on the amusement in his voice.

I took a deep breath and lowered myself down.

Jack never said a word, but I could feel his energy. He didn't think I was ready for this, but I would prove him wrong—somehow. The claustrophobia I had experienced in the underground passageways was nothing compared to the anxiety squeezing my chest now. At least the tunnels were the width of three feet. Here, four sides of packed earth hugged me, as if a substantial inhale would expand me to the confines of the space.

"I'm coming." Again, Paige's soft voice had a way of soothing me despite the tight quarters threatening to take my last breath and smother me alive.

I looked up. Paige's face filled the opening, and her red wavy hair framed her face. The vision was replaced by the bottom of her shoes.

I continued my descent, one rung at a time, slowly, methodically. I tried to place myself somewhere else, but no images came despite my best efforts to conjure them—and what did I have waiting for me at the bottom? *What nightmares are made of.*

Minutes passed before my shoes reached the soil. I took a deep breath when I realized the height down here was about seven feet and looked around. The room was about five by five, and there was a doorway at the backside.

One pigtail fixture with a light bulb dangled from an electrical wire. It must have fed to the same circuit as the underground passageways and been connected to the power generator as it cast dim light, creating darkened shadows in the corners.

I looked up the ladder. Paige was about halfway down. There was movement behind her, and it was likely Jack and Zachery following behind her.

"You're almost there," I coached them.

By the time the rest of the team made it to the bottom, along with the deputy and a CSI, I had my breathing and my nerves under control.

Paige was the first to head around the bend in the wall.

"The sheriff is going to stay up there an' take care of things." The deputy pointed in the direction Paige went. "What they found is in here."

Jack and Zachery had already headed around the bend. I followed.

Inside the room, Paige raised her hand to cover her mouth. It dropped when she noticed us.

A stainless steel table measuring ten feet by three feet was placed against the back wall. A commercial meat grinder sat on the table. Everything was pristine, and light from a bulb reflected off the surfaces.

To the left of the table was a chest freezer, plain white, one owned by the average consumer. I had one similar, but it was the smaller version because it was only Deb and me.

My stomach tossed thinking about the contents of this one. Paige's feet were planted to where she had first entered the room. Zachery's eyes fixed on Jack, who moved toward the freezer and, with a gloved hand, opened the lid.

Paige gasped, and Jack turned to face her. Disappointment was manifested in the way his eyes narrowed. "It's empty." Jack patted his shirt pocket again.

"If you're thinking we found people's remains in there, we haven't," the CSI said, "but tests have shown positive for human blood."

"So he chopped up his victim's intestines? Put them in the freezer? But where are they?" Paige wrapped her arms around her torso and bent over to look into the opening of the grinder.

"There are many cultures, the Korowai tribe of Papua New Guinea, for example, who have been reported to practice cannibalism even in this modern day," Zachery said. "It can also be involved in religious rituals."

Maybe my eyes should have been fixed on the freezer, on the horror that transpired underground in Salt Lick of Bath County, Kentucky. Instead, I found my training allowing me to focus, analyze, and be objective. In order to benefit the investigation, it would demand these three things, and I wouldn't disappoint. My attention was on the size of the table, the size of the meat grinder, and the size of the freezer. "Anyone think to ask how this all got down here in the first place?"

All five of them faced me.

"The opening down here is only, what, two feet square at the most? Now maybe the meat grinder would fit down, hoisted on a rope, but the table and the freezer? No way."

"What are you saying, Slingshot?"

My eyes darted to Jack's. "I'm saying there has to be another way in." I addressed the CSI, "Did you look for any other hidden passageways? I mean the guy obviously had a thing for them."

"We didn't find anything."

"Well, that doesn't make sense. Where are the burial sites in relation to here?"

"It would be that way." Zachery pointed at the freezer.

We connected eyes, and both of us moved toward it. It slid easily. As we shoved it to the side, it revealed an opening behind it. I looked down into it. Another light bulb spawned eerie shadows. I rose to full height. This find should at least garner some praise from Jack Harper.

"Nothing like Hogan's Alley is it, Kid?"

Also available from
International Bestselling Author
Carolyn Arnold

ELEVEN

Book 1 in the Brandon Fisher FBI series

In this international bestseller, rookie FBI Agent Brandon Fisher takes on his first case with the Behavioral Analysis Unit, but will he survive long enough to catch the killer? Eleven is a fast-paced, spine-tingling thriller that will have you gasping for breath at every twist…

Eleven Rooms. Ten Bodies. One Empty Grave.

When Brandon Fisher joined the FBI Behavioral Analysis Unit, he knew he'd come up against psychopaths, sociopaths, pathological liars, and more. But when his first case takes him and the team to Salt Lick, Kentucky, to hunt down a ritualistic serial killer, he learns what nightmares are truly made of.

Beneath a residential property, local law enforcement discovered an underground bunker with circular graves that house the remains of ten victims. But that's not all: there's an empty eleventh grave, just waiting for a corpse. The killing clearly hasn't come to an end yet, and with the property owner already behind bars, Brandon is certain there's an apprentice who roams free.

As the FBI follows the evidence across the United States, Brandon starts to struggle with the deranged nature of his job description. And if the case itself isn't going to be enough to push Brandon over the edge, he's working in the shadow of Supervisory Special Agent Jack Harper, who expects nothing short of perfection from his team. To make matters even worse, it seems Brandon has become the target of a psychotic serial killer who wants to make him—or his wife—victim number eleven.

Available from popular book retailers or
at CarolynArnold.net

CAROLYN ARNOLD is an international bestselling and award-winning author, as well as a speaker, teacher, and inspirational mentor. She has several continuing fiction series and has many published books. Her genre diversity offers her readers everything from cozy to hard-boiled mysteries, and thrillers to action adventures. Her crime fiction series have been praised by those in law enforcement as being accurate and entertaining. This led to her adopting the trademark: POLICE PROCEDURALS RESPECTED BY LAW ENFORCEMENT™.

Carolyn was born in a small town and enjoys spending time outdoors, but she also loves the lights of a big city. Grounded by her roots and lifted by her dreams, her overactive imagination insists that she tell her stories. Her intention is to touch the hearts of millions with her books, to entertain, inspire, and empower.

She currently lives near London, Ontario, Canada with her husband and two beagles.

CONNECT ONLINE
CarolynArnold.net
Facebook.com/AuthorCarolynArnold
Twitter.com/Carolyn_Arnold

And don't forget to sign up for her newsletter for up-to-date information on release and special offers
at
CarolynArnold.net/Newsletters.

www.ingramcontent.com/pod-product-compliance
Lightning Source LLC
Chambersburg PA
CBHW061336190726
48288CB00005B/1477